IMPULSE CONTROL

Book Two of the Red Creek Series

Rachael Llewellyn

An Imprint of Sulis International Press
Los Angeles | London

ISBN (print): 978-1-946849-70-0
ISBN (eBook): 978-1-946849-71-7

Published by Riversong Books
An Imprint of Sulis International
Los Angeles | London

www.sulisinternational.com

Contents

For George,
Because I'm so into you

Prologue

When my daughter was six, she cut her hand chopping some carrots. She said that I used to chop vegetables too big. Fiona insisted that she wanted to do it. I would let her lay the table and pour our juice, little things like that, so, I suppose in her mind, chopping up carrots didn't seem like too much of an upgrade.

I was against her using a knife. I knew that she'd rush it or mess around, impersonate those disturbing looking turtle men from the television. The other mothers say how quiet and well behaved she is, and I'm sure she is, in front of them, but I know how clumsy she is when we are alone.

But, of course, she didn't like being told no. My elder sister was the same.

She argued and argued until not letting her use the knife was more grating than the ramifications of letting her try. So, I put her red footstool up against the kitchen countertop and gave her a very small kitchen knife and the smaller and sturdier chopping board to cut the carrots.

"You have to hold them steady," I said, "Or they will slip and you could cut your hand."

"I can do it!" she said in the voice she uses when she hasn't truly listened.

And naturally, within about two minutes of awkwardly slicing at the carrots, of saying 'I know!!' whenever any advice was passed over her way, of course Fiona managed to slice the top of her index finger.

She didn't cry. She watched the blood drip down her finger and onto the chopping board. She can't stand blood. It makes her boneless. I saw her hand go to the counter to hold herself upright.

"Ow," she said almost silently.

"Oh, look what you've done," I said, bending down to examine the cut.

"Nooo."

"Come on. Don't be silly. Let me see."

Becoming significantly less irritated when she stopped squirming to let me bandage her up. The cut was small and with a Disney Princess sticker over the top of it, now smiling again. But doesn't dare ask to carry on chopping the carrots, big or not. I add her carrots to my chopping board, finish them quickly and put them in the oven with the rest of our meal.

Her chopping board I kept aside to clean, the small splash of blood across it like a tiny miniature murder. Fiona sat with her head in her hands on the countertop, bored and feeling sorry for herself while I finish. She itched at her Disney princess bandage and kicked her feet against the countertop as I sprayed her chopping board with anti-bacterial spray and begin wiping it down with a paper towel.

The kicking now louder.

Thud, thud, thud.

"Fiona, stop that."

"Stop what?" she asks.

I sighed and gestured for her to come to me. "Stop being a nuisance and come and learn something."

She sighed heavily and climbed down, walking over to stand beside me.

I showed her the chopping board.

"Nice and clean, right?"

She nodded, but I shook my head.

"Actually, the blood stain is still there, even after I cleaned it up. We can't see it, but if we had one of those special lights, like the ones the police have, this would still show that there had been blood spilled on it."

"Gross," she said. "So, do we throw the chopping board away?"

"Oh, no, Mom would have practically no belongings at all if that was the case," I explained, shaking my head. "You can completely remove blood stains using this useful little tool. Hold on, I should have some down in the basement."

She never follows me down into the basement anymore. I watch her, waiting nervously at the top of the stairs behind the creaky red door. She was frowning as me as I return with one of the spray bottles from my gardening kit.

I bent down to show it to her more closely.

"This is called hydrogen peroxide," I said. "If you rub it in very thoroughly, it will clean up all the blood so that even the police wouldn't be able to find it with one of their lights."

"That's neat," she said.

Chapter One

On my lunch break, I find out that they are making a movie about her.

A movie.

I mean, she's probably never going to see it. I doubt they're going to flash up a movie on the big screen for a bunch of criminals serving life sentences for murder. But she'll know it's out there. I dread to think what it will do for her ego.

Maybe she'll find out from one of those trashy magazines, or through her secret cell phone, or maybe her gal-pal, total hack journalist/author Winnie Gails, leaked it to her months ago. But my mother is the inspiration for a three-hour feature about her life choices.

Sure, the film has arisen a fair chunk of controversy around its inception. For one, the victims' families are all still out there, protesting that it's in very poor taste to make a movie about Red Creek. Particularly as the director leading the project is known for making big, gory, flashy movies. I hardly think it's going to deal with the way 59 people died with dignity, sensitivity or caution.

Additionally, there has been criticism that making a film about a serial killer—particularly a living one—glamorises the things that they did. That this film is in particularly poor taste as Red Creek was only caught six years ago. One online search and you can find an onslaught on Twitter insisting that the final victims' families deserve longer to grieve. That it's morally wrong to put them into contact with a heavily stylised version of their loved one's death up on the big screen. But as usual, for every one of these people, you can find ten more saying 'Well, they don't have to go and see the movie though'.

The element that has caused the most controversy, however, is the fact that they cast Scarlett Johansson to play Sarah White/Sylvia Taylor as an adult.

I wonder who will get to play me. Probably someone hot and maybe slightly weird looking and…I don't know, like in their early thirties and barely able to pass for a high schooler. I have never been one to dwell on who would play me in the movie version of my life. I am pretty much on board with the people in the comments saying that the movie shouldn't be made at all.

Winnie Gails is a fucking creative consultant.

Oh, fuck me.

*

At some point in your life, someone will tell you to try to find a career where you can do what you love. It's why they gave us those bullshit career aptitude tests in middle school. It's why they started going loco about college credit in our first year of high school.

You go to school, you do the whole college thing, you do some jobs along the way, something in retail or bussing tables, but then you find your forever job. The job that you love and you love going to work for. Maybe you start your own business, or you get to play Captain America at Disney World or you become a professional athlete or…Well, nobody thinks of their forever career, their best life, sat around in an office, surrounded by dull paperwork, getting calls from dull people with complaints or an inability to process basic information.

They tell you to do something you love, sure, but you're a kid then. One day you grow up, you realise that the whole 'Do what you love thing' is horseshit.

As I look around my office, the bright Santa Cruz sun blaring offensively in through the back windows, I try to imagine that anyone here would have imagined this as their forever career. Behind me is Tanya, playing Fantasy Football and trying to sell her Ikea coffee table on Facebook, using one of the student applications as a makeshift fan. Rajish is by the printer, low-key on his phone. Kiko is doing her lipstick using the black mirror of her monitor.

I watch Claudia from her seat across from me. She is subtly giving herself a manicure and at a guess, possibly googling holidays. Behind her, I can see Jack, our moronic boss, rolling himself a cigarette and humming tunelessly to himself.

Sat at the desk next to me, there is Donnie, who has been looking at the same Excel spreadsheet for twenty minutes—this is a cover of course, for the fact that he's on Tinder on his phone, under the table.

I bet none of them imagined that their lives would turn out this way.

"Claudia, coffee?" Jack says as he heaves himself upright and breezes past the rest of us to the front door.

"You'd like a coffee?" she asks, shoving her nail file under the keyboard.

"That's what I said, isn't it?"

He slams the door behind him and Claudia flips him the bird once his back is turned, before getting up to her desk, muttering under her breath as she makes her way over to the kettle. I bet she did not imagine that this would be her forever job. I bet she wanted to do something fancy, like, with fashion or something.

"Sonova bitch, he should shove his coffee," she mutters. "Can you believe him?" she asks when she notices me looking. "He never asks anyone else to make him his fucking coffee."

"He's scared to ask anyone else," Donnie says. "He asked me on my first day and I cracked a joke about him making me his slave. That man is *very* uncomfortable about his race." He laughs and shakes his head. "So, that's me out, that's Sookie out, that's Rajish out, that's Kiko out, so you and Tanya are promoted to being his coffee bitches."

"Coffee bitches, that's real nice," Claudia says, folding her arms.

"Hey, you forget that I'm his cigarette mule," I say. "The man hasn't brought his own cigarettes in months. His wife gives him three in the morning, he smokes them on the drive to work and by 10, it's 'Oh, Sookie, can I nick a smoke?'"

"You should tell his wife, man," Donnie says.

"Oh, right, sure, I'll tell his wife."

"You should, you're like his cigarette woman, it's basically cheating," he says, shaking his head. "It's sordid."

"Why don't you tell his wife, Donnie?" Claudia asks. "Since you're such a good friend of theirs."

"I saw them at the hardware store once," he corrects. "That doesn't make us friends."

"Woah, that's cold," she says. "At last year's Christmas party, you practically went home with them."

"Erm, nobody needs that particular image in their heads," Rajish calls from the far side of the room.

"Sorry, Rajish." Claudia puts down a mug of coffee onto Jack's desk before flopping back into her own and letting out a heavy sigh. The nail file comes back out from under her keyboard and she leans back before going at her nails with a newfound ferocity.

The door opens and Jack strolls back inside, reeking of my cigarettes and takes a sip of his brand-new coffee without thanking Claudia. After a moment of leaning back into his chair, he spots Kiko applying a second coating of bright red lipstick and moves to loudly berate her in front of everyone.

Of Jack's management style, we are kind of dead inside.

I don't think anyone planned their forever job to be like this.

I would be depressed that this is how I'm spending my life. Only, I'm not. It could be worse. I have a fake name, a fake high school diploma; in real terms, I don't even have one full year of high school education, so getting a job like this is actually a relief. It would be too risky to apply for college with fraudulent paperwork. There are too many facts to check, too many questions that could be raised. I didn't really mind. My desire to go to college died a long time ago.

The people I work with have mostly all finished high school, been to college—heck, Claudia even went to grad school—only to find their way to this particular office at the mercy of a manager who often comes to work wearing his shirt inside out.

I think the whole 'What are you doing with your life' thing is only on my mind because today is actually my birthday. I'm twenty-one, despite what it says on my ID. Twenty-one. I know, big birthday. The last big birthday before society dictates that I get snippy about my age. So yeah, it's my birthday, but nobody knows. Not because I'm prone to early self-consciousness about my age or I'm ridiculously private or whatever—it's because technically all the documentation that exists around me states that I'm twenty-five years old and that my birthday was four months ago.

To be more accurate, and accuracy is important—*Sookie King*, had her twenty-fifth birthday four months ago. However, *Fiona Taylor*, soon to appear in a major motion picture about the Red Creek Killer (played by some successful white girl presumably), believed to have been murdered over five years ago, turns twenty-one today.

I'm not celebrating for obvious reasons.

Though, as I do every year, I will buy a doughnut on my way home as a makeshift-just-for-me birthday cake. Why not enjoy the two birthdays thing a little, like the Queen of England or one of those girls from the Sweet 16 show who spreads their birthday out over six months?

Work finishes for the day. I end up staying late because the mother of a student will not get off the phone. Jack turns out the light on his way out even though he can see me still sat there. So, I sit in near darkness, tapping my pen on the desk. It's not the first time this has happened, not even with this particular woman. She wants to know her daughter's grades, she doesn't have permission to check these, but every few months tries, anyway. She doesn't trust her child to be honest with her about how she's doing in school and if I was her daughter, I wouldn't want her to know that I'm failing either.

Eventually, I get bored so I pretend the connection is bad and hang up.

The hallway outside is empty, except for Greta, the cleaner, who is scrubbing away at a blood stain on the floor.

"Kid came out of Chem 1 with a nosebleed," she says to me. "Pretty gory stuff."

"Ew, not nice. Hope it doesn't keep you late, Greta."

She won't get it out like that.

But this is information that I keep to myself.

*

Part of what pushed me to apply for work at Preston College—other than their policy of hiring people with nothing further than a high school education—was its close proximity to my apartment. It's always a short walk home so staying late never pisses me off that much. I stop off at the shitty supermarket at the end of my road to buy a jelly doughnut and some beers for the fridge. I'm planning on spending this birthday night in, possibly watching a bad movie. Nothing by a certain director and nothing with any slashers.

Tickle me put off.

The cashier asks me for ID and says, "Twenty-five, really?"

I got that for a while. Always the moment of panic at the beginning, age fifteen, terrified that the person behind the counter would call out my ID for what it was. F-A-K-E. But no, I paid good money to be Sookie King. So, the most I get is a disbelieving roll of the eyes or a 'Seriously?' but am otherwise left unscathed.

"Yeah, twenty-five," I say. "Haven't lost my baby face yet." I pinch my own cheek and he laughs, shaking his head.

"Man, I don't remember the last time someone asked to see my ID."

"Blessing and a curse. Have a nice night."

I take my brown bag of birthday treats and stroll home. There is a couple fighting outside a café, a drunk old guy wandering around, muttering to himself. My apartment is across the street. My flatmate Leda is out, but I can hear the TV is on.

Believe it or not, I actually hate the thought of living alone. I've never been able to do it. I lived with my mother and then I lived with roommates. I've only recently made the cut down from two to just one. I met Leda through my friend Gabbie. Leda is nice and very beautiful, but a complete scatterbrain. With very little prompting, I can make her think that we were hanging out all night—you know, if anyone asks. We have been living in our current apartment for just over a year and for the most part it's fine.

Often, there is also Leda's ex-girlfriend, Tammy, the worst person in the world, so more frequently than not, there are actually three of us. Tammy is kind of sponge, she sits around the apartment when nobody's home like a really greedy burglar alarm. She watches our Netflix and eats all the toast. They have been off/on for the last two years. Personally, I wouldn't mind if they were permanently 'off', but on this matter, I get zero say.

So when I come home to the TV on and the smell of popcorn, I know that Leda and Tammy are 10/10 back on.

I climb the stairs from the front door to the living room and find Tammy sprawled out on the couch, wearing the big blanket and eating an enormous bowl of popcorn. She looks up when she sees me and waves, leaning back on the couch.

"Hey, Sookie, did you know you guys are out of milk?"

"Woah, seriously," I say but don't really address it.

Tammy never contributes anything anyway.

I kick off my sneakers and leave them on the rack.

"Oh yeah, I texted Leda about it earlier. She should be home in an hour. Hey, have you seen this documentary? It's about people who get their pets to enter talent contests and stuff. It's totally wild."

"No, what?"

I glance up from the fridge and spot a Persian cat sat in the middle of a red carpet, glaring at a wild-haired old man, trying to lure it along the literal cat-walk with a plush fish on a stick to little effect.

"This is the weirdest fucking thing I've ever seen," Tammy says, laughing. "Want to watch with me?"

"Thanks, Tammy, but it's been a long day and cat-walk pets are a tad too weird for me right now."

"Suit yourself," she says, leaning back into the sofa. "But on a less long day, you should totally check this out. There are like twelve episodes and I literally cannot see how."

I leave her chuckling to herself as I take my beer and my doughnut to my room and kick the door shut behind me, drowning out the rustling of popcorn and displeased meows of the contestants.

*

In TV and movies and stuff, serial killers are always shown as minimalists. You go into their room and there's like a bed, plain white sheets, blinds, a really organised desk and a wardrobe with like a variant of the same outfit.

Maybe there's a handful of books about Satan or Nazis or Japanese prison camps or something else super unpleasant. The books are usually tucked away so that later on, when the police come and do a really thorough scouring of the room, they find them and get all like, 'Oh, here's our sicko'.

My room is kind of the opposite. For one, I have always found the whole minimalist thing to be incredibly difficult and pretentious. Also, why would a serial killer own white bed sheets? It's almost like owning a white car and then getting pissed when it gets dirty, which is, well, every time you drive anywhere. My desk is a kind of organised chaos, my tablet is propped against a pile of books—notably not books about Satan or prisoner of war camps, you know, normal books, about coming of age losers or inventors or lonely women going on holiday and finding love with a hunky barman or waiter.

My wardrobe looks like a bloated holiday maker, bright flashes of blouses and skirts popping through the doors and spilling across the desk chair and the bed. I relocate the ones on the bed to the chair and flop down on my bed, readjusting the cushions and leaning down.

"Happy Birthday, Taylor," I say to myself, taking out the doughnut and carefully biting in to avoid getting jelly spurt all over me.

My second phone buzzes.

Only one person has the number, of course, so I know who it's from.

I take it out of my bag and glance at the screen.

From M:
Happy Birthday.
I hope you are staying out of trouble.

I smile, despite myself, and text her a picture of my birthday doughnut and beer to which she responds with a thumb's up emoji.

From M:
Goodnight X

I lean back against the pillows and close my eyes as I finish my doughnut, fishing for my tablet to put something rubbish on to watch. As birthdays go, this one has been ok. Minimal annoyance at work. Minimal annoyance at home. The most birthday card a mother can send her dead child.

I don't mind no presents or anything fancy.

She's done more than enough for me.

Chapter Two

Fiona Taylor knew how to clean up. It's what her mother taught her. And boy, did the two of them *have* to know how to clean up because they liked to make a mess. I would say that I am more cautious than that. Despite making certain promises to certain people at certain times, I could never bring myself to stop my little bad habit.

So once a month, I like to go out and commit a murder. It doesn't have to be someone that I know, though I am not below making it someone from one of my circles. Once a month, like clockwork, or I get all bent out of shape. Well, maybe not every month, sometimes I'm not in the mood or it's the holiday season so I don't want to mess with people's celebrations too much. And you know, even though we are living in a more digital age than ever before, I have not, in six years, been questioned by the police.

You see, I've found my niche.

I have become a master at committing murders that look like accidents or suicides. It really shouldn't be as easy as it is, but it really is. Especially when you know what you're doing, you know exactly what to look for. And like I say, we live in a digital age, more specifically, a lonely age. You would be surprised how easily people believe that their friend or relative would take their own life. These are miserable times to be alive.

So sad. Too bad.

I have washed away a lot of blood in the shower in this apartment. Our bathroom is always immaculate because of this fact. Four walls and shiny, clean perfection—if anyone came and checked, which they haven't. I'm a pro at cleaning. In fact, the toughest thing is to get the blood out of my dreads. Always an area I try to avoid, but you can't always be so lucky. Cold water works the best, tried and tested and of course, totally ruins the whole notion of having a nice hot shower. Follow this up with applying baking soda, which I will still not get used to.

Now I'm lying in bed, trying to get the smell of baking soda out of my nostrils when I hear a tap at the door.

"Sookie, are you awake?"

Leda is outside, sounding drained. She pokes her head around, her long silvery hair poking out from the bright pink towel wrapped around her head. She is bright eyed and fresh from her morning shower.

"Can we go and get breakfast?"

"Sure," I say. "Will Tammy be joining us?"

"God no," she says, wrinkling her nose. "I've had more than enough Tammy time."

Ah, off again.

*

Leda orders beer with her halloumi and avocado toast. She makes eye contact with me right after she does, daring me to challenge this or say something. When I don't, she settles back into her chair and swigs straight from the bottle, ignoring the too-hot glass straight from the dish washer.

"So, you and Tammy are off again?"

"I'm so sick of her," she says. "She comes over for days, eats everything, borrows my pyjamas, uses up all my shampoo. She's like a little kid."

"She'll be back," I say with a sigh, taking a sip of my coffee.

"Sookie, come on, she won't. I told her this morning, we are done. For good. No more of her attitude, stinking up the place."

"Until next week, don't you dare trick me into talking shit about her and making it super awkward when she's back next week, telling me to go buy milk and eating all the bread."

"Aha!" Leda says, pointing at me. "You do hate it when she comes to stay!"

"Aha yourself," I say. "Is this why you're taking me out for lunch? To tell me that my two mommies are getting a divorce?"

She laughs at that and leans forward. "Oh yeah, you want me to get custody of you, right? You're at an impressionable age and this must be hard for you." She snorts into her beer, before glancing back at me. "Nah, I just wanted to get out of the house."

"Always advised."

"You came home late, didn't you?"

"No, I came straight home after work."

"We heard you get back this morning, right before the dumping happened," she said. "Was it some guy?"

"You do realise that we aren't a bunch of lonely housewives, right?"

"Was it a guy? Come on, I'm just asking."

"No."

"Liar! I can tell!"

She really can't.

"No, I just went out for a walk."

Leda doesn't look convinced.

"Hmm, sure."

"I really did. I went for a jog. It's a nice time to go."

"It's a stupid time to go. You could get hurt by some drunk. Go in the morning like a normal person. You do know that this is why I don't believe you, right?"

I mean, yeah, to a degree it was a guy. And to a degree we had been involved—he grabbed my ass on the subway the other day and I've been low key following him for a week, checking out his social media, seeing where he goes. It took about a week to see where he went, how easy it would be for his wife and daughter to believe that he might be so inclined to drive his shitty company car off a cliff. The hardest part, honestly, was shifting his fat ass into the car before I sent him into the water.

"Believe whatever you want, Leda, it's a free country. So, what did Tammy do?"

"Tammy, really? What didn't Tammy do?"

I raise an eyebrow and see her smile.

"Ok, ok, she made a comment about how the place could be a bit tidier. And I lost it because me and you are at work, Tammy is an influencer, living out of her mother's pocket, who lummoxes around our house eating our food."

"And you kicked her out?"

"Really surprised you didn't hear us yelling."

I was having a euphoric sleep.

"You know me, when I'm out, I'm out."

"Tired from a good, long, hard..."

"Don't be gross," I say. "Finish your food."

I met Leda through my old roommate, Gabbie.

Gabbie was my first friend when I moved to California, the two of us bonded over a mutual love of superhero movies and both being in possession of fake IDs. Mine being slightly better; Gabbie said her surname was San Diego for crying out loud. She got rumbled within nine months of our cushy Santa Cruz life—her parents showing up at the apartment one night, red-faced and angry. But by that time, Gabbie genuinely had turned eighteen so they could do very little in terms of forcing her to go back to Georgia.

The experience rattled me. I worried about my new identity being seen through and getting exposed and brought back home or potentially to juvie because how on earth could I explain why I'd gone into hiding?

But that day never came and I stayed Sookie King.

Gabbie got a proper ID with her proper name on it—Gabriella Amber-Lee Jackson and after much flirting with Leo, our Batman-obsessed landlord, she was allowed to resume her residency same as ever.

"You better not be a secret kid too," he said to me once.

"Ha, as if."

Gabbie worked with Leda at a tattoo and piercing place a few years ago. They got on pretty well, they were both very tall and beautiful and arty. Leda ended up crashing at our place a lot, usually because she'd fallen out with Tammy or whoever her girlfriend was before.

Then just over a year ago, Gabbie got engaged to Leo, our old landlord and my living situation became very *crowded*. I figured it was best to leave the happy couple to it and Leda seemed the obvious choice for a new living situation.

"So, what are you up to today?"

"I have no plans," I said. "How about you?"

"I was going to go to the beach, catch some sun," she said. "Want to go?"

"Yeah, I can do that."

"Maybe you can tell me about this guy you're seeing?"

"Maybe we can invite Tammy."

"Oh, you are hilarious."

*

Part of the reason I chose to escape to California was the prospect of being close to the sea. I'd never seen the ocean before, other than in films or online. I always think that if I'd been caught back then, I'd have gone to prison without ever seeing the sea like this.

We are lounged out by the boardwalk, screams and music from the fairground in the distance, Leda is asleep with her sunglasses on. Or at least she looks asleep.

I wave a hand in front of her face and hear her make the slightest snoring sound. I chuckle to myself and lie back against my towel, inhaling the smell of sunscreen and a BBQ from further down the beach.

Somewhere nearby there are some guys throwing a beach ball around, being loud, making a ruckus. I hear the click of a camera and the loud chatter of tourists and feel the hot sun on my skin.

I sigh and lie back down, taking in the smell of the sand and the sea.

I wonder why she never brought me to a beach when I was young. Did she ever go to one? Maybe when she was a kid? Or when she was living in Atlantic City? I wonder what she thought to all of this...

I frown and shake my head and try to push her from my mind.

I really need to stop doing that.

It's guilty and unrewarding.

Still, I text her a photo of the sea for good measure.

She will probably think I'm being overly sentimental.

"Sookie, do you think it was stupid of me to dump Tammy over cleaning?" Leda mumbles in a tiny voice.

"No," I say.

"Don't you get scared of being alone?"

"No."

"Not ever?"

I sit up and turn towards her. "Leda, come on," I say. "Don't tell me that you just date Tammy because you're scared of being alone. You're twenty-six for God's sake."

"Well, I wouldn't phrase it like that," she says.

"You implied it."

"I just don't want to be still dating when I'm in my thirties."

"Yes, but you also don't want to be dating someone who irritates you."

"So, good idea?"

"I won't say it again."

"Thanks."

*

The walk back from the beach is short and warm. Leda stops to buy milk—one useful thing Tammy did remind her of—and she picks up some margarita mix from the discount counter.

"Little cocktail party tonight?" she asks.

"As long as it's roomies only," I say.

"You're never going to meet anyone with an attitude like that," she says, shaking her head. "But, yeah, I totally agree."

Recently, and I think it's the whole twenty-five thing, Leda has kept making comments about me being single. Because of my…extra-curriculars, I have never really had time for a relationship. The concept doesn't interest me. A relationship would mean being asked waaaay too many questions, you know…Where are you going, where were you last night, how did you get that bruise on your arm, why do you own a bone-saw, etc?

I like my privacy. It's what keeps me safe. It's what keeps my lifestyle *safe*.

I like having someone to live with, not someone who watches to see how I live. I think I've long since given up on a need to be understood by others, anyway.

"Come on," Leda says, fumbling in her beach bag for the keys. "Margaritas and something to binge watch?"

"Sure, whatever. Just no Tammy."

As we reach the stairwell to our apartment, I spot a straw fedora and the sharp, cocky-looking face of P.J., our landlord poking around from around the corner. This is echoed by Leda muttering 'fuck' under her breath.

"Oh hey, P.J," she says.

"Hello yourself, milady," he says.

This guy. This fucking guy.

He's twenty-eight, about 5' 9", skinny with long pale arms and legs even though he's always in a vest and shorts. He wears them like a uniform with that goddamn stupid hat. He's prone to a sociopathic smirk and I'm sure I've seen him wearing an MAGA baseball cap on his one-day ditch from the straw fedora.

His eyes skim over me and settle on Leda, where his entire face creases into a smirk. His lanky arm comes to rest against the wall, cutting off our access to the stairs.

Now, typically, you might think we would be trying to dodge out on the landlord because of being slow on the rent or something.

Ha, as if.

No, one thing we have never been, particularly after this clown took over as landlord from his father, is late on rent. He's the kind of scumbag who has watched too much porn. You know, the drugged-up looking thirty-something in dress-up as a college girl, tugging on her cheer uniform while she tells her junk-in-the-trunk landlord that she couldn't possibly pay the rent this month, but maybe they could come to some kind of arrangement *wink wink*.

Only this creep thinks that's how life works.

This guy has been the most irritating thing in my life for the last six months, ever since he became the landlord of this building.

After seeing his father once—save the day we moved in—we have suddenly started seeing the new guy around the place a lot. Whether he's leaping from his office, the second he hears Leda coming or popping by the front door to check everything's alright. One time he even showed up late at night with a bottle of wine and stinking of whisky to celebrate his own birthday.

He has been very clear in his intentions.

"So, Leda..." He pronounces her name as Lead-daaah. "Good day at the beach?"

"Oh yeah," she says, "Got to love some beach time."

"Nice bikini," he says, lowering his sunglasses and raising them back up again in mock but totally sincere admiration, "Bet none of the guys there were complaining."

This dumb bastard probably thinks that Tammy is just Leda's *good* friend, her pal, her close personal gal pal.

He interprets the lack of men hanging around the place as Leda being a good girl, smoking hot, but pure, not slutty like all those mean girls from high school who definitely never gave him the time of day.

This type of man probably sincerely believes that lesbians only exist for porn.

"So, you ladies having a little party?"

He turns the leer on me as well and I suppress the urge to vomit… barely.

"Nah, just a girl's night," Leda says, stressing the word 'girls'.

"Well, do enjoy," he says, doing an awkward little bow that takes his eyes closer to our crotches than I would really ever like. "Mi-ladies."

Leda shoots me a smirk before dashing up the stairs. I follow and watch how his eyes follow my friend's long legs and he—he actually licks his lips.

Animal.

"Oh, ladies, while I remember," he said, "I popped in earlier. Hope you don't mind? One of your neighbours mentioned some damp coming through her wall? I just wanted to make sure there wasn't a leak."

"Oh no way," Leda says, "Was it ok though?"

"Completely fine," he said. "You guys keep the place looking tidy."

"Well, we do try," she says, laughing.

"Sorry, but next time, could you let us know if you're going to pop over?" I say, raising my eyebrow.

"I was concerned about the leak," he says and I notice how his eyes harden ever so slightly. "Can't have any damage to my property."

Your dad's property, I think but don't say.

"Yeah, I totally get that," I say, "But as tenants, we have legal rights. If you want to check out the place, you have to give us sufficient notice. You have Leda's phone number, right? You could just call her and let us know."

The smile is glued onto his face.

I don't like the look in his eyes. He doesn't look mad exactly, I have undermined him before and seen him look mad. No, he looks smug.

"Sure, whatever you say," he says and offers that creepy bow again before slinking back into his office.

This requires…more thought than I would perhaps like to spend on my creepy-ass landlord, but there we go. We climb up the stairs and Leda starts laughing when the door is shut.

"Milady, shall I fetch you a glass?" she says, doing an exaggeratedly flourished bow.

"I shall fetch it myself," I say, joining in. "Then to the television for some sofa masturbation."

"Ew! Don't! He's harmless," she says, laughing and shaking her head. "Though, could he be any weirder than this? I don't even want to know!"

"I don't think he realises you're gay," I say.

"What did he think Tammy was doing here?" she asks, fumbling around the counter for some glasses. "That she was my sister? Who I sometimes kiss? Kister."

"Guy that lonely probably thinks that's what really good sisters do," I say to watch her cringe and shake her head in disgust.

"Ew! Ew! Sookie, cut out that talk!"

*

I don't notice P.J's little scheme right away. For that I only have myself to blame. I never like to think of myself as slow on the uptake, but I guess everyone has their off moments.

It all starts that day, of course, not that I knew it then. We get back from the beach and I notice him giving us this smug little smirk and think nothing of it other than how irritating and gross he is. Me and Leda get drunk on cheap margarita mix and fall asleep raggedly, tossing and turning. In the morning, I wake up blearily to Leda telling me that we are out of sugar and that she was going out to buy some.

Only then I hear her talking to creepy P.J of all people. He was randomly walking past our apartment after picking up some sugar from the store and actually had spare. They are chatting for a few minutes and then she sends him on his way.

The weekend ends and I go back to my desk job and Leda goes back to selling lower back tattoos to tourists and talking to Gabbie for hours about how she'd like to try rainbow hair for the millionth time. In the morning as I am getting ready to leave the house, Leda mentions that the shower head is running slow again.

I get back from the office to find P.J fixing the shower, eager for praise, eager for compliments from Leda, who is sulking about Gabbie's less-than enthusiastic reaction to her rainbow hair goals.

"She said that I have zero follow-through, zero," she says, "Can you believe that?"

"It'd be like really tough to grow out," I said.

"I think girls who dye their hair look tacky," P.J said, though nobody had asked. "I think you look beautiful natural, like you are."

Leda glances at me and snorts, shaking her head.

"Dude, I'm a redhead naturally."

He chooses to ignore this and continues to talk for another ten minutes about girls wearing too much make-up or girls making themselves bald with all the crap they put in their hair.

Did women need that stuff in caveman times?

We call him 'Ug' after he leaves and spend the next few weeks muttering 'Ug' to each other when we see him watching us from the reception window.

But then there are other little things, weird, hardly noticeable stuff. Like, he strikes up a conversation with Leda about what happened on *Dancing with the Stars* the night before, despite it being painfully obvious that he's never seen it. In fact, he practically quotes something Leda yelled across the room to me, while she was watching it.

Then, I start to think that he might have cottoned on to 'Ug' being him—because just like that, he wasn't around so much. I mean, yeah, he was present-present, but he was less creepy, less pushy. He got less needy, less over the top, less desperate for any affection from Leda. We start joking around that he's getting some. I mean, even Charles Manson had a girlfriend. But no, we saw him every day, he lived in the building, he was all alone. There's nobody else there with him.

Then one evening when I get back from a jog, I notice him watching me from his office and he is staring at me. He's staring at me in a way that makes me stop. And as I go past him, I'm not going to cower or act all shy and scared, so I look him straight in the eye and say, 'Good evening' before reaching for the stairwell.

And he says, "Going to run yourself a nice hot shower, are you?"

I glance back and notice in the reflection of his screen that he is rubbing the front of his pants under the table.

So, I go home and I turn the bathroom upside down. At first worrying that I'm being suspicious or paranoid or delusional or grossly overestimating his intelligence. But then I find it.

A tiny little camera that he's tucked into the extractor of the shower.

The realisation comes over me all at once and I feel terror rising in me like vomit. My hand covers my mouth and I smash the thing with one of Leda's heavier shampoo bottles.

That bastard.

He's been watching us shower; he's been watching what we do in the bathroom.

I try to remember when was the last time I came home and cleaned a bloody knife in this bathroom, when was the last time I washed the blood off my hands, when was the last time I did something that I really wasn't supposed to. I can't get caught out—not after all my hard work, and not by some pathetic guy like this!

I clutch at my chest and cover my hands over my head and try to calm down.

One.

Two.

Three.

Four.

Five.

Deep breaths.

It had to be that day that he went into the flat to check a mysterious damp patch that definitely never fucking existed. I haven't been out for any…fun since then. There's nothing I've gone and done in this apartment, since that time, that I wouldn't be comfortable describing in court and anyone else seeing.

Only, nobody should have the right to watch me like that.

Nobody.

Leda isn't home for another hour.

So, I go through the rest of the apartment. I find one tucked behind the television, mixed in with Leda's fairy lights. I find two in the kitchen, one in a cupboard, one by the extractor fan. My room is free. But there's one in the hallway and four in Leda's room.

I smash them all to bits.

I imagine confronting him, threatening to call the police, I mean there has to be a law against this. But at the same time, I don't want to draw attention to myself. I don't want to go down to the station, to answer questions, to file a police report. I don't really want to make unnecessary contact with the police with my forged documentation and backstory that has no witnesses past five years ago.

So when Leda comes home, I don't tell her.

We hang out and watch a movie.

She gets a call from Tammy and goes out onto the balcony to take it. She's there for about twenty minutes and I hear giggling and flirting and get the dreaded feeling in my stomach that Tammy will be back again very soon. But the front doorbell rings.

He is outside, looking irritated and frantic.

"Can I help you?" I ask.

"I think there's a leak," he says, glancing past me. "I think there's been a leak, can I come in and check your shower?"

He steps forward as if to come in.

"Sorry, it's not convenient," I say.

He doesn't seem to have heard.

"It. Is. Not. Convenient. No."

He blinks in surprise.

"But there's a leak, one of your neighbours said-" He steps to the side as if to bypass me, I move with him, raising one arm to cut off his entrance.

"Which neighbour?"

"Sorry?"

"Which neighbour? Is it Mrs. O'Riley or Jonah?"

He doesn't seem to have thought that far ahead, so he steps back looking nervous.

"Fine, fine, whatever, when would be a good time?" he asks.

"Alone? Never," I say.

The colour vanishes from his face.

"I found those cameras you put up in our apartment," I say coldly.

His bottom lip trembles. "I don't know what you mean."

"Really? So, it's not a coincidence that the day I find the cameras and smash them, the mysterious leak is suddenly back? You're a lousy fucking liar." I watch the colour come back to his face, watch his long nose and high forehead turn a sickly red. "So, yeah, unless you want me to tell Leda and call the cops, I want that footage you have of the two of us. And I want you to keep the fuck out of our apartment."

"You don't have any proof."

"Are you going to delete the footage?" I step forward and jab him in the chest with my finger. "Because what I'm hearing is bullshit excuses."

He seems to get over his initial shock. He's not big or strong, but he is a pig. He's not going to get talked down to by some woman, some woman who is beneath him.

"How would you like that footage to go viral, skank?" he snarls.

"How would you like to get charged for revenge porn, you dumb bitch?" I say.

His ears turn scarlet. "You can't talk to me like that!"

"Delete the fucking footage," I say, taking another step forward.

He seems to realise that he's now stood with his feet against the top of the stairs, back facing the long way down.

"You think you scare me?"

I don't say anything.

He nervously turns around and starts walking down the stairs.

"Goodnight, Ug," I call after him.

*

The next day I tell Leda that I lost my key and arrange for a locksmith to install new locks. I tell Leda that I'll let the landlord know but obviously, I don't. I bet he tried his luck once anyway but whether he did or not, that isn't my problem. Not at the moment.

Or, that's what I thought, anyway.

Then this morning, I'm at work, I'm sat talking to a tearful student who is flunking absolutely everything. She leaves to go and calm down and I head back into the office. Claudia is on the phone and drawing crude graffiti onto a photo of Jack she has had to blow up for a meeting later.

Kiko is making coffee and Tanya and Rajish are talking quietly over a bunch of paperwork. Donnie looks up when I get to my desk and gestures over at Jack's chair.

"The boss is looking for you."

"Oh, no way, what did he say it was about?"

I glance down and see that my own coffee has gone cold during my meeting with that last student and go to make myself another.

"Actually, man, it seemed kind of urgent, I'd just go. He's in the consultation room." Donnie winces and shrugs his shoulders. "You getting in trouble or something?"

"Oh yeah, you know me. Trouble is my middle name."

Actually, it's not. Sookie King doesn't have a middle name. Fiona Taylor had one—Annabel—I'm glad Mother liked her grandma enough to name me after her instead of giving me a name she must have liked enough to pick it out from like every other name on the planet.

"Good luck," Donnie calls as I head back out the office door, still holding my mug of depressingly cold coffee.

Now, a meeting with the boss is never good. Even if that boss is Jack, who is a moron. But as I try to convince myself, I'm basically his dealer for cigarettes, so whatever thing he has to give me shit for, can't be that bad.

I'm like 90% certain that his cigarette privileges matter more to him than this job.

I knock on the door and Jack waves at me through the glass.

He is sat behind the little round desk with his laptop in front of him. He tugs on his tie awkwardly. He looks weirdly flustered.

"Hey, Sookie," he says, "Have a seat, have a seat."

Repeating himself isn't good, it's something he only tends to do when he's nervous or babbling for time.

"Am I in trouble?"

"Oh no, no, no, no," he says, continuing to repeat himself. "I mean, a little bit, but it's nothing to do with your work, it's nothing like that. This is actually a bit personal. I..." He sighs. "I was sent this earlier."

He turns the screen towards me.

I frown and feel my heart grow tight in my chest as I look down at a photograph of me. It's blurred and steamed up from the shower. But it's me. Naked and rubbing shower gel underneath my arm, one breast covered by my wrist, the other on show.

"What the fuck?"

He reaches past and clicks off the screen.

"This was sent to me this morning from a weird-looking account. I would usually have just deleted it as spam. I just thought I should make you aware of this before I take this matter further."

My stomach is in my shoes right now. My face burning with shame.

Already I know that the bastard was probably angry about me changing the locks, so he looked up where I work. They have this stupid webpage on our department with phone numbers and photographs of the team. He would have looked up who my manager was, hoping to humiliate me because I humiliated him. My nails dig into the skin of my palm and I start to feel blood, the half-moons of my nails finding old indents, old wounds to dig back into.

"Sookie, are you alright?"

"Jack, I'm really sorry you got dragged into this," I say. "I'm so embarrassed..." I blink a lot and start dabbing my eyes with my sleeve until he looks away. I make my voice tremble, the way I've practiced well. "I can't believe this..." I even manage a little choked sob. "I-Is there any way we can keep this between us?"

"Sookie, we really do need to report this. This could be a police matter, I mean, this is..."

"It's just...I recently split up with my boyfriend. He's not taken it well. We've been fighting, saying a lot of ugly stuff to each other. I know he's done this to try to get back at me."

"That's not legal," he says.

It's so weird to see him putting on his professional hat.

"I know, look, could you…just forget about this? I'll talk to him, get this straightened out. I promise it won't happen again."

"I really would feel more comfortable…"

"Please?" I say. "Please, can you just sweep this under the carpet?"

"I mean, alright, if that's what you want. But this isn't how I'd really like to see my team," he says, laughing nervously. "Not that you aren't…you know…" He gestures strangely with his hands.

Ew.

"Erm, yeah, can we really just forget all about this?"

I wipe my eyes with my hands.

"I promise, he won't bother you again."

"Sure. Consider it gone."

We shake hands and he asks me for a cigarette which I even roll for him because I do not want to think about my fucking idiot boss seeing my tits ever again. We head back into the office and he falls asleep at his desk.

"So, are you getting fired?" Donnie teases.

"Oh yeah, I'm waiting for security to escort me off the premises," I say.

Then I take some calls, answer some emails and make arrangements for an upcoming exam board. But it's background noise. Mostly, I am making a mental note of what time P.JT tends to leave his post at the reception area he calls his office, whether it's late, whether there's a little kitchen out back there. I swear I have smelled pop tarts coming from the door as I passed it before.

Like I said before, sometimes, as much as I love keeping my life and my extra-curricular life separate, there are definitely occasions where you just have to mix it up.

Chapter Three

I like to think of myself as someone who doesn't get mad easily. I mean, look at my track record, if I lashed out every time I got angry with someone, I'd have been arrested like two weeks into the first grade after Mrs. Philberts, my teacher, told me that I wasn't allowed to go to the bathroom without her permission.

Fascist.

But, still, I would *like* to think of myself as someone who doesn't get mad easily. However, I know when I break into P.J's office, that it is going to be *so* hard not to fucking mutilate this guy.

I am fucking furious. These last three days after I had to sit and have my boss tell me that he'd seen me naked, I have been like a clenched fist. I've walked past this office every day, said a polite 'Good morning' or 'Good night' and watched him smirk at me.

Bastard even asked me 'How's work?'.

But today's the day, I won't need to see that little shit sat behind his desk smirking like the cat who got the cream ever again.

That obnoxious, arrogant little...

You know, this is the kind of behaviour I hate the most. Generally, I have always found men to be difficult to deal with. Firstly, got to add the 'not all men' disclaimer; there have been lots of guys I have gotten on great with. But if we were to narrow down to the most toxic kinds of men to know, there would have to be two in particular.

In high school there were guys like Riley Sanders, who was big and tough and made his way through high school devouring everything in his path. He'd call anything that didn't fit into his world 'GAY' and lash out. It was a nuisance when I was a teenager. But I've noticed after high school, guys like that still exist: some of them become gas station attendants or work behind the till at a movie theatre or they take over their daddy's business. Sometimes they marry the prom queen, sometimes they have kids real young. I guess we'll never know with Riley Sanders.

But no matter what, these types of toxic guys end up frequenting bars, red-faced and fatter, grumbling about the good old days parading around campus as a big football player. They are gross has-beens, they probably try to pick up college girls and get mad when they don't give a shit about what a stud some old guy was when he was a quarterback a billion years ago.

But there is a different breed of guy that are just as irritating as the self-important former big man on campus. These are the entitled baby-men, who find themselves approaching thirty single and furious that women aren't just dropping at their feet. These are men that send dick pics, harass, start rumours and attack. Men who see women as property, as something they deserve due to their right as a man on this earth.

Men like fucking P.J.

Sure, it's just watching us shower and shit and sleep and eat now. But he's already peddling out our naked bodies as crude revenge. How long before he decides he's not ok with just watching? How long before he knows when Leda is in and out of the apartment? How long before he starts coming in and helping himself to her things, a pair of underpants here, a few of her personal items there?

How long before she gets back with Tammy and he realises that he doesn't stand a fucking chance?

How long before he gets angry because he feels duped?

How long before he hurts Leda, or Tammy?

How am I meant to not carry on like I do, knowing there are men like this guy out there?

And Leda wonders why I'm in no rush to date.

Ha.

I watched him for a few days to see when the best time to strike would be. He's always here, but he does go for long walks sporadically throughout the day, to stretch his legs and probably catch a view of unsuspecting ladies. I know when the other tenants are around and when they aren't. With my hobby, it's kind of my prerogative to know things like that.

i'm tired of living in a world where girls only want to date guys who are bad for them. what's the point in being a nice guy like me if you're alone for the rest of your life? i help people, i do my best to be the right sort of man but nobody will even see me. i don't want to spend the rest of my life alone in this building. leave my things to my mom and dad. i'm sorry i have to go out like this.

P.J.

And no smiley face, that would be inappropriate.

I close the book and put it back in his drawer.

The big knife stays with me.

P.J. comes back from the toilet or wherever the hell he's been and sits back in his squeaky chair. But he doesn't see me. I'm hiding behind the door to his pseudo-kitchen. I watch him jerk off at his desk, clumsily plugging in sticky-looking headphones to the PC.

Well, that's hygienic and mentally scarring.

He finishes, misses the bin with his tissue and does up his pants before staggering towards me in the kitchen to get himself a beer, or maybe a pop tart or something. I guess we'll never know what he was after.

Delirious from his orgasm and tired from a long day of being completely useless and creepy, he doesn't notice me until he's in the kitchen.

I cough and close the door behind us both.

"What the fuck!"

Not uncommon last words.

I hit him hard where his neck meets his shoulder to temporarily weaken his right arm. He yelps and I grab hold of one of his wrists. He sees the knife and his weakened arm comes and tries to grasp at the handle. He is clasping onto it with me, grunting from exertion.

Thanks for the prints.

I cut his wrist nice and deep and hard and let go of his arm.

He lets out a horrified gasp and staggers against the countertop.

I grab hold of his other arm and pull it towards me.

"No-no-no!"

Very common last words.

I cut his wrist jagged and awkward, like he was struggling to make the cut with his left hand. I've cut enough people to know when I've sliced an artery nice and wide. He is weeping and trying to pull away from me. He falls onto the ground and starts gasping.

"I'm sorry! I'm sorry! Oh God, call an ambulance, call an ambulance!"

"I'm not calling anybody," I say. "You're pathetic."

I drop the knife on the ground. From the wrists...a nice wide cut to an artery could cause a heart attack to occur within about 2-3 minutes.

"Take it. You can do fuck all with it. Like that shrivelled little thing you call your dick."

He starts to see red through the panting and the exhaustion and the fear. He snarls at me and scrambles for the knife, he brandishes it at me. He's wheezing, his sentences slurred.

I guess I'll never know what his last words are.

He slashes at me once, uselessly, bloody hands over his knife.

I snort and step around him to go through the door. I close it behind him and flip his notebook over to the page with his little goodbye. I hear him groaning as I walk out into the sun. I peel off my gloves and pocket them for now. They are due a soak.

On the way back to the office, I pick up my dry cleaning and spend a few minutes chatting to Mari-Lee behind the counter, joke around about the crazy old man preaching the end of the world outside, to give the slightest hint that I was hanging around the dry cleaners the whole time.

You know, if anybody asks.

But they haven't so far.

*

Upsettingly, it's Leda who finds him.

She calls me at work hysterical and sobbing.

She was coming back from work and saw him propped up against the door and called an ambulance. Of course, he was long dead by then, but I'm still sorry she had to go and see something like that.

She was there when they found the photo of her in his desk and she's basically convinced herself that she may as well have murdered him herself.

Like that even makes sense.

"I can't believe it," she says, weeping. "I mean, I didn't like him overtly, but he was harmless. He was a nice man! I saw him just this morning. I just… I can't believe it. Can you come home?" she asks, "I-I can't be here on my own. It's horrible!"

"I'll talk to my boss, let me call you back," I say. "It'll be ok."

Jack is, of course, super sympathetic. He tells me that male suicide rates are an epidemic in this country, then turns it into a long story about him going on a road trip with a mopey friend of his in college. I pretend to be very upset so I can get away from him and take some solace in the women's toilets. My sanctum of refuge.

I walk home, dry cleaning intact, I buy a bottle of wine and some ice cream, Leda's custom comfort food and head back to the apartment. The police are there, the office has been sectioned off. I have to show my ID and explain who I am to get inside.

The detective is young and pretty.

"Can I ask where you were between the hours of one and two?" she asks.

"I was on my lunch break at the office," I say, "I picked up some dry cleaning from Blue Moon and hung out around there mostly."

She writes it down and gives me the OK to head back up to my apartment.

I open the door to find Tammy's red sneakers on the mat, next to Leda's impractical heels. I walk up the stairs to find the two of them sat on the sofa, watching the cat catwalk show, Leda crying into Tammy's shoulder.

"Leda, hey," I say, "I have wine and Ben and Jerry."

"Hey, see," Tammy says, "Everything is better with wine and Ben and Jerry's." She shoots me a smile and shifts along on the sofa to make room for me.

Leda wipes her very red eyes and sniffs loudly.

"I wish P.J. had some wine and Ben and Jerry's earlier."

"Oh, honey, I doubt it would have helped at this stage," she says, smoothing her hair. "He's in a better place now."

The morgue, I think, but don't say.

"I just feel like I've been shot in the stomach," she says. "It's not fair-"

"There was nothing you could have done," I say. "He was a lonely, complicated guy. It has nothing to do with you."

"I just feel so helpless," she says miserably.

"Well I'll stay as long as you need," Tammy says. "I won't leave your side." She hugs her tight as Leda starts to cry all over again.

One necessary evil for another, I think as I pour the wine.

Chapter Four

After a full week of Tammy time, our bathroom is back to having three toothbrushes, and Tammy's Instagram is full of images from hanging out around the flat or cute photos of the two of them #truelove. Leda is back to being 'in a relationship' on all her social media. She tells me that Tammy has really matured from them being apart, which is not true, but it makes her happy so whatever.

Too happy in fact. There have been a few instances where I've had to sleep with headphones in and ACDC blasting me to sleep to cover certain intimate sounds…I realise that they are probably going to stay on from now on.

We grieve for P.J by drinking at home, by putting down flowers outside the reception area. The police have ruled his death as a suicide. His scrambling around the kitchen was in an attempt to use a phone, maybe he'd changed his mind, they suspect. His father has been around, grey-faced and quiet. He removes the cheerleader calendar and the handful of other things P.J. kept in the office.

I find out that P.J. stood for Peter Jerome, which is a way less irritating name.

We do a lot of mourning. Leda in particular is inconsolable. I suspect P.J's father discovered the surveillance videos from our apartment because he tells us not to worry about the rent that month and never explains. I think he suspected the sort of man his son was. Leda thinks it's because she found him. But I am less sentimental.

After nearly two weeks, Tammy insists we go out on the town. We need to be living life, she says, as if we were basically living an unlife before. And of course, that somehow means go to a bar and pay way too much to be hot and squashed and molested.

This bar they picked, for example, is called The Orchid, for fuck knows what reason, and is loud with an incredibly sticky floor. This is something I don't realise fully until I'm sat at the table and my foot is firmly stuck to the floor. As I raise my heel, I feel my foot come away without my shoe. I am sat awkwardly, trying to get my left shoe free from the sticky ground without drawing too much attention to myself.

I think Tammy has noticed, she's frowning slightly.

Over the music, Leda is yelling something, when I don't respond, she waves an empty beer at me.

"No, thanks!" I yell.

"No, my round!" she calls back, before disappearing through the crowd to the bar with Tammy in tow.

I roll my eyes and finish the rest of my martini, stabbing at the olive with a cocktail stick lazily.

This will be my first properly legal drink. 21 or over, now officially not a lie. I smirk and eat the olive, enjoying its saltiness. I lift my foot and rest my bare foot against the cold metal of the chair, glancing down at my lone heel embedded into the floor. Well, that's that. Goodbye all hope of having my shoe restored to me easily.

I don't like nights out. They can be good for dancing, for blasting it out with noise. But, it's never just about that. These sorts of places become a low-key breeding ground. Guys come here to grind up against girls. Not to say that girls don't do the exact same thing. But you never find a club full of people who genuinely came to dance.

It's depressing.

Or maybe I just started being allowed into clubs when I was still too much of a kid at heart and also secretly/actually.

I'm not good at the whole dating thing, much to the horror of all my friends. But I only have myself to blame.

Thanks to certain extracurricular habits, I'm pretty good at noticing things about people. Spotting out little weaknesses, bad habits, ways of talking, sometimes even deep dark secrets.

People are a lot easier to read than you might think.

Like my shitty boss, you can tell from the off that he's a smoker who is supposed to be trying to quit, that he's married and has kids that he adores. Ok, so he always stinks of cigarettes—you can smell it before you physically see him—which lets you know he's a smoker. Within minutes of talking, he may ask you for a cigarette—which tells you that he has run out and can't just buy more. You could assume that he's a cheapskate, but he has a Subway sandwich on his desk and an expensive watch—showing that he doesn't mind spending money on the casual.

Then, big hint, he's wearing a wedding ring—so he's married—therefore he's hiding the quantity of his smoking from his spouse, who probably doesn't enjoy kissing an ashtray so much anymore.

Finally, on his desk, he has two framed photos, pictures of his kids. Plus, if he gets the chance, he will rant about his kids for any amount of time. You might think this would give away that he loves them, but you'd be wrong. When he talks about his kids, he's always moaning—about lack of sleep, about dirty diapers, about the two of them attacking each other. I was once in the office when he referred to his three-year-old daughter as a 'dickhead'.

What shows that he loves them are the photos on his desk. Usually people use nice pics of their kids. You know, the professional ones every parent gets done, where you have the weird background and the kid looks either super smiley and adorable or secretly constipated.

The photos my shitty boss keeps on his desk are candid shots, pictures of the kids pulling weird faces. The little girl who is apparently a massive dickhead covered in jam and laughing a toothless laugh. The little boy covered in spaghetti pulling a demonic-looking expression and holding a fistful of spaghetti up at the camera.

Here's an idiot who loves his kids.

This has always been my little extra, something from my serial killing that I can apply to real life.

Sure, sometimes it isn't the most useful.

You can pretty much always tell when someone is lying to you, or spinning you a yarn to try to get into your pants. You can always tell when someone is going to leave you.

"Hey," I hear a guy call over the music.

I glance up and see a tight t-shirt-wearing guy with a shaved head and a realtor-style smile.

"This seat taken?"

"Yeah," I yell over the music, "My friends are at the bar."

He leans in and I repeat it and point over to the bar. However, I notice that Leda and Tammy have noticed me talking to a guy and why am I struck with the sneaky feeling that those bitches aren't coming back any time soon?

"Mind if I keep you company while they're away?" he asks and sits down anyway, regardless of what I might have said. He takes the seat beside me and leans back, resting a thickly muscled arm behind me against the countertop. "So, what's a pretty thing like you doing alone?"

"I'm not alone," I say. "My friends, I mentioned them a second ago."

He laughs and shakes his head. "Girls night then?"

"Yeah," I say.

"Cool, cool, cool," he says, "I'm Todd."

"Natasha," I say.

"So, what do you do?"

Now, I have never been asked this question by a man, without it being a really obvious way for them to say 'uh-huh' before humble-bragging about themselves. I have found a couple of different solutions for this:

Say something like 'office worker' or 'hairdresser' and they will think they have you all figured out. They then start to brag about their personal fitness trainer gig or their band or their 'assistant to the regional manager' job, etc.

I mean, the fallout from this is annoying, but deep down, you can feel smug knowing that you've won.

> *1. Say something super intellectual or high powered, like 'judge' or 'researcher in biomedical science with a background in finding alternative food sources' or 'Miranda Priestly'.*
> *The best outcome from this would be that they are intimidated and suddenly remember that they have somewhere to be.*
> *The fallout from this one is having them roll with it and mansplain your career to you anyway, before somehow, linking it back to their personal*

fitness trainer gig or their band or their assistant to the blah blah blah, you get it.

2. *Say something that is from a movie, maybe elude that you're Black Widow from the Avengers or the Terminator.*
   The perks of this one is watching them get more and more confused as you continue to explain, with a straight face, that you are having a night off from hunting Sarah Connor. They may think you're nuts and find an excuse to slink away. Or, they get pissed off and leave, claiming they were only trying to start a conversation with you, God. But deep down, you'll know that they are bummed out about not having the opportunity to talk about their personal trainer gig or band or whatever.

"I work for an agency which doesn't technically exist on any government register," I say. "We wear these really smart black uniforms and have to investigate all kinds of unusual activity."

"What?" he asks, confused.

"Yeah, I shouldn't even be mentioning it, but I have become inebriated," I say, waving my hand dismissively. "It's my night off, but it's hard to know that the galaxy won't have me to defend it while I'm off drinking my ass full of martinis. But everyone needs a break, right?"

I can see the cogs in his head turning.

"Are you making fun of me?"

I smirk at him.

"No way, why would you think that?"

"You know, there's no need to be a dick," he said coldly. "I was just trying to start up a conversation."

"Did I ask you to sit down?" I ask.

"Bitch." He bashes his fist down on the table.

The realtor smile is nowhere to be seen now.

"Hey, baby, thanks for holding the table for me," another voice calls over the music.

There's a guy tucking in on the other side of me now. And he is… like ridiculously good looking, like, what the fuck…? He's slim and tall with light brown skin, dark brown eyes and brown hair and an awkward spread of peach fuzz across his chin and cheeks.

"She's with you?" Todd, who looks ugly when he's mad, says.

"Yeah," he says, brightly. "Hey, baby, how you doing?"

I slip my arm through his and smile back at Todd. "Just chatting to this guy here."

"She's got a weird sense of humour," Peach Fuzz says. "Sorry, man."

"Whatever," he says, getting up and leaving.

Peach Fuzz laughs and shakes his head.

"And presto, the alpha male disappears," he says, flashing me a big easy smile.

"What are you, a freelance creep remover?" I ask, retracting my arm.

"I mean, it is something I could charge for," he says. "Good to have a career that's in demand. What are you, a freelance comedian?"

"Well, I am offended. I could work for the Men in Black."

"I mean, that is true, but I don't think they get nights off, that was kind of where your story fell apart to be honest."

"How do you know I'm not working a job?"

He lifts my empty glass and sniffs it.

"I doubt Men in Black drink on the job."

We both laugh and he offers me a hand.

"I'm Rick Fumero."

He smiles at me and I realise that I've forgotten my damn name. I've opened my mouth and 'Fiona Taylor' has nearly spilled out.

"Sookie King," I catch myself and say, shaking his hand.

He raises an eyebrow. "Is that the truth?"

"Yes," I say.

"Because you paused there, so if this is an alias…"

"Hey, you want to see my ID?"

"I mean, yeah, if you have an interesting photo," he says. "Mine is awful." He reaches into his wallet and produces his ID. "I had really long hair."

I check.

He did.

"And a zit on your nose," I said. "Damn, this is an embarrassing ID."

He's twenty-three and actually suited the strangely crimped waist length hair in a way that a person just shouldn't.

"Whatever, let's see yours then."

I pass it over and he scoffs.

"Well, this is fake."

I smile and think how he's the first to ever say so.

"Twenty-five years old? You look like a high schooler in this picture alone. There is no way in hell you're older than me."

I snatch it back and stuff it back in my handbag. "I'm baby-faced. Maybe you're just haggard."

He laughs and leans back.

"So, I know you're in the Men in Black, but what is your cover job?"

"Oh, don't make me say it, it's so boring, I'll actually bore myself to death talking about it."

"Come on, try me," he says, "I want to know."

I laugh and nudge him.

"I work in college admin."

"And what is that exactly?"

"I tell students when they fail, if they can have extra time to submit their work, I hold meetings where their grades get approved. It really isn't interesting work."

"But it's the perfect cover."

"Exactly. Now, can we talk about you, like you clearly want to?"

"Oh, me, pfft, no way," he says, shaking his head. "I want to hear more about these meetings of yours."

"My ass, you do."

"Do you have issues with the copier? That's just the worst."

He laughs and nudges me back.

"Yes, we do. And it is."

"Well, I mean, it's no Men in Black, but I do work for a company that makes office supplies."

"That is so interesting."

"Oh, it is. Next time you staple something, please remember that it could well have been me who processed the order for that stapler."

"So, do I blame you if the quality is crap?" I ask.

He smirks and shrugs helplessly. "I mean, I could take your comments on board."

"Are you really an office supplies guy?" I ask.

He smirks and shakes his head. "No, I'm a proofreader for an indie publishing house."

"So, your job is reading? Nice. But, is it books or catalogues?"

"Yeah, it's books, but it's mostly English language teaching books for foreign countries, they aren't interesting," he says, shaking his head. "I thought it'd be all, proofing badly written erotica or the Man Booker prize, or whatever, but no. It's crosswords and short articles on the Statue of Liberty."

"Sounds thrilling."

"You have no idea," he says, "So, if you're ok with drinking on the job, how about I get you another?"

"Sure," I say, "That'd be nice."

"Don't disappear," he says.

"Hey, I won't, God, paranoid."

He waves as he slips into the crowd towards the bar. And I can't stop goddamn smiling.

Fiona, I'd nearly introduced myself to him as Fiona.

*

Fast-forward four hours—count 'em—four. We are sat on a bench in front of the darkened beach, my legs tucked over one of his. We are sharing a bag of soggy-looking fries dowsed with ketchup and *way* too much salt.

I left the sole of my shoe back in the bar and he has lent me his Vans. His socks are filthy from the floor but he tells me, laughing, that he really doesn't care.

I don't think I've smiled this much in my entire life.

When I see him, there are no red flags. Nothing that leaps out and says, 'This! This right here! Watch out for this, you idiot!' or something that says, 'Yes, he's cute, but THIS will annoy you in six months'.

No, when I look at him, all I can think about is…how much I want him to keep looking at me.

Of course, there are other things. I mean, we've been together for a whole four hours, come on.

Rick talks fast and *way* too much, he says he thinks fast and gets distracted easily and you can tell. He is a total flirt but insists he's not when you call him out on it. His parents are divorced, his mother is from Mexico City and his father from Dallas. He has one older sister, Maria, who lives in Vermont and a younger sister, Veronica, who lives in Santa Cruz. He lives in an apartment with a guy he met on Craigslist, Phil, who has a high squeaky voice. He has a huge group of friends he's known since forever and a day, but his best friend, Luis, lives in New Orleans and owns a sandwich van that is definitely in vague copyright violation of a popular franchised chain.

But there are some things I know without him having to tell me.

Like, he's a good dancer, much better than me, who to be fair, cannot dance. He has a scar on his left hand and he never knows the lyrics to songs but that never stops him from singing along, anyway.

"Those could be the lyrics," he says, "Ever think of that?"

"Well, no, because they aren't." I lean back and glance up at the dark sky above us. "Good attempt, though, I guess?"

He smiles and rests a warm hand on top of my leg.

"So, I feel like I've talked non stop. Tell me about you, when did you move to California?"

"When I was nineteen," I say.

"You come alone?"

"Yeah, it was my big thing I had to do at that age."

He whistles, "I mean, that's pretty hard-core."

"Yeah, I guess it was."

"So, what made you move?"

"I was this bored city kid from Chicago," I say with a shrug. "I wanted a clean break from everyone I knew back there. You know, I was going to settle into the kind of life my parents had, I could see all my friends turning into people I didn't want to be. So, I figured

I'd just leave, try to make something of myself somewhere totally different."

"And I mean, why not start in the Golden State, right?"

"Yeah."

"You didn't miss home?"

"No," I say. "Everything I could've missed was gone."

It's why I took her name.

To keep her with me.

He whistles and pats my knee, calling me morbid.

I always find this kind of thing hard, it's hard with work, with friends. There's only so much backstory I can produce. I don't want to lose track of convoluted lies about old friends or amusing anecdotes about people based on people.

I keep my backstory vague.

I came from a suburb in Chicago. I have a bad relationship with my family and don't keep in touch. I was a chronic under-achiever when I was in high school.

"Your folks visit?"

"No way," I say.

"That's sad," he says and he genuinely means it.

"Nah, it's all good."

"Friends visit then?"

"Like I want to be surrounded by people who remember me as a spotty little shit. No thanks." I laugh and shake my head. "I was not a fun person to be around when I was back there. I think my life took off after my big California move."

"I mean, sure," he said. "But I couldn't just leave it all behind like that."

I smirk. "Are you saying there's something wrong with me?"

"Maybe," he says, leaning in. "You're being unnecessarily mysterious, you know? Are you going to turn out to be a vampire or the queen of England or something?" He laughs at his own joke and shakes his head, putting his legs down on the ground, soggy socks and all.

I knock the fries out of his hand and slip onto his lap, resting my arms on his shoulders.

I get three very quick reactions because I'm watching for them.

First, his eyes go wide and his lips twist up in horror—the loss of the lukewarm, horrible food.

Then his cheeks go slightly pink as I slide my leg over and sit down in his lap.

Then, ever the 'Oh yeah this happens to me all the time' flirty guy face comes in and his hands come to rest on my hips.

He raises an eyebrow and says "Hey," in a slightly lower pitch.

"Do you have a sore throat?" I ask.

He colours up and coughs. "Erm, no."

"Good," I say and kiss him.

Chapter Five

My early childhood was perpetuated with a sense of complete and utter helplessness. I mean, now I feel guilty whenever I think about how frightened of her I was when I was a child. With all she's done for me. It feels wrong, but the truth is that I *was* scared of her for a very long time.

Growing up, I saw my mother as a bad person, a dangerous person. I knew that if she *wanted* to hurt me, she could. And there would be nothing I could do to protect myself from her.

It was scary to feel so helpless every day.

I knew that she was my mother and therefore she would never hurt me, but not knowing exactly why that was.

I mean, she hurt all kinds of people. She did it all the time. She always had.

So, what made me different?

Did I just think that she wouldn't hurt me because of how all the moms acted in films and on TV? I genuinely couldn't imagine why she chose to have me, why she chose to keep me around when it was nothing for her to wipe out anyone she wanted.

I worried a lot about it. But she never did.

But I was growing up, I had friends. There were other ways she could hurt me, so that sense of helplessness continued.

My friends were loud. Not the loudest, but I mean, they were little kids. I'd have them over and we'd make a mess in the garden or run up and down the stairs. And when their parents would come and get them, after they left and the two of us were all alone, Mother would make idle threats or comments every now and then.

She only ever acted on it once.

My best friend Sukhy saw her in the basement one night, there was too much blood for Mother to pretend that anything other than what it looked like was happening. So, like a completely rational person, she chased her upstairs with a big knife.

My brilliant, brave best friend lived another eleven years because I woke up that night.

I remember getting between the two of them, shielding Sukhy from the knife. I remember her fist around my arm, trying to separate us, trying to tug me free. I remember thinking that she was going to cut me to make me let go. I remember how much I cried; we were both crying. I started elbowing her and biting her. I was so sure she'd lose it in the end and kill the two of us.

But she didn't.

And even though she didn't, there was that feeling again.

Helpless.

I am so fucking helpless.

You know, I really hope that scene doesn't get put in the fucking movie. I mean, cinematically, it would probably look *great*, it'd probably be a good prophetic scene given in mind what the rest of the world thinks happened in the end. Morally, not great, to put very young child actors in a scene like that.

And also, from me, this is my actual life point of view, I would really not like to see that part in particular.

There wasn't much I wanted for myself in the future when I was growing up. I mean, there was a time I imagined college by the sea, me and Sukhy living it up together. But that was childish of me.

Overall, what I wanted for my future was to grow up and never feel helpless again. For a long time, I've had that with my new life here and I have felt in control. What happens to me is because of me. There's no fear or uncertainty anymore.

However, at the ripe old age of twenty-one, twenty-five if you ask me out loud, I find myself helpless again. Completely helpless. In a way, I actually don't mind. I know, who would have thought such a thing existed?

It's his doing, of course.

Rick Fumero.

I honestly didn't think I had the capacity for this sort of thing. I didn't get lonely the way my friends did. I didn't get invested when I was seeing someone. It's like I was defective in some way. Like, I'd never evolve past a few apathetic, practically joyless dates and awkward sexual encounters.

But no. No, that's not the way it is with me and him.

When this man smiles at me, I'm so freaking helpless.

*

The sun comes in through the dusty blinds of an apartment that isn't my own. It is in my eyes though. I roll over into the warmth of the body beside me. His arm comes over my back and tucks me in against him.

This is snug.

I take in his smell, his stupid stubble against the top of his head. The warmth of his arms and the ugly little Diablo tattoo on his wrist. A friend of his had done it in high school—they were bored in class and wanted to piss off their moms.

The bedroom is warm, but my feet feel cold out of the covers. I curl them up and rest them against the back of his thigh. He shivers in his sleep and mumbles incoherently in a strangely serious tone.

It's hard not to laugh.

I don't remember the last time I slept next to someone. Most likely when I was dating Reggie…two…years ago? But that little sleepover was due to alcohol, rather than a need to stay beside someone all night.

Rick is peaceful when he sleeps. He is completely out. He pulls faces too; he looked angry last night, like someone in his dream had really made him mad. Now, he looks the opposite, the most relaxed anyone has ever been.

I wish for the first time in a very long time, that I was a normal girl, with normal girl problems. That's stupid really. Even if I was still Fiona Taylor, I'd be Fiona Taylor with the scary mom in prison. Fiona Taylor who everyone would know must have known about her mother's nefarious basement.

It's better he meets me as Sookie King, with her clumsy backstory and no family to speak of.

One brown eye opens and he smirks down at me.

"Are you staring at me?"

"No," I say. "I'm asleep."

"A likely story," he says, shifting up and resting his head in his hand. "Some girls might start their three-month anniversary by waking up their guy with coffee and pancakes…But no, you choose to start this day by staring at me like some freakin' owl."

"Oh no, it's our three-month anniversary?" I gasp in mock horror, one hand over my mouth. "Whatever shall I do? Oh yeah, nothing, because I'm not in junior high. Also, neither are you."

Rick laughs and slides down on top of me, hands finding mine and holding them down to the bed.

"So, that's how it is. You gonna make fun of me for wanting to make today a bit special?"

"Oh, well, you should have said. A bit of a special day, that's something I could get excited about."

He kisses me and I wrap my legs around his hips, pulling him against me. He laughs and nearly loses balance. I flip him onto his back and slide my legs either side of him.

"You're so cruel to me," he says, his hands sliding onto my hips.

"I'm sure you can handle it."

*

The pancakes are from the bakery at the end of Rick's street. This is a good thing. I am no good at pancakes. I am good at some things, but not pancakes, or cake actually. Rick says his speciality is ice cream…he can scoop it from the tub and present it real nice.

We debate whether or not that's the same as cooking.

The seats are high here and unsteady. It's all about arranging your limbs on them carefully. He keeps teasing me by putting his arm on the back.

"Are you trying to get me to knock my plate over? Because if I lose these, you aren't having them," I say.

He laughs.

He has an adorable laugh, like a kid.

"No way," Rick says. "I just want to put my arm around you."

"What a gentleman," I say. "Has it really been three months?"

"Yeah," he says. "We met on the 6th, remember?"

"Soooo, it's from the day we met?" I tease, reaching over to steal a strawberry from his plate.

"Well, it's not like my intentions were hidden," Rick said. "We didn't have several weeks of beating around the bush before I asked my friend to ask if you had a crush on me."

I laugh at that.

"So, yeah, anyway, I booked a table at Maurice's. I can meet you there after work? The table's booked for five-thirty. Is that ok?"

I've been there once with Leda. The food is fantastic, but the owner is this really awkward guy. He is the only one who seems to wear a uniform and comes over to ask if you're enjoying your meal, like he's some frightened school boy. He sort of lurks by the table, then mumbles his question so you only catch one proper word.

Leda flirted with him last time, which seemed to terrify him away from our table.

"Yeah, sure," I say. "I'll meet you there."

"Sweet," he says, leaning down to kiss my cheek. "I'll get the bill. Want to put in for the tip?"

I fish out four dollars from my wallet and go back to my breakfast. He has a spring in his step and waves at me cheerfully from the counter. He's like a freaking four-year-old. But I wave back. Of course, I wave back.

Three months, I can't believe it's been three months.

Three months is a milestone for me. It feels like no time at all. And yet, I find myself wanting to be closer, wanting to trust, like we've known each other all of our lives. By three *weeks*, Reggie was getting on my nerves. Within three days, I'd decided I was going to start ignoring Mo's texts. By three hours, Sam had pissed me off and I knew that I was going to sneak out when he left the table to go to the bathroom.

You get the idea.

Read into it what you will, but I struggle to trust.

Rick comes back and slides his arms around my waist, resting his head on top of mine. "Want me to walk you to work?"

"I mean, if you want?"

"Of course," he says, squeezing my hand. "I can go in a bit later today. Let's get you to work."

Rick is a hand-holder. Seriously, he's like the most affectionate person I've ever met. He enjoys closeness. He spoons me when we share a bed. I feel so at peace that honestly; my little hobby has just ceased to exist for the last three months. Look at him, unknowingly saving the state of California.

Not that this means I've stopped.

Oh no. No.

I know they say love can heal the world or whatever.

But let's not go crazy.

This is a break. A nice time. The start of something new for me. There's not always time for a hobby. Leda has a jewellery-making kit that she hasn't touched in months.

So, this little break of mine, it's really more of a sabbatical.

I shake my head and link my fingers through his tighter. He is chatting about work and this weird new editorial assistant who takes suspiciously long bathroom breaks. Then he catches himself talking too much and laughs, embarrassed.

"Sorry, I'm all hyper."

"It's fine. I'd be hyper too if my job was more interesting."

"Oh, don't even. Your co-workers sound nice and your boss sounds like something…else."

"That's one way of putting it."

"Well, exciting or not, we have dinner plans. Maurice's at 5.30? Shall I meet you there or try to pick you up?"

"Let's just meet there," I say. "I won't have time to change after work though."

"Well, I will," Rick says, grinning. "I'm gonna wear a tux. Gonna bring a corsage for you. It will not look out of place with your grey jumper."

"Wow, a corsage. What next? You going to take me to the prom?"

He laughs and shakes his head.

Leda and Tammy approve of him. He laughs at Tammy's dumb jokes and hasn't gotten impatient with Leda's back and forth-ing about her hair. I came home from work the other day to find the three of them hanging out listening to music and shooting the shit.

It feels…nice to have someone to come home to.

Look at me, fucking *s-a-p*.

*

"Well, check you out, eating face outside the office," Donnie says, raising an eyebrow as I walk over to my desk.

"Well, check you out, staring out the window like a little orphaned Annie," I say, putting down my bag.

"We both were," Claudia says brightly. "So, that's the guy?"

"Yeah," I say.

She nods approvingly and settles into her chair. "So, you two been dating long?"

"Three months," I say.

"Honeymoon period," Donnie says. "That explains a lot."

"Honeymoon period," Kiko agrees, glancing up from the printer.

"Oh, shut up, Donnie," Claudia says. "Just because you're like a savage when it comes to women."

"I am not," he says. "I just don't have time for needy women."

"That sounds pretty disrespectful," Rajish says. "Maybe you're just lazy."

"As if!" he says, laughing and shaking his head. "Just because I don't want to carry a girl to work with a winged carriage and a falcon and shit."

"Are you sure it was me you saw through the window?" I ask. "Is that what you think women like?"

The others laugh, Donnie shakes his head, swatting me with a folded-up envelope.

"Didn't you tell me that you split the bill by item the last time you had a date?" Tanya asks quietly.

"She had a sharing plate to herself and had like…three mojitos!" Donnie protests. "She spent like $15 more than me."

"Donnie, that was two years ago," Tanya says.

The door crashes open and Jack struts in, shaking off his coat so the zipper very nearly collides with Claudia's eye. "What's this? Sounds like you guys are having too much fun in here! Back to work!" He cracks a mimed whip with his hand and makes a clumsy 'cracking' sound. He then pales a bit when he sees me and Donnie share a glance. "I mean whenever you're ready. This is a place of business!" He sits behind his desk and instantly starts rustling through his pockets for his leftover cigarettes.

"Fuck's sake," Donnie mutters under his breath.

*

Work is boring. Rick texts me about the weird new editorial assistant. He Snapchats me a photo of the ugly sandwich platter they got in for the writer's lunch. I send back a photo of me rolling cigarettes on my boss's orders. Jack is feeling extra lazy today and just wants to chat to everyone about…any topic that will stick.

Jack took it upon himself to explain the whole plot of *Jurassic Park* to Kiko, who didn't want to write up her meeting minutes so humoured him by pretending that she'd never ever seen it.

"Only every day from the ages of six to seven," she says to me as we sneak away for a coffee break. "I was super into dinosaurs."

"I like how he kept referring to Laura Dern as the 'lady scientist'."

"Lady scientist, so rare, so shocking."

"Like a girl, but with science and stuff."

"A bigger mystery than the actual dinosaurs." She snorts and sips her coffee. "I think I could get out of doing any work at all if I just pretend that I know…like, actually nothing about 80s and early 90s culture."

"You should actually put that to the test."

"He is being extra dumb today. When you were on lunch earlier, honestly, he was trying to talk to Donnie about politics," Kiko says. "Donnie was pretending to be a massive republican."

"Man, I can only imagine how that conversation went."

"Jack kept telling him that he's not *allowed* to be a republican and black. And Donnie asked him if he was telling him as a black man, how he was allowed to vote."

"Ouch. I'm cringing just *hearing* about this."

"I hoped that would keep him quiet for the rest of the day. That was stupid of me," she says, grinning. "I don't think I've cringed that hard at something he's done since he started explaining how Diwali works to Rajish."

"I had to leave the room for that." I hold open the break-room door for her with my foot as she follows me back out into the badly lit corridor.

"I know. Someone needs to like, film him and send it to SNL."

"They wouldn't even need to recast him. Just raw footage."

"We're pretty lucky to work here," she says, rolling her eyes.

"That's what I'm thankful for."

We laugh and dodge our way past a gaggle of students waiting to go into one of the classrooms.

"Oh, hey, I almost forgot. I saw someone super suspicious earlier."

"What?"

"It was this weird guy hanging out by reception earlier. He was like…really tall and swaggering around. He looked like a crook."

"Ew, no way."

"Yeah, I can tell he's making Maureen on reception, like, super nervous. And Maureen is adorable, so I wasn't having that. So yeah, I go over and ask him if he's here to see someone. And he asks me if I work with any Kings or Queens."

"What? That's super weird."

"It was!" she says. "Sooo I tell him that unless he's a student or staff, he has to leave. Like right now. Or I'd call campus security."

"What did he do?"

"He called me doll-face and left. Doll-face, seriously."

"Ew, that's so gross."

"I know! He did leave, I watched him go across the street into this proper 'Hey kids want some lollypops' white van."

"That's so weird, Kiko."

"Maureen reported it to campus security. But yeah, he had proper serial killer vibes. What an absolute freak."

She holds the office door open for me as we walk back inside.

"But actually, I suppose I do work with a King," she said, "I mean, that's your name, right?"

*

The others leave early, Claudia has a date; you can tell from the 4 o'clock reapplication of her foundation (she has missed a spot, right above her perfectly groomed right eyebrow, I noticed it when her coat knocked her bangs askew as she flustered to leave). There was also the bolder lipstick, the reuse of her eyeliner. She basically looks like a whole new Claudia.

Jack is humming tunelessly as he strolls out the door with my last cigarette. The others follow suit not long after. Tanya sneaking out just before 5, Rajish on the phone to his roommate, who, from what I can gather, is very impractical and is always getting into dumb situations. As usual, I spend the end of the day alone.

Mother texts on my dodgy second phone.

M: Did you know they are making a film about me? I met S.J. in person.

Me: No way. I haven't heard anything about that. What was she like?

M: Very polite. Not like you.

Me: Haha!

M: Are you up to anything?

Me: No. I'm being vv good.

M: Why do I not believe you?

I smirk and slide my phone into the secret compartment of my bag. Rick has seen it. I told him it was my very first cell phone and I'm sentimental. I hope he thought that was weird and endearing, rather than suspicious.

Mother texts like someone's Grandma, I think, smirking to myself as I shut the blinds and re-adjust my monitor before sitting back to reapply my lipstick using my main phone's camera.

Much like Claudia, I also have a date.

I text Rick back to remind him about the movie tickets for Friday. I text him a goofy picture of myself pulling a face with the caption 'Your hot date'.

I leave my sweater at the office because it's way too nice a day for any more layers than you really need. *And* I kind of feel like I'm in a romcom from the eighties when he wraps his jacket around my shoulders on the walk back from the restaurant.

I put my phone in my pocket and look both ways before crossing the street as the street sign turns green for pedestrians.

I take a deep breath and wonder briefly if the restaurant will have menus in just French or English too this time. I never did tenth grade French so my knowledge is always limited to the basic-basic, to insulting tourist levels, you know, pointing and speaking English very slowly.

I smirk and dismiss it.

"Miss. King?" a voice asks from beside me.

I'm practiced. I'm used to responding to a name that doesn't quite fit me.

"Yes?" I turn my head to face them and someone grabs me from behind.

Then I feel very genuine fear as hands grab hold of me around the waist and I am dragged into the white van waiting at the lights outside my office. Kiko literally warned me about this fucking van earlier! King or Queen! FUCK!

I kick and lash out and scream as someone forces a detergent-stinking rag into my mouth and yanks a canvas bag down over my head while someone forces me into a seat. Strong hands hold both of my wrists in one as someone else straps me into a seatbelt.

My feet slam against the floor and I struggle against the grip around my wrists.

My heart is racing.

What is this?

I know better than most that there are some sickos out there. It's the unspoken mantra of my life. But this isn't a 'me sicko', this could be something so much more terrifying.

Because, let's face it…women have to be so careful. There are so many ways to become a statistic. Dead, but somehow our outfit choices are what is discussed, like that has anything to do with it.

For me to become a number in the statistics of women murdered in 2017—my case less to never reported on (I mean, come on, I'm not some little white girl college student, smiling on a beach)—I want to be scared, but right now I'm way too fucking angry!

These three men—there are three of them, I'm almost sure. My killers, my would-be killers. I can't believe I could be potentially murdered by three fucking men. Three fucking men, after all this time!

You'll only hear about them if they ever get convicted and go to court. Then it'll be sympathy. Fucking sympathy for them. But they're family men, look at photos of their kids, their multiple fucking kids, their wives.

Maybe they'll say that they are *intimidated* by black people, not racist, just intimidated by the way they talk and walk. This man, this family fucking man panicked when he saw me, wanted to protect his family, so he and his buddies went and took me out on my way home from fucking work. That was the reason my body was burnt up after they were finished with me.

They'll tell that fucking story and the sympathy will be with them! Them and not me!

I don't want to die!

I start twisting and kicking out as I feel handcuffs around my wrists.

Handcuffs.

Ok, calm down.

You've read too much…of the news.

The fucking news.

Three men. You're sure of it.

One driver. One sat opposite. One beside.

Handcuffs, nice ones, sturdy ones, not 'I read a kinky book once, look I'm so BDSM for $3'. Professional, steely. And that suits. The guy who strapped me in did it quickly, business like. There was no inappropriate touching, no frightening words, no lingering hands.

These men are silent. They know why they are here. And they must know enough about me to make sure I can't get my hands free.

I consider wetting myself to freak them out, using their disgust to get my hands free and cut them with the knife in my purse. I know they put it by my feet.

But would that be enough to get them to back off? Could I get into my handbag while in handcuffs?

Why was I never handcuff adventurous? So many people are, but not me. Fuck me.

I scream into the gag and twist to one side, kicking blindly at the doors and the sides of the car. My healed shoe collides with a window hard and pain shoots through my ankle. All too quickly there are hands on me, restraining my thigh, the other on the back of my neck.

"Do not make me hurt you," the man says in a clipped steely voice that is almost completely without an accent.

Baltic.

I'm almost certain it's Baltic.

I am forced upright and give the seat another kick for good measure.

He sighs. "Nobody has to hurt anyone," he says. "Just sit fucking still and enjoy the ride, ok?"

I nod and think fleetingly of Rick, of him waiting at the restaurant with the stupid French menus I can't read and wine and I want to kick myself for being so unbelievably fucking stupid as to get caught.

We drive in silence for thirty minutes. I think they are doing it on purpose, trying to confuse me with some mystery location. Mostly it just makes me feel carsick. I was right, there are definitely three of them. A driver. One next to me, the guy with the Baltic-sounding accent, and a guy opposite, I kicked his shoe earlier when I was flailing around.

Eventually the car pulls to a stop. The big guy next to me, I'm guessing he's a big guy from the way his palm enveloped my entire neck, unbuckles me from my restraints. I hear a door slide open and someone else gets out. A huge hand encases my wrists and I'm pulled out of the van, stumbling unsteadily from the slight step.

"I-van, hey!" someone calls from a few feet away.

I hear a scraping noise, we are in a factory, I think?

Apparently-Ivan, who is holding my arm with his massive hand, grunts. "Hey, moron, do you see what I'm doing here?"

"Shit, sorry!"

My shoes skid slightly on the tarmac. Apparently-Ivan says, "Look, either walk properly or I'll carry you."

I want to tell him that it is incredibly difficult to walk properly when you can't see and have zero idea where you're going and are being dragged along roughly by a guy who does know all of those things.

But whatever. Even if I wasn't gagged, I doubt he'd want to hear it. So, I awkwardly walk/am dragged with him another thirty paces before I hear a door open. It's a harsh, metallic sound, like we are definitely in a warehouse.

"Hey, boys, you fetched our guest!"

Now this accent is pure Californian.

I'm drawn to a complete stop by Apparently-Ivan. My feet screech uncomfortably loudly against the squeaky plastic.

"Woah there," someone says, laughing. "Hey, did she give you any trouble?"

"No, boss," Apparently-Ivan says. "Spit."

I realise he's speaking to me and I feel his hand on my mouth to remove the gag. The taste of cotton gone from my tongue fills me with relief. But I find myself panicking about what to say now that I have the privilege of speech back.

Play dumb?

Cry?

No, I doubt men like this would respond to weakness very well at all. Playing dumb and crying would be a sure-fire way to become a statistic. The canvas bag comes off all the way now and my vision adjusts to the bright light of a warehouse.

Called it.

I glance to the side at Apparently-Ivan, who is not only tall, but fucking massive. His neck is thicker than my whole torso.

I look over at his boss and see a little white boy, aged…between twenty-five and thirty. He's wearing a leather jacket and looks like he does CrossFit. His blonde hair is too long and makes him look like a failed male model. He is sat down on a fold-out chair crotch-first.

"Hey, so do I have the pleasure of speaking to Miss. Sookie King?" he asks loudly and cheerfully.

"Yeah," I say, "Who are you and why are you messing with my Thursday?"

He snorts. "Well, it's hardly your Friday. I'd get over it if I were you." He puts his head in his hand and frowns at me slightly.

I glance behind me and flinch as I hear the chair screech as he leaps off and bounds over towards me. He stops way too close and surveys me carefully.

"Personal space," I say coldly.

He smiles and I see all his veneers.

"Ha, you know, I like you, Miss. King. You don't rattle easy."

"Call it a life skill."

He folds his arms and leans back. "So, me, you don't know. But we have a connection. Care to guess what it is?"

"Nope."

He sighs. "We've got the same nose, the same eyes. Come on, our Grandma couldn't get over the resemblance."

I frown, and with prompting, I can see it.

"Your old landlord was my cousin," he says with a sigh, puffing out his chest and flicking back his long hair.

"Oh, I didn't know that."

"Yeah, P.J and me go way back, all the way to Pre-K. I like his Pops, got a lot of respect for him. P.J, I mean, it stinks to say because he's dead now, but he always rubbed me the wrong way. Too... creepy. He looked like a panty-sniffer, right?"

He clicks his fingers and sighs.

"Are you bringing all his tenants here?" I ask.

The boss shrugs. "Nah, just the one that killed him."

I feel my blood go cold.

"That's a harsh accusation to make."

He shrugs his shoulders. "It ain't wrong. He called me, see, right before he died. He had a burner phone. I doubt you bothered frisking him to check. Panty-sniffer, right?" He smirks. "He'd called me a few minutes before, he owed me some cash—so he still had the phone on him. You cut his wrists and he managed to get the phone out and call me back. I bounced his call, didn't want to hear his sorry excuses. But he left me a message. Hold on...Let me..."

He produces his phone from his jacket pocket, swipes along the screen and then holds it up.

"Barry, she's trying to kill me. That black bitch in 301 is trying to kill me. Can't go to the hospital. Call your guy, please call!"

I hear a grunting, a gargling and the line goes dead.

"I've got a cop working for me," he says. "He recovered the phone lickety-split. Don't you worry."

I feel sick. Like someone has punctured me with tiny holes and I'm bleeding through onto the floor.

"I could delete this recording," he says, holding the phone to his lips. "But I just don't want to." He meets my eyes. "I mean, I know he was a real piece of shit, but P.J was my flesh and blood. And I like his Pop. Always very, very good to me growing up. Some men, particularly in my line of work, do not like harm coming to their family. Some take it as a personal insult. Some might make a blood oath, some might swear revenge."

He steps closer and raises an eyebrow.

"Some guys would get really fucking nasty if they ever found the sonova—or, sorry, daughter of a bitch who insulted him and his clan so thoroughly."

I wish this guy would stop talking.

"And you know, a guy could really enjoy taking his revenge one piece at a time. Particularly if the one who wronged him happens to be a beautiful woman."

I flinch and squirm back and feel Apparently-Ivan behind me, thick hands holding me still. The boss comes closer and grabs me by the collar. He then raises his hands over his head and laughs.

"Nice try, sister," he says, "But I'm a married man." He flashes a tacky-looking gold band in my face and I imagine embedding it in his eye socket.

"Bastard," I hiss, tugging free from Ivan's grip. "Keep your god-damn hands off me."

"Sorry," he says. "That wasn't nice. But, you did kill my cousin, so consider that little scare as getting off light." He straightens his collar. "Listen, Miss. King, I don't like to bullshit around the bush, I know that you like to make people disappear."

I go to interrupt but I doubt this guy ever hears much over the sound of his own voice.

"No bullshit," he says. "You like making people disappear. I have people I need to disappear. You could say we're a match made in heaven. That the two of us could make real music together."

I say nothing but I can feel the walls closing in around me.

He reaches out and unlocks my handcuffs.

"From now on, Miss. King, you work for me."

Chapter Six

Apparently-Ivan drives me home, fortunately in a car and not a van.

I've been issued a phone and told that my new employer, Mr. Barry Ames will be in touch. He shook my hand aggressively, and that alone makes me want to smother it in sanitiser and then cut it clean off.

The car is expensive and smells of cleaning products and pine. I spy a little green pine tree air freshener behind the screen between me and Apparently-Ivan.

"So, Ivan, right?" I ask.

He doesn't respond.

"Is it not Ivan then?"

Blue eyes flicker over to me then back to the road.

"What do you want?"

"Well, we are co-workers, sort of," I say. "Shouldn't we try to get along?"

"No."

I sigh and lean back into the squeaky leather and wonder briefly, as the smell of anti-bacterial spray fills my nose, what kinds of bodily fluids have been splattered across these seats?

"So, you know my neck of the woods?"

"Do you see me use SatNav?"

"Why the hostility, man?" I ask.

"What hostility?" he asks.

Definitely with an edge.

"Never mind, I'm sure we have plenty of time to get close," I say.

"Oh yes," he says, smirking now. "I doubt he will be letting you go anytime soon."

He is good.

On a lesser person, it likely would have filled them with dread. But I've always been an optimist. Well, to a degree. So, I try not to register what he said. My burner phone and my secret second job, they don't seem real right now. Despite the smell of anti-bac telling me again that yes, this is actually happening to you.

I think I can deal with this as long as it's not real just yet. Later maybe it will become harder, but not now.

We pull up outside the supermarket near my apartment. He gestures with his thumb for me to get out. I can't think of anything witty to say at the moment so I just get out of the car. Apparently-Ivan drives away and I watch the car turn into faceless evening traffic.

Part of me registers that I can't just stand here. An old woman with a pile of shopping bumps into me and I stumble, a man's shoulder collides with my back. I realise that I should get going. I should be walking across the street. I should be getting ready, I've sweated through my clothes. I should be texting Rick with some excuse, some lie, some reason why my patient, ridiculously kind boyfriend is sat in a fucking French restaurant alone.

Sookie King, internally known as Fiona Taylor, could have dealt with tonight. This wouldn't even be a thing that could hurt her.

But Sookie King, externally known as Rick Fumero's girlfriend—no. This is scary this is damning.

This is kind of what you might call a split in ideals.

It was hard enough knowing that Rick was unknowingly dating Fiona Taylor, daughter of the Red Creek Killer. But now, this is Rick dating Fiona Taylor, who works for a fucking sleazy gangster because she was stupid and got caught.

I don't think I can move. I don't honestly know where to go from here.

Fortunately, the decision is quickly made for me.

"Sookie, what the hell are you doing?" Tammy takes my hand and physically moves me towards my apartment. "You can't just stand in the middle of the street like a lobotomy patient!"

We get outside the building and I notice that Leda has apparently restored Tammy's key. The keyring charm is a tiny rectangular photo of Tammy and Leda wearing Minnie Mouse ears from a trip to Disney World last year.

"Leda has Pilates," Tammy says. "I'm making lasagne for when she gets home. Do you want some?"

"No, I'm ok."

"What was that about?" she asks, raising a pencilled-on eyebrow—showing the natural expressiveness of her face. "I said your name like four times, you space cadet."

"I think I'm just tired," I say.

"Ok, I'm not stupid, Sookie," she says, taking off her boots. "I mean, is it Rick? Did you guys have a fight?"

"No, no, I was meant to meet him after work and I got all distracted, I was..."

Her eyes widen at that. "Did someone hurt you?" She glances sporadically over to see that I still have my purse, then over my clothes. "Did!"

"No, I'm fine."

"We can call the cops, Sookie!"

"Nothing like that happened, seriously, you watch too much CSI. Calm down, ok? I just had a really shit day, I got chewed out by my boss at work and I was upset and just walked home. Forgot my date, you saw me as I just realised that and I felt like an asshole and...eurgh."

Tammy sighs in relief and folds her arms. "Well you scared me, you idiot. Look, just text him and explain." She scans my outfit again. "And wear something sexier so he will get distracted from being mad."

I laugh and take out my phone. "Thanks, Tammy."

"If anyone is good at getting out of the shit for being late to a date, it's me," she said. "You sure you don't want in on this lasagne? It's my grandma's recipe."

"Well, I mean, if you have leftovers?"

*

Lucky me again, Rick hit traffic getting out of work. He'd only been waiting for ten minutes by the time my Uber got me to Maurice's. And of course, he's more worried than angry.

Of course, he is.

"I ordered us wine already, it's nice," he says. "I mean, I think it is, but I basically like any wine."

"Sounds refined."

"Oh, it is," he says. "I'm glad you're here, anyway. I was starting to get a little panicked."

"Stupid work," I say. "I was all thrown out by today."

"Your boss sounds like an asshole," he says as he tucks me into my chair.

"Oh yeah, he's the worst," I say with a shrug. "Sorry about traffic."

Sorry, Jack, but you are an asshole like 85% of the time.

"Traffic is traffic, my own fault," he says. "I pulled in to see my sister after my shift. It can get crazy busy by her place."

"It's useful that you both live in the same city," I say.

"Oh, it can be," he says. "Always kind of jarring when we run into each other in clubs and bars though. Like, I remember her playing with Barbies and holding weekly weddings for the cat and the dog."

I snort with laughter. Rick chuckles into his wine.

"Seriously, babe, she would force our dog into this raggy-ass veil once a week from the ages of like five to eight. It was basically like watching a crime against nature."

"What was the dog's name?"

"Officer Pickles."

"And did you name her?"

"Aha, no, that was Veronica again."

"I'm starting to think that she's the creative one in your family."

"She's the something one alright," he says, laughing and shaking his head. "So, how about you? Any pets?"

Beth's dog and so many slain stray cats come to mind. So many unmarked graves. Practically a pet cemetery behind our house. I don't like to think about it.

"No."

"You don't like them?"

"I'm allergic."

That's my line and I'm sticking to it. What it means more is, you know, 'Please don't put any small animals in my general vicinity'.

"That's too bad, they are a lot of fun when you're a kid."

"Yeah, I could have thrown a wedding."

"She also tried to ride Officer Pickles around the house. Like a dog jockey."

"And that was definitely Veronica too?"

"Well…ok, maybe that was me."

"Dog jockey, I really missed out."

"Allergies, so depressing," he says.

"I mean, I got a little bit of the pet experience, other than a lot of coughing…A friend of mine had a dog when we were little kids, but he ran away. So, it was kind of the hard stuff with pets rather than the good. You know, teaching kids about grief and stuff."

"Oh, no way, that's so depressing."

"Totally depressing."

He smiles and I almost—almost forget it all.

"So, shall we order?" he asks, brandishing the menu. "I had this amazing pasta dish last time, but the menu is in French so I have no idea what it's called."

"Right," I say. "Well, just to warn you, I will be of absolutely no assistance."

"I failed French in high school like…twice."

"I did it, but I remember nothing, I'm like a shitty tourist."

"I'd have my French teacher insisting that French and Spanish are so close, so I should just get it."

"We could have gone to a Spanish restaurant," I say.

"And miss out on Maurice?" Rick points carefully over at Maurice, who has snuck up on two old ladies to ask them in his signature hurried whisper if they like the food.

"Maurice kind of makes the date. When do you think he'll come and take our order?" I ask.

"Oh, please, we don't even know what we're having."

"I'm going to be adventurous and try this!" I point. "Don't make me pronounce it and don't judge me for pointing."

He laughs and shakes his head. "I wouldn't, I wouldn't!"

"Seriously, this is nice, but next time let's go somewhere we can order without looking like a pair of jackasses."

"Sure thing, Sookie," he says, "I just figured for this occasion that a French one is more romantic, you know, for a big event like a three-month anniversary," he says, smirking. "At least one of us is invested in this relationship," he teases.

"Oh, cut it out," I say, laughing and shaking my head.

A waiter, who is thankfully not Maurice, comes and takes the order. He re-pronounces the dishes we pick—Rick's so much that when the waiter asks if that is everything, Rick doesn't look entirely certain when he says yes.

"So, I'm not sure you're getting pasta," I say.

"Me neither, but it's my own fault. I should have kept a better grasp on my high school French."

"And I should…point more politely, I guess?" I say, shaking my head. "I guess we can enjoy some mystery meat when it gets here?"

"Mystery meat, wow, there are nicer ways to phrase that," he says, shaking his head. "That's a mental image I don't need."

"Call it a perk of dating me. Happy three-month anniversary."

Rick laughs and leans over to squeeze my hand. "Seriously though, I can't believe it's been three months already," he says.

"I know."

"Like, it's just so…natural being with you. There's no drama, we don't try to act all complicated to be interesting."

"I hate it when people do that."

Rick smiles again and I feel warmer.

"Look at us, judging people together," he says. "We make quite a pair."

"Pair of what…"

"Honestly, it's nice to have no mind games," he says. "It's so easy being with you. I feel…pretty lucky, I guess."

I smirk. "Well, it's good to find a guy who thinks I'm easy."

*

When Rick is sleeping, he looks mad, like someone has wronged him in a very frustrating way. It's really funny to watch. Or it usually is. But now our date is over, now it's time to sleep, the whole day has started to creep out from under my skin.

I try not to shake.

I curl myself into a ball against him and close my eyes tight.

My body feels too hot and then too cold.

Mostly, I just feel sick.

I've had a day like this before. I know people have them all the time. Sometimes these days are self-inflicted, like mine. You know what I mean…Days where everything you know is wrenched out from under you. Days where you end up leaving everything behind and your life isn't the same anymore. It won't be the same again. It's a lonely feeling, a panicked feeling, like bees that live in your stomach and thrash around your organs trying to get out.

I want to panic.

I want to run away.

I can't live with being me and being recognised. For someone to know who I am and what I'm like. To get used by someone who really is bad news and might try to make me worse news than I already am.

I like my little…extra-curriculars. But they are mine. They are on my terms. What if he asks me to hurt someone that I don't want to? What if he wants me to hurt kids or old ladies or…I try not to gag and cover my face with my hands.

What the *fuck* am I going to do?

Chapter Seven

My first week as a mafia employee passed fairly inconsequentially. That doesn't mean to say that it was easy. I've barely slept and my seedy third phone seems to burn a hole in my handbag. Every time I passed a window, I'd look for a white van, I'd flinch every time I saw a particularly tall, scowling white guy. I'd panic that it was Apparently-Ivan in his casual sportswear.

We go out for drinks with Rick's friends, who are the best and I can't even relax. I have to force myself to pay attention to the jokes and the chatter. His friend Miguel texts Rick to ask if I'm ok and I feel like I will never be able to cope with this double-double life of mine.

The lack of communication from my creepy third phone could almost make a gal believe that the whole thing had been a really irritating nightmare. Only there it is. The stupid phone in my bag that I'll have to explain away to everybody when it inevitably goes off.

Claudia asks me if I'm ok in the break room. I tell her that I'm just feeling a bit sick. Only for Jack to loudly and *sensitively* ask if I'm pregnant.

I use the 'feeling sick' line a lot lately. I use it to get out of talking to Leda and Tammy at home. I use it to get out of drinks after work. I even use it to get out of seeing Rick, which makes me feel like the worst person alive.

So, yeah, it's been a week and I'm holed up in my bedroom, eating Cheetos and watching an old episode of *The Simpsons*. I feel sorry for myself, it isn't a dignified picture.

And then my phone buzzes.

Cautious, I lean over and lift it from my bag.

There's a text.

It's an address and a photo of a cocky-looking red-headed guy. He's wearing a baseball t-shirt and pouting like a teenage girl.

At least this looks like the sort of person I'd usually go after, you know, under the usual circumstances.

The address is in a really crappy neighbourhood on the other side of town.

I take a deep breath and try to rationalise how I can make this happen in my head.

Maybe I'll head over there tomorrow after work, scout out the place, find this guy—check his social media, check his schedule, see where he goes and see if I can work out the best way to get at him. Monitor him for a few days and voila, head back and finish the job.

I can work this out and do this my way. And if all these guys want is for me to get rid of creepy-looking douchebags, then maybe it won't be too...

Then ping, another text.

By midnight.

My blood runs cold.

What the actual fuck?

Midnight.

I glance at the clock, it's nine-forty-five now! He wants this man dead by midnight? But he's given me no time, no room for manoeuvre, to plan!

There's another text, this one from Rick.

Sorry you're feeling gross
Want some company? Can bring horrible medicinal
tea?

My heart melts and then hardens again very quickly. I have a job to do or all the good things in my life will have to disappear. And I worked really fucking hard for this life. I just had a three-month anniversary. I pay my taxes. I talked my way into a job that pays well and that I am completely unqualified for.

It isn't fair to do a do-over at this stage.

I text Rick back to say that I'm drowsy and in bed with a hot water bottle, but would welcome some company and gross medicinal tea tomorrow.

Then I put my phone away and take another deep breath.

Tonight, there is work to be done.

Thanks, lousy second job.

*

What has two jobs, three phones, two thumbs and can't catch a break?

Yup, that's me alright.

I get an Uber halfway to the crappy neighbourhood, then I walk the rest of the way. I Googled the address and managed to find out the identity of my target. His name is Adam Liverston. He's a personal trainer and lifestyle coach. He has a very minor Youtube channel where he starts each one with a burly 'Hey guys'—in a way that gives the impression that he personally knows his 56 subscribers IRL.

This guy is a show-off, he seems the sort who would marry himself if he could, the whole time yelling 'no homo' for anyone who'd listen.

There's a video where he walks through a gym, telling women who are trying to run on treadmills in peace, the best way to bulk up —and it leaves me like completely convinced that he has about 5% knowledge of female anatomy. Oh, and he advises them strongly, that it's not hot for a girl to be too buff.

What a car crash of a human being.

No, thank you.

However, as I'm halfway to his crumby flat, I check his Twitter feed and discover that he is out on a night with the boys. Unfortunately for him, I recognise the bar from the terrible quality photo.

It's only another twenty-minute walk which leads me to where I am now.

Despite being dressed in yoga pants and a very well-worn hoodie with a Cheetos stain on the left sleeve, I get into the club, emergency knife hidden in my underpants.

The bar is mostly a sausage fest. The music is too loud for a Wednesday. Seriously, the dotters around at the bar are literally yelling to hear each other yack, they scream at the bar staff and probably get their orders about half correct.

But, my guy I spot easily.

Redheads.

He is leaning against the bar, trying to chat up this girl, who, and I can see this from the other side of the room, is 10/10 not interested in whatever he's selling her. But there he is, flexing his muscles, he waves his credit card in front of her face when she attempts to pay the bartender for her martini.

She glowers at him and says 'No' over the rumbling music.

She walks away, her drink clenched in her well-manicured hand. And I hear Mr. Charming call her a fatso as she walks away.

I bet, like $100 that he tells women that he's a nice guy who tells it like it is and not a lot of people can handle it.

Warning. Asshole alert.

However, this aside, how am I going to get him alone without being caught on camera or make myself noticed?

My third phone vibrates. A text from my new boss, who like Jack, fucking loves to micro-manage—reminding me that I have an hour.

Like I don't know that, jerk.

This isn't fair. It's not how I do this.

The phone makes an uncomfortable sound in my clenched fist and I put it back into my hoodie pocket to avoid the temptation to squash it.

It's fine.

This is fine.

Do a good job here and Barry Ames might pull back on the douchy tactics. This is a first—to prove yourself. This is like an after-interview test. This is like the time Jack put you in charge of student orientation on your first day.

And your job with Jack is just a job.

This, what you do here, this is you.

And you know, depressing as it is, the suicide rate for men is at an all-time high. A douchebag guy like this would probably be happiest dying in a club, surrounded by friends and hot girls.

I take a bottle of beer and smash it against the wall, the sound drowned out over the radiating music. I take the sharpened top and hide it in my hoodie pocket as I watch my guy stumble from his seat at the bar and try to dance with one of the four girls in the club tonight.

She slides away from him and back to her friends, laughing.

He mutters, what looks like a very rude word, though it's hard to tell in this lighting. Then, woozy from drinking, he staggers into the disabled toilet. Honestly, it's like he wants me to do this. I tuck in behind him, burly arm missing my head as I duck under him.

There are no cameras in here.

He starts when he sees me, and stumbles at first. Then he laughs and tells me that, no offence, but he's really not into black girls.

I lift his ill-fitted tie and push it up into his mouth. He gags, laughing. Or he does, before I cut his wrist. Nice and deep. I'm something of an expert by now. I hear a crunch of bone. He stumbles against the toilet and tries to take a swing at me.

It's easy to dodge him as he is, drunk and bleeding to death.

He manages to get his phone out and instantly drops it to the floor.

I snort and pick it up.

Why does nobody password protect their devices in this day and age?

I tweet something vague, drunken and depressing.

He has vomited and passed out.

The phone goes back into his pocket.

I wait until his pulse stops before I take out my third phone and snap a photo of him lying there like that. I return Barry Ames's message with one of my own.

And forty minutes to spare. Any notes?

Then I walk out of the toilet, careful with the lock, careful to avoid eye contact. I walk right out of there, past the bouncers and into the night. I take a deep breath, inhaling that boozy night air.

Then I notice Apparently-Ivan stood outside a blue sports car on the other side of the sidewalk. He waves—which would look friendly—but his face just doesn't have the capacity.

"Yo, Ivan," I say.

"The Boss wants to talk to you."

"Right now?"

He gestures to the car. "Get in."

"Can I ride shotgun?"

"No."

I climb into the back and he adjusts his seat a few times, it's got to be hard with those long legs. I cross my arms and lean back, sighing.

"So, no blindfold this time?"

"No," he says.

Then he puts on some creepy classical music, possibly just to destroy any chance of a conversation. Which to be honest, is fine by me. I'm trying not to let on that my hands are shaking. The car has heated seats, which is actually a huge factor in calming me down. I tuck my trembling hands under my legs. I lean back and close my eyes and try to tell myself again, that I probably would have targeted that guy if I'd ever walked into him on the street.

Sure, this isn't how I usually do it.

Sure, I'm scared that someone will recognise me, that there was a very well-hidden camera in that toilet. That maybe nobody would believe that he would kill himself. If I'd had more time then...

*

The car pulls up on the boulevard by the sea, near to a crappy disused fairground that used to be here. Apparently-Ivan turns and gestures roughly for me to get out of the car. He turns up the music when I open my mouth to ask him a question.

So, I just roll my eyes and get out.

Fortunately, he doesn't drive away and for that I am relieved because I am not 100% clear on how I'd get back from here. Unsurprisingly, there has never been a reason for me to come to this side of town. I shiver in the cold evening air and walk out until I notice Barry Ames, waving at me from a bench facing the sea.

"Hey," he calls.

"Hello," I say. "Thanks for the tight deadline."

"Hey, as I'm sure you know from your career as a...college administrator, there are times when you need to get the job done fast."

He claps his hands together for effect before tapping the seat beside him. "Won't you have a seat?"

"I'd rather stand."

"Nah, sit, it'll look weird."

I do, sliding my hands into my pockets.

"So, how did it go?" he asks.

"You saw the photo," I say.

"Yeah, that was satisfying, but I mean, how did it go? Was it tough? Or are all those big muscles of his just for show?" he asks, smile bright, eyes engaged, genuinely interested.

I sigh.

"I mean, the guy was wasted. It was pretty easy."

"And you tweeted from his phone, I take it?" he asks, holding up his phone and flashing Adam Liverston's Twitter feed at me.

"Yeah," I said.

"You've got a knack for suicide notes, particularly given the short notice here," he says, whistling. "So, do you want to know about this guy?"

"Not especially."

"Oh, don't be boring. Come on, you have to be a little curious about how this wannabe Youtube fitness star ended up swimming in my ocean," he says.

I shrug my shoulders.

"He is dating my older sister," he says with a sigh. "He's been on-again off-again with her for the past two years and I mean, you saw him tonight. The guy is a freaking animal."

"Right," I say. "And obviously, you know, *this* was the best way to handle the situation."

He shrugs. "Well, you can say that and imply that this was an over-reaction, but I've tried everything." He presses an arm back against the bench, waving his fingers in my face as he counts off his methods, "I buy him off, give him a lump of cash and tell him to move town, and to never bother my sister again. And he agrees, he accepts the money, he breaks her heart, he vamooses. Then, six months later, he comes back 'cos he ran out of cash. So, I threatened him, got Ivan there and a couple of my boys to try to intimidate him, and what does he do? The bum just went straight to my sister for help. She is a good woman, but she's not smart when it comes to the heart." He sighs and rubs his head. "She swigs down his bullshit every time like it's Pinot Grigio."

I sigh and lean back against the bench.

"So, what was the final straw?"

Barry smiles, "Oh there was always gonna be something. I figured it'd be when he proposed or something. But no…So, recently I found out that the chances of me having little nieces and nephews has diminished *significantly*." The arrogant smirk is gone from his face and for the first time, I think he looks scary. This looks like a man who you wouldn't want to cross. "I should have put a stop to this a long time ago."

He smiles at me.

"Thanks again, Miss. King," he says. "You've gone and done me a favour."

"Well, I can't say I had too much choice in the matter," I say.

Barry smirks and shakes his head, chuckling to himself. "No, you don't." He offers me a cigarette. "Hey, you want one?"

"No, thanks."

"Come on, smoke with me. I know you smoke. Be polite."

I take a cigarette and reach for my own lighter. The cigarettes are strong and leave a bad taste in my mouth. He sighs and rests back, closing his eyes as he exhales a grey cloud into the cold night air.

"So, now can I ask you a question?"

"Shoot."

"Ok, well, will it always be like this?" I ask.

"How'd you mean?"

"You gonna give me five minutes notice, text me every two seconds and then invite me out for a smoke on the beach?" I ask. "Because if it is, you should know that I'll get caught. I need time to plan."

Barry snorts and shakes his head, stubbing out his cigarette on the polished wood of the bench. "Nah, I was just messing with you, Miss. King. I wanted to see if you could deliver. And hey, I wasn't disappointed either."

"So, next time?"

"I'll get in touch with you next week. A photo, a name and an address, just like today, or roughly," he says. "You can do it in your own time, plan, go through their garbage or whatever, whatever method suits you best. But if the target isn't dead in a week, I may get in touch to ask, like, what the fuck you're actually doing."

"A week would be better," I said. "I shouldn't need much more than that."

He nods and brushes back his greasy hair. "Glad to hear it. Anything else?"

"Will it always be guys like Adam Liverston?"

"Hey, what are you trying to say about my sister?" he asks, raising an eyebrow. "No, she doesn't have a load of awful ex-boyfriends I need you to go and get rid of. But…all of them will be people I need gone. That's all you need to know. For the record, that's all you will ever need to know."

He gets to his feet.

"Ivan will take you home."

He gestures with his hand and I glance over my shoulder to see Apparently-Ivan get out of his car and stand there in the dark, looming and waiting for me.

I sigh and stretch. "Thanks for the cigarette," I say.

"Keep up the good work, Miss. King," he says brightly. "I'll be in touch."

I stub my cigarette out on the ground and stamp on it more times than I need to.

Chapter Eight

I think all things considered, I'm a well-adjusted person.

All things considered.

*

"You have a lot of scars," he says, tracing a finger along the thin pale scar along my forearm. "You a clumsy kid or something?"

"Oh no," I say, "I'm an assassin. These be battle scars." I flex my arm for him and watch his face crease up into a grin.

"Well, that makes sense," he says, rolling his eyes. "An assassin, sure."

I rest my head on his shoulder. "Okay, you caught me, yeah, I was a clumsy kid. I was always... falling off stuff and crashing into things. Never got invited to birthday parties."

"Poor thing," he says, "So, tell me, how did you get... this one?" He pulls back the covers and presses a finger gently along the long thin scar across my thigh. "This must have hurt a bunch."

And I could say, 'Well, Rick, when I was fifteen, I wanted to cut someone, *anyone*, but also I didn't. So, I cut me. I cut me all over. Most of my scars made that way healed up. All except this one and one on my wrist that I hide behind that silly friendship bracelet Leda made me.' But, am I going to say that? Pfft. No.

"I climbed over a fence playing with some kids in my old neighbourhood, there was a nail. It bled a lot! Agony!"

He leans down and kisses it lightly, his stupid not-quite-there stubble tickling the skin.

"And how about this one?" He reaches up and slides his fingers through my hair, just above my ear, revealing the paler skin of a scar hidden by my hair.

I tell him that I bumped my head falling off a swing when I was a stupid drunk teenager so he'll kiss it better and I won't have to tell him about the night my friend Jason bashed my head in with a rock.

"How about this one then?" He lifts my forearm.

These are all Jason. He was and is, to this day, the only person I have killed who I also loved very dearly. So, I suppose it makes sense that he did a number on me before I put my knife through his left eye. It's crazy… despite what he became, despite what he did, as time passes, all that remains is the good.

"I got that in school, I got clumsy in wood shop and sliced my arm on one of those machines they probably shouldn't let idiot kids any-where near."

He kisses it gently. "Poor Sookie, you needed someone to look out for you."

"You should've tried telling that to teenage me," I say.

"How about this one?" He reaches between us and touches the scar on my side.

Jason and his knife. I close my eyes and I remember his wild, crazed expression. I remember the water, the dirt. I remember cling-ing to his leg, vision stained with blood, trying to keep him away from Sukhy. Failing… to keep him away from her.

"So, what about this one on your hand? Another wood shop acci-dent?"

"No, that was from when I was little, I was helping my step-moth-er cook," I say. "I got clumsy. It should have healed better, but hands are one of those places where you end up catching it on everything."

He kisses it softly. And I try to stop my eyes from watering.

But I'm a well-adjusted person, so it's not that hard.

*

A week later, as good as his word, I get my next job. The phone goes off while I'm in the shower late one night. I take it out of my bag and despite knowing this was going to happen, my heart sinks.

My target is a fifty-three-year-old drug dealer, who lost a shipment of Class A substances he was procuring for Barry and his cartel. The going theory is that the shipment went straight up his nose.

I guess I can get behind getting rid of someone like that. I mean, who would even miss him? And you know, he's an addict, he's sick. I'm helping him. I'm making it all ok.

He is sleeping when I enter his apartment. The door isn't even locked, the knob is hanging from its hinges. There's boxes and shit all over the floor. Our guy is curled up on his couch under a thin blanket. And the man looks like a scary ad from the 90s to discourage teens from smoking or whatever.

He looks weak. I can see all the bones in his arm through his papery skin.

He's clutching onto a photograph in his bird-like hands. I don't notice that the photo is of his wedding, with a wife with sandy hair who is no doubt, long gone. I don't notice that at all.

I put a really big dose of whatever he was injecting earlier into a syringe and re-open one of the many holes in his arm.

He vomits, he contorts, he trembles.

But in the end, he is still.

I guess that's how we all are in the end.

*

We are at the movies, sharing nachos, fighting off a hangover and ready to get scared by the latest feature about a spooky doll. Rick's slushy spills bright blue ice onto my leg as he leans over to get some salsa and I shriek loudly over the bloated car commercials.

His hand in mine as the movie starts and I feel fine.

I feel fine.

No, really, I do.

The movie ends and we're in a diner. The seats squeak uncomfortably in the heat and I am aware of every butt that has graced the seat today. I tell Rick and he laughs like a child and I feel fine.

I feel fine.

Breathless laughter and bad impressions. He does a terrible British accent, impersonating the old scientist who widely disputes the evil nature of the doll—right before he gets paid a nasty late-night house call.

Rick smiles and I am helpless.

*

The next one is a burly middle-aged man with an arrogant smirk and a beer gut that could possibly maintain its own centre of gravity. He's a taxi driver in the next town over. Apparently, he's been hassling one of the girls who works as a hostess at Barry's nightclub.

I take a train and then book a taxi from a movie theatre downtown. I chat a lot, I reach over and touch his flabby shoulder when he turns a corner. I let him look at me in a way that makes my blood boil.

I direct him to a lonely looking warehouse by the sea.

He pulls to a stop and smiles at me and calls me a dirty girl when he realises that I've led him to a dead end.

He is half facing me, still smirking when I shoot him through the temple.

*

The others are gone, it's dark and I fumble with my phone as I walk out the front entrance, fiddling with my headphones. But then, there he is, waiting for me outside the office.

Rick waves at me and before I can react, is suddenly bounding over. He picks me up, squirming and struggling and spins me around.

I'm laughing as I punch his shoulder playfully.

He carries me, laughing to his car.

It smells of cotton candy—a freshener he got as a present from Veronica, his sister. I settle into the front seat and lean over to kiss his cheek.

He laughs at me and squeezes my knee before switching the car into ignition. "So, I thought I'd kidnap you after work?"

*

He is forty-three, an ex-employee. It is not explained what he did to get on Barry's bad side. But he lives in a fancy apartment complex and wears sunglasses all the time, even at night, like he wants people to think that he's some undercover celebrity.

I get into the building easily enough. A neighbour, struggling with a screaming toddler leaves the door open for me. I am inside and thanks to the mail slot, I can see which apartment he lives in.

My guy isn't home.

Unfortunately for him, I know a thing or two about getting into a room. Buildings like these, particularly the fancier apartments, don't tend to splash out on sophisticated locks, they assume the key card access to the building will protect the tenants from anyone who might do them harm.

All too easily, I am inside. I don't pay any attention to his personal items. I don't read into the lack of family photos, the depressing contents of his fridge or the leftovers in the sink. I find his gun in one of the kitchen cupboards. Like, what the fuck? I don't notice the dried saliva around the barrel. No, I don't notice at all.

His wardrobe smells of dust and somehow even his outfits look depressing, limp on plastic hangers. I climb inside, amongst his dusty suits and a few alternating pairs of black shoes.

I wait around all night until he comes in.

Alone, because of course.

I was sort of worried that as an ex-employee, he'd be a little on the paranoid side. I mean, he must have known who he was working for. But no. Not this guy. He slopes miserably through his apartment, opens up one of the beers from the fridge and drinks it on the toilet. Then he staggers into the front room where he watches *Family Guy* for twenty minutes. Then back to the toilet for round two. He doesn't brush his teeth. He doesn't wash his face. He just shuffles to his bed with the same flat expression on his face and drops down flat onto his back.

I watch him in the dark. He just lies there, staring at the ceiling.

It's like he's already dead.

But I don't think about that as I use his gun to put an end to it.

*

He is sleeping with his chin against his chest on his sister's sofa, arms wrapped around his middle. He either looks cross or happy when he sleeps. Today, it's happy. He's smiling like he has a secret.

I smirk and tuck one of the grey blankets over him.

"He's so creepy when he sleeps," Veronica says, shaking her head and settling down into the very patchy-looking armchair she assures me is vintage and so adorable. "Like, look, he's sleeping like he's farted and nobody knows."

I laugh and top up her wine.

"Has he always done that?"

"Oh yeah," she said. "He also tends to fall asleep after dinner if he's had too much wine."

"Like an old man," I say and she laughs.

"Oh yeah, he's basically like a grandpa," Veronica agrees. "And, I mean, whatever, if you want to spend your life with a grandpa, then that's on you."

She looks like him, they have the same eyes, the same smile.

We're the same age, I realise when we've been talking for a few minutes.

"Well, I guess it's important for the elderly to have a companion in their golden years?" I suggest.

This really makes her laugh and she nudges me as she takes her wine.

"Ok, *please* don't dump my brother!"

*

Apparently-Ivan drives me to an apartment on the other side of the state. The journey is long and I'm glad I'd packed my earphones as it's creepy classical music all the way.

He doesn't talk to me, just shoots me disapproving looks if I make any sort of sound in the back seat. I hum to get on his nerves, but he won't speak to me.

Eventually we pull up at this really dull-looking apartment in Sacramento. Apparently-Ivan turns down his music and shows me a photograph of a woman with iron-grey hair and a tired-looking expression. He doesn't tell me her name or anything about her, but he tells me that I need to make it look like a robbery and jerks a canvas black backpack in my face.

I get into the apartment easily enough. The old woman is in. I pretend that I don't hear her singing in the shower. She has a shelf full of antiques—nice of her to put her valuables in one place. And as I browse her shelves, careful not to notice anything…about her, I spy a few nice copies of books by Charles Dickens. Those all go in the backpack Apparently-Ivan shoved in my face.

Before I leave, I shoot the old woman in the back while she showers.

The singing stops.

*

Rick is singing in the shower as I creep in to get my make-up wipes. He pokes his head out from around the curtain and waves at me.

"Care to join me?"

I laugh and shed out of my pyjama shorts to clamber in after him —only to discover pretty quickly that it's too cramped. Rick winces as his warm back presses against the cold tiles.

I'm laughing as I wrap my arms around him to try and cushion him from the cold a little. He wipes his wet attempt at facial hair across my forehead and I press him back against the cold tiles to watch him squirm.

One of his hands comes up and pulls out the chunky hairclip keeping my dreads mostly on top of my head, causing them to spill out across my shoulders, damp from the shower. I nudge him and the two of us crash into the shaky metal shampoo rack. My foot slides up against the hard side and I wince and cling to Rick as I hop up on one foot.

"Ow!"

"So, showers together are a bad idea?" he says.

"Yes!" I say, trying to glance down at my throbbing big toe. "That kills!"

*

His name is Officer Vince Cho. He is twenty-eight and he found out about one of his superior's working with Barry Ames. He's young and honest and doesn't want a career to be tarnished by some gangster.

He won't listen to his boss. He won't make a deal with Barry. He won't play the game.

I contact him from a burner phone and ask him to come and meet with me in a warehouse, near where I killed the taxi driver. I tell him that I have irrefutable evidence of what has been going on. I tell him that I'm an ex-girlfriend of Barry's and I'm scared.

He wants to be a hero.

He shows up, ready to tell me that it's going to be ok, that I don't have to worry, the police are here now.

He is young, I try not to notice.

He has his whole life ahead of him, I try not to notice.

My instructions said 'Leave no trace'.

So, I keep cutting him until there's nothing left of him but blood and teeth and sawed up chunks of bone.

Then I burn him up.

I think about the last time I did this.

Then I think about Detective Brankowski and the way his mother cried at his funeral and I feel sick.

I shower until my skin feels cracked and I still don't feel clean.

But I don't want to think about that.

*

"So, I feel like you know my whole family history," Rick says, "But I know like…nothing about yours!"

"Well, there's not much to tell," I say. "I don't have like…a million cousins like you. Hell, I don't have any cousins."

"Hey, I sometimes forget my family, it's crazy extended—Sandra, my cousin in San Francisco, she has like…five kids, triplets last year and I feel so guilty that I don't remember their names!"

I laugh and squeeze his hand across the table. "You're not really selling the whole big family thing to me, you know?"

He chuckles and glances up at me. "Yeah, maybe not. Hey, Sookie, if you don't want to talk about your family, that's ok. I just, you know, I'm a little curious is all. I mean, I heard you talking to someone this morning? Your mom, right?"

I try not to freak out. I try not to let it show that my heart is beating like crazy right now. I try not to sweat or flinch or...

"This morning?"

"Yeah, I was half asleep."

She called this morning. She doesn't get a lot of privacy so she doesn't do it often. So, when she calls, I make myself *available*. I'd crept out into the hallway and whispered. I thought he was asleep. I thought...

"Yeah, well," I say, trying not to falter. "My stepmom. We don't get along. Every now and then she calls. She's basically a terrible person."

"Sookie, honestly, I feel like such an asshole for prying, I just!"

"Babe, it's fine," I say, leaning over to squeeze his hand. "I know how weird it must look to you. I really don't want you to think I'm being purposefully cryptic or mysterious. I just don't want to bum you out with the whole thing."

Rick squeezes my hand back.

"You know I care about you, right?"

I lean over and kiss him.

"And I care about you. I ran away when I was fifteen, my dad died and left me with my stepmom. We clashed, I was a dumb teenager, she was, awful, so I left. I was in foster care for a bit, then I got a job and became independent and yeah, we're caught up."

I feel like shit for lying.

"Family was just never part of my whole...thing. This is going to sound a bit, dramatic, I guess, but my life isn't the happiest story, I've been on my own for a long time." I glance down at my feet, "And I'm not saying that just so you'll feel sorry for me, I just-" He leans across the table and takes my face in his hands as he kisses me.

My heart is beating fast and he smiles at me.

"Besides," I say, "you, Rick, have enough stories for the both of us. And I like hearing them. I really do."

*

Her name is Lydia and she has dealt with Barry a few times over the years. She sells information for a living and moves around a lot. I struggle to track her down. Lydia isn't her real name and she's wearing a wig in the photo I am issued.

I end up going back to Barry asking him how the hell he expects me to get rid of a woman who doesn't even exist. He does a bit of digging and eventually, an address is provided.

It's an office she used a few times, she still pays for it, the lights are still on. But she hasn't been there for a while.

I call in sick at work and watch the place for a few days—a few days *wasted*! Then, one day as I'm giving up, I notice a woman who roughly fits Lydia's description enter the building. She has a shaved head and big sunglasses, but it's her.

Though the building looks crappy, the locks are excellent and I can't get in.

But I don't need to get in.

I smash a window and stand on a box, waving my lighter around until I set off the alarm and the sprinklers.

She leaves through a side door into the alleyway I'm waiting in: I knew she wouldn't try and leave through the front or back door, she's too cautious, she won't do anything that might put her in immediate danger

She sees me and knows who I am; I wonder briefly if she was the one who looked me up for Barry Ames in the first place.

That makes it a little easier to shoot her in the head as she yells, 'Wait! Wait!'

*

"I don't want to wait!" He rushes up behind me and I laugh as he scoops me up into his arms. "Come back to bed, you!"

I'm breathless from laughing, sweaty from trying to squeeze out of the black dress Tammy recommended for our special six-month anniversary dinner. My underwear came from a shop I honestly felt embarrassed to walk into, and quite frankly, it should have come with a manual on how to put it on.

I shriek and flail around as he flings me back onto the bed.

"Rick!"

He is laughing as he gets down on top of me.

"So, quick question, how on earth did you get this on?" He asks, tugging at one of the straps around the top of my thigh. "Was there a manual?"

I smirk and lean back against the pillows. "I thought the fun would be getting me out of it?"

His head moves down and lips press against my inner thigh. I sigh and close my eyes, lying back against the bed, legs trembling as he touches me.

"I love you," I say much too quietly.

"What was that?" he asks, looking up.

"Oh, nothing!"

*

The hotel is fancy. If it wasn't about to be tarnished in my memory forever, I'd book me and Rick a room here. It really is nice. I lie back on the bed Barry has booked for me and close my eyes.

The guy I'm after works in the kitchen, and on late shifts, he gets to kip in one of the empty rooms, if they have one available. He's in his late twenties, and lives with his mother who has had to pay off his gambling debts to Barry once before.

"She said she wouldn't pay my guy again," Barry said. "Guess a mother's love has its limits, eh?"

I try not to think about it to be honest.

I wait for him to finish his shift and go into his hotel room which is just down the hallway from mine, I can see it through my peephole. I'm stood around, trying to plan the best way to do it. When something unexpected happens, my guy calls one of the maids to his room—I know her from the staff rota, and more importantly, from his Facebook page, this is Shana Lewis, an ex-girlfriend. I hear them arguing from across the corridor.

Note to self, not the best hotel for soundproofing.

Shana leaves after ten minutes, clearly angry, and in her hurry, she knocks straight into me, who just happened to be leaving my room. Embarrassed and flustered, she rushes past me with a quick 'Sorry'.

She won't realise that I took the master key she was holding right out of her hand.

He is on the toilet when I enter his room.

"Shana, hey?" he calls.

I use a knife, not dissimilar from ones he would use every day in the kitchen, to slit his wrists. He was so embarrassed about me walking in on him on the toilet that it gave me time to cut him deep before he could really try and fight me off. I muffle his yelling, his dying breaths with one of the towels and hold him there until he is still.

Then I leave and drop Shana's key in the corridor, so she might think that she's dropped it.

I try not to think about it too much as I go back to my hotel room to try and sleep.

*

"So, when is the wedding again?"

He is bent over, frowning at the price tag on a plush-looking armchair at the front of the display.

"Next month," he says. "She has family coming from Europe, so they have to do it while everyone is in town."

"And how does Marco feel about it?" I ask.

"Pretty great actually. He thinks the longer you spend planning something, the less joy you get out of it."

"That is actually a really good attitude," I agree.

"Yeah, he's pretty much the most laid back guy in the world." Rick stands up and dusts down his jeans. "I'm gonna get them something else. This chair is way over-priced."

I lean down and lift the tag up.

"Well, it's expensive because it's real leather and super nice. How about we get it for them together?"

He flushes a little. "Sookie, no!"

"Come on, it'll be easier if we do that," I say. "You know, actually affordable! And you won't get a nicer chair than this."

"But they're my friends, I'd feel bad you having to chip in."

"Well, I'm going to their wedding so I should get them something. Don't be dumb, let me help?" I reach for his shoulders and kiss him.

He wraps his arms around me and smiles.

"You really are the best."

*

This guy is a teenage drug dealer who isn't making payments or delivering on his end. Barry tells me not to kill this boy, but to teach him a lesson that gets him off the criminal circuit.

I tell him I'm not a corrections officer. He offers to get some of his boys to go and do it instead. I don't like the expression on his face when he says it. So I go over to the park where this kid operates.

He's younger than he looks, and I wonder if his parents know what he does when he's supposed to be in some dumb after-school club. I buy shitty weed from him and he follows me for two blocks. He's probably going to grow into a right little creep, I tell myself for reassurance.

I feel less guilty when he follows me into an alleyway. I hide behind a bin, put on a dumb Halloween mask Barry asked me to bring along for Christ knows what reason, and proceed to beat the shit out of the kid.

I force feed him some of his own material and kick him in the crotch and face until he cries for his mother, drugged up and delirious. I tell him bad men are going to come after him and fuck him up. I tell him they are going to burn down his parents' house with his mom and dad in it. He cries and cries and I tell him to stay away from Barry Ames.

I leave him weeping and bloody in the alleyway.

I hope he goes home to his mom and dad and never tries any of this fucking shit again.

*

Rick's friends are the best. He is part of this big group that have known each other forever. And they have all been so great and welcoming to me. We go out for drinks at least once a week, sometimes twice if there's something going on.

There's his best friend, Marco, who he's known since they were in diapers, and Marco's fiancé, Starr, who they met when she was an exchange student at their high school and officially moved to the states for college. The two of them are witty and sweet and drowning in wedding planning.

Carla, who he met through his older sister, who is stunningly beautiful and owns a small art studio downtown. She drinks red wine and promises to tell me all the embarrassing stories about young Rick that Marco is too gentlemanly to share.

Then there's Miguel, his college roommate, who smiles constantly and his boyfriend, Rory, who frowns a lot. Miguel actually works at the same college as me, he's an MFA candidate who works as an assistant to one of the professors.

There's Dan and Jandro who are both friends from college and their girlfriends, Alex and Libby, who are both incredibly sarcastic and funny. Apparently, there was another girl, Amber, who used to tag along with them as well. Jandro and Dan talk about her fondly, but the girls seem less keen.

"You'll meet her eventually," Jandro says, "Amber makes the whole town stop when she comes into town."

"She likes to think she does," Libby says. "She thinks her life is a reality show, I swear."

Everyone laughs and it's warm being here. They all fit together, it's all in-jokes and new jokes and goofing around and it makes me feel good. It makes me wish that I was good. Everyone made me feel like I belong and it's…a feeling I haven't had since… Well, it's something I haven't felt in a long time.

*

Barry tells me over a drink that he has been with a lot of beautiful and sophisticated women. He touches my arm when he says it, and the look I give him gets him to back off, laughing.

"One of these women, is my ex-wife. Her name is Carmen, she works as a record producer in San Francisco. Have you ever been to San Francisco?" He doesn't listen to my answer and instead tells me that I'm going to spend my weekend there with Apparently-Ivan.

The ex-wife, he suspects, is going to talk to the Feds about him, or she might one day, anyway. I try not to think about the implications of that.

I ditch plans with my friends and Rick, insisting that I have to go and see an old friend in Illinois. The lie feels that much worse this time and I try not to think about that either.

Apparently-Ivan is in a terrible mood and refuses to speak to me on the drive or when we get to Barry's apartment there. He dumps the information about the former Mrs. Ames on the kitchen table and uses his height as a way of avoiding eye contact with me.

I do some sightseeing, get dinner at this really bad hot dog stand and eventually find myself walking over to Carmen Ramera, née Ames's, office. She works at a record company, she's an agent. Older than Barry and incredibly beautiful. I googled her and found that she's worked with some pretty big names over the years.

The gangster ex-husband doesn't suit her, which is why she left him.

She works later than everyone else.

She leaves the building just before security leave.

I watch her in her car. She is talking to someone, her perfect face crinkled in rage. She hits her iPhone against the steering wheel a few times before sighing and covering her face with her hands.

I wait for a while, wondering why I hesitate, trying not to think about why I hesitate.

Then I walk over, holding my phone and tapping her window, gesturing nervously, I'm asking her for directions. I don't know San Francisco that well, I don't know the area at all.

 To my surprise she rolls it down.

I tranquilise her with the syringe Apparently-Ivan left on the table for me.

Her eyes cloud over, then she closes them forever.

She doesn't have to be there for what comes next.

*

The wedding is beautiful and bright, and Rick nails his best man's speech. My dress has a wine stain on the skirt, but this is why it's always ok to wear black!

We're sat on the stone steps of the hotel where Marco and Starr tied the knot, sharing a cigarette and sipping red wine. My feet hurt from dancing and the booze has made me feel light, like I could fly.

It's a magical night.

I rest my head against his shoulder and take in his smell.

"It's beautiful here," I say.

"I know, this is like, the nicest wedding I've ever been to."

"The nicest ever," I agree.

"Thanks for coming with me," he says. "Sookie, you know I love you, right?"

Then he turns and smiles at me and I love him.

I love him so fucking much that it makes me *ache*.

"I was wondering," he says, "Phil is moving out next month, he's got a new job in San Francisco. How would you feel about maybe moving in with me?"

*

Thomas J. Anderson is something of a property giant who lives in a big ugly house up in the hills. He is, on paper, a typical goody-goody rich guy. He's sleazy in the way that his wife is a nineteen-year-old, Miss California contestant. However, in a less socially acceptable way, he is also massively addicted to the races and he owes Barry huge amounts of money and is refusing to pay.

I get into the house easily. Their security guy, Ali, doesn't work on Thursday mornings, he has a daughter who needs serious dental work and on Thursdays he drives her to her appointments.

I take a day off. Mr. Anderson has Thursdays off, he sleeps in until late, then spends his afternoon making loud angry phone calls to his assistant, Peter for the rest of the day. His wife is usually at her aerobics class. She was supposed to be at her aerobics class.

I walk in through the door and find Mrs. Anderson coming down the stairs in her dressing gown, with a set of glasses and an empty bottle of champagne.

I have been told to get rid of her if she's in the house when I come to take out her husband.

I stab nineteen-year-old Mrs. Anderson with a butcher knife I've taken from their kitchen. I close a hand over her mouth to muffle her scream. I stab her five times in the stomach.

I slit her husband's throat while he sleeps, wipe off the handle of the knife and leave it by his hand.

I walk past his wife's body on the stairs. Her robe has come undone in the struggle, revealing her naked body. I want to cover her back up, but if her husband had done it, as I want everyone to think, I don't think he would have.

I wish she'd been at aerobics.

I wish she'd been at fucking aerobics.

*

I am curled up in a ball on the bathroom floor. Aching from sleep.

I want Mrs. Anderson to be a bad dream. I want to believe that the whole thing was just a really, really bad dream.

But it's not and I wake up in a cold sweat. And it makes me sick.

I hold my knees against my chest and try to breathe normally.

In and out.

In and out.

There's a knock at the door.

"Babe? Babe, it's me."

I open it up and manage to open the door and find Rick staring down at me, rubbing his tired eyes in the hallway. Concern fills his face when he sees me and he bends down, holding my hand in his.

"What happened?"

"Bad dream," I say. "It…it was just a bad dream."

He drops to his knees and holds me until I manage to breathe properly. He holds me until I stop shaking, and suddenly I register how weird this must look, how crazy I must look. How many nights I've spent like this on the bathroom floor.

"I'm sorry, Rick," I mumble.

"Geez, that must have been some dream."

I laugh and rest my head against his chest. "I'm sorry," I say.

"Oh, come on, don't. Everything's fine."

I groan and rub my hands over my face. "No, I mean, I must look completely nuts. Like, I don't want you to see me like this."

"Well, I'm glad I'm here," he said. "Hey, Sookie, how about we get out of the city for a little bit?" he asks. "Tiny vacation? Would you like that?"

"Yeah," I say. My body is so tired I just want to sink. "Yeah, that'd be nice."

I think I need a break.
I think I just need some time.

Chapter Nine

My three phones are at home, stuffed into my pillowcase, out of sight, out of mind. I am here, driving along Route 5 and for the first time in a very long time, I feel really good, almost like I can breathe.

*

Rick says that his mom taught him to drive—she became a driving instructor after her divorce. She was giving lessons while she was pregnant with Veronica and in time, taught all three of her kids how to drive.

"She could teach you?" he says, "You know, if you ever wanted to learn?"

"I'm a pedestrian," I protest. "I know I'd be dangerous behind a wheel."

He laughs at me. "No, you're about the least dangerous person I know."

Oh boy.

I hand him his sunglasses as the light starts to come in bright along Route 5. He takes them and slides them up his nose before leaning back into his chair. He looks good like that: I sit back to take him in as we race past rows of little green trees, stretches of brown fields across the horizon.

The power lines cut across above us and verge off into the distance.

I don't think I've ever been on a trip like this. It feels good, driving to nowhere in particular, watching the skyline change and turn around me.

We pass a row of parked up pickup trucks along the freeway, one has a set of portable toilets on a little trailer out back. A handful of people are delving through the green fields. I wind down the window and hear music playing.

We cut through small towns, trailers parked up and decorated with little gardens in between them. Small, dusty-looking houses with people sitting on porches in the shade. The smell of dust and oranges in the air.

We stop and use the bathroom at a rest stop on the outskirts of one of these little towns and I come out to find Rick chatting to an elderly couple. He smiles when he sees me and introduces me to his new friends.

We pass a garden with the tallest palm trees I have ever seen. I make Rick stop so I can get a photo. He jumps in, arms outstretched, beaming as he reaches, trying to stand just as tall. We drive away, laughing as the crotchety-looking old woman who lives there comes out onto her porch, walking stick raised and fierce.

"This is fun," I say, leaning over to squeeze his knee.

"That's the idea."

*

We go to a beach on the coast. Rick parks up wonkily and practically leaps out of the car. He tugs off his shirt and tosses it through the window. I'm laughing as I climb out. The wind feels good on my face and I take in the smell of the sea, of a hot dog stand, of sunscreen and a family barbecue somewhere close by.

I push up my sunglasses and start tying back my hair.

"Come on, let's go in!" he says, and I realise to my horror that he means it. He really means it.

"No, Rick, wait!"

But he's ditched his shoes and dashed out across the hot concrete, onto the sand, past the hot dog stand and a somewhat obvious sign that reads 'Beach'. He races past a family sprawled across beach towels and a couple of teenagers playing frisbee. He rushes into the sea and jumps right in, no hesitation, no customary pause, not even a screech of complaint.

I watch him amongst the gentle waves, bobbing up and down in the bright blue waters, rocking back and forth, so carefree. His hand comes up and he waves at me, beckoning me forward.

Despite myself, I step out, following him from concrete to sand, past families and frisbees. I stand at the edge of the shore and take out his phone and snap a few of him bobbing up and down in the water, smile stretched across his face.

"Not coming in?" he asks, "It's nice in here."

"No way, someone has to watch the electronics," I say, gesturing to his phone and the car keys in my hand.

"Booo!" he yells and dunks his head under the water.

I sit down on the soft sand and watch him for a while, taking in the sound of the sea, the bright horizon, the screech of seagulls and the warm sun coming down on me from above.

This is…this is nice.

*

We check into a motel near the beach. Rick parks the car, better this time. We find a little convenience store where they confusingly sell champagne, which we obviously buy. The motel is a stone's throw from the beach but I can see why it's not very popular, despite its beautiful location. I mean, it looks like something straight out of a horror movie.

The clerk behind the counter has a patchy goatee and a dead-eyed expression. He is palming his way through a battered-looking Stephen King as we enter, and does not put it down as he checks us in.

"Have a nice night," he says in the same bored monotone.

"Oh, we will," Rick says, smiling.

I elbow his side and he laughs, scooping an arm around my shoulders.

We pass a pool on the way past the car park and towards the stairs to our room. It is covered by a layer of flies.

The room smells musky, in fact as I flop backwards onto the bed, I notice a small cloud of dust rise into the air behind me. It creaks and I feel all the springs press along my spine.

This will not be an easy sleep.

Rick laughs and wafts the air with his hand. "Ew, well, at least we know there was no funny business in here recently."

"Unless we get a blacklight on the sheets? Old stains still show, you know?"

"I'd really rather not." He reaches up high and opens the narrow window at the top with some difficulty as it creaks uncertainly in response. "Oh wow. Does nobody stay at this motel?"

"Probably not. Hey, maybe we have the haunted room?"

"Wooo," he says, before laughing and shaking his head. "Sounds spoo-kyyyy."

I sit up from the bed and pat down my hair, increasingly aware it's probably dusted with grey now. I frown and fold my legs up against my chest. "No, but seriously, I like it. It feels like we're in an old movie."

Rick grins, "Well, I guess it does have the whole authentic road trip aesthetic."

"I mean, we have our early 90s TV that looks like it won't even work," I say, gesturing to it. "Oh wow, yeah, I hope you're prepared to watch a movie on my phone instead."

"Fully prepared, let's see…there's the shower," Rick dashes over to the bathroom door and cracks it open, "That looks like it's straight out of *Psycho*."

"Straight out of *Psycho*," I agree.

"And I mean, this wallpaper…"

"Yeah, I'm not sure where to begin."

I get the impression that maybe it was red once, but the light has faded it to a kind of very shitty brown and it's decorated with little flowers—or maybe that's what they were meant to be. It looks like little scribbles, really.

"This one looks phallic," Rick says, gesturing with his thumb. "Seriously, I can't tell if it's graffiti or not."

"And I'm not exaggerating, but you can feel every spring on this bed."

"How are the pillows?"

"Limp."

He nods, "I guess this is what $50 a night gets you."

I smile at him, "At least we have champagne."

"Right, but do we have ice?" He goes over to the metal bucket left on the little brown table by the window. "Clerk said there'd be some in the room and…Ok, to nobody's surprise, we're out of ice." Rick says, holding up a bucket filled with water. "I think we had some…a long time ago." He heads to the bathroom and pours it out into the sink. "Oh, hon, the sink is green! Blergh!"

I shudder and climb off the bed. "That's horrifying. Hey, I'll go get some more ice," I say, squeezing his shoulder as I take the bucket from him.

"Ok, thanks, babe. I'll see if I can de-limp these pillows."

"Well, I mean, you can try."

I hear him flapping one of the dusty faded yellow pillows against the bedroom wall as I close the room door behind me. Glancing along the stairwell, I can see some badly lit vending machines and… yes, upon approach, a disturbingly loud ice machine.

Thankfully, at least the machine is working and full of ice. The coolness feels good against my hands as I open the lid and grab the scoop. I'm bending down to scoop some into the bucket, when I hear a voice that I haven't heard in a very long, long time.

"So, like, I haven't called him, because I honestly don't feel like I should have to, you know? Like, I know feminism blah-blah-blah, but sometimes it's nice to be made to feel like a lady and have the guy be a little…persistent, you know, Marsha?"

It's a highly elevated Downtown Abbey style British accent, but with an awkward American twang. And I am fucking frozen to this spot, awkwardly bent over, my hand holding the scooper shaking.

"Sure, Lisa, but, if you don't make a move at all, it's football season and you won't see him at all next semester, you know?"

I fucking make it for six years without running into anyone.

I have *never* been recognised.

I stopped wearing my coloured contacts like…four years ago.

And this little bitch just happens to wander into the same motel as me on my escape from the city break?

"Oh, *whatever*, if a man won't make the time for me, then he's not interested."

"Well, just don't complain to me when you have nobody to bring to Mindy's party next month."

"Come *off* it, just because I'm not going with him doesn't mean I'd have to go alone, Marsha!"

I feel my blood go as cold as this ice box as two women pass the vending machines and come up behind me at the ice box.

I'm watching out of the corner of my eye and it is her, it is undeniably her. Maternal cousin of my old friend Beth, Lisa Jones, who moved from the UK to our sleepy wood-side town for high school.

Oh, fucking hell, of all the people I could have run into, it would have to be her.

Same long blonde hair, same pointed nose. Same *loud* voice.

She's taller now, wearing white shorts, a blue bikini top and a man's letterman jacket. She has grown a fringe to hide the scar on her forehead where Jason hit her with that rock.

I put down the scoop and hope that their inane conversation about whether to call what's-his-name or not, distracts her from seeing me. I'm nearly past her, when a well-manicured hand clasps hold of my shoulder.

"Hey, do I know you?"

I look up and even with my bullshit drugs store glasses, she has to know it's me. Like, she has to. And she had to come with a friend so I can't just…hit her over the head with the ice scoop, finish what Jason started…

Marsha, who has a wild-looking blood red afro, glances up at me from her phone. Lisa is frowning, trying to place my face. And I feel like everything is being drained out of me slowly, like my stomach is in knots because I'm caught. She has to know me. Like, my mother's status as a hardcore serial killer, Lisa's own bludgeoning, and the death of me and like…two of our friends, wouldn't have painted her high school career with some serious bad vibes.

"Erm, sorry, I don't think we've met," I say.

"Nah, you have like, such a familiar face," Lisa says. "Do you go to San Francisco State?"

"No, not me," I say.

"Oh, hmm, ok," she frowns. "But you have, like, *such* a familiar face. You definitely look like someone I know."

"I think I just have one of those faces, seriously, I get that a lot."

I don't. I have only ever looked like one person.

"Oh, I hate when this happens, I know I've seen you before."

"Lisa," Marsha interrupts, "Is this like when you insisted you knew that girl from Burger King before?"

Colour flushes to her face and Lisa laughs. "Hey, no!"

"Sorry," Marsha says, elbowing Lisa playfully, "This one is a complete nut. She insisted once that she had been at school with this random girl at Burger King, she wouldn't let it go for like twenty minutes." Marsha laughs, "Lise, stop harassing innocent people on vacation."

I feel relief like never before.

Thank God, Lisa is still an idiot.

"Hey, no worries, could happen to anyone," I say, smiling. "Like I said, I kind of just have one of those faces." I nod brightly and walk back down the corridor and out towards my motel room. And honestly, I didn't imagine doing this as easily. I have to compose myself before I walk back into the room, try not to show that I'm sweating.

"And we have ice," I say, dramatically waving the bucket as I enter the room.

"You took a while," Rick says, "I was about to come and check on you."

"Nah, I ran into some sorority girls, one of them kept insisting that she recognised me," I say with a shrug.

"That's so weird," Rick says, kissing my forehead as he takes the bucket from me, putting it down on the little brown table and dunking the champagne bottle in amongst the ice. "So, you've made friends with some sorority girls?"

"Oh, yeah, like, best friends."

"You gonna go to an *awesome* party with them instead of hanging out with me?"

"Duh," I say and push him back onto the dusty bed. He laughs and yanks me over to him, the springs screech uncomfortably and I curl into his arms, tucking my legs over his. "Nah, I don't much like *awesome* parties."

His arms wrap around me and I sigh, content.

"I'm glad we got out of the city," I say.

"Tell me about it. Creepy motel or not, I'm up for it."

*

At night, I dream of the woods behind the house I lived in with her.

When I was very little, I used to be afraid of them; I'd picture myself like Hansel and Gretel, I'd wander in and get lost until I found a witch's cottage. They were…ominous looking, they probably still are. So big and dark. My bedroom was at the front of the house, facing the street and looking out on my friend Beth's home. Mother's room faced the woods.

Sometimes when I'd pass her room, I'd see her stood, staring out of the window.

I wonder what she thought about at those times?

As I got bigger, I stopped being afraid of the woods. I had problems closer to home, things in the walls and below the house for me to be afraid of. The woods seemed like a jungle, a maze I could enter and hide away in forever. It became my playground, where me and my friends would go to drink and get stupid.

It felt reassuring that nobody could find us there, not easily and not on purpose.

But tonight, my dreams take me back to the woods of my childhood.

I wander through, frightened and covered by the trees and their shadows. I creep through the undergrowth and flinch at every snap of a twig, at every bird who flies through the cage of branches. I try to peer out for the footpath, I search frantically for some light.

I hear my friends running around in the woods, just out of sight.

I hear them laughing like the children we were.

Then I hear my friend Matt begging for his life as the sounds of fists and blows clap through the air.

I hear Beth, her voice shaking with accusations and fear.

I hear Jason's laughter turn to pure mania.

A stone narrowly misses my face.

Then a hand on my shoulder and I scream and struggle, only to see Sukhy, my Sukhy, just as she was when we were children, but as she staggers towards me in the dark, I can see that she is bleeding and bruised.

"Run away, Fiona."

I cling to her and tell her that we can find a way out.

Sukhy grows bigger and taller than me, her cuts growing deeper, her bruises wider, she stretches until she becomes as she was on the night she died.

"I SAID *RUN!*"

And, just like that, the dream is over.

I lie there and catch my breath as I watch the sun rise through the blinds. I take in the stale smell of the motel room, the warmth of Rick's arm around me. And it's just a dream. Just a stupid dream.

I curl into a ball and cover my face with my hands.

I watch the sun as it rises through the blinds and I wonder what my mother thought about as she watched the woods all alone in her room at night.

But, I guess I was never much good at knowing what she was thinking.

Chapter Ten

The drive back feels shorter than the drive away. My stomach is in knots and I tell Rick unconvincingly that I'm carsick. He stops to buy me water to calm me down. As he buckles his seatbelt, he reaches over and touches my arm.

"Sookie, it'll be ok when we get back. There's nothing to worry about."

I tell him I'm not worried, but I'm not entirely convinced that he believes me.

I want him to believe me, but…

We have the radio on for most of the drive home, Rick sings along and I think about Sukhy doing that when we were kids. I close my eyes and try to relax and imagine a time where I don't do any of this. I'm dreading going back to my phone, to my missed calls, missed messages, I dread picking up my phone and seeing the face of the next person he wants me to hurt.

This isn't my hobby, this isn't me controlling my compulsive behaviour. This doesn't make my heart feel calm the way it used to.

I wonder how long this will last with fucking Barry.

Will it last so long that it starts to feel good? It just becomes like it was before when I just hurt people because it was an itch I needed to scratch? Or will it get worse? Will it be like how she cured me of it for a time, when I was young. Will it make me sick? Will it affect my crappy job? Will it affect me when I'm with the people I love?

I take a deep breath and sit up, pushing my sunglasses on top of my head.

"Thanks for this," I say, "I was feeling all…weird and tired back in the city. Can we do this again sometime? Just drive off like some Bonnie and Clyde shit?"

He chuckles at me and glances over, smiling. "Any time. I get the same. Sometimes you just need a change. When was the last time you left our neck of the woods?"

"Not for a long time," I say. "I came here at nineteen and I've mostly stuck to being California bound. Don't remember the last time I left the state."

"Babe, we didn't even do that this time. Right, next time, we are going on a proper adventure, somewhere far, far away. Gotta get you more worldly and wise," he says, nodding his head. "Seriously, any time. It doesn't have to be beaches and stretches of highway with us."

And honestly, I want nothing but this, us, nothing but us.

I lean over and kiss his ear, smirking. "Hey, Rick, pull over somewhere."

"You need to pee?" he asks absent-mindedly.

"Rick," I say, firmer this time, one hand running down the front of his pants. "Pull over somewhere."

*

We get back to mine to find Tammy and Leda sleeping on the sofa to *RuPaul's Drag Race*. I grab a change of clothes for work tomorrow. Rick is in the bathroom as I turn on all three cell phones.

The main cell is all Leda sending me Snapchats from a night out, a message from Tammy asking if she can use my shampoo (at least she's asking). The WhatsApp group from work has blown up, but that will require further investigation later.

A text from Mother on the second phone, asking me about the weather.

She *so* texts like a Grandma.

Then comes the third cell. An ominous text from Barry telling me to have fun on my little trip out of town: an unofficial 'I know where you are' kind of message, great, that's not creepy at all. I can finally feel my heartbeat returning to normal as I see that this phone has been quiet. There're no threats, no fear, no build-up. There's just one job, Apparently-Ivan will collect me on Thursday after work.

Thursday is like four days away and I can handle that. I let out a sigh of relief and silently curse myself for letting this play on my mind the way it has.

The phones all go back in my bag, along with a change of clothes for tomorrow.

"Ready," I tell Rick as he returns, and I mean it. I'm ready.

*

We get back to Rick's place and the second, literally the second we get inside, Phil is waiting for us looking freaked out. Before either me or Rick can say anything, he pulls in close to Rick and whispers something frantically that I don't quite catch, but I don't like the expression clouding over Rick's face.

He glances nervously at me, then at Phil, "Why did you!" he hisses, gesturing at the closed living room door. He looks panicked.

"What's going on?" I ask.

"Sookie," he says, moving to stand in front of the door. "This is..."

But then the door opens and there's this woman stood there with her arms folded. She has near waist-length light brown hair and big black hipster glasses. Her long thin nose is pierced with a little silver hoop, and she's wearing a green parka with a man's shirt tucked into tight black jeans.

She snorts.

"Don't even want to say hi to me, Rick? That's just peachy."

He looks nervous as he turns away from me to face her. And there's an iciness in his tone that I don't…that I don't know.

"What do you want, Amber?"

Amber from the group, Amber?

Amber who Jandro and Dan like but Libby and Alex don't, Amber?

She snorts again and peers around him at me. Hazel eyes narrow in amusement. "So, this is Sookie, right?"

He stands so stiff and firm, but I can see the way his hand is shaking.

"If you don't want anything, you need to go," he says.

Amber rolls her eyes and glances from me to him. "Does she talk or is there a switch you have to push?"

And before I can say anything and believe me, there are a *great* many things I would like to say, Rick steps back and opens the front door wide.

"Get the fuck out," he snaps.

Amber sighs and holds up her hands in self-defence. "Wow, so, this is how it is? This is how you're going to talk to me from now on?" She looks sad, or at least, that's how she wants us to see her as she walks over to the door. "We can't even be friends now?"

Don't fall for it, I want to say.

But Rick sighs, "See, Amber, friends call first to say they're coming over. They check a good time, a good day, they *ask*."

Amber closes the door.

"I'm sorry, I just wanted to see you, to catch up. It's been ages. I was hoping to run into you at Marco and Starr's wedding but my invite never came and..."

"Well, if you want to see me, you know what to do next time," he says, opening the door again. "It's not a good time. Good night."

Amber smiles, eyes narrowed behind bulky frames. "Sure, next time you can introduce me to your mute new girlfriend. Oh God, Rick, I'm kidding! Clearly kidding! Ok, bye!"

The door closes and Phil instantly starts apologising and I realise that I'm blindsided. I can't remember the last time I had a conversation where I've been this completely absent.

Ex-girlfriend, of course he has an ex-girlfriend, probably more than just the one, actually. But I didn't think meeting one of them would be this...aggressive.

Rick tells Phil to forget it, very coldly and takes my hand as we walk over to his bedroom. "I'm sorry," he says to me. "I'm sorry you had to meet her like this."

"So," I say. "You two used to date?"

"Yeah," he said, and he's so rattled. His hands are shaking so I reach down and take one of them in mine and he looks at me properly for the first time since we got out of the car. He smiles and pulls me close. "Sorry, yeah, we dated in college and it ended badly. I wasn't expecting her to just show up out of the blue."

I rest my head on his shoulder, frowning. "Do you two keep in touch?"

"Not really," he says. "She dips in and out of my life…It's complicated, I guess. Mostly because she's still friendly with the gang."

"Do you still *see* her?"

"No, no," he says. "It's just you, it's always been just you," he says firmly. "Me and Amber have been broken up for a year and a half. We were always, off and on, but then we were properly off. Look, I'm sorry I didn't mention it. We haven't really talked about exes or past relationships and it's just…ugly and dramatic and I didn't want you to know that side of me."

I squeeze his hand. "It's ok. I don't mind. Sure it was shocking, but the ex thing has never come up. I didn't think you were hiding it."

He tells me that her name is Amber Bayley and they met in their second year of college at a mixer. She was his girlfriend off and on for two years and they lived together when things got serious after college, for six months. This was where things got bad. The two of them were just incompatible as a living together couple. It started out as dumb fights over the laundry and the dishes, basic stuff. But soon it changed, these escalated to screaming matches, jealousy, passive-aggressive displays in front of their friends. One really horrible fight between Veronica and Amber.

He looks ashamed and defeated as he tells me that a year and a half ago, he was arrested after a neighbour called the police on them during one of their screaming matches. Amber had smashed up their coffee table with a baseball bat and the cops arrived in time to find Rick trying to wrestle the bat away from her.

Amber cleared things up with the police and explained that Rick wasn't the one being violent, but not after he had been dragged out of their old apartment like an animal, in his pyjamas and handcuffs. His hands are shaking as he tells me how frightened he'd been that she'd just let him rot, how scared he'd been that he might have bruised her in their struggle over the bat.

"We were wrong for each other, it just took us a long time to have that kind of clarity," he said. "It got so ugly before we ended it. I really am sorry I didn't tell you. But it makes me so ashamed. Like I'm some violent piece of shit like my father. Or like people will think that I really did hit her and she's covering for me or…" He hugs me tightly and apologises over and over again.

He struggles to sleep and when he does, it's a fitful rest. He tosses and turns and mutters anxiously.

But as he does, I go through his Facebook friends and easily find Amber Bayley. There are no old photos of them together, no coupley bits, I suspect these were removed after the break-up. There are a few old group photos from college, one of Amber sat on Rick's lap, head tilted back in laughter at his birthday party.

Her own profile doesn't give much away. Her profile pics are all selfies where she pouts flirtatiously up at the camera. Her job isn't listed, her bio is a pun. Her tagged photos are all from nights out with a gaggle of similar-looking women. Her relationship status is set to 'It's Complicated'.

Doesn't seem complicated to me.

Chapter Eleven

When I was young, I relied on getting the drop on people. I mean, it made sense. I was fifteen and skinny, *nobody* expects to get stabbed to death by a person like that. Plus, I lived in a small town, people aren't as cautious, they think serial killers only exist in movies or fantastical documentaries which are so sensationalised, it's like it couldn't even be based on true events anymore.

So no, I didn't fight; I don't fight. I wasn't the type of kid who got into fist fights or caused a scene in the lunchroom. But I knew little ways to hurt people, sensitive areas, it was one of the things my mother told me, grabbing hair at the nape of the neck, eyes, throat, I suppose little things she picked up from her hobby and I don't know, maybe she attended a self-defence class or two when she lived in Atlantic City.

Mother was stronger than she looked and was also *very* good at getting the drop on people.

The first person I ever…consciously remember killing was a six-foot-tall football player who was built like freaking Captain America. If I'd had anything but the element of surprise on my side, well, I suppose my life would have turned out very differently.

I didn't know how to physically overpower someone, how to defend myself against a counter-attack. I knew how to gauge, where to aim my knife, the parts of the body that are weakest and easiest to cut.

Back then, it was all I needed to know.

But then I grew up.

And you know, even if my hobby wasn't what it is, then I'd still have needed to take a rigorous course of self-defence classes. It got recommended to me by Carmel, my first ever boss and saviour when

I moved to Santa Cruz. I'd go down to the community centre twice a week. The instructor was this tiny old woman named Midge. The class was mostly made up of women, housewives, college girls and busy-looking office workers.

Midge was patient, a woman of few words but she totally knew her stuff.

She was pragmatic, practiced, and could train us on exactly how as women, we could disarm and defend ourselves.

She told me once that I had a killer instinct and I chuckled at how on the nose she was.

Whenever I'm in a spot like this, I internally thank Midge for everything she taught me.

This man was expecting someone, and unlike the last one who had expected a retaliation from Barry, today's man has absolutely no intention of letting me kill him. When he realises I'm in his home, he comes at me with a kitchen knife. I duck under his swing and strike his armpit with my palm.

Ew, sweaty.

But I hit him hard enough so he drops the knife. I smack him in the throat with my fist, knocking the air out of him. I kick him in the groin and hear Midge's words: 'All you need to get away is one swift, very hard kick to the groin'. He falls to the floor, gasping for air, wheezing, hands frantic on the ground.

But he lurches forwards, nearly crashing into me.

He tries to get up, but I pick up a rolling pin and bash it down against his head. There's blood and I keep hitting him. He lands on his back and his arms come up to try to protect his face.

I stamp on his stomach and bring the rolling pin down again and again and again until he doesn't have a pulse.

Then I go and wait for Apparently-Ivan to come and pick me up.

*

First morning back at the office and I come in to discover a bunch of cardboard boxes on my desk. Donnie is already trying to remove them.

"What is this?" I ask.

He groans. "New intern…"

"New what?"

"His name is Corey," he says, "Trust me, you'll be way familiar soon."

Claudia comes in through the door. "For fuck's sake, I asked him to take those before I left yesterday. Fucking Corey."

"Fucking Corey," Donnie says, "Come and give me a hand."

Wincing, probably over the expensive-looking nails, Claudia comes over and takes a box from me. We place them out in the hallway. Who doesn't like starting their day somewhat sweaty and uncomfortable?

"So, who is Corey?" I ask.

"Jack hired him the day after you went on holiday," Donnie said, rolling his eyes. "And honestly, he's terrible. Jack was all, wow, the office will be so much more efficient with this bright young man around…"

"He's making more work than anything else," she says, rolling her eyes. "And he's a massive misogynist."

"How do you mean?" Donnie asks.

"Ok, so you remember yesterday when I asked him to send out the emails to students asking them to go and check the exam timetable?"

"Yeah."

"Yeah, he told me that he was busy checking his email and he'd try to make time to do it later. And then what?"

"Oh," Donnie says, wincing awkwardly. "Ok, yeah, I get you. Sookie, honestly, I asked him ten minutes later and he did it instantly."

"That's not a good start for his first week."

"I know," Claudia said. "I think he's gotta be Jack's nephew or something. He's instantly cozied up to him—he asked me to make coffee for him and Corey yesterday morning. I swear if that little bug asks me today, I'll lose it…" She scowls and starts furiously typing away at her desk. "The two of them went to the same college. It's like being around the world's shittiest frat."

Twenty minutes later, a tall, skinny guy with a shaved head arrives. His trousers are really high, like, perhaps where some man seventy years older would wear his trousers. He's picking his nose—literally doing it as he enters the room.

He wanders in aimlessly, without saying hello to anyone, and takes a seat beside Claudia. Five minutes later, so in no way on time, Jack parades in.

"Ah, Corey, Corey, good to see you, good to see you," he says brightly. "Good to see our bright young thing arriving on time."

Corey is older than me, I realise. Twenty-two. I'm watching him pick his nose from the other side of my desktop.

"Oh, Sookie, you're back to grace us with your presence?" Jack says, seeming to notice me for the first time. He wanders over to my desk, confusingly bringing Corey with him. "Corey, Sookie is kind of like my corner shop round here. Care to lend your boss a cigarette?"

"Well, I don't want it back," I say, reluctantly handing one over.

He laughs and pats my chair.

"I forgot my lighter today, do you have yours?"

"Sure," I say, trying not to scowl. Boy, am I bitter my vacation is over now...

"Corey is our bright young intern," he says, gesturing to him for dramatic effect. "Graduated from the same school as me. You should expect good things from him."

"Cool," I say, "Hi, Corey."

He doesn't respond.

Jack breezes out of the office, telling me that my lighter is shit. I go to go back to work, when I notice Corey is still stood there, itching at his nose.

"Erm," I say helplessly.

"Corey, man, go sit down," Donnie tells him.

"I'm Corey," he tells me before wandering back, limbs lolloping.

Well, boy, do I feel special now.

*

My day does *not* improve.

I spend the morning dodging round the papers, answering angry emails, I end up on the phone to one particularly nasty parent for twenty minutes. Then I foolishly go and help Claudia explain to Corey the intern how the exam packs need to be put together.

He stares at her tits so unashamedly that it actually makes me want to slap him. Claudia, frustrated in the end, particularly after he manages to staple a stack of invigilator forms together, clicks her fingers in his face to draw his attention upwards.

"Up here and again, you need to stick one of these in each pack, not put fifty in together. How would that be useful?"

"Ermm," he says, but then looks away to check his phone.

"Put that away," I say, "Look, we'll go and fix this. Can you start putting the papers into the boxes here?"

"Erm," he says slightly more affirmatively.

"Come on," I say to Claudia, who is surprisingly more red-faced than before. "Let's go get coffee on the way back."

She looks slightly like she wants to start stapling things to his head, but agrees. She curses quietly as we walk on over to the staff room.

"Hey, it's ok," I say.

"He asked me to get him a coffee this morning," she mutters. "I'm so sick of all of this bullshit!"

"I hope you told him no."

"Oh, I did. You better believe it. Though I can think of some things I'd like to have said." She grins wolfishly and stretches. "I'm sick of this, Sookie."

"Where did they find this kid? Was it off the street?"

"No," she said, "Jack spent ages telling us that they both went to the same college. He's like a proper applicant, they interviewed him and everything."

"Fucking hell."

When we return, we find him sat next to a stack of papers, browsing the contents of his phone. He looks up, knees to chest, where his vacant expression remains.

"What?"

He sits there, watching as me and Claudia assemble the packs without him. He starts picking his nose at one point and doesn't seem to register it when we start openly staring at him while he does it.

"Do you think you've gotten the hang of it now?" Claudia asks.

"Yeah, sure," he says.

I don't think that convinced anybody.

"Hey, why don't you pop back to the main office?" I ask. "You can see if Jack needs your help with anything."

"Nah, he told me to shadow you two," he says.

"Well, there's not much to see here," I say. "Why not pop back over?"

"Nah, he was pretty clear," he says, stretching and leaning back in his chair. "This is pretty boring, right?"

Maybe this is why Mother made such a solid attempt at clearing out Franberg when she was a teenager. People really are irritating. Life can seem fine and then bam, suddenly your life is full of problem people. Barry Ames, Amber Bayley and now this fucking guy.

*

Now it's not that I mind Amber…No, that's a lie, why am I lying? I can't fucking stand Amber. My life is complicated enough without my happy times being disrupted by some stupid power play by Rick's ex.

And like, what is her play? Because clearly she has one.

I don't want to be this person, but it's clearly 'Dump your girlfriend I'm bored'.

It's been two weeks and she's fully back on the scene. I don't know where she went for the last year, but now she's everywhere.

I come by Rick's place after work and she's already there, making herself coffee like she owns the place. She gets on with Phil, Rick tells me, that's how she gets in. I find myself panicking that she has a key…and I'm not this person.

She's at the bar, she's posting on his Facebook wall. She called me Little Sookie King with this self-righteous smile on her face.

I don't know why she's here and I don't want her in my life.

Mentioning it to Leda is a bad idea because I don't want it to include Tammy. So I try to bring it up with Gabbie, my first ever roommate. She was my first friend in Santa Cruz, who I started to see less after she married our old landlord, Leo, and even less after she had her baby.

I don't get babies. As a woman, any interaction that includes babies usually ends with the baby being dumped unceremoniously in your arms. Heck, I was once left alone with a former co-worker's baby while she was in the bathroom.

And it's like, come on!! I'm an actual fucking serial killer. Do not leave me alone with your child.

Gabbie's baby is called Lucas. He is eighteen months old and drools on everything. Kitted out in a little Batman onesie, his dad is a comic book nut, he rules over his household by gurgling, screaming and shitting.

It's strange how quickly Gabbie stopped having things in common with me and Leda after Lucas was born. Mother told me that can happen, that things can change, priority-wise after you become a mother.

We meet in a cafe outside the Mommy and Baby dance class Gabbie attends. Again, I don't get it, she gets to careen around the room like a wobbly samba dancer with Lucas in arms. I'm not sure what kind of actual exercise benefits it would offer, but again, I cannot claim to know much about the subject.

Lucas is chewing on a plastic rabbit while me and Gabbie share a plate of nachos.

"He tries to eat everything," she says, "And he keeps pulling my hair, really giving it a yank, you wouldn't think he'd be that strong but...yeah, he is. That's why I hacked it off." Her formerly Rapunzel-style locks have been trimmed down into a stylish pixie cut.

"Well, he certainly looks carnivorous with that rabbit," I offer with a shrug.

She laughs and sits back. "Sorry, I've been so off the radar lately. This motherhood thing is a lot more full-on than I expected it to be. Not that I'm complaining, no way! And Leo has been incredible, but we're just not a match for this little guy!" She smiles down at her drooling son. "I don't know how we'll keep up when he's bigger!"

'Don't ever have a kid,' Mother told me once, a long time ago, 'That's where it all went wrong for me.'

Honestly, she said it like this, this right here, would be something I would ever actually want.

Lucas squirms and bashes a chubby fist against his highchair and Gabbie coos as she picks him up, babbling at him in soothing nonsense speak.

Conversation is harder now.

"So, how's Rick?" she asks.

"He's good, yeah."

"I loved those photos he put up from the other day, that long trip you took? I miss doing spontaneous things like that," she says, attempting to eat a nacho over her son who is attempting to grasp it with his chubby hands.

"It was fun, really great. But something…happened when we got back. I was actually hoping to get your advice?"

At this, Gabbie's eyes light up. Girl talk has always been her absolute favourite and since the arrival of her son, I doubt she's been having much of it. The other mommies she has been hanging out with don't seem like the type to offer her the calibre of what she's used to.

"Some advice? Well, I mean, I can try. What's up?" she asks brightly.

So I tell her about Amber, I give her the abridged version of Amber and Rick. I ask her if I should be…worried.

Am I worried?

I don't really know what to do in this situation. Is there etiquette? I don't want to look crazy or controlling. I don't want drama. I have other things on my mind.

"Leo had this super serious ex before me," she says, "I mean, she wasn't like bad or crazy or whatever. Seriously, never trust a guy with a lot to say about his crazy ex-girlfriend, it just reeks of oh wow, I'm dating a jerk, but anyway, when me and Leo got serious, she was still on the scene. They were friends, still on really good terms, aaaand, she naturally hated my guts."

And I think I actually remember this.

"Greta, right?" I ask.

"Yes," Gabbie says laughing, "Fucking Greta! Oh!" She looks, panicked, down at her son, who is absent-mindedly chewing on his rabbit. "Oops, I keep doing that. I'm so convinced his first word will be like…well, never mind. But yeah, Greta, she kept showing up all the time, and she'd be all, 'Oh hey, Gabbie, how's school?' That sort of thing, like, petty stuff. And it'd make me so mad because she clearly wanted Leo back, like she felt he was her property or something! But it was the kind of passive-aggressive where I'd look really psycho if I retaliated or made a big deal out of it."

I remember Greta, with her tight business curls and beige blouses, coming up into our apartment when Leo was fixing the TV. She smirked at the two of us and asked Leo if he was running a half-way home for girls.

Bitch.

"So it all builds up for ages and ages and ages, until Leo's birthday. Do you remember? I made him that Batman cake? You were pulling one of your little vanishing acts so you missed all the action, but, I bought this cake along and fuck-fudging Greta wouldn't let me put it out on the table."

"Wait, she did what?"

"Yeah, so I tell her no, I made this cake for Leo and I'm putting it out. She has done all this fancy catering shit and she says the cake is childish and tries to yank it off me. She's calling me a child and I'm really upset and embarrassed because, I mean, you remember, I spent ages on that cake. But then Greta suddenly lets go, and I end up wearing the cake. And I'm furious at this point and I want to hit her, but I'm covered in three days' worth of hard labour, so I just burst into tears because I just did not know what else I could do. However, this is when Leo comes in. Greta tries to tell him that it was an accident and I'm overreacting, but no. She played her hand and came across as a total bit-belittling person, right, Lucas?" She rocks her son in her lap and he giggles, delighted.

"So, you're saying I just have to wait it out?" I ask, exasperated. "And what, hope she does something really awful to me in front of Rick?"

"Afraid so," she says, "If this girl is going to be crappy, I mean, crabby, crabby, Lucas, to you, to try to get Rick back, she'll make it really obvious soon and he'll know that she hasn't changed one bit and send her packing. But, if they are really ok and are just friends now, then you have nothing to worry about. I mean, you both want the same thing, for Rick to be happy. Right?"

I mean, that sounds logical.

"Right, I guess."

*

To be honest, I can't get over how weird it is that we dated for like over six months without any hide or hair of fucking Amber and yet now she's everywhere. And I mean everywhere! She has pushed her way back into the friendship group so easily.

Carla tells me—when the guys go to get the drinks and Amber is outside having a cigarette—that Amber likes being 'the girl in the group' and not to take any of her bullshit personally. Carla, Libby and Alex have all had it directed at them at some point.

"I kind of thought we were finally rid of her," Libby says with a sigh.

"It's been nearly a year," Carla says, "I thought she would go and bother someone else."

They avert their eyes back to their phones when Amber returns and settles in next to Libby, halfway through rolling another cigarette.

"So, little Sookie King," she says, "How long have you been with my ex now?" she asks me brightly.

I smile at her. "Oh, Rick? Nearly seven months now."

"Oh, puppy love, how cute," she says, stabbing at the ice at the bottom of her old drink. "Everything is so…honeymoon phase at that stage, right? I bet you like to think he doesn't even snore, right? So naïve."

And like, what the fuck am I even supposed to say to that?

Rick sits down beside me, passing me a beer. "Hell, I don't snore."

She laughs, "Oh, I beg to differ."

Miguel, Dan, Rory and Jandro join us, crowding around the table bearing drinks. Fortunately, Miguel starts talking about work over anything else Amber might say. She sits there, laughing along with the others, sipping her drink. Only, every now and then I notice her give me this look, like she's sizing me up.

"Where did you go to college, Sookie?" she asks me.

"I didn't," I say.

"Oh, you didn't?" she repeats. "What a shame. It's where we all met. You make good memories there."

"Kind of," Alex says. "I think you make better memories after college." She smirks at Amber lazily. "I mean, we're older, wiser, richer. I prefer this."

"Don't we all?" Amber says, "I just mean, it's a shame Sookie never got to go."

"It just wasn't for me," I say.

"Nor me," Rory adds.

"Yeah, not everyone can deal," she says, nodding. "Wait, don't you work in a college? Isn't that kind of depressing, seeing all those people go through and study and graduate and stuff, while you just push papers around?"

I smile at her. "I never thought of it like that. Wow, what a thing to say."

"So, you're like twenty-five, right?" she says, smirking. "What did you do instead of college?"

"Just worked," I say, "I was a waitress for a while, then a hotel receptionist for a little while, then at a movie theatre, before I started working in college admin."

"Yeah, ok," she says, not missing a beat. "But I mean, we all have resumes like that, plus college as well, do you just find it hard to settle down on one thing?"

Rick is frowning now.

"Do people usually have a response when you ask stuff like that?" I ask.

The others laugh, Amber included.

"Oh my God, I'm sorry, ex-girlfriend's prerogative. Got to be a bit protective of our guy, right? Make sure Rick moves on to the right sort of woman."

"Amber," Rick says coldly.

"Come on, Rick," she says, "Lighten up, Sookie knows I'm teasing, don't you, little Sookie King?"

I hate you, I think, imagining how much better it would be if her head was completely separate from her body.

But I laugh and squeeze Rick's hand under the table.

"Babe, you heard her, she's *teasing*."

*

I find out why she wasn't invited to the wedding when we pick up Starr and Marco from the airport after their honeymoon. Possibly the only person who dislikes Amber more than I do is Starr, who is freshly tanned and utterly furious to hear that Amber is back on the scene.

She rants for the whole car ride home and despairs at Rick, who mutters something non-committal about trying to tell Amber nobody wanted her around.

"Well, I don't want to see her," Starr says coldly. "She better not be at your place, Rick. I don't want to see her."

We pick up Chinese takeout for the four of us and drive back with their bags. Their house is having some work done which isn't finished yet, so they are currently crashing on the couch at Rick's place. I've missed them, I think I need someone else to be unabashedly unimpressed with fucking Amber for being around all of the fucking time.

Only, of course, when we get back to the apartment...

"The fuck is she doing here?" Starr hisses at Phil when we arrive to find Amber making herself a sandwich in the kitchen.

Amber is on them in a second of course, she squeezes Marco's bicep, hugging Starr and calling her Twinkle and dropping little passive-aggressive digs about her lack of a wedding invitation. Marco looks worried at his wife's expression and I hear a couple of somewhat frantic-sounding whispers of 'Babe...Babe!'

"I just popped over to bring back some of Rick's old records I held onto," she says brightly. "See, I have them all here. Want a look?"

"Oh, fuck this," Marco hisses at us. "Guaranteed she'll try to gate-crash on dinner too."

We all eat smaller portions of kung-pow chicken than we intended to. Amber sits at the head of the table and talks through old college stories so I can't join in. Starr breaks her smoking ban and joins me on the balcony.

I try not to let it bother me when I hear Rick laughing along with her jokes.

*

I checked Reggie's phone once upon a time. I know it's bad, I know it's a massive invasion of privacy. I know it's a shitty thing to do.

But I'd find myself drawn to it when he slept. I was intrigued. Who was he talking to when he was out with me? If there was someone else, and I found out, would I care? Would it matter to me?

So, every now and then I'd check his phone. Usually it was nothing. He'd just be scrolling through Twitter while we ate dinner, while I was talking. Just before I ended things, there were messages from Omara from his office. Nothing that he couldn't have read out in front of his mother, but it was…the beginning of something private, something more.

I never checked Rick's phone. He only ever picks it up to take a call, usually his sister, or to take a photo of the two of us.

I never felt the need to check up on Rick. I know how he feels about me. I knew…

It's her I don't trust. And it's not like I can go through her phone.

So I check his while he sleeps. There are recent texts, recent Facebook messages, recent WhatApp messages. He doesn't have her on Snapchat, which is the only thing that makes me feel better. It's all basic stuff, catch-up stuff, but there's a lot of it.

And then...

Amber: I miss you

She sent this to him after fucking drinks the other night.

Rick: Don't, ok?

Amber: No, but I do. I miss you.

Rick: I have a girlfriend.

Amber: She doesn't suit you.

I hate being right, my blood burns.

Rick: Don't be an asshole.

Amber: I'm sorry. I didn't mean it like that.

Rick: We didn't work. I moved on. You know that, right?

Amber: I'm sorry. I get that. I do.

They bounce back to normal after that, back to talking shit about college and records and I want to fucking scream. I hate this so much. I don't want this bitch in my life. I don't want to be this woman, sat going through my boyfriend's phone like some jealous self-esteem-complex-ridden teenager.

I'm not equipped to deal with stuff like this.

*

Phil moves out at the end of the month and Leda helps me load my stuff into her car. I've moved before but never in with a guy, with my guy. It feels…intimate, and proper. Also, I cannot believe that all my stuff fits into just six boxes.

"I can't believe you're leaving me for a boy! I'm going to be all alone with Tammy!" Leda says, throwing her arms around me.

"Hey, I can hear you," Tammy says. "And I'm fucking carrying your boxes. Come on."

"Sorry, Tammy."

"Sorry, babe."

We park up outside Rick's building, my building. I'm all excited and…I don't know, I just couldn't have imagined this for myself before. The three of us are met in the stairwell by Carla, who has Jandro and Rick come and help with the boxes instantly.

Our groups mix easily. This isn't so much a Helping Us Move party, as it is a drinking beer while we try to unpack gathering. Leda has always been able to charm everyone she's ever met, and Tammy is dry and sarcastic and easily fits in with Libby and Alex. The table and chairs had belonged to Phil, so we have the task of assembling new ones, courtesy of Ikea. I am disappointed by the lack of hammering involved; everything seems to slot together. Rick is confused by the manual, in particular the illustrations included.

"Babe, what is this even supposed to be?" he asks.

Alex orders pizzas, Leda puts some music on Rick's record player and for an hour or so, I feel truly and honestly content, like maybe pretty close to how I felt a long time ago, sat around a campfire in the woods with my friends.

But much like back then, all good things come to an end.

I answer the door, expecting pizza but instead finding fucking Amber stood there. Without a word, she brushes past me and strides inside, wielding a bottle of tequila and a rolled cigarette between her lips.

"Hey, y'all, guess who brought tequila to this shindig?" she announces, like she was fucking invited. The guys all start cheering, I catch Alex rolling her eyes at Carla.

"No, no tequila," Rick says, looking up from the chair leg he had been attempting to insert into the base. "Not today."

"Oh, come on, Rick," she says, "You can't say no to tequila, you remember that night in Vegas, we were drinking it out on our motel balcony? Come on, it was our anniversary, I crowned you the tequila king." She laughs and waves the bottle in his face. "You have to!"

Jandro, Dan and Leda all start chanting for tequila.

Amber starts going through the kitchen cupboards for glasses, knocking things askew.

"Amber, let me," I say.

"No, no, it's cool," she says, "God, where are your shot glasses, Rick?" She peers around me to address him.

"We don't have any," he says bluntly.

"What? No way, you used to be cool! What happened to you?" She cackles and scoops out a selection of whisky tumblers and tops them and the countertop generously with tequila. The others take theirs, Leda is complimenting Amber on her glasses. The guys are sprinkling their hands and the floor with salt. Amber starts chopping a lemon against the countertop, completely ignoring the chopping board by her hand.

She perches down next to Rick and calls him a grandpa before passing him a chunk of lemon and his drink. He's frowning, but he takes it, rolling his eyes.

I suddenly realise that everyone seems to have a glass but me. As the gang counts down 5-4-3-2, Tammy hands me hers. "Here, you need this more than I do."

1.

It's coarse and burns bitterly in my throat. Amber bashes her glass against the kitchen floor hard. I flinch and try not to think about the amount I paid for nice whisky fucking glasses.

"Watch it," Rick snaps at her.

She snorts, "Sorry, I didn't realise I was partying with the Queen of England. God, you used to be cool, Fumero."

She then proceeds to fucking take over building the last of the chairs and of course, she's really fucking good at it. For fuck's sake.

"Oh, please," she says, "I had to do all this stuff when me and Rick moved in together," she says, "He was so useless, I had him fetching me drinks while I did all the actual work!" She shakes her head laughing, "I honestly expected him and Phil to have freaking playschool furniture when he moved out."

Miguel smacks Rory for laughing with the others. I am attempting to clear up after the pizza after fucking Amber insisted that we wouldn't need plates. Does she fucking live here?

"So, you and Rick used to date?" Leda asks her and I'm 100% certain that I see Tammy roll her eyes.

"Oh yeah, we're just friends now, top pals," she says, "We dated all through college and even lived together after we graduated. So, Sookie, little Sookie King, if you want any warnings about what you're getting into, any hints about the real Rick, ask away."

The others laugh, except Miguel and except Rick, who I see has shaking hands. So I take his hand and squeeze it because it numbs the very real, very actual urge to force-feed Amber her own tongue.

Almost numbs.

When it gets late, the others all start to leave: Dan and Alex first, then Jandro and Libby who cab-share with Leda and Tammy, Tammy promising to come and collect her car in the morning. Leda drunkenly tells me that she won't buy a cat to replace me, then bursts into tears. Tammy drunkenly tells me that Amber is such a cunt which makes us both laugh a little too loudly and suspiciously.

As Miguel, Rory and Carla are waiting for their cab, Amber chooses now to curl up on the sofa and pretend to be asleep. She curls into a ball, hugging my favourite pink fluffy cushion. Carla tries to rouse her, telling her that she can't sleep there, she calls her name, she shakes her, but it doesn't work.

"Could you just let her crash here?" Rory asks.

"No," Rick says, "No, it's inappropriate. I'm not babysitting her tonight. Amber, Amber, come on, wake the fuck up."

She groans nonsense.

"She's pretending," Miguel says, angrily.

"Pretending? She's not six years old," Rory says. "Babe, come on, she's just wasted."

"Exactly, she's not a child," Miguel snaps. "Amber, get the fuck up, now! Amber, stop being an asshole."

"Don't yell," she slurs.

"Amber, get up!" Carla says, "I've called a cab. Get up."

"No," she moans.

And I am so not having my first night living here with Rick's fucking ex on the sofa. So I walk into the kitchen and fill one of my whisky tumblers with water. I get back and both Carla and Miguel are attempting to shake her awake. I lean over and drizzle the water over her head.

She screams and bolts upright like the water is burning her like she's the fucking Wicked Witch of the West. There are comparisons. Damn right, there are comparisons!

"What! What the fuck?"

Miguel is laughing.

"Awake now?" Rick asks coldly.

She shoves him before realising that I did it, her eyes narrowing on the glass in my hand.

"What! What the hell is wrong with you?" she yells, tears brimming in her eyes.

"We couldn't wake you," I say flatly, "I was concerned."

"Like fuck you were!"

"Amber, we have a cab outside," Carla says, "Come on, let's go home."

She starts crying then and she hugs herself. "Fine! But there's no need for her to do that to me! I'm all wet!" She walks off to get her coat, crying audibly, or at least that's what she wants people to think.

Did I just fuck up? Am I Greta smearing Gabbie with cake?

I try to read Rick's face but he's walking after her. Miguel touches my shoulder and says, "I'd have done the same if I were you. She was really fucking out of line."

Rory doesn't look impressed.

Carla chuckles to herself and hugs me around the shoulders. "I was wondering when you would lose your patience."

"I just want to go to bed," I say, my hands are shaking. "I don't have the patience to be in the fucking Amber show."

The others laugh and I pretend that I don't see Rick hugging her as she cries.

*

I check his phone while he sleeps.

He texted her to ask if she got home ok. She tells him that she did.

133

Amber: Has your gf always had a temper?
Rick: Even saints can run out of patience.
Amber: Is she jealous of me?

And I want to scoff and say that I'm not, but here I am, going through my boyfriend's phone.
It's my first night here, living with a guy, living with my guy.
And I just want to cry.

Chapter Twelve

Living together is easier than I expected it to be. I had my doubts before, but we fit, it's like it was before, but better.

I know people who say that men start being super gross after you move in, or like any shred of their independence vanishes and you get lumbered with a pouty man-child who accumulates piles of laundry, who is allergic to chores and practically incapable of good hygiene, someone barely able to wipe his own ass.

At work, in all places I have worked, they have loaded me up with living together horror stories. And I must admit, I have been kind of nervously waiting for my grown-ass man boyfriend to devolve into a man-child, but it didn't happen.

We share. It's equal, it just works.

I like how we live. I like how I live.

We set alarms to get up for work; we stagger down into the kitchen; he does breakfast and I do coffee. His shower is better, bigger, enough room for two. He drives me to work, hell; he makes me lunches. I go and start each day at work feeling like my stupid job contributes to my immediate happiness.

After work, on every day but Wednesday when he works late, he picks me up from the office. We go home together; we cook together. I chop the meat and the vegetables, he seasons and prepares, does all the oven stuff. Sometimes we listen to music while we cook and it's just...nice, safe.

I remember a time, a long time ago, when I used to cook like this with someone else. That really was a long time ago.

We eat together; we get to sleep in the same bed every night. Even if it's stuff we've always done, it's happier, it's all ours, there's no limit until I go back to my place or Phil comes home. Plus, we get to fuck all over the apartment now, you know, without Phil walking in on us. We can go out with the gang without doing the whole 'your place or mine' afterwards.

Sure, Amber is still present. She shows up at the bar or at a house party. She'll ask how we're coping, have we been fighting, are we driving each other crazy? When she does, Rick always jokes, 'Oh yeah, we're trying to kill each other'. Then he grabs me and tilts me back for a kiss. And we laugh until the rude, personal questions stop.

Once she cornered me in the ladies' room of a bar, she moved in front of me in the queue and wrapped her arm through one of mine. "So, he isn't here now, you can be honest, how are you holding up, little Sookie King?"

And she's right, he's not here right now.

"No, was he supposed to?"

She folded her arms. "Oh, come on, don't go all Stepford on me. I lived with Rick, I know how he can be."

"Yeah, you did, but wasn't that a long, long, long time ago? And for like three months? Maybe you were just super hard to live with? I'd move on if I were you." I tugged my arm free and pushed past her to get into a free cubicle.

*

Unfortunately, there is a downside to living together. It's my second job, my hobby, my secret nasty side. The work is still coming in, and Barry didn't seem overtly sympathetic to my request for Wednesdays specifically.

Fucking Barry.

All he did was ask me what I wanted for a moving present, then he laughed. He just likes to let me know that he knows where I go, what I do, who I'm with. I say nothing to try to shrug off how much I enjoy his lowly concealed threats. Much like Antagonistic Fucking Amber, it's all a power play with him.

Motherfucker.

I have to make up some lie about working late due to student orientation, which is complete and utter bullshit. I'm ridiculously relieved when Rick gets wrapped up in the publicity behind a new book and ends up working late.

It eases off the uncomfortable feeling I get in my stomach when I lie to him.

Since moving in together, I've made my way through five people. No more beat-up jobs, just straight-up removals.

It's actually been a really good way to work out some of my Amber-based frustration. There was definitely a hard gambler dock worker I didn't need to hit that many times with a wrench. A rival gang member I didn't need to drop an anvil on. An underpaying junkie with bulky hipster glasses and ratty brown hair that I didn't need to drown slowly.

It does help for when I have to deal with the real thing.

It doesn't help my increasingly bad relationship with my pseudo-chauffeur.

Apparently-Ivan hates killing. I'm pretty sure he's muttering in Russian about me right now as he drives me home.

"Sorry, I didn't catch that last bit," I say.

He rolls his eyes and averts them back to the traffic. "Nothing you'd pay any attention to, I'm sure."

"Oh, try me," I say.

"No."

"You do know that it wasn't my choice to work for your boss, right?" I say, stressing the word 'your.' "Like, you were even the one who manhandled me right off the street."

He doesn't respond.

"So, it's actually pretty hypocritical of you to sneer at me for doing the work that your boss insists I do. What am I gonna do, Apparently-Ivan? Say no?"

He glares at me in the mirror.

"He is asking you to do nothing you weren't already doing. Killing."

"That was on my terms," I say, "It wasn't every week."

"A week, a month," he says dismissively. "You are a person who kills people. It is all the same for me."

I roll my eyes.

"And I suppose you were off teaching ballet before he had you working for the mob?"

He glares at me.

"You are very annoying."

"Why thanks," I say, "Your judgmental tutting was annoying me."

He tuts and goes back to watching the road.

"If you don't enjoy the work he gives you, you can at least enjoy the money he gives you," he says.

And that, I suppose, is the point. I tell Rick that I was just always really good at saving. I don't. I'm not. There has never been a brunch I skipped out on. Never a latte I haven't treated myself to. Over six years of full-time jobs, I have never saved more than $50 at a time… not until I went onto Barry Ames' payroll. Now I have savings, money put aside for a rainy day.

I just let Rick believe I'm good at saving and rely on him to be too polite to really question it.

I suppose that no matter what you do, a job is a job and you just gotta keep slogging away for pay day. If that's how Apparently-Ivan copes, then who am I to complain?

Rick is worth it.

I want to give us a good life. Even if this whole secret job thing is going to be the fucking death of me.

*

The man Barry sent me to kill was surprisingly taxing. Not only was he expecting someone, but he was a fucking gun-nut, who very nearly took my head off with his revolver.

This guy was a fucking former navy seal, who had a leg injury preventing him from active service, but he had not let up on the lifestyle. There wasn't a speck of dust on his weights. Barry had said so little about him, but his name, his gambling debts, the threats against a few of the hostesses who worked for him. All he said was that this guy knew Barry wanted him dead.

But that didn't bother me. I mean, I was ready.

But he was ready too.

He found me in his house when I broke in and if it hadn't been for the drag of his bad leg, I'd have had my brains splattered all over his fucking living room. I would have died. I remember seeing Rick's face flash before my eyes before I hit the deck.

And just then, it was like I couldn't breathe. My body was still moving, still responding, but it was like it was happening in fast-forward but my brain was in rewind.

I ducked underneath the sofa and tried to stop the trembling of my hands when I heard his gun go off, sending plaster across the carpet near my feet. He fired another shot at the sofa, this one scathed just past my shoulder, leather and sofa stuffing splattering across the floor.

Our guy, the former navy seal, was yelling, saying Barry Ames'll have to come kill him himself.

He said he'd send my head back to him in a goddamn box, along with other, interesting threats.

He was slurring his words and he was big and dumb and had a gun. I crept behind the sofa and he fired a warning shot up in the air. I kept low, I crawled and when I got close, I stabbed him in his bad leg, right at the top.

He screamed like a pig and shot his gun off in the air by accident. I thought I had him. I thought I'd take out my gun and get him up in the head. But as he screamed out in pain, he turned, looked down and then he took a swing at me.

The blow smashed into the top of my head and cracked my skull back against the wall. Then I heard the click of the gun going off in my face.

Click. Click.

A grunt of frustration, he'd used up all his bullets.

A hand grabbed hold of my leg before I could get away. I screamed out as he dragged me out from my hiding place. He got down on top of me, practically drooling at the mouth and tried to snatch the knife out of my hand.

I couldn't hear what he was saying. It was like the ability to understand had been smashed out of my head.

I wouldn't let go of the knife, so his fist came down on my face, once, then twice, then again.

I reached up and cut his face with the knife, right below the jaw. He howled and hit me again in the mouth as hard as he could. My head was spinning, I remember thinking, I can't let him hit me again.

Then I managed to hook a leg free and over him. I slammed my foot down into his bad leg. This dislodged him and he grunted in pain like an animal. I punched him in the jaw twice, as fast as my limbs would take me. For a second, I thought it wouldn't fall, that he would withstand it, that another one of his blows would land. But then I felt him move under my fist and I sent him onto the ground on his back.

He clutched at his leg in pain.

My vision blurred, I managed to get a hold of my gun and put a bullet in his head.

I put a bullet in his head *four* times.

I don't remember much after that.

I don't remember calling Apparently-Ivan but I must have done, because he came to pick me up. I don't remember what we talked about. But I think I must have cried at some point because he helped me out of the car.

I wonder what the hell I must have said to make him do that.

I breathe slowly, in and out. I tug my hoodie up over my head and try to light a cigarette. I don't want him to be awake when I get inside. I don't want him to be there. I just want to…I cover my face with my hands and wince as my fingers collide with my bruised face.

What the fuck am I going to do?

Calm down, I imagine Mother saying. First, Fiona, you need to calm down.

*

I sneak into the bathroom as quietly as I can, locking the door. My hands are shaking violently as I twist the lock and turn on the light. My face is bloody, my eyes are already starting to swell. My bottom lip has swollen and cut along the side. I wish my hands would stop— stop shaking as I put in the plug and start filling the sink.

There's so much blood.

I keep thinking about the bullet smashing into the wall by my head. How he nearly stabbed me in the stomach.

I can explain—I'll have to explain away the black eye, the split lip, but I can't explain it away if it's my life, if it's a stab wound or a gunshot wound or…I can't! I want to scream until my lungs explode. I want my hands to stop shaking.

I dunk my face into the cold water and feel the sting of it against my eyes, against my lip. I keep my face under the water and hope the cold washes the tremble out of me, clears away the shock.

I stand up and take four deep breaths.

The shaking is getting less and less.

I close my eyes and hold my wet hands over my face.

I pull the plug and watch the red water vanish. Then I scrub out the sink and run a shower. My wounds ache even more under the shower, but it makes me feel calm and clean and safe and...

A knock at the door.

"Just a second," I call.

"Babe," Rick calls sleepily. "You there?"

I turn off the shower, tug a towel around myself. "Rick, go back to bed, it's fine."

"When did you get home?" he asks.

"Just a few minutes ago."

"I was worried."

He knocks again.

I open the door and he gasps, sleepy eyes instantly becoming awake and alert and terrified.

"Sookie! Sookie, oh my God, what happened?" He steps into the bathroom, hands reaching for me, frightened. He touches my cheeks, tilting my head back in the light. "Who did this to you? We have to call the police!"

I shake my head and struggle free of him.

"No, no, look, it looks worse than it is."

"Were you mugged?"

He looks heartbroken.

"No," I said, "It's stupid, I tripped and fell off the bus. I missed a step getting down and smashed my face into the floor. I bruised my knee too, see?"

He doesn't look convinced.

"On the bus?"

"Yeah," I say, "I was trying to get off the bus and I slipped and my face hurts so much!" I reach out and hug him and he clings to me tightly.

"You poor thing," he says. "Oh, Sookie, it looks so painful."

"It's ok, it just looks so, so bad."

He kisses my forehead. "Did anyone help you?"

"The driver was really nice about it, considering, you know, they say to sit down until the bus actually stops...Man, I feel stupid."

He hugs me tightly. "We should get you a steak or something for that shiner or frozen peas or something. Oh baby, no."

I'm sorry, Rick.

I wish this wasn't our life.

*

I knew it wasn't going to be an easy sell at work. Once Tanya had eczema on her face and Jack loudly asked her if she had been burned. I got to work earlier than the others and really shoved myself into a pile of paperwork that didn't require much more than a non-committal 'Morning' when someone else arrived.

Or that was the plan.

At nine-forty-five, over an hour later than even Kiko got here, Jack prances into the office, jacket flailing behind him. He tells Claudia to go and get him a latte before his eyes focus on me as he gets to his desk.

"Jesus Christ, Sookie, is that man of yours beating you?"

Sensitivity of a fucking dead badger, that man.

So of course, all eyes fucking avert to me.

I frown at him.

"No, Jack, no he's not."

"Phew," he says, "Because that would be awful! You ok? Sure you should be in today?"

"It looks worse than it is," I say.

"Oh, cool, cool," he says, nodding a few times for effect. "Well, alright, guys, your fearless leader is here! So, back to work with you, yah!" He mimes cracking a whip before looking nervous and sitting back down.

Donnie twists his chair and rolls on over to me.

"You sure you're ok?" he asks. "That looks nasty."

"I tripped over getting off a bus," I say. "Went WHAM into the floor. I feel like a fucking idiot. I can't believe he asked me like that..."

"You are a fucking idiot," Donnie says, "What are you doing jumping around on the bus?" He smirks before patting my shoulder. "Sorry, man, hope your face gets better."

And it's like this all day.

I have Tanya cornering me in the toilets and checking that everything is actually fine. She insists that her sister kept 'tripping over' when actually it was her husband drunkenly lashing out. She insists I take her phone number and I insist again and again, that I would never date someone who'd hit me.

I get Kiko and Claudia double-checking that I definitely fell before teasing me about falling over on the bus. At least they double-checked.

I have Jack loudly telling me to send someone else out when I get called outside reception to speak to a student.

"Can't have the students think we have thugs working here with two black eyes," he says. "It gives the wrong impression."

I text Rick to tell him that I'm miserable and he promises a quiet movie night with soothing aloe vera for my eyes and a back-rub and whatever I want to be honest, which makes me feel a lot better; that is until Barry texts.

*

Barry comes to see me himself after work. He's waiting in his car and texts me his registration plate number so I know where to come meet him. I don't much like meeting with him without Apparently-Ivan, but I have had to deal with a lot today. He's parked out in the student car park in a red sports car, reading a magazine. He waves when he sees me and gestures for me to hop in.

Barry winces when he puts down his magazine—it's a *Deadpool* comic and not a magazine, upon closer inspection—and actually looks at me, lifting his sunglasses in shock.

"Woah, Ivan told me you took a beating, but boy, oh boy, look at that face!"

I glare at him. "Your empathy is touching."

"Hey, I warned you that our boy was dangerous, didn't I warn you that?" He clicks his fingers at me and smirks, settling back into his chair. "Sorry about the eye...eyes anyway, that does look nasty."

"Thanks, Boss," I say.

"Not a problem," Barry says, "Anyway, I figured I'd give you a little break. Say, two, three weeks? It wasn't cool of me to work you so hard, particularly with your big move with your guy." He nudges me playfully. "And also, those injuries make you pretty hard to blend in. I could see you coming from across the street, you look obscene."

"Obscene, thanks."

"Well, I'm nothing if not honest," he says. "Take some time, Miss. King. Maybe a month, maybe longer, get back on your game. I need you at the top of your game." He taps the steering wheel. "You want to go for a spin?"

I glare at him.

"No."

"Whatever, whatever," he says, reaching past me to open the car door for me. "You catch a bus or something instead, text lover boy. Boy, I bet you've had some questions about that. Ouch...Look, I'll be in touch. Later, Miss. King."

I watch him speed away and glare at the marks of his tyres on the ground.

I try not to smile, my busted lip hurts too much, but I want to smile so bad.

Some time off sounds just what I need.

*

Rick hugs me around the middle when we settle back on the sofa. I rest my head against his shoulder and take in the smell of him. He strokes my hair and switches up the volume of the dumb zombie movie we're watching.

"You ok?"

"I told you already, I'm fine," I say, nuzzling in. "I love you."

"And I love you," he says. "You are never catching a bus again."

"Oh babe, you are so romantic," I say, laughing.

"Hey, you joke, but I worry," he says seriously. "It scared me seeing you like that, all bruised up."

"I'm sorry," I say.

"For what?" he asks, "Falling over? Come on, Sookie."

The doorbell rings loudly, breaking out over the zombies munching on the screaming hillbillies. Rick groans and glances up. "Who the hell is that?"

I have my theories...

"Ignore it," I say. "Probably Mormons."

"I'll check," he says, kissing my forehead. "You chill."

He gets up and walks over to the front door. I hear him groan as he spies through the peephole before opening it.

"Amber," he says, "Seriously, you can't just show up here."

She laughs, she's drunk. "I know, I'm sorry, I'm just out with the girls and I got lost, see?" She holds up her watch and staggers in past him. She stops when she sees me and loudly gasps, "Rick! What happened to Little Sookie King?!" She claps a hand over her mouth in shock. "You have two black eyes!"

"Do I?" I said, "Oh shit."

He looks uncomfortable. "Amber, can you go home?"

"I just wanted to say hi. I got churros, remember how we used to eat churros after a night out?" She holds up a bag of very crushed, greasy-looking churros.

Rick looks over at me, "Babe, I'm sorry."

"You should be," Amber says, "Giving her not one but two black eyes, Rick! Really!" She puts a hand on her chest in shock, then cries out in alarm when he grabs her by the shoulder and manhandles her towards the door.

She drops the bag of churros, laughing as he pulls her to the front door and opens it wide.

"Hey! I'm sorry, I'm sorry! It was a joke!"

His hands are shaking. "Well, it's not fucking funny, is it? Do you hear anybody else laughing?"

"I didn't mean it! I know you aren't like that!" she says, holding her hands up in defence. "I really didn't, Rick! It was a nervous reaction, I mean, she has two black eyes, I didn't know what to say! It was a joke, it was so obviously a joke."

He growls in frustration. "You're psychotic showing up here, you know that, right?"

"I was confused," she says in a tiny voice.

"You never lived here," he says, "So that's bullshit. I'm sick of your bullshit. We're having a special night and you interrupting is ruining that."

"I didn't mean it," she said. "Look, I want your girlfriend to like me. I don't want it to be weird. I thought I'd show up, surprise you guys with churros and we'd all just get along?"

He groans in frustration.

She is such a fucking *liar*.

"Amber, you know you're a grown-ass adult woman, right? Not an extra-terrestrial child?" he says, "Look, even if you and Sookie become, like…BFF or whatever, it will never, ever be acceptable for you to just show up at our freaking apartment in the middle of the night, out of your face."

"I'm sorry."

"If you really do want the three of us to get along, you call to check, you stop calling Sookie 'Little Sookie' or whatever, it's rude and weird and shitty." He sighs. "You have to respect boundaries."

"I really didn't mean…I can imagine how this must have looked," she said in a hushed whisper. "Can I go apologise to Sookie? I really didn't mean to spoil your night."

"Sure," he says. "Want me to call you a cab?"

"Nah, I'll get an Uber." She pokes her head around the corner. "Sookie, hey, I'm really sorry for interrupting your evening," she says. "I'm useless with people, really. Forgive me?" She holds her hands up in mock prayer.

"No worries," I say, "Bye, Amber."

She beams, hugs Rick around the shoulders and dashes out the front door, phone in hand. Rick sighs and locks up before walking back over and sliding in next to me.

"I have anything to worry about from your exes?" he teases.

"Nope, nothing like this," I say, whistling. "She is…something else."

"She was my best friend," he said sadly. "A long time ago. I wish things didn't get so ugly." He squeezes my shoulder. "I'm sorry. I really hate dragging you into this."

"Do you wish you had worked it out with her?"

He blinks. "What? No way!" Rick says, "We broke up for a reason. I wouldn't…Oh, Sookie, have you been worried about that?"

"A bit," I say. "Not really."

He kisses me, stroking my cheek, "Baby, I love you. Me and Amber have been over a long time. I want us." He holds me close against him. "I'm sorry that she can be such an asshole. She shouldn't bother us again."

"I just don't see *why* she has to be part of our life. I mean, she's always around now and she's such a…"

He frowns a little, then tries to hide it with a smile. "She isn't a bad person, she can be sometimes, but that's all bravado. Her being my ex aside for a moment, Amber's actually very sweet, just insecure. And she's hilarious, she's got this sharp, dry sense of humour. She can be great. I don't think she wants to get back together or anything either, I think she just…feels protective of me, probably because of how long we dated, how close we were, but also, I imagine, because of how we ended things." He strokes back my hair. "I promise you have nothing to worry about."

"Ok," I say. "I trust you."

I just don't trust Amber Liar-Liar Pants on Fire Bayley.

Chapter Thirteen

Barry has been as good as his word and his frantic murderous requests have stopped. He checked in once to ask how my face was healing up, then sent me a GIF of a race car driver, I wasn't sure what to read into there.

Amber has stopped calling me Little Sookie King, in fact, she's been on her best behaviour. She follows me out for a cigarette and pretends to care about my job. She got my number off Rory and sends me Snapchats. This is a development I do not like, particularly as ignoring her makes me look like I'm the one with the problem. This is less than ideal.

The polite bullshit ends when the others aren't watching. When we are alone, she smirks, she stares, she finds ways to talk about the good old days with her and Rick. She asks me about Rick's mother and says 'Oh, that's no good' when I say I haven't met her yet.

"Aleida loves me," she says, "She still sends me cookies on my birthday."

Then she blows smoke in my face and parades back inside to the others, full of smiles and topped to the brim with bullshit. I think I preferred it when she was just outwardly being an asshole.

*

It's a Friday night, and I have neglected my staff nights out for far too long! I mean, in my defence, I have been suitably busy. And now my black eye is healing nicely, I'd say it's definitely time to get back out there.

We eat out at the same bar as usual, order jalapeno poppers and fries, but we all know we aren't there to eat. Jack has come along as well, which means we can't start bitching about him yet, though from the way Donnie is drinking, I'm not absolutely certain the two things won't align.

"You don't have to help out the wife tonight?" Donnie asks, leaning down to Jack as he returns from his cigarette.

"No," Jack says, "She can do her own dirty work for once."

I notice Tanya roll her eyes.

"So, you're staying out with us all night?" Donnie asks again.

"Yeah, can't have my team off partying without me," Jack says, scooping an arm around both mine and Kiko's shoulders. "We're getting crazy tonight. It's such a shame that Corey couldn't join us!"

"Yeah, such a shame," I say, trying not to roll my eyes.

My phone buzzes and it's Rick, he's out tonight at a concert with just the guys, or that was how it was going to be until Amber invited herself along, bought herself an extra ticket and since then, it's all she's talked about.

"We finally get a night away from the girlies," she said at the bar three days ago, "Just us, the guys, guy time!"

Ergh.

> *Rick: Hope you're having fun! We just got to the arena.*
> *Amber is driving me nuts...*

Nice, but she's still there…

Donnie hands me a shot of tequila, "Sookie, have one of these, we're going to need it if he is intending to stay." He sits down opposite me and hands me a chunk of lemon. "Believe me, we need this."

Jack is attempting to talk to Claudia about issues with the photocopier.

Right, fuck this.

I neck the shot and push my leftover French fries aside.

It has been *way* too long since we all knocked back like this.

*

My phone buzzes, I glance down and see a Snapchat from Amber. Snarling under my breath, I click it and switch up the brightness on my phone. It's a short video clip of the band playing in the background, Rick is loudly singing along, Amber is on his back, hanging from his shoulders. They are both laughing up at the camera.

My heart sinks and I slam down another shot of tequila.

That fucking bitch.

"My boyfriend has this awful fucking ex," I tell Claudia, who looks up, interested. "She's just this big, bitchy glasses woman."

She snorts with laughter, "What a bitch."

"What's wrong with her?" Rajish asks.

"She's just always being really slyly rude to me, like she always calls me Little Sookie King. Even though I'm older than her."

"Ew," he says, shaking his head. "Is she good friends with your boyfriend?"

"That is weird by the way," Claudia says. "Whenever I had a guy who was really close with an ex, it always meant they were like… friends with benefits or something."

"Nah, I don't think they are," I say.

"But they could be," Rajish says unhelpfully.

I squint at him, "Hey, Rajish, how's your love life?"

He swats me, "What are you, my mother?"

We laugh and "Summer of '69" starts to play over the speaker system and we lose Claudia to the sort-of dancefloor in the corner.

Rajish winces.

"She is…not a good dancer."

"No, she is not."

Jack returns to the table with more shots and some beers, he offers one of the shots to Rajish, then looks panicked and drinks it himself before breaking out into a coughing fit.

"He apologised to me for drinking an hour ago," Rajish whispers to me, snorting with laughter. "He apologised on behalf of all white people."

"Oh, fucking hell," I say, before adding, "Thanks for the beer, Jack," to our coughing idiot boss.

Claudia is now attempting to get Donnie to dance with her, mostly by jumping on his back. Kiko returns from the toilet and sits down next to me.

"So, your boyfriend has a dumb glasses ex-girlfriend?"

"Yes," I say. "She sucks."

"You should tell her," she says.

"I so should."

*

I stagger over to the toilets with Kiko, who rushes off the second we are close to the mirrors to tell a gaggle of girls fixing their makeup, that she loves their makeup. That's probably the best thing about nights out, girls being sincerely nice to each other in the toilets.

I once had a girl try to fix my broken heel in the toilets, she tried to use eyelash glue, which didn't work, but it was a kind and thoughtful gesture.

I climb up onto the countertop after I've used the bathroom and try to tug up my tights.

My phone buzzes, it's a text from Rick telling me the concert is over and him and the guys are all going home. I get another Snapchat from Amber, who is chanting 'Out on the town' over and over in a crowded cab. She scoops an arm around Rick and kisses his cheek.

I accidentally rip my tights by digging my nails in.

I'm tired of this.

*

I wonder if Barry would get all asshole about it if I killed someone while not on duty. I haven't ever since he employed me and ruined everything.

Would he mind if I arranged a little accident for Amber?

I bet he wouldn't. Or if he would, maybe I could engineer some way for them to meet? I bet she'd get on his nerves.

No, that's dumb.

I pick up the tray of drinks with some difficulty and stagger over to the table. Donnie takes them from me part of the way, laughing and shaking his head.

"We're sat over there, dummy."

"I know!" I say.

Did we move?

I sit down and don't bother with salt and lime and just knock back the shot. Then I tuck into a large glass of red wine. I Snapchat Amber telling her to get a life. I show it to Kiko and she laughs until she nearly falls off her chair.

"So, gang, is this how it usually goes?" Jack asks, tapping too loudly on the table. "Claudia, you look a wreck."

She glares at him before remembering to smile, "Nah, I don't."

"Did I hear workplace harassment?" Donnie asks.

"We're not in the office," Jack says, leaning back. "So, I can talk to you jerks however I want."

Tanya sighs and mutters something about finding another bar.

Jack laughs and claps her on the back, causing her to nearly spill her wine.

"So, which one of you girls is gonna be leaving on maternity next?" he asks, pointing a sausage-like finger at us. "Kiko, you're married, right?"

"Divorced," she says.

"Not you," he says, waving a hand to dismiss her. "Sookie, you just moved in with your guy, right? You pregnant?"

I gesture to my wine, "Well, I hope not, Jack."

"Don't get pregnant," he says, "Especially you, Claudia."

Claudia looks disparaged and folds her arms. "Are you gonna ask the guys which one of them is going off on paternity next?" she asks.

"Don't be dumb, guys can't get pregnant," Jack says, laughing and swigging back his beer. "But probably me, got to support the wife. I gotta worry though, what are you idiots going to do without me?" He goes to clap an arm around Donnie, who ducks out of the way. "A team needs a boss to keep 'em in shape."

*

Somehow, I end up stood up on a barstool singing along to "Mr. Brightside" with Claudia, with Kiko attempting to coax us down. I jump off with a flourish and land awkwardly on my ankle.

I wince as Claudia sways into me, our voices hoarse from singing and yelling. I grab at a wall and tell Claudia that the bar smells of spunk.

Rajish calls us the Spice Girls before picking up his coat and telling us he's heading home. Jack tries to scold him for doing it, but is unsure of how to word it without somehow sounding offensive… so he offers Rajish a little handshake.

I hear him laughing as he walks out.

"I love Rajish," Donnie says with surprising sincerity.

I lean against the table to attempt to finish my wine. I check my phone to see that Amber hasn't responded to my message.

Good, I'm glad. She can finally *fuck off* and let me live my life.

I struggle to get it back into its zipper and in the struggle, my bag falls out of my hands and spills its contents over the floor. I climb down from the table to pick it up and Donnie moves down to help me.

"Your purse has a unicorn on it," he says, raising it up.

"Thanks, Captain Obvious," I say.

He lifts up my second phone. "Why'd you have two phones?"

"It's my old one," I slur, "I'm selling it."

"Naaah," he says, "Are you a drug dealer?"

"Yes," I say and snatch it off him. "Gimme some drugs."

He laughs and helps me to my feet. "You're crazy."

"No man, you're crazy."

He hugs me around the shoulders. "You're alright, you are, Sookie."

"Nah, you're alright."

I sit back down and finish the rest of my wine.

"Anyone else want another shot?"

"Shots, shots, shots!" Claudia and Donnie cheer, batting on the table.

I edge my way through the crowd, duck under a very tall man's arm and squish through to the crowded bar. It's sticky to the touch so I move my dreads away from it as much as I can.

"I made it to your concert," someone says to my right.

I look up and see Apparently-Ivan stood there, blocking out the bright lights behind him with his huge head and neck.

"Apparently-Ivan!" I yell, punching him in the arm. "What're you doing here?"

He frowns at me. "None of your business."

"You heard me sing," I say, laughing. "Oh man."

"Yes," he says, "It is brave of you to sing with a voice like yours."

"Thank you," I say, hugging him around the arm. "That's so kind."

He rolls his eyes and points down at me when the bartender makes her way over to us. "Serve her," he says, "Get rid of her please."

I edge past him and the crowd of others with a tray of shots and a couple of packets of salt and come back to the table. I sit down next to Jack and start passing them out. As I hand one to him, he hands something back to me.

"This yours?" he asks.

I look down and see him holding my third phone.

"You had a missed call from your boss," he says.

He looks…frighteningly sober and suspicious.

"You have another job?"

"What?" I say, "No!"

I glance down at my phone and see a missed call from Barry and a couple of texts, demanding an update on my current assignment.

Fuck. Fuck. Fuck. Fuck. Fuck. Fuck. Fuck. Fuck.

Fuck.

"Why're you going through my phone, Jack?" I ask.

"Why do you have three phones?" he asks.

"One is my old phone," I say, "I'm selling it."

"And who is this guy?"

"It's an in joke," I say, "It's one of my dumb friends being a dick."

"Sookie," he says, "I'm pretty easy going as a boss, aren't I?"

"Jack, it's not like that," I say, "It's really not."

"I'm not sure I believe that."

*

My head is spinning and the thought of Jack's hands on my seedy third phone makes me feel even more queasy.

My head is pounding as my key misses the keyhole and scratches noisily against the door.

I laugh and flop down on the doorstep, slumping uncomfortably against the door. I start singing, I'm not sure what, but I know that I'm not singing particularly well because I hear someone in the distance telling me to shut up.

The door opens behind me and I fall backwards, hard, against the ground. I see Rick's face above me but upside down. Then I realise that I'm the one who is upside down.

"Heeeey," I say.

"Hey," he says, "You ok there?"

"Yeah."

"Want to come in the house?"

"Naaah."

"Come on, Sookie, I'll make you some coffee." He bends down and I scramble for his shoulders. My head is spinning as I am pulled into an upright position. I chuckle and cling on as my feet get caught up in tangles.

Rick grunts and tugs me into his arms, holding my legs either side of him as he struggles to gain his balance.

"That's not very flattering," I say. "Stop grunting."

He laughs and kisses my forehead.

"Hold still then, princess. Or do you want to try the stairs with me?"

"Noooo."

He chuckles and slowly begins to make his way up the stairs. I press my face against the crease of his neck and feel myself slowly drifting.

"So, was it a good night? Your texts stopped making sense."

"Nooo."

"Drinking to make it a better night?"

"Yes," I say. "Can I have a juice?"

"Sure, whatever you want."

He's out of breath as he sets me down on one of the kitchen chairs and laughs breathlessly when I don't want to let go of his hand.

"Gotta let go, babe," he says, "Or it's no juice for you."

"Oh no."

"Oh no is right."

He kisses my forehead and I stagger to use the countertop as a balancer after he lets go.

"You want a sandwich?"

"No."

"I can make you a PB&J sandwich?"

"I want pizza."

Rick smiles at me. "Babe, would you prefer pizza or to go to bed soon?"

"Pizza in bed."

"Ok, well, I'll make you a sandwich for now."

"Oh nooo."

"And I'll order us a pizza for after. This is just to tide you over until it gets here."

I groan and rest my head in my hand. "Well, ok then."

I blink and there's a sandwich in front of me. I laugh and smack the table with my hand in disbelief. Then I rest my head on my arm and chuckle mindlessly.

I don't remember the last time somebody took care of me like this when I was wasted. It's been just me and friends since I was only fifteen.

Seriously, when was the last time somebody took care of me like this?

"Good sandwich?" Rick asks.

"Yeah."

Oh, I do remember.

I remember… The pang of my sneakers against the glass doors of the kitchen as I kick them off. The sound of footsteps and the creaking of the red door to the basement. I chuckle from my place, flat on my back on the ground.

Mother sighs and wipes bloody hands on her apron.

"I thought you were a burglar."

"Ha!" I snort. "Poor burglar!"

She rolls her eyes and walks over to the kitchen to wash her hands in the sink.

I lie back and watch the ceiling as it spins.

Then, the gentle clatter of a plate beside me on the floor. A peanut butter and jelly sandwich.

"At least line your stomach if you're going to be stupid."

I frown at her.

"Is this poisoned?"

"Fiona."

A strong hand around my forearm and she pulls me into a seated position. I lean against the sofa for balance. The sandwich tastes good, like…when she used to make me packed lunches when I was in elementary school.

"Mom, I don't feel good."

"Water. Here, small sips."

I drink and cough.

"I said small sips."

"Don't be mad at me."

She sighs and gently pats my back as she sits beside me.

"Ergh. You stink of spirits. So, what are you irresponsible kids drinking?"

"R-uuum."

"Oh, Fiona, *really*."

"I said don't be mad at me. Don't be mad."

Mother rubs the bridge of her nose.

"Come on, let's get you to bed."

*

"Do you miss your mom?" Rick asks in the morning as he brushes an unruly dreadlock of hair out of my face.

I blink sleepily.

"What?"

"Last night, I made you a sandwich and you cried. You kept asking for her."

He looks so sad for me.

"I know you probably don't want to talk about it…But I remember you said you and your mom didn't get along?"

I sit up and rub my head, trying to remember the stupid backstory.

"No, that's my stepmom…My actual mother died when I was little. It was really long ago. Sorry, I must have been pretty drunk. I'm sorry for making a scene."

I avoid his eyes when I say it. I really don't like lying to him.

Rick's hand is gently on my lower back. "You sounded so sad, Sookie."

I lean against him. "Sorry, it gets to me every now and then. I guess I've just been on my own for a long time."

"How did she die?"

This question I don't like. I don't want to predict the future here… I mean, probably of old age in a prison cell or in some kind of prison hospital. I don't think I could stand it if it was anything worse. I think my heart would break.

"My mom…left me and my dad. Got into a car accident. I was really little. My dad remarried, then passed away not long after. Then it was just me and the evil stepmother until I ran away. Oh hey, hey, it's ok, God, don't look so sad!"

He laughs, self-conscious and hugs me tight against him.

"I promise you won't have to be alone again."

And…I don't deserve this.

I really don't deserve this.

Chapter Fourteen

As I sit back in the waiting room, I find a leftover copy of *Empire* magazine in the rack and lo and behold, the front cover is the movie about her, about me and her…It's got a close-up of a river running red and superimposed onto the image is our girl, Scarlett Johansson, staring dead-eyed at the camera.

I still don't know who gets to play me. It doesn't say in the article.

Detective Brankowski is being played by Matt Damon though, which I think he'd have been pleased about. I read an interview with him on page 12 where he talks about getting the family's permission to read Brankowski's Red Creek notebooks. That's unnerving, and you know, kind of what the fuck when you think about Matt Damon scrolling through a book I've read.

I mean, he had it on him when he died.

What was I going to do? Not read it?

There's a cliched Halloween release date and a couple of pictures from on-set. Also, much to my surprise, at the end of the article, there's a small comment from Mrs. Green, who was slamming the gore-happy director for trying to get creative input from her daughter, Beth, 21, studying at Yale.

Yale, wow, nice one, Beth.

Apparently, he has reached out to Beth on numerous occasions to provide a bit of realism to the bits with 'Fiona and the gang'; you know, it makes my heart leap whenever I read my old name, part of me still wants to respond 'Yes?'.

Mrs. Green talks about years of therapy being undone by the sociopathic way the director has been hounding Beth and the others involved. She stresses that she and her family will not be going to watch the film, she claims it glorifies a very real, very human tragedy for bloodthirsty entertainment.

You know, I can even imagine her saying it.

I put the magazine down and glance up as Rick comes out of the dentist's office, rubbing his jaw and frowning at his wallet.

"I resent having to pay for the privilege of having that man torture me," he mutters. Rick hates the dentist even more than little kids after Halloween. "I swear he enjoys it."

"He might do," I say, linking my fingers through his. "You ok to drive?"

"Yeah, all he did was try to prod my gums open with little scalpels," he said. "I'm good to go." He kisses my cheek and then winces at the movement of his mouth. "Ow."

Mother's contact couldn't provide dental records for me, so I start fresh and hope that nobody ever needs to know about me before age nineteen. It's always one of those things that makes me panic. Like handing over my 'totally legitimate' high school diploma when I got my job for an identity check. Pretending frantically that I had a full high school experience and did not fake my own death and run away before the end of freshman year...

"What were you reading? You looked…engrossed," he says as we sit in traffic, the radio a low hum in the background.

"Oh, about that movie, you know, the Red Creek Killer," I say, "You know Matt Damon's in it?"

Rick whistles, then winces from the movement of his mouth.

"You wanna see that?" he asks, "The movie I mean?"

"Maybe, it's not out for a little while," I say. "It could be interesting."

"Poor taste though," he says.

"Well, I guess all these things get a movie version sooner or later," I said.

"The whole thing freaks me out, like body parts floating down a river is nightmare fuel enough," he says, "But all that later stuff, about hulking body parts around in a cello case?" He shudders. "Haven't been able to look at one of those things since."

Mother dearest.

I find myself smirking.

"Yeah, it's pretty nasty shit."

"The nastiest."

*

The worst thing about working to earn a living is the fucking mundanity of it all. I really hate it some days, I really get why Mother put so much time and effort into becoming her own boss: I was so dismissive of it then, I thought of her career as her little fake job, but to be honest, now I'm there, I totally get it. I bet she hated being bored like I do.

There are some mornings it won't bother me. I mean, I know all this pays for me and Rick to live the way that we do. But on others, that doesn't matter, I don't want to get up at that time, I don't want to sit in traffic, I don't want to sit in that room, and I don't want to talk to those people. I don't want to read my emails and I don't want to answer that phone.

I know it's part of the deal, the whole productive member of society thing. You know, all the freedom of earning a living but constrained between working hours, rent, the water bill, the Wi-Fi, all that shit.

Today is one of those days.

It's raining and nobody is in the mood to talk or think or really do anything.

Claudia is sat with her face nestled in the palm of her hand. She is scowling at the screen and using one finger to punch in student results. She yawns aggressively and occasionally closes her eyes for too long.

Donnie is watching *Hey Arnold* on his phone with one headphone in. Every now and then he hides the screen beneath the same spreadsheet. He has turned his phone down to the lowest volume and picks it up quickly so that Jack never catches on.

Rajish drops me a message on work Skype to send me a quiz about *Game of Thrones* and Shakira songs: 'Everyone is a combination of One Game of Thrones character and One Shakira song, which are you??', basically very crucial stuff. I guess there can't be much work going on there either. I glance behind me at Tanya, who is definitely playing out her Fantasy Football.

He informs me that Kiko is essentially asleep.

Not much work going on here.

I smile to myself and try to get interested in the same email I started forty minutes ago.

We have to see all Rick's friends tonight. It's Amber's birthday and we are all going to a house party to celebrate. I honestly think I'd rather spend the evening scrubbing ancient asses with my own toothbrush than go and wish her a happy birthday. We signed a card together. Signing my fake name never felt so good.

No, I don't wish you a happy birthday, bitch, this completely fictitious person does.

That's me, basically.

Not real.

I sigh and push my keyboard away, and avert my attention to the rain outside my window. I hate the cliché of feeling down when it rains, but I do. It used to rain a lot where I'm…where Fiona Taylor is from. So whenever it rains in Santa Cruz, I find myself getting a little bit sad.

I open Facebook and search for Beth Green.

She's easier to find than most. She's strangely got a mutual friend with one of the professors who added me a while ago. Dereck is a junior lecturer here, he did training at Yale, where he got his MBA. Beth's one of his former students, from what I can tell.

Her profile is private.

But she looks almost exactly like she used to.

Hair just above the shoulders, blunt fringe, black hairband. She wears makeup to try to hide her freckles now. In her profile picture, she is smiling and confident and dressed in a black sparkly dress, like she's out somewhere fancy.

She looks happy.

A few clicks and I find Matt. They are still close. There's a photo of the two of them hanging out together at a lake somewhere, last summer. Matt is still short and slight, but handsome, you can see that more without all that shaggy brown hair over his face. The two of them are smiling, and that makes me feel lonely, even though I'm happy to see them.

That's what I'd like to say, that I'm happy to see them.

Social media is the fucking worst.

Jack leaves the office early, claiming to have better things to do and better places to be. He reminds the rest of us that we all need to stay until five before he strides off, snorting about it.

Claudia leaves as soon as he clears off, muttering something about fascism.

I contemplate joining her.

I could use a few drinks before I'm back in Amber's super sweet sixteen, knowing that no amount of booze will rescue me.

Plus, I wish it wasn't a house party. Historically, house parties do not agree with me. There's a high school quarterback would could elaborate on that, or there was…

Rick texts at quarter to five to say he's in the car park, he suggests that the earlier we get to Amber's party, the sooner we can leave. And I really hope that he means that. I wave goodbye to the others and on my way out, I hear the buzz of a phone in my handbag going off.

Hands trembling as I close the office door behind me, I pull my stupid third phone out of my bag and my heart sinks as I see a message from Barry Ames.

Long time no speak, Miss. King, he says, like this isn't a message that he knows will pulverise me. It hasn't been a month. It's not been as long as he promised…Well, I always knew that about his promises. I take a deep breath and wipe a hand carelessly over my eyes.

There's a little problem called Dwaine Anderson living at the address enclosed. Can I ask you to get rid of him tomorrow night? I'll be in touch with more information shortly. Glad to have you back, of course. Laters, Barry xx

I want to scream. It's not fucking fair. I can't get news like this tonight and have to fucking talk to Amber the Ex. How is this fair to anyone?

I pinch the bridge of my nose and text Barry to tell him, sure, because I know that the easiest thing with him is to just say yes, yes, of course, that's fine. Because he would be so much worse, so much more cruel, if he knew how much I wanted to say no.

"Are you ok?" Rick asks when I get into the car.

"Yeah, just the after-effects of a long day," I say, squeezing his arm. "Do we have to stay long tonight?" I pout and make my best and most adorable face. He laughs at me, of course, and kisses my forehead.

"It won't get late."

"That's how every late night starts out," I say.

"Hey, hey, no it doesn't. I mean it," he says. "I got meetings in the morning. Also, it's a house party, I don't get why she even needs to throw it on a Wednesday."

I laugh and buckle in and try to forget about the actual fucking criminal texting me from the other phone.

"Okay, well, you owe me if we end up staying late."

*

So, she doesn't actually live here. Amber's big soirée is being hosted by her friend Heidi, who owns a house in the suburbs. Heidi seems to be like what I've seen a lot of Amber's friends are like, she wears the same glasses and a version of the same outfit, even tonight.

The birthday girl herself is on full form. No sooner than we enter through the front door, she's on us. She runs—actually runs—at us and dives into Rick's arms, causing him to stumble back into Miguel. She hops down, laughing and excited before assaulting me with a hug.

"Little Sookie King in the hooouse!" she says, snorting with laughter. She grabs hold of my bun with her hand and ruffles it aggressively, before bodily shoving me aside to hug the others. I frown at my reflection in the ornate silver mirror across the hall. She has, in five seconds, ruined twenty minutes of styling.

This fucking woman...

You know, I'm glad I didn't bring a gift. I open the wine I brought in the kitchen while Amber takes her time taking a selfie with Rick and our friends. Nobody seems to notice that I'm not there. I bet they have a lot of old pictures like that.

Fuck, I think I'd rather be at Barry's beck and call tonight.

There's quite the crowd here. They all seem to be Amber's colleagues from work and their boyfriends.

Heidi, the hostess, inherited this place from her dead grandma. Amber delights in telling the whole party that Heidi would not have been able to afford to even *rent* a place half as nice as this on her salary!

Heidi goes a colour somewhere between red and really-really red. I take a strange sort of comfort in knowing that Amber is just as big a dickhead to her enemies as she is her friends.

I think about pouring drain cleaner into her next birthday cocktail.

Amber is in her element, she flitters about the place, holding court, like some social butterfly conducting an anthropological experiment. She makes a big thing of introducing me to the one other black person at the party—the boyfriend of one of her best girlfriends from work. She introduces him as Mark; rolling his eyes, he tells me he's actually called Alan. Aside from both being aware of Amber being the worst, we quickly discover that we have *absolutely* nothing in common—Alan went to MIT, works in IT and is a gym devotee. We make awkward small talk for ten minutes before he pretends that his phone is ringing and goes outside.

I return to Rick, who is having a cigarette in the garden.

"Can you believe her?" I ask. "Hey, Sookie, I know who you'll want to meet, the one other black person at my party."

Rick cringes. "I promise, we'll leave after two hours."

"Two hours? No, that's right before things get really good!" Amber declares, leaping out from behind us. "Now, Rick, Rick, you have to come and meet my friends from work! You will just LOVE them!" She links his arm through hers and steers him back towards the house. I go to follow, when she turns and says to me quickly and quietly, "Actually, Sooks, the girlies aren't really your sort of crowd. Why don't you stay put?" She smiles. "Mark not with you?" she adds.

"Alan, actually, and no."

"Whatever," she says brightly, closing the back door in my face.

I light up a cigarette and sit down on the garden wall. I check my phone and read through two nonsense messages from Barry.

I can get through this. This is easy compared to what I'm usually up to.

I take a deep breath and within minutes, Rick returns, smelling of tequila, rolling his eyes and taking my hand. We laugh and wander back in, a change of location to avoid the birthday girl. We are sat around the dining room table, chatting to Jandro and Carla and within minutes—minutes—Amber pounces again: 'Riiick, Sue is here! You must remember Sue! Sue! Sue-Sue? Oh, she'll want to see you, you guys haven't hung out since we broke up!'

And then, all too soon, I find myself…alone. Cramped against a wall in the living room while everyone talks over the TV. Then cramped outside the bathroom in a never-ending queue. I move around, but I don't see you, Rick, not anywhere. I run into Amber every now and then, who, if it's in front of one of the gang, throws herself at me and gushes and makes a fuss. And if she's caught me alone, she smirks and breezes right past me.

The two hours we were supposed to be here pass with unending slowness. I find myself anxious. You know it's bad when I'm wishing that I'd picked up a call from Barry rather than come to a party here. Starr is sat with me at the top of the stairs, we're sat on the top step, sharing a bottle of wine. I don't think she's having any fun either.

"He's probably just run into someone from college," she says for the third time, slurring her words. "I wouldn't worry."

"I'm not," I say. "I know how parties can be."

Yeah, terrible and noisy and everyone talking and nobody listening.

I jerk my hand back in time as a girl with very long straight brown hair comes clattering down the stairs in dangerous-looking heels, nearly taking out my fingers. Her bag slides off her shoulder and collides with the side of Starr's head.

"Watch it," Starr snaps at her.

She turns around, drunk and laughing, "Sorry, sorry!" Before her eyes settle on me, she gasps in delight and reaches down to try to grab a fistful of my hair. "Oh, I love dreadlocks, so pretty!"

I swat her hand away, "Don't touch me."

She looks stunned, rubbing her hand like I've poured boiling oil over it. "Ouch! Hey, I was just being nice!"

"How would you like it if I grabbed your hair?" I ask.

"And like pulled it? What's your problem?"

"No," I say, and I can feel my temper in my voice now. "But like, you wouldn't go and start trying to pat *her* hair, would you?" I say, gesturing to Starr. "It's what you'd do to a fucking dog, so keep your hands to yourself!"

She folds her arms, red-faced and annoyed. "You people just like being offended."

"Wow," I say, shaking my head. "Just wow."

"You people," Starr repeats. "Listen, can you fuck off, ok?"

"Rude," she says and turns, bag swinging from her shoulder and nearly catching me on the arm.

"Ugly bitch," Starr calls after her. She slides over to me and wraps an arm around my shoulder. "Fuck her."

"Fuck her," I agree and take the wine from her, having a swig. "And fuck this party."

"Fuck Amber," Starr says. "I didn't even want to come."

"I hate parties," I say.

"Noooo," she says, "Parties are fun."

"I hate them," I say. "Your wedding was different. I mean parties like this. This is a high school party."

"It *so* is, why aren't we past high school?" she says, laughing. "This is a fucking Grandma house high school party."

I laugh and shake my head. "I never even liked them in high school. I went to this one once, and man, it was such a bloodbath."

Starr swats my shoulder, laughing. "High school is a bloodbath, Sookie."

I shake my head, leaning back when I spot Marco at the bottom of the stairs. My heart sinks when I see that he's holding their coats, mock pleading.

"Fuck," Starr says, "Sookie, I'm sorry, but I really do have to go. Marco has a huge meeting in the morning and I really did promise we'd only stay an hour."

"It's fine," I say, "Honestly, you guys go."

Marco edges his way up the stairs and asks me breathlessly if I'd like a lift home. "It's really no bother."

"It's ok," I say, "Rick'll be done soon. Wherever he is... Hey, you haven't seen him have you?"

"No," he says. "You sure?"

"I'm sure. You guys go. Good luck in your meeting."

Starr hugs me before following Marco downstairs, offering me an apologetic smile.

And this is fine, only now I'm alone and hating it here, which is way worse. I check my phone again and try not to cringe at how desperate my texts are starting to sound. Oh God, it sounds like I'm pleading with him to go.

Someone bumps into me hard on his way to the toilet.

"Watch it!" I snap at him and receive a derisive snort in response.

Of course, Amber would be friends with the worst people alive.

Where are my friends? Why did only Starr bother to stick it out with me? Where's Rick? He's got to know that there's nobody here to help me, right? He's got to… I hold my breath. I can handle this. I slice people up for a dodgy second job. This is just a shitty party.

I brush back my hair and walk down the steps, through a hundred and one conversations. I've finished the crappy bottle of wine and it's just not giving me the buzz I need to tolerate these people. I can't even pretend that none of this bothers me. Someone bumps into me and someone's heel comes very close to squashing my sneakers.

I stumble on the last step and hear someone to my left stage-whisper, "Oh, is *that* her?" I glance over and see two of Amber's friends giving me the side eye. I recognise these two from her social media. These are the 'girlies' who dress and do their hair like her. I mean, who started the trend? Do they all coordinate outfits before they go out or are they really as unoriginal as that?

"Yeah," the other identical girl sniggers behind her hand. "I thought she'd be prettier."

"She's exactly as I imagined her to be," the taller one of the two says. "Rick's dating some angry black girl with a stick up her fat ass."

They both snort with laughter and like… no! No fucking thank you. No, I'm not dealing with this. I'm not going to stand here while Amber's fucking racist friends stare at me and spout that hateful shit. I'm a dangerous person. I shouldn't be in a situation which inspires that side of me. I'm finished with this.

I grab my coat from the rack by the wall and book myself an Uber. I glance around the party—more as a formality—for Rick, knowing that I won't see him. I send him a last text—the last one, I promise myself.

Enjoy the party. I'm going.

I hear Amber's friends snorting with laughter as I slam the door behind me.

My Uber is here and they can go to hell.

"Sookie!"

I walk down the steps of Heidi's dead grandmother's porch and spot Rick sat on the front lawn with two other guys. My hands are shaking so hard I can barely hold up my phone.

"Sorry, Rick, my Uber is here."

"Wait, wait what?" He's wasted, staggering and using one of the guys next to him to stand up fully. "No, don't leave!" He laughs and clasps hold of my hands. "Look, Amber invited my boy, Paulo! It's Paulo, Sookie! I haven't seen him since college!" He's laughing, bright-eyed, trying to steer me towards Paulo.

"That's great," I say, "Nice to meet you, but I'm going. I'll see you back at the apartment."

"Nooo!" He pulls me close to him, smile brilliant on his face. "No, please stay! I insist!"

I want to settle into this, but he's so drunk and happy and I'm upset. I want to scream until my lungs explode. I can't calm back into this setting. I can't calm down. I can't…

"Rick, no, I'm having, look-" I pull back to make him look at me. "Rick, listen, I'm having a horrible night. I just want to go home."

"Oh no," he says, "I'm sorry!" He's still smiling though. "Come and sit down with me. Chat with the guys! We'll cheer you up!"

"Turn that frown upside down," Paulo says, patting the grass. "Come sit!"

"Do it! Do it!" the other guy I don't know starts to chant.

"No," I say to the guys, "You guys have fun!" I steer Rick back to look at me. "Babe, I'm going. I'll meet your friends another time. I just want to go."

I pull myself out of his grip and then feel someone slam into me from behind, pale arms around my shoulders.

"Little Sookie King, there you are!" Amber says cheerfully, her breath stinks of strawberry booze. "Are you leaving? Hey, no leaving my party!"

My phone flashes telling me that my ride is here.

She's sweaty, pressing against my back, laughing, nails digging into my dress. I wriggle out of her grip and see that she's smiling this shit-eating fucking smile.

I ignore her. It's all I can do peacefully.

"Rick, I'll see you at home."

He looks baffled as I walk off to my Uber. I get in and glance through the window, watching Amber hanging off him, laughing as he watches me drive away.

I don't cry right away. I don't cry in the car. I don't cry when I get back to the apartment. I wash my face. I make myself drink a herbal tea. I settle back into bed and that's when I cry. And it's ugly! I ugly cry for a long, long time. But not long enough because he doesn't come back. And I pretend I'm not crying because I'm so angry it feels like my insides could burn.

*

In the morning I wake up to an empty bed. There are three missed calls from Rick, lots of texts that just stop making sense towards the end. He says that he's sorry and asks me to come back to the party. I'm guessing that he ended up staying the night because he's not on the couch.

Despite everything telling me what a stupid idea this is, I click onto my Instagram and search out Amber's account. Of course, the whole party is up there already, did it really happen otherwise… Fucking phone, why am I doing this to myself?

It's all there. It's all filtered to make it look like the best night ever and not an evening that made me want to rip my own skin off. Everyone is smiling and having fun, chatting and dancing. Amber features in most of them. There's a few of Rick with the old friends from college. A few of me in the background, looking tired and sulky. But of course, Amber Bayley has been kind enough to tag me in them, anyway. Thanks for that…

And then there's this one taken early this morning, you can see the sun rising in the background. It's the two of them, just Amber and Rick sharing a cigarette and smiling, cozied up on the garden bench.

I feel… I feel… I feel way too much to deal with this healthily.

Rick keeps a baseball bat and a punching bag in Phil's old room. I swing for it until it cracks. I bash it with my fists until my knuckles bruise and swell. I go for it with a kitchen knife and manage to stop myself before I do something I would need to explain.

Then I shower, get dressed and go out because I don't want to be here when he gets home. I don't want to hear excuses. I don't want to discuss this. I don't want him to see me when I'm literally vibrating with rage and pain. I don't want to have a fight where he says, frustrated, that he just wanted to spend time with his friends.

I just... I can't.

And as angry as I am with him, as much as I want to yell at him and tell him that's he's bullshit, that his friendship with her is bullshit, that that evil bitch is playing us and he's letting her do it, not giving a shit how much it messes me around—just eating up the shit she serves up. I don't want this to be the thing that breaks us up...

This isn't me.

This isn't what I want.

I stomp along the beachfront, up and down. There are joggers, and I think about jogging. I try to almost instantly regret it. Now with my boob aching and my ankle feeling irregular, I stagger down onto the beach and throw rocks into the water. I ignore my phone, buzzing in my pocket, I don't know what to say. I don't need to have this conversation. I don't want this to be over.

But I can't and won't do this again. This pattern of behaviour is thankless and tired. She butts in. He asks her for boundaries. She gives some excuse and promises she'll keep to them. She doesn't.

Maybe I need to consider, and I don't particularly want to consider this, but maybe... he keeps putting up with her and the things that she does because he has every intention of getting back together with her one day.

My stone narrowly misses a seagull bobbing along on the water's surface.

Fuck.

I leave the beach and think about calling Leda or Gabbie. Only if I do that, then I'll turn Rick into the dickhead boyfriend, the shit, the shithead, the bastard. I'll never be able to mention him again without getting a lecture about how I should dump him.

I think about speaking to Mother—then laugh myself temporarily out of depression. Wow, ok, that's the wake-up call I need. Could I even imagine how that conversation would go? I doubt she has ever had any sort of boy trouble in her life, and I mean, from prison, I doubt she's about to start.

This wasn't her world and ultimately, it's not mine either. But I'm trying to live here, nonetheless.

Rick's number flashes up on my phone. I let it go to voicemail. I scroll through the missed text messages, his WhatsApps, his Facebook messages. Damn, he's covered all the stops.

Where are you?

Sookie, I'm worried, will you please call me back? Please?

I'm sorry.

I'm so sorry.

Please, I'm sorry, just let me know you're ok.

I know I've fucked up. Please come home.

I sigh and text back to say that I'm on my way home.

And look at that, the angry tremor has gone. I'm definitely ready to go home.

Chapter Fifteen

For the first few minutes, it's quiet. He's made me a cup of coffee when I get in. He smiles, and I feel helpless because he's so gentle and good.

But he's wearing last night's clothes. I think about that fucking photo again. So, I take a deep breath and then I yell.

"I won't do this again."

"I'm sorry."

"No, you don't get it," I say.

"try to help me to," he says. "You left last night, I was really just hanging out with my friends. I'm sorry I… I'm sorry! I don't know what else to say."

"I love you, Rick. I love you so much, but I won't go through this again. You and fucking Amber have put me through this way too many times! I won't be some fucking pit stop on your big romance with her!"

"Romance?" he says, eyes widening. "Sookie, no!"

"I don't care if she's still your friend or like a big part of your life from college or whatever or if your mom still makes her a birthday cake every year or fucking! She is vile to me. She's vile to me and you let her!"

He reaches down and takes my hand, bringing it to his chest. "I know I fucked up and let you down last night. I know how… this must look. But Sookie, I don't want that. I have no intention of ever getting back together with her or anyone. It's you. It's just you. I'm so sorry."

"No, Rick," I say, pulling away. "Ok, you know that we've had a version of this conversation at least three times since she came back on the scene? I feel like… I don't know, in like two weeks, we'll be having this conversation again. I can't do it, not anymore."

He takes my face in his hands. "I love you. Tell me how I can fix this. Please, I don't want to lose you. I love you." He kisses the tip of my nose, fingertips stroking my face. "Please, I don't want this to end. I'm so sorry."

I pull away and hold my hand over my eyes. "I don't even know how to play this. I know she was a big part of your life. And your friends like her and… your mom likes her. But she doesn't like me, babe. She's always fucking with me."

"I won't see her," he says, and I can tell from his eyes that he means that. "She's being awful to you. I won't see her. I'll block her on everything. I'll cut off contact, I'll!"

"She's friends with your friends, Rick," I say. "If you cut her out for me, it'll be oh look at Rick's mean jealous girlfriend who won't let him see his friend."

"It's not like that."

"Do you honestly think that's not the spin she's going to put on it?"

His expression falters. "I…"

"Babe, you know she will. It's what she does. She's like a poison. I will never be ok with her. If she says things are fine, I guarantee she'll find some other way to make me miserable."

"Well, I promise to be more united," He says, "We'll close ranks around her. I won't let her pull stuff like that anymore."

"Rick!"

"No, I won't. I won't let this happen again. I'll be better. I'll talk to Carla, she'll back me up. She's never liked Amber, I promise. We can do this. Please, please say you'll let me try. Please? Please don't leave me over this."

"Alright, ok, ok," I say, hugging him then. "I wouldn't do that, you know? I love you."

He hugs me back. "I love you too. I love you so much. God, I was so scared that I'd fucked everything up."

*

"So, you didn't enjoy the party?" Leda says, "The pics looked great."

"And why would pictures lie?" Tammy adds sarcastically.

I smirk and shake my head. "Leda, honestly, that girl hates me. She violently hates me."

"She was sweet about you when I spoke to her," Leda says, frowning at Tammy as she goes to interrupt again. "I'm sorry, babe. I wish we could just get rid of her." She rests her head on my shoulder. "I'm glad you and Rick talked things out."

It's always easier to manage a narrative with your friends once the issue has mostly been resolved.

"Me too. If she wants him back, she can fuck off and build herself a time machine."

Leda laughs and shakes her head.

"Leda," Tammy calls from the kitchen. "The popcorn looks wrong."

"What's wrong with it?" I ask.

"It's all hard," she says uncertainly.

"Oh, for God's sake," Leda says, "You have to put it in the microwave. I swear…" She rolls her eyes as she gets up to follow her away.

I take a deep breath and lean back. This is nice. This feels back to normal again.

And you know, any leftover frustrations over certain parties is resolved by getting stuck into my latest assignment from Barry. On my way home from movie night with Leda and Tammy, I catch up with Carl, a DJ at a club who has gotten on Barry's bad side in a big way.

I bash him around with a lead pipe I found in an alleyway outside the club, then arrange a car accident in the quarry near his apartment. Carl the DJ looks nothing like her. But when you're angry enough, anything vaguely the right shape will do.

"You're in a bad mood today," Barry says when I meet him at his office.

"You don't say."

He taps his desk. "Come on, Miss. King, tell me what's up. I'm a good listener. You have your boss's ear."

"Well, you can't think all of this is making me feel on top of the world," I say.

"Come on," he says, "This isn't anything you weren't doing all on your own before so don't give me that."

"I don't see how that's the point," I say.

"If you're growing frustrated with your circumstances, surely, I am providing the best outlet for that, right? And much better than when you were pulling this shit on your own. With me, you've got back-up, security, all the stuff millennials tend to lack in their respective workplaces. I thought you'd be happy?"

I sigh, "Yeah, I meant to ask you this, but, say there was someone I wanted to remove on my own terms…"

"Another panty-sniffer like my dear departed cousin?" he asks, not without edge.

"This is a hypothetical situation, Barry, I'm just checking up on my role here."

His eyes narrow. "Well, hypothetically then, no. If there's someone you want to remove, you put up with them like a goddamn normal person. You can't just get rid of everyone who happens to irritate you, I mean where would that leave you, huh?"

"You know, that's kind of a confusing thing to say to your hitman."

"I'm the boss," he says, prodding his own chest with his thumb. "I say who goes. If you start picking again, then you'll get caught. And before you get smart, remember that you got caught by me. It's why you're here." He taps the desk again. "So, if there's some chump getting on your nerves, some bitchy gal from the office, you suck that shit up and act like a normal goddamn person, you got it?"

I really, really hate it when he pulls his boss hat on.

"Do you understand what I'm saying here, Miss. King?"

"Perfectly," I say.

He beams at me. "Come on, don't look at me like that, this isn't forever, so ditch that glum face and give me a smile."

I do a big fake smile, but doubt he knows the difference between the two.

*

On the drive home, stuck in traffic, Apparently-Ivan is incredibly quiet. He drums his fingers on the steering wheel and occasionally makes eye contact in the mirror which is frankly too intimate for my liking.

"What?" I say in the end.

"I did not say anything to you."

"Sure," I say.

But after five minutes, he's doing it again. And his tapping is actually out of tune with the classical music on the radio.

"Look, what's wrong with you?"

He sighs.

"When he says, not forever, well, don't hold your breath."

"Is that why you're here?" I ask.

He is frowning at me, wordless, mouth a cold, stiff line.

"So, before you were Barry's tough guy, what did you do? Ballet instructor, art dealer, geography teacher?"

"Security guard," he says. "Not that it is any of your business."

"And you ended up working for Barry how? Come on, Apparently-Ivan, you can't give me 'don't hold your breath' then go all quiet and mysterious again."

"My daughter… I left her mom when she was only seven. It was ugly, so I kept my distance. I paid child support, I did my best. But I didn't want to intrude…" He sighs and furrows his brow. "My daughter was unhappy. My ex-wife's new boyfriend hit her, knocked her around, made her feel worthless. So, she started using… bad drugs when she was just a teenager. Which is how she ended up in the same circles as people who work for Barry Ames. She racked up a debt."

He pauses, and I can't look him in the eye from the mirror. I have to look away. His face is racked with pain.

"One day I get a call from her, she was scared. She begged for help. I came. She owed Barry Ames impossible money. I couldn't pay what she owed. They were going to make her do… awful things to make her pay it off. I said I would take on her debt, that I would work for him instead."

My stomach has sunk into the soles of my feet.

"How long ago was this?"

"Twenty-three years ago," he said.

"And your daughter?"

He sighs, a heavy, defeated sound.

"She overdosed eighteen years ago."

*

True to his word, Rick had worked on the Amber situation. There were more occasions without her. She tried to pop by our apartment once. I was in the shower and I heard her knock. I heard her on the answering machine as I got out, listening to it rumble through the door. The knocking continued.

"Rick, I'm outside, are you home? Come on, I bet you're home. I thought we could head out. There's live jazz three blocks from here. Hello? Pick up?"

The knocking continued.

Rick turned up the TV and waved at me as I poked my head out of the bathroom door.

"Hello? Little Sookie King, you there?"

I pop out of the bathroom, hair up on top of my head, towel-clad and sit down beside him, curling up on the sofa. He wraps an arm around me. "Just us tonight," he says, kissing my damp forehead.

"I mean, this is kind of stalking," I say, gesturing to the footsteps outside the apartment door.

"She'll learn," he says.

"She better."

*

I suspect Carla has been a big influence on his new cut-throat approach to Amber's neediness. It is so often Carla who makes arrangements for nights out. Carla who has suddenly started hosting movie night at her place and Carla who has started a Facebook group-chat which excludes Amber.

One Tuesday after work, I meet the others at the bar. As I'm waiting with her, Carla turns to me and says, "Just so you know, you won't have any more trouble from Amber."

"Doesn't feel that way, I mean, she rocks by the apartment whenever she wants."

"I've never liked her," Carla says. "The guys are friendly idiots. I'm sorry about them. But she's always rubbed me the wrong way. She was bad for Rick back then," she says. "His sister Maria was my best friend growing up, I've watched Rick make a lot of stupid mistakes over the years. Mostly to do with styling his hair. But nothing would come as close as letting that psychotic little girl mess stuff up between the two of you." She squeezes my arm gently. "I've got your back, ok?"

She says it so sternly, so confidently, I believe her. I believe every word.

She smiles and slips back over to the bar. I sit between her and Rick and when Amber inevitably shows her face an hour later, I don't have that knee-jerk reaction of complete and utter dread.

"You guys, I never see you anymore, what is up with that?" she says, wedging herself between Jandro and Libby. "What is up with that?"

"We're busy," Carla says, "Busy, busy, busy."

"As if," Amber says. "Rick, they had live jazz right by your apartment the other day. It was awesome, I tried to drop by but you weren't home."

"You should have called," he says. "You know, to check I wasn't busy."

We leave early, I make up some story about having a meeting. As we leave, Amber gives me a huge hug and digs her fingernails into my arms as she does. Then she smiles and bops me on the nose like a dog.

"A catch-up is due so so soon!"

*

She invites us for a dinner party, at her apartment, she insists on wanting to show it off to us. Rick declines, tells her that he's snowed under at work.

Miguel and Rory go along and she sends photos to Rick while it's going on, to try to show him what he's missing.

She invites me, Carla, Libby and Alex out for a girls' night. Carla tells her that she has a date before Amber can even reveal the approximate date of girls' night. Dan begs Alex to go along.

We get Instagram photos of the two of them sat together in a bar. Amber has her arm around Alex's shoulders. Alex looks uncomfortable, smiling vacantly at the camera. Alex texts Carla's group chat saying 'Save meeee', while Dan pesters her with apologetic emojis.

She invites Jandro, Dan, Miguel, Rory and Rick out for a boys' night, just the lads and her, classic, just like old times. Jandro and Dan go. Rick doesn't bother replying at all.

*

He turns his phone towards me one night, there's a message from her.

Amber: *Are you mad at me?*

He snorts and puts his phone down and carries on chopping the onions for dinner.

"Unbelievable."

I hug him from behind, rest my head against his shoulder blades. But I keep an eye on his phone and see her other messages as they drop in, needy and fake and sorry for themselves.

Amber: You're being really off. Did I do something wrong?

Amber: You promised if I did something wrong, then we'd talk about it. Why are you ghosting me?

Amber: Shutting me out like this isn't fair, Rick.

Amber: We've been friends for years—years!

Amber: Hey, look, this is just a gamble, and don't read into it if I'm wrong, but is this about my birthday party?

Amber: Rick, I like us being friends. If YOUR girlfriend is the jealous type, that has nothing to do with me. Ok?

Amber: It was my birthday. I was just having fun. You were having fun too. I'm sorry I didn't stop and babysit

*your girlfriend through my birthday party. Are you se-
riously going to cut me out because your girlfriend
doesn't like me? The gang are my friends too. This isn't
fair. You never used to be like this.*

"Are you ok?" he asks, glancing back.

"Yeah," I say.

*

Even on my best day, my very best day, I expected this good time without Amber to last…for a few weeks, maybe a month. But no, it lasts. Rick has her on mute on WhatsApp, he ignores her Facebook messages. His phone will buzz on the table and he won't even give it a glance.

It's making her desperate.

"She called me from her friend's phone," he says, rolling his eyes. "Can you believe that?"

"What? Seriously?"

"Yeah, I got a random call, which I stupidly answered because it was a local call and I was worried it was like my sister or something." He sounds more amused than cross. "So, I answer it and it's Amber. She's like 'So, your phone's not broken then'—and I just hung up."

I snort. "You didn't."

"Hey, I did, I can be Mr. Aloof."

"You hung up on her?"

"Yeah, then she texted me from this other number saying, 'Did you just hang up on me???'"

"Oh, my God!"

"Yeah, then the girl whose phone she was using clearly took it back and sent me an apology text a few hours later."

"It was probably just Amber," I say, shaking my head. "I bet she'd buy a new phone just to push her stalking to the next level."

He winces. "Wow, you're not wrong."

*

Ok, so since the party, one, two, three months—*months*—pass without me having to interact with her for more than maybe half an hour. Carla knows the manager of the bar Amber works at and managed to sneak a look at her schedule (on a near permanent basis). Suddenly the gang is meeting whenever Amber is busy. There are whiny WhatsApp messages, a few run-ins where she arrives as we're leaving. But Santa Cruz is a big place, and suddenly three months pass without me having to get talked down to or condescended at.

We have our cute little one-year anniversary celebration without her being any part of it. We wake up and do presents and it's silly but also kind of like Christmas. We go to work, I pretend I don't care when Corey spills coffee over all the exam documentation. We talk about maybe going to Maurice's for dinner.

I'm finishing off the last of the paperwork while Jack congratulates Corey on letting him know about the coffee spill—when the phone rings. Wanting to take a break from this bullshit anyway, I slip outside.

"I'm sorry, babe," Rick says, "There's been an issue with work, I've gotta stay late. Will you be ok getting home?"

"Sure," I say. "The walk will do me good. Too late for Maurice's?"

"I'll get us pizza," he promises. "I promise it'll be a special night."

All of this for the last three months has felt easier, happier. There's been no tension, no nagging sensation in the back of my mind. It feels like it did before. Just us. The gang is just fine without her. Sure, Jandro says that he feels bad we all haven't seen as much of her, but he's the only one. I wonder how it'd make her feel to know that life goes on without her. Like it did for us six months ago.

This, I can get on board with.

I head home, feeling light and optimistic. I'm humming on the bus and don't give a shit who wants to give me a funny look over it. Rick texts a photo of himself at the office, doing an exaggerated weeping face. I'm still chuckling about it as I slide my key into the front door and freeze as I enter the apartment and hear a creaking in our bedroom.

Oh no.

I'm unarmed. My tools are in a box in the wardrobe in our room. That creaking sounds close. I wouldn't have time to get there. An intruder—someone has tracked me down through Barry—fuck, maybe this is Barry? No, no, that wouldn't…Amber! Fucking Amber has broken into our apartment. I should've fucking!

Oh God, what if it's not Amber?

Not wanting the intruder to hear the creaking of the cupboards as I go for one of the knives, I opt instead for the mallet Rick has left out on the drying rack from last night's dinner. Frowning and nervous, I creep through the apartment, phone in one hand, mallet in the other.

I don't want to shit where I sleep.

Oh man, why did this have to happen today?

There's a clinking sound, like glass knocking against something.

I leap into the room, mallet raised, "Arms up, shithead!" and freeze as I see Rick, in the process of scattering confetti over our bed. He's leapt into the air and managed to scatter it all over the floor.

"Sookie! Babe, is that a mallet?" he asks. "What were you planning on doing with that?" He laughs, reaching up to take it from me. "Oh my God, my heart!"

"You said you were at the office!" I splutter.

"I shouldn't try to surprise you again," he says, shaking his head, still laughing breathlessly. "Lest I get malleted!"

"It was the closest thing to grab," I protest. "You said you were at the office!"

Still laughing and reminding me that if I attack an intruder, I'll be the one in trouble (sure, if they find a body), Rick takes me from the confetti-covered bedroom, out to the living room window, up the fire escape and onto the roof.

"This was supposed to be a better surprise," he says, kissing my forehead. "But I was really running late."

There's a little table, set with a cloth, two garden chairs and a pizza box. Two champagne flutes and a bottle to one side. He's put up fairy lights and covered the rooftop with more confetti, most of which is blowing away in the gentle breeze.

"So, is this nice?" he asks.

I'm laughing as I kiss him.

"Awful," I say, "It is in no way, the nicest thing anyone has ever done for me."

He's laughing and tilts me back, smiling down at me. "I'll guess I'll have to keep trying to impress you, huh?"

*

Rick is snoring, peaceful and happy. I glance at my phone and smile down at the photo of us he put up on Facebook. There's the table, the pizza box, the champagne and the rooftop. The two of us smiling, glasses raised.

For the first time in my life, without any disguises or make-up, I don't look like *her* daughter. I look like me. I want to look like me all the time.

Turning my eyes down to the comments section, I notice Amber has left one already. Pre-emptively rolling my eyes in sheer frustration.

> *Aww, I remember when he used to do stuff like this for me.*

*

So, this all started when Barry sent me after this guy José. José worked for a rival gang and Barry had me pretend to deliver a pizza to his apartment before I decapitated him and chopped him into several pieces. He said I could keep the pizza after, but to be honest, after all that I wasn't much in the mood. And besides, it was cold by then.

I never did find out what José did to earn such a violent reaction—usually Barry likes to regale me with an explanation—but no, in this case, my instructions on his demise were particularly detailed. And not just the actual act which Barry asked to be present for. Which felt…weird. He wore sunglasses indoors and sipped a glass of rosé. That part didn't make me feel great. It felt…dirty, intimate, like he'd asked to watch me undress. It felt too personal. But he did stress what a one-off this particular gruesome event would be. So, I did what I do and I tolerated it.

My boss was a captive audience. You know, I don't think I've really had an audience since my friend Beth saw me cutting up a groper one night in the woods when I was fifteen. I don't know why I ended up thinking about that. But it was a good distraction as Barry cheered and gasped. And in the end, he called me a sick fuck, then he offered me some of the cold pizza he had been eating the whole time.

As Apparently-Ivan drove us away, I felt particularly dirty and wrong. But Barry's instructions continued from there. He explained it, twice when he got the strange impression I wasn't listening.

This fucking guy.

Barry said I had to get rid of the body parts, so I did that too. It was actually very nostalgic. I burned a lot of José to be honest, but Barry said I had to get rid of some of the less critical areas (hands, bits of arm etc) in ways so that they could *potentially* be found. And finally, the head had to be dropped somewhere it could definitely be found.

I joked about leaving it in a playground, mostly out of curiosity, and he seemed to show genuine disgust. I don't know what the rules are with this guy, I swear.

So I dug a hole and buried the left hand in a ditch out of town. Apparently-Ivan helped me dig the hole, he was much quicker than me. I left a chunk of forearm in a bin downtown, wrapped it up in kebab wrapping like it was a leg of lamb. I had some fun with a wood chipper back at the warehouse. But then I had the head. I had it in a jar for a few days, musing over where to ditch it—the plan was to toss it off the end of the Santa Cruz Wharf. I mean, it's a nice view, it's a very public place, people toss shit off the edge all of the time.

Give José something to see before he ends up as fish food.

So, we're out there one night, walking along the boardwalk; Carla and Libby pose like they're holding up the moon all by themselves with some careful camera work. Alex buys us all hot dogs because she won her office raffle this week. Then everyone chooses to vanish into the arcade, goofing around, there are shouted promises of Rick winning me a bear or something cute. And it's honestly such a perfect day, I could almost forget that I have an actual human head in my freaking backpack.

Almost.

But yeah, we're eating fries, hanging out, watching the sea and fucking *Amber* arrives. Suddenly it's all, 'Oh remember when we all came here before'—which is super rude anyway because, you know, we're here now, we're having the same experience, so just do that.

"I texted you the other day," she says, prodding Rick.

"Did you?" he says, uninterested, before going back to the zombie shooting game he's playing.

It doesn't deter her. She sits up on the vacant chair beside it.

"So, this is so nostalgic," she says, "Remember when we used to come here all the time? I was like, the queen of that game-" She points to another shooting game, "That game!" A driving game, "And that one, bet my high score is still there!"

She takes out her phone. "Look, look, I was looking at this the other day, there's a photo from back then!" She holds it up. Rick doesn't look up from his game, but Jandro and Dan and Rory have gathered.

"Look, look at Libby's hair!" She shrieks with laughter. "A perm! Hello, what was it, 1985?" She cackles, and then pointing, says, "Oh, wow! Libs, you are so so red! Oh my God!"

Laughter subsiding, she leaps up and prances over to a basketball game. "Yep, my score is here! Look!" But the others seem to have gone back to their respective games.

I roll my eyes and check my phone and try to forget about the severed head in my bag as Rick plays. Amber cheers as she gets a high score on a basketball game.

"Little Sookie King," she calls. "Come over here!"

Rick kisses my cheek as I wander over.

"What?"

She's smiling, bright-eyed.

"Look at this score! You too chicken to face me?" She tosses the basketball hard at my chest.

"Nah, I'm not very competitive," I say. "Couldn't even play sports in high school."

"This isn't sports, Sookie," she says, like I'm an idiot, "This is an arcade game. Children play these."

She's picked her moment to be an absolute fucking asshole well. Rick is playing a loud zombie shooting game with Alex, the others surrounding them, pointing and cheering along.

"Yeah, kids' stuff doesn't really appeal to me," I say. I turn and walk on over to Carla, who is smoking outside the big entrance doors. She winces at me in warning when she sees Amber following me.

"Can I have one of yours?" she asks me, "I can't be bothered to roll one right now." She pouts, holding her hands together in mock prayer, it's a thing with her.

"Sure," I say, passing one over and really resenting it.

"Hey, Carla," Amber says, dismissing me now, "Do you remember when we all came here like…years ago? You were dating that guy… Dean? He was so handsome, God, why did you *ever* break up?" She laughs before turning to me to add, "Sookie, you didn't know Dean." *Obviously*. "Anyway, do you remember, we had those really nasty nachos? Like the cheese tasted like plastic? They were so so disgusting!! Then after, the four of us went and took photos in the booth outside? We should totally recreate that, like, you me and Rick, like a before and after?" She nudges me out of the way to scoot in closer to Carla.

"No thanks, I'm having a bad hair day," Carla says, "The after photo is meant to be an improvement."

"Aw, no way! Hey, we have so many good memories of just messing around here," she says, "Carla, do you remember…"

Fucking hell, I think.

"We're here now," Carla says, genuinely surprising me, "Why not just enjoy that instead of aggressively talking about the past?"

Amber frowns a little, "Hey, who's being aggressive? It's nice to reminisce."

"No," Carla says, "That's not what you're doing and you know it."

Amber looks angry. "Is this because I mentioned *Dean*? There's no need to take it out on me. You know, you should move on, you know? Much healthier."

Carla stubs out her cigarette and laughs.

"I should move on? Wow. Wow, bitch." She tugs her jacket tighter around herself. "Listen, I'm going to go and tell the guys that we're moving this back to my place. Do us all a favour and don't come, ok? I'm done with your bullshit."

Amber reaches out and grabs hold of her arm. I can see her nails digging in.

The two of them freeze up, staring at each other.

Then Amber lets go and dashes past her back to Rick and the others, yelling, "Hey, guys, we should go to The Asti!"

"I've had it with her!" Carla snarls, "I've fucking had it!"

She storms on over after her and as much as I would like to witness Carla losing her shit at Amber, now is probably the best time to slip outside and towards the end of the wharf. There are not many people around, just stragglers, a few tourists, nobody who looks like a cop and nobody who looks like they might come over to bother me, no staff.

It's ideal.

I take a moment to stand back and check out the view, take in a moment before I toss the head. But then…I hear Rick's voice calling me. I close my backpack and turn to face him.

"Hey, babe."

"Hey," he says, "So, Carla and Amber are pretty much going to kill each other." He sighs and brushes back his hair. "They have never really been…best pals or anything, but yeah."

"I know, I came outside," I say, "Uncomfortable."

He hugs me around the middle. "Sorry about that…Anyway, I think the plan is we're going back to Carla's? Amber may or may not be invited."

"Hopefully not," I say, "She's on the war path."

He kisses my forehead, "So, you're coming to Carla's?"

"I'd love to, but I'm meeting up with Leda and Tammy for drinks in town." I say with a shrug. "If we get bored, we can always head over to Carla's place?"

"Sounds good," he says, "Listen, I'm gonna try to get everyone in an Uber as quickly and war-free as I can. Text me, ok?" He kisses me and dashes back into the arcade.

I can hear Amber faintly and Carla, wow, I have never heard her yell.

I text Leda and Tammy to make sure they're still coming and suggest dropping by Carla's later. Tammy responds instantly saying that she's not coming if Amber will be there, to which Leda starts defending her sincerely.

I pocket my phone again and decide to walk up and down the wharf before I come back to this point. That seems sensible.

I buy some candyfloss and sit eating it watching the fairground in the distance. I check my phone, Rick has texted to say that Amber is blowing up everyone's phones with angry texts.

I really wish I was enjoying it with them.

I smirk and pocket my phone again.

Time to ditch the head.

I'm at the edge of the wharf, again, it's ideal, there's nobody around, it's dark. I take out the cardboard box from my bag, unwrap the head from its careful packaging, tossing it out over the side. Then I stand, holding José's head by the hair, just out over the edge.

"So long, José," I say and drop him.

That's when I feel a hand clasp hold of my shoulder. I think for a second that it's a security guard, or that someone has seen me. I turn and stare right into the wide, terrified eyes of fucking Amber.

She is staring past me; she's watched the severed head hit the water.

Did she see what it was?

"Hi, Amber," I say carefully, calmly. "You ok there?"

There's not an ounce of colour in her face.

She *saw*.

She saw me just now.

"I'm fine," she says, her voice trembling a little. "I'm..." She attempts to cough into her hand. "I'm fine, I mean, I'm actually not feeling great. I just...I just remembered that I need to be heading home."

"Really?" I slide my backpack up over my shoulder. "That's a shame. I thought you wanted to head to Carla's?"

"Carla's?" she says, her eyes are wide and it's like she's scared of blinking. I didn't imagine she'd spook like this, she's like a rabbit in headlights. "N-No, no, I'm just going to head home."

"Give me your phone," I say.

She hands it to me instantly. "It died," she says, the word even seems to scare her. "I-It died while I was trying to call..."

"Oh, of course, Rick said you were spamming everyone," I say, handing it back to her. "Well, I don't want to keep you from heading home."

Her eyes are brimming with tears, real ones this time; so this is how she looks when she cries.

"Go on," I say. "Off you run."

I wonder if I look like Mother right now?

She turns and starts walking very quickly, she gets a few feet away and breaks out into a run. My heart is racing in my chest. She saw me. She saw me.

So, that means I have to make her…un-see me, right?

I text Tammy to let her know I'm going to be late—I've spilled something on my top and am gonna go home and change—before I make my way down the wharf and follow Amber out into the night.

Chapter Sixteen

I thought she might try to run to the police or a security guard. But no, she went straight out into the streets. She's looking behind her, stumbling, scrambling. A woman stops to ask if she's ok, but Amber doesn't stop.

I watch her from a distance. She finds a pay phone. I see her hands rattling with the change, dropping it on the ground, scrambling to pick it up. I wonder if she's going to dial 911. That would be smart. But she doesn't. She dials a bunch of numbers and I realise that she's trying to call Rick.

Enough quarters for one call and she tries to call Rick.

I sigh and dial Rick's number before she can finish tapping his digits in with her shaking hands. Of course, she knows his cell phone by heart. Of course, she does. I'm dealing with his stalker here.

"Hi, babe," he says brightly. "You girls having fun?"

"Yeah, I'm just walking to meet them now. Just wanted to check in," I say.

"We're having a good one," he says, "Amber's been calling just about everyone…Carla really sent her off on one this time."

"I know, it was pretty badass of her to be honest."

He laughs. "You promise you'll come and meet us here after?"

"I promise."

I watch Amber hitting the sides of the phone booth as her call inevitably goes to voicemail. I see her trying to gather up change again. Hands visibly shaking now. I can see that from here.

"Ok, I gotta head back in, but I love you, Sookie."

"I love you too."

She is weeping in the phone booth as I put my phone away.

A man taps the side of the booth, asking when she'll be done. She shrieks and rushes out. I watch her walk, looking over her shoulder, scanning the darkness of the crowd for me. She doesn't go into any shops though, any late-night places. She just keeps walking and looking around. She isn't looking for shelter. She's…

I guess it's an animal response in the end. Fight or flight.

And as I know, she's all about the fight.

She stupidly wanders into an alleyway. She arms herself with a broken bottle she's found in the dirt and waits there, crouched amongst the garbage cans. She shrinks back when she sees me, stepping further out of sight and into harm's way.

"I've told Rick about you," she calls. "I told him everything."

"Sure you did," I say. "Could have called 911, instead called Rick, that seems smart."

"Fuck you!" she hisses. "You keep away from me!"

I step closer.

She brandishes the bottle in front of her.

"I knew there was something wrong about you! I knew it! You're a murderer! What, are you going to hurt Rick? I had to warn him! He knows all of it!"

"I called him," I said. "Just to check in when I saw you counting your change. Figured you wouldn't have the survival instincts for 911. So, why don't you stop lying?"

She waves the bottle in front of her frantically. "Keep back!"

"You're pathetic," I say. "What do you even expect to do with that?"

She throws it at me, I duck and it shatters against the wall. She shrieks and leaps back, grabbing another bottle to defend herself, miscalculating in her panic and crying out in pain as she slices the tip of her finger on it.

I just stand back and watch.

"You're a psycho! He should know!"

"You know what's psycho?" I say, "Coming by your ex's apartment every night, knocking the door and yelling through the letter box instead of moving on with your life."

"He loves me!" she says, stepping back, frightened now. "You were just a holding space!"

I sneer and she shrieks and waves the bottle frantically in front of her.

"Stay away!"

"He'd never believe you," I say slowly.

"He would!"

"Not ever."

"He would! He would! *Keep away*!"

"Amber," I say calmly. "You know, I've never enjoyed our little chats. If social decency didn't expect it, I'd have made that a lot clearer."

She swings the bottle in front of her again as I close the gap between us.

"So, I'm not going to debate with you about if Rick likes you more or if he would believe you or whatever," I say. "I don't care. Nobody's here but us and I don't have to pretend I want to talk."

"Stay away!" She flings the bottle again; it narrowly misses my face and smashes against the wall. Then she turns and runs as fast as she can, body trembling, up further into the alley.

It's not much of a chase.

I've imagined doing this often.

I knock her face-first into the wall and she scrambles, kicking blindly, right elbow flailing for me. I reach around her and stab her in the torso, just above her belly button. She stiffens, her arms stop flailing, her legs stop kicking.

She turns and looks at me.

And there's fear.

There's confusion.

Then there's blood.

Now, this is what I do.

I pull out my knife and she gasps, frightened and confused, hands clutching at her wound as she tries to remember how to survive this.

Spoiler, she won't.

She steps forwards, eyes wild and tries to turn to face me, perhaps thinking she can run. Her eyes meet mine and she suddenly has a striking, exact resemblance to my high school quarterback.

She seems to realise that she won't be able to outrun me.

"Help!" she says it softly first, then wincing from the pain in her stomach as she tries to scream, "HE!"

I punch her in the mouth, stuffing her cry for help back inside her.

My foot smashes into her leg and topples her to the ground.

She lies on her back, bloodied hands over her wounded stomach. Her eyes wide in fear, glasses askew across her face.

She's bleeding faster now.

I sit down on her thighs.

She brings her hands up to protect herself as the knife comes down.

Again.

Again.

Again.

Again.

Again.

I slash her wrists. I stab her chest. I cut her face nice and deep.

She wails, undignified and incomprehensible babbling, tears running down her cheeks.

Eventually she stops.

Her bleeding arms come down to her sides and she is quiet.

All is quiet now.

Then in the perfect silence of the city, I detach her torso, I remove her wrists and hands and fingers. I clean her nails and wash her hands to remove any trace of touch from them. It's as I'm removing her ears from her head that I suddenly stop and think, oh fuck.

This is Mother's way. This is Mother's style. This is Red Creek.

And rationally, there's a movie coming out.

Irresponsible it is, really, to make a film about something as sick as that, something as graphic as that, and expect copycats won't come weeping out of the woodwork.

No.

I rub my head with a bloody hand.

No, no copycat.

No messing around with this. She gave up so much for me.

But what to do now...?

I glance down at Amber's ear-less head. She has such a wide forehead. Maybe she'd have hidden it better with bangs...I left it up and smirk and start etching a pentagram into it.

Yeah. Yeah. People are doing satanic murders all the time. Read a history book. Men love to kill women, turn them into mincemeat and decorate the area with pentagrams and all sorts of crazy shit.

I laugh at my own idea and start taking my time, etching out little symbols and markings over her detached arms and legs. I rip a sun onto her stomach. I cut crude hands onto the palms of her hands.

I leave her head on top of her hands and put her heart in her mouth.

I juggle with the idea of making a pentagram out of her limbs, but it seems a lot of effort; like where a perfectionist would start to lose their temper with proportions, etc. So I just leave her there. Maybe a rat or an alley-cat will come by and ruin my crude masterpiece.

But one thing's for sure, she won't be darkening our door any time soon.

*

I call Apparently-Ivan to come and pick me up. It is so much more convenient to have a getaway driver. The only thing that concerns me is if he tells Barry. I stand there in an alley, a few blocks away, waiting.

He shows up. I've put my jacket on over my blood-stained clothes. I smile and he frowns at me deeply.

"I don't recall you having a job tonight," he says.

I climb in anyway and sit down carefully. "I was seen getting rid of the head. When Barry said he wanted it left somewhere obvious, I doubt he meant to do this with witnesses."

Ivan frowned deeply.

"Have you told him?"

"No," I said. "I don't think he'd understand."

"He wouldn't."

Apparently-Ivan turns back to the road and drives me away from there. He takes me home and says nothing. He doesn't even put on his favourite jams. He's as silent as the grave and that's kind of what I need right now.

When we get outside my apartment, he taps the glass so I come to his side of the window.

"Don't slip up again," he says.

He means it.

I nod, but he shakes his head and grabs my covered wrist.

"Really. Don't slip up again."

Then he releases me and drives off into the night.

And I start to wonder how he slipped up. What did he do? What did Barry do? What did it cost?

These thoughts don't last long, I don't have much of a window to shower, clean up and get dressed again. My clothes, I plan on destroying later, they go in a sweaty-smelling old gym bag from my brief dalliance with the gym. I get dressed, texting Rick to let him know I went home briefly to change because I spilled ketchup over my top. He drunkenly tells me that I'd look gorgeous if I spilled all the condiments ever over my top—which is sweet, if slightly odd.

And for the sake of argument, I take out another white strappy top —this is why it's important to have these things—and squeeze out a deft portion of ketchup over it. I then stick it in the washing machine with a bunch of my other clothes.

My hair, I tie up, still slightly wet on my head, wrap it with a scarf and re-do my make-up. Then I call an Uber and wait for it outside, smoking a cigarette. I want to feel stressed—in a few hours, maybe a day—soon enough, in some capacity, I will be informed that Amber's body has been found.

Having avoided getting rid of anyone I directly know for a long time, means that there will be more need to cover up than usual. Nobody is going to haul me in for questioning over the death of a man who groped me in an elevator once six months ago. Amber, however, the irritating ex-girlfriend of Rick? That could require either Rick or myself being questioned at least provisionally.

You have to imagine the worst-case scenario. You just do. Or when things blow up in your face, it will be worse, so much worse and you'll create more chaos from that.

So, in terms of witnesses, alibis, cover-stories, Rick is out with witnesses all night. Another reason why it's so good to have such a big group of friends. As for me, I have witnesses too, Tammy and Leda. And if they want to know where I was for that hour…hour and a half when I was alone, well, sure, I went home to change.

Yes, that stain really is ketchup.

Do I have an interest in the satanic? Erm, no, I do not. I can't even watch *Sabrina the Teenage Witch* without doing a few Hail Marys.

Thank you, shoot me up if you have any more questions.

My Uber arrives and I stump out my cigarette.

Ultimately, this will be a good thing for everyone.

"So, Tammy, where are you guys? I'm on my way!"

*

The media cycle around Amber happens quickly. Her body gets found that night by a group of guys on a bachelor party. One of them vomits all over the crime scene—which is as helpful to me as it is unhelpful for the police investigation. It makes the morning news and Rick tells me about it as I make us hangover coffee.

Her name, of course, hasn't been released to the press.

Just most of the horrifying details.

"This is some serial killer bullshit," he says, "This is terrifying. Hey, we are never splitting up on a night out ever." He wraps an arm around me and pulls me close, and it's sweet, but I find myself smirking into his dressing gown.

"It's terrifying," I say, as the reporter goes on in further detail about the occult-looking symbols that were scratched onto the victim's skin with a sharp object. "It's got to be some sort of cult thing, right?"

"I feel sick," he says, covering his mouth. "Oh, fuck. I'm texting Marco about this. Hold tight." He reaches over to grab his phone. "I'm texting Veronica. I don't like the thought of her going out by herself with this sort of shit happening. Oh, my God, I'm turning into my abuelita and I don't even care. Sookie, you text Marco, I'm gonna call Veronica."

"She won't be awake," I warn him as he gets up to take the phone into the bedroom. "She'll be mad."

*

The notion that anything bad has happened to Amber doesn't come to mind right away. We go about our lives the same as usual. The media circus continues. Lots of shocked citizens, an interview with one of the guys who found the body—that sort of thing. It's different from my accidental murders, and it's a different world to Mother's heyday. Something horrible happens every day in this country. As a culture, we eat it up, spit it out and move on.

It's callous, but it's a way of life.

The grisly murder becomes background noise.

Amber still hasn't been identified, which to be honest, demonstrates how many people she pissed off. I can only imagine her friends are enjoying the break from her blowing up their phones to explain how superior she is (was) to them. I certainly find myself enjoying the lack of late night knocking on my door.

So, a whole week passes and the group of us are crowded around a booth in a bar and the same grisly story comes up on the news. There's a police push requesting people come forward with any information, that sort of thing.

It's background noise, but it catches Carla's attention.

She smirks and says, "Hey, maybe that's why we haven't heard from Amber."

And the guys laugh and tell Carla that she's so cold! We all laugh and then Libby shivers and says, "Yeah, but seriously, has anyone actually heard from her since that night?"

Jandro starts to say that he has—and I know that's bullshit—before frowning and shaking his head. "No, no, not since Carla and Amber's throw-down."

"I figure she's just sulking," Rick says, "You know how it was last time she felt like we ganged up on her. Radio silence until I changed my relationship status on Facebook." He rolls his eyes and scoops an arm around me.

"She's probably using this to make us worry," Starr says, "That is so like her."

Rory shrugs and says, "I mean, probably, but I feel kinda spooked out now, so I'm gonna text her, ok?"

We make ghost noises as he types it up and presses send.

"Don't expect a reply," Rick says, "This is the sort of thing she does. God, I can't believe her. She's a fucking piece of work."

Pieces, more accurately.

But still true.

*

One night, nearly two weeks after I'd killed her, Rory called up Rick, crying. Rick was cooking and dropped a glass on the floor. I rushed in and when I saw the colour drain from his face, I knew. They'd finally identified her.

"He said he went to her apartment after he couldn't get hold of her," Rick said miserably. "He said there was mail lodged in the letter box and it smelled of old food. He spoke to the landlady, who said she hadn't been able to contact Amber either. After that, he went to the police station and…"

He covered his face with his hands.

"She's been there all this time, all alone."

I trained my face into an expression of surprise, then felt relieved when I got to hide it in his shoulder.

*

Slowly, we all get called in for questioning about the night she died. Rick and Carla go first and go under the most scrutiny. Rick as the ex-boyfriend, Carla as the one who started a fight with her hours before she was killed.

The gang is their alibi, of course, I accounted for that. They have receipts for their Uber, witnesses who saw them. So, at last, they call me in, as the only other person who was there that night, who stayed out when the others left.

"How did you and Amber get along?" the detective asks.

He's bald and handsome with bags under his eyes.

"To be honest," I say, because honesty is always the best policy, "and I feel bad for this, after what's happened, but not great. She didn't like me, I didn't much like her either."

"How come?"

"I think she didn't like the idea that Rick had moved on with his life. I think she…maybe thought one day they'd patch stuff up, get back together, pick up where they left things."

"And how'd that make you feel? With him keeping her around?"

I shrug, "Not exactly great, but Amber is, no…wow, fuck, sorry," I pause for effect. "Amber was friends with everyone in the group, I didn't want to be that girl, you know? Telling a guy he has to choose you or his friends."

He nods and rubs the bridge of his nose. "So, Miss. King, that night, can you describe what went down between Amber and Carla Fortuna?"

"Yeah," I say, "We were at the wharf, playing arcade games, Amber hadn't been invited, by the way. Amber…used to do this thing, like, if we were all out, she'd corner me and make mean comments, like while the others weren't listening. Only this time she did it in front of Carla, and Carla called her out on it."

"So, they started arguing?"

"Yeah, Amber made some remark about Carla's love life or whatever and Carla told her not to come out once we left the wharf. She went to walk off and Amber grabbed her."

"Amber grabbed Carla?"

"Yeah, on the arm, she dug her nails in. They sort of froze up, I think Amber realised what she'd done, but then Carla stormed off to tell the others they were leaving and Amber ran after to try to persuade them to go to the Asti instead."

"The Asti, right," he says, writing something down. "You didn't go with them?"

"No way," I say, "I try to keep out of all that, drama, you know? Rick came over a few minutes later to tell me they were all going to Carla's, without Amber. Amber was really mad about it. The others left without Amber, they got an Uber, I think, and I stuck around because I was meeting up with my old roommates for a drink."

"Did Amber talk to you after the others left?"

"Yeah, not at first, like, I wandered around for a few, but she found me, came over and asked me to call Rick for her. She was really mad, I told her to call him herself and she showed me that her phone was dead. I told her mine was too and she got annoyed and walked away."

"Was your phone dead?"

"No," I say, "I just didn't want to get dragged into it anymore."

"Did you follow Amber?"

"No way," I say, "Like I said, I'm sorry she's gone, I really am, and I feel sick knowing that she died that night, but she was…awful to me."

He seems satisfied with that.

"So, what did you do next? You mentioned you were meeting friends?"

"Yeah, I got delayed, I bought a hot dog for dinner and got ketchup all over my white tee. Embarrassing, right? Why wear white? So, I went home to change, met up with my girls around 10.30, I think?"

"And nobody was with you?"

"I called Rick," I say, "But yeah, I went back there alone."

"You didn't see anyone at the wharf acting suspicious, did you? Notice anybody following Amber after she walked away?"

"No, nothing like that."

He pauses. "And your boyfriend, Rick Fumero, has he ever been physically violent towards you?"

"No."

"If you'd be more comfortable, I can go and get a female colleague to-"

"No," I say more firmly. "No, he's never been violent. It's not in his nature. I'd never be with someone like that."

"Then I'm sure you're aware that Mr. Fumero was taken into police custody for exhibiting violence towards Amber-"

"And I'm sure you're aware," I say calmly, "That no charges were pressed against Rick and the only thing he was exhibiting that night, was self-defence."

He smiles then, sitting back. "Anyone ever tell you that you come off a little intense, Miss. King?" His smile is more flirtatious than I'd like.

"Yeah," I say, "It's been said."

He puts down his pen. "And you can't think of anyone who'd wish any harm on Amber?"

"Not in any way that resembles our current predicament, officer."

*

Rick mourns her. I knew he would. Despite everything, this has hurt him so badly. He misses work for a week after they identify her body. I hear him crying on the phone to Amber's mother in Florida. He doesn't sleep. He picks at his food. He doesn't talk or smile.

Whenever I try to make him talk to me, he clings to me and begs in the smallest voice, that we just leave it for a little while.

He blames himself.

It gets harder to sneak off to work for Barry, Rick tails me everywhere. This has made him petrified of me getting hurt. I almost feel sorry for getting rid of her, I hate that I've done this to him. He wears his grief like a wound. He doesn't smile. He doesn't laugh, it's like all of that stuff is a betrayal of the fact that she is gone and she can't anymore. He doesn't want me to touch him, but when we do, he clings on like he can't bear to let go of me.

He doesn't sleep. I wake up to find him staring out the window, off somewhere else. Maybe somewhere with her. I want to turn and make him look at me again, but it's not the time for that. I have to just let him mourn her away.

It is hard though.

He finds an old photo of them in one of his college albums and he cries miserably over it. He tells me that it makes him sad that Amber and I never got along. He says that we could have been friends. He fights with his mother when she suggests that he talk to someone, a professional.

"Where are you going?" I ask.

He's up and dressed on Saturday morning, red-eyed.

"To Amber's place," he says. "I'm helping her mom clear out her apartment."

"Rick, do you have to?" I ask.

He looks startled.

"What do you mean?"

"Clearing out her stuff. You don't have to do that, do you?"

He looks at me like he can't believe what he's hearing.

"You've been finding this so hard. I'm really worried."

"Sookie, there's nobody else," he says.

"Rick, I don't want to see you do something that messes you up. Her family is there. You don't need to hurt yourself this way."

"There's nobody else," he says sharply, eyes glistening. "Nobody. It's just her mom. Her dad left when she was a kid. And her friends —none of them care, not past just doing a fucking Instagram post about her—no. Nobody will help. She had nobody watching her back." His voice catches in his throat. "She died frightened and alone and now her mom has to sort through her things and I can't-" He covers his face with his hands. "I feel sick. I wasn't there for her when she needed me the most."

He gasps and sits back down on the bed and sobs miserably.

I crawl closer and cling to him. He wraps his arms around me and cries into my shoulder.

"I can come with you?" I say. "Today's going to be so hard, please let me..."

He shakes his head. "No, it's ok. It should just be me and Gloria. It's...God, I'm sorry. I just can't believe this. I know how she could be." He coughs, sitting upright and rubbing his eyes. "I know she could be...a real asshole sometimes. But she wasn't a bad person. She didn't deserve something like this and I'm so angry with myself that the last thing I said to her was cruel."

"You had no way of knowing," I say, stroking his hair out of his eyes. "It's alright. I'm sorry."

He hugs me tight to him.

"I'm so scared of anything happening to you."

"Hey," I say firmly, taking his face in my hands to make him look at me. "Believe me, nothing is going to happen to me. Got it?"

He laughs and kisses the tip of my nose.

"I love you."

Chapter Seventeen

I've never been to the funeral of someone for whose death I was personally responsible for. This is kind of a first. They can't bury her body yet because of the ongoing investigation. Everyone stands around an empty casket and we all pretend Amber is inside. I even pretend to be sad.

Amber's father comes and stands at the back, he doesn't stay for the wake; he doesn't say anything. But I spot him after, stood by her grave, silent and trembling. Her mother is the main character of this event. For the most bizarre reason, she actually reminds me a lot of Mrs. Sanders. Her son was the first person I ever killed. It's her anger. They don't look alike—Mrs. Sanders was a soccer mom with her son's Captain America jawline—Amber's mother, Ms. Belflower, is short and tiny with strong arms and short dark hair. She's grieving and in pain, but it's there on her face, she's so unbelievably angry with Amber for leaving her. She speaks with a controlled calm. During the funeral, she refers to Amber bitterly as a 'friendly wise-ass who always got the last word in'. She loses her composure towards the end of her speech and Rick gets up to help her back to her seat. I watch her during the wake, I don't think she really hears anything anyone says to her.

Rick is distraught, red-eyed and silent. He lets go of my hand three times in total. His grip is tight. The boys are all devastated and quiet. Libby and Alex stand guiltily together, knowing they never liked her either. Carla cries bitter, angry tears when she thinks nobody is looking. Starr avoids Rick's eyes and lets Marco talk to Amber's mother. She hands me wake-wine while Rick goes to sit with Ms. Belflower.

Everyone looks…the right amount of sad. I match it and try to pretend I'm not excited. I am excited, really fucking excited. I mean, I don't get to do this. This is the first funeral I've attended that I've caused.

I wonder if this is why Mother went to the Red Creek memorial service every year. A person could get addicted to this.

The ceremony was sombre, they played some Rolling Stones.

As I stand here, sipping wake-wine, I can't help but find a bizarre sense of amusement at Amber's best girlies taking selfies by the flowers. It's Starr who notices them first, she wrinkles her nose in disgust.

"The hell is wrong with them?"

It's the selfie stick, the four of them all gathered together in front of the flowers for a photo. They aren't even like…looking sad or the least bit sombre. These are fully posed pictures, smiling and pretty and…at their friend's funeral…? I guess there really was nobody else.

Holy shit, I'm actually starting to feel sorry for Amber.

I just don't even…?

"Talk about tone-deaf," Marco says.

"I know," I say. "Like, they do know this is a funeral and not a surprise party, right?"

"Don't make me laugh," Starr says. "I'm gonna go tell them to cut it out before her mom sees them."

"Starr," Marco says nervously, following her as she stomps on over.

I watch Starr as she approaches them, knocking the selfie stick aside with a well-manicured hand. She points around the room; I can see how mad she is without seeing her face. I guess grief can even affect you when you didn't like the person at all. Maybe yelling at Amber's strangely identical friends is kind of like closure for her, getting to yell at Amber one last time.

Amber's friends at least have the brains to look embarrassed. Starr keeps away, hugging Marco and trembling. The gaggle of near-identical friends approach Amber's mother with big tearful red eyes and toss the phrase 'thoughts and prayers' around a lot. As if any one of them has ever prayed for anything in their life.

*

I hold Rick's hand when he returns and don't let go until we're in the car on the way home. He didn't see the funeral selfie crew and for that I'm glad. He is quiet, thoughtful and fragile. In the car, he doesn't speak, he switches on the radio and I watch him in profile, notice how his hands stay on the wheel, firm and strong. His eyes are red and sore, but his hands are steady. I know that as much as it hurts now, he will live through this.

When we get home, he goes to bed without a word. And it's alright as I know all this will pass. It may take time, but it's going to pass.

After I'm sure he's asleep, I open a bottle of wine and wipe that stupid sombre expression off my face. I can't stop smiling—and yes, I know how fucked up that is—but I really can't. This has been a rush. This is what my work with Barry is missing. Just wiping people out on his orders doesn't interest me, it's annoying, it's…a chore that makes me feel dirty. But this—this is what I *do*.

This is me. I feel like a freaking teenager again.

I cover my face with my hands and try to get this stupid, gleeful smile off my face. This is like cutting off Riley Sanders' head all over again—without all the teen angst. This is taking the nastiest, shittiest person in my life and getting rid of them, without trouble, without strife.

I finish a second glass and lie back on the sofa, letting out a deep sigh of relief. This is the one thing my world has been missing. The thing that's made me feel so good and so messed up for so many years that sometimes it's like I can't breathe. This is what I do and I'm good at it. Getting rid of Barry's guys isn't the same. There's no choice in it. I'm the gun that lets loose the bullet. I'm the hammer that smashes down doors, that cracks skulls. I am Barry's fist. And after, when the deed is done and I have to be me again, it feels wrong. Like someone else has been wearing my skin and taking my body for a walk.

I sip my third glass and settle back, admiring one of the old scars on my wrist from where I used to dig in my nails so deep and hard. A tiny crescent moon, pale on my skin. It's the only one left, I remember a time my arm was a swarm of them.

This is what I do. Like in high school, with Riley dead and gone, I knew I could pass through those corridors without the same cruelty, without incident. My friend Matt would be safe and sound, without Riley's fists smashing down on his head.

Amber won't come calling here at night. She won't darken our door. There will be no more vile birthday parties for me to attend. Her mother said that Amber was a 'wise-ass who always got the last word'—not anymore.

The leftover wine goes back in the fridge and I walk to bed, feeling settled in my own skin.

The world is just a little bit brighter now.

*

Of course, any feeling of joy or excitement is soon squashed out at work the very next day. I'm sent a strange, nonsensical message from Barry first thing, which he depressingly finishes off with 'More info to follow'.

Great. That's one thing to look forward to.

I return to my desk to find a stack-load of papers all over my keyboard and chair. Gone one day and they turn it into a freaking storage facility. Fan-freaking-tastic. I shift them around and manage to sit down. The others arrive, Claudia mentioning, irritated, that Jack had Corey print the papers and he did the first 200 of them completely wrong—something about the cover-sheet.

"So, he hasn't improved at all?" I say to Donnie, who shakes his head.

"Never in my days, have I met anyone who didn't give a shit so much," he says.

Stacking the papers precariously around my desk is the best Donnie and I can do to shift them for now. I open my Outlook to email-maggedon and try to focus on this—my official, on-the-books job—and not stress about whatever Barry wants me to do. I want to wear the glow I had yesterday. I want to feel good again. Of course, this doesn't happen.

Rick texts me to say that he's up and meeting Marco for brunch this morning to try to cheer himself up. I'm texting my reply when Jack arrives—forty minutes after the office opened but whatever—with Corey the intern, making Claudia's nephew theory seem more likely.

"Sookie, phones away, this is a place of business and not your bedroom," he bellows across the room.

"Sorry, Jack," I say, trying to keep the irritation out of my voice and withholding any remarks about the opening hours of this particular place of business.

He laughs at my response and strides over to the stacks of exam papers piled in the gap between mine and Donnie's desks and Tanya and Rajish's. "And speaking of not treating the office like your bedroom, can I ask why these very important papers are stacked around the floor?" He nudges one with his foot and sends it spilling out across the carpet. "See, things could get lost."

"Temporary solution," Donnie says, "They were standing up on their own *just* fine a second ago."

"As the boss, I've got to keep these things considered," Jack says. "This is what keeps you in your pay-grade, Don." He pats Donnie's seat, laughing again.

"They were all over my desk and chair," I say, "I figured since we'd be working on the exam packs today, it wouldn't matter if we kept them on the floor temporarily."

"I'm the boss and I told Corey to put them there," Jack says—he's very fond of telling us that he's the boss, like we could ever forget. "That's what you get for skipping out on us yesterday."

"I was at a funeral," I say coldly, hoping this will embarrass him into just leaving it alone. However, he has an audience: Corey, the vacant-looking intern, who has, I've just noticed, had his mouth hanging open for the whole of this encounter.

"Whose funeral was it anyway?" he asks.

I blink. Wide-eyed, fucking disbelief here.

"Jack, you can't ask that," Tanya says sharply, minimising her Fantasy Football and swivelling around in her chair. "Come on."

"Hey, it was an honest question," he says, shaking his head. "Come on. I'm just asking, don't mind, do you, Sookie?"

"I mean, sure, some could call that a personal question," I say, "But not me. It was a funeral for my friend, who got murdered recently. She got chopped up and left in an alleyway. You might have heard about it on the news?"

I smile.

The colour drains from his face, and if his expression had a name, it would be called 'Fuuuuuuckkk'.

"Right, right," he says when he's gathered himself. "Back to work, people! Boss's orders!" He goes to make the whip crack noise, but his immediate proximity to both me and Donnie seems to shock him out of it. He awkwardly walks back to his desk, leaving Corey stood, still mouth-open in his place.

"Do you need something?" I ask.

"Erm," he says.

"No?" Donnie offers. "Go sit down."

*

My day does not improve. Corey gets confused about how to use the printer and keeps pushing the same button over and over again. The process of trial and error seems completely lost on him. He chews his bottom lip so much that I want to put some sort of gag in his mouth to cut off his access.

I see him itch his crotch more than once before going and helping himself to the communal cookies Rajish brought in this morning.

"Honestly, he's disgusting, I don't think he even owns a washcloth, man," Donnie says as we walk out to our ten o'clock meeting. "I don't want to upset you more, but I left the bathroom at the same time as him earlier and he did not wash his hands."

"Donnie, you need to keep that shit to yourself," I say, nudging him. "I hope you told him to get back in there and wash his hands."

"Oh, I did," he said with a sigh. "But he just kind of stared at me like I was a freaking space creature or something."

"Hey, if anyone's a space creature…"

He snorts with laughter, then straightens up really quick, "Oh, hey there, Corey, fancy seeing you around."

I turn and see him vacantly staring at us, itching a nostril.

"Hey," he says. "Jack said I should come with you to your meeting or whatever."

"We're good," I say. "Do you know what this meeting is for?"

"No," he says.

Well, at least he's honest.

At least he has that in his court.

The meeting, though I doubt he'd know even after attending, is a board meeting for the improvement of student experience. Jack has upsettingly requested that Corey take the minutes, so I'll have fun trying to decipher his notes later.

Sat around the table, I lean back in my seat and know I won't be able to relax through this one. No way. I glance at Donnie, who is already wincing. I glance at Corey and see that he is already picking his nose. Fantastic.

We go around the table, giving out names due to the slight change in membership. I know everyone here, so I should be able to fix whatever train wreck Corey makes of his minutes… I should probably make some notes of my own.

"Sookie King, Professional Services."

"Donnie James, Professional Services."

I glance at Corey, who is staring off into space. Sensing my gaze, he looks up at the others and says, "Donnie James, Professional Services."

Oh, fucking hell. No, no, why is he still here??

*

At least telling Rick about the nose-picker gets a laugh out of him for the first time in weeks. I get the bus home as I want (and need) Rick to see that I won't die if he isn't there to watch me. I get back to the apartment and loudly tell him about Corey in the meeting while I take off my shoes. I hear him laughing from the kitchen and feel warmer as I haven't heard him laugh in such a long time.

"Hey, you like that, huh? Why not come and try working with him," I say, walking into the kitchen.

"Ha, nice try, no thanks," he says.

He smiles at me and I'm…helpless. He's back.

He's made carbonara, bought us wine, he's shaved off the peach fuzz and put on clothes that aren't sweatpants and a heavy sweater.

He looks like himself again.

"So, is this ok?" he asks, "The wine doesn't taste like vinegar, I sampled it." He offers me a glass. "Well, maybe a little bit?"

I laugh and slide in against him, taking the wine and kissing him gently. "This is certainly a nice surprise to come home to."

Rick grins, "Well, I know things have been… awful lately. It's been hard to see an end to it. But, I needed you to know that it would end. I promise things will be better, I'll be better. Stronger."

"It's alright," I say, "I can't even imagine what you've been through, how you must have been feeling. I hope I've been… supportive enough?"

And you know, long term, I've done him such a favour. His life will be enriched in every way with her gone from it. No more haunting our door, no more crowding, no more emotional manipulation. I know he will never see this as a good thing the way I do, but in the back of his mind, he will know, how could he not? That everything is better because she is dead.

He hugs me close, taking my face in his hands. "Hey, don't talk like that. You have been. You've been so great. Honestly, Sookie, I couldn't have come back from this without you."

I let myself smile and rest my head on his shoulder. "Thank you for this."

I really don't deserve it, but I will.

*

He sleeps easily. That's good, so much better than he's been in a long time. I don't have that luxury yet. Barry's job is playing on my mind, along with the day's annoyances. I close my eyes and itch my brow, flicking through my phone. One nuisance after another, when will I ever have time to rest?

I glance down at Amber's social media profile; her mother is still operating it. It's all baby photos and tiny pieces of her childhood. There's an amusing school report, a funny drawing. It's so weird to think of her like that, as a child, as someone… There wasn't anything like this for the others. Riley Sanders was pushed into my face from the minute he was declared as missing. But we weren't Facebook friends, I was a freshman nobody, he was the quarterback. Sukhy's account was private and her parents shut it down after she died. Jason never had one. It's another first. I've never seen the social media profile continue after a victim is long gone.

I don't like it. It feels too intimate.

Boring.

I close it down and lie back on the bed, scrolling through my next job on my burner phone. It's close by, something minor, just taking out an IT technician in San Francisco. Manageable and irritating. This will mean another drive with Apparently-Ivan and his unfathomable ability to guilt-trip. I slide the phone back into the cubby hanging off the bed and close my eyes.

Best try to sleep.

Sleep is always the solution.

Chapter Eighteen

The technician is cowardly and talks too much. His shorts have a burrito stain near the crotch and there's something really embarrassing about being pleaded with by a man five times my size. He quivers and whimpers and at one point attempts to bat me away with a desk chair he can't quite get a handle on, it's the wheels. The wheels throw him off balance.

I'm wearing a stupid Halloween mask Barry presented me with the second I was in the car. I feel stupid but got the impression that arguing about the costume would result in something much worse in the future. I don't want to get known as like the Lingerie Killer or something. It's the kind of sexist, Hot Murder Girl chick that Barry would know I'd hate.

"Come out from under there, you look stupid," I tell him as he attempts to scramble under the desk, twice bumping his head against the wood.

"No," he says, "No, no, please! Please, I have a family! I have children!"

"No, you don't," I say.

"I might one day," he stammers.

"Come out from under there now. I'll make it painless, like falling asleep."

His eyes are watering. "Y-You promise?"

"Yes," I say from behind the mask. "Come on out."

He staggers out from behind the desk, arms over his head defensively. "I-I can give you money! Not much, but I can!"

"Shut up," I say. "I don't give a shit about money." I wave the gun at him. "Turn and face the wall."

He is crying as he does so, hands clenched into fists. His jaw is quivering. He mumbles something under his breath. I don't catch what it is exactly.

"What are you babbling about?" I ask.

He glances over his shoulder, calming, and as he opens his mouth to explain, I shoot him in the side of the head. He slumps, falls against the wall and is still. I bend down and put the gun beside him. Then I pick up the desk chair and put it back in place. I fix up the desk he bumped into. I take the Starbucks he had just bought and bring it with me as I walk out of the building and out into the light.

*

"I can't believe she's gone," Carla says to me as the two of us wait for the others to arrive. "I have so many mixed emotions about it, you know?"

"It's complicated," I say, "I'm just glad to see Rick is coming back to life."

Carla squeezes my hand. "You don't think I'm a bad person for how I acted towards her that night, do you?"

"No," I say firmly. "Carla, hey, I feel bad for what happened to her. I really do. Nobody deserves that, but… just because it happened doesn't mean that she couldn't be… well, how she was. You argued with her for perfectly sensible reasons that night."

She rubs her hair out of her eyes. "Thanks, Sookie. I didn't know who to talk to about this. Starr has been really confused as well. Amber and Libby feel too guilty and the boys are genuinely missing their friend. I didn't know who else I could talk to."

I smile and shrug. "She was lousy to me. It's been hard to act like… well, how the others are, with all the history there. Mostly I just try to be supportive. She was how she was. But the way she died was awful." Pretty exciting though. I mean, Amber could get her own Wikipedia page, something, I might add, she never would have gotten without me.

You're welcome.

Carla stretches in her seat. "Thanks for this, and for the drink."

"Don't mention it."

Look at me, enjoying a night out with my friends without that little worry in the back of my mind that Amber could appear. Rick arrives with Jandro and Dan. Libby and Alex come from work. Carlos and Rory get there last and the group of us sit and talk and it's all that much nicer. There's an air of her here of course, the ghost at the feast, but it's almost like an unspoken rule, not to mention her.

I'm a fan to say the least.

I ignore the buzzing of my burner phone and find myself relaxing. I can get used to this for a while. I can tolerate all of this bullshit with Barry for moments like this.

*

I get back from work to the smell of dinner cooking. I kick off my shoes and swing off my jacket. "Hey, babe, I'm back!"

But then I see him sat on the sofa with this look on his face, he's pale, drawn and... scared. I can see how scared he is in his eyes.

"Rick, what's wrong?"

He stands up, using the sofa to balance himself. His bottom lip is trembling.

"Rick?"

Then as I lower my gaze, I see that he's got my knives. Ironically, though not in a way I can appreciate right now, the same knives I used to kill and dismantle Amber. He has them all spread out over our coffee table, some taken out of the pouch I keep them in, some still locked in place.

"What is this?" he asks in a small voice.

And there's a chill running through me because I'm not sure how to answer him. What ideas has he already started forming? What does he think this is? What will he believe? Did I clean them well enough? What would he believe?

"Rick," I say.

Already I can imagine him talking to Carlos about this, talking to Jandro and Dan. How would they feel if they found their partner's supply of... knives?

"Why do you have these?" he asks, his voice catching. "Sookie, why do you have these knives?" I look at his face and he's close to tears.

And, Rick, baby, I love you, but there's a knack to you.

I cover my face with my hands, I can get my eyes watering, I can get my bottom lip shaking. I can look so, fucking hurt. I groan and grip my hair and sit down on the sofa and take it as a good sign that he doesn't flinch and move away from me. I say 'goddammit' a few times because it feels about right.

"Fuck," I say and cover my face with my hands. "Fucking hell…"

He waits, eyes on me. I can see how he shivers.

"I just… I…"

He touches my arm. "Sookie, just talk to me. Help me try to understand."

I let myself cry a little, let out some of that stress about something else entirely and brush my hands over my cheeks. "I… I just feel so stupid. I… I have those from like ages ago. When I first moved here, I was just a kid. A-and I was scared. I was so scared. Once, this guy came and he took my phone and my purse and I felt so powerless. I'd taken self-defence classes and even then, I just locked up."

Ok, so, kind of true, he had taken my phone, he grabbed my crotch through my jeans too. But then I stabbed him in the eye with a pair of scissors I kept in my handbag. It wasn't my smartest move, but I was fifteen and really shocked.

"You brought these into our house?" He sounds exasperated. "Sookie, do you know what could happen if you're stopped by the police with these?"

"I know!" I can get my voice to do this horrible, achy tone. It sounds really good! "I know how it would look, I know… But after it happened, I bought a knife… I bought a few, it was like an obsession for a while. Like, if I had one on me then I'd be safe. It's crazy and I haven't carried them with me in years, I really haven't. But I felt safer with them. I put them away, but ever since… well, ever since Amber… I got them out again. I didn't feel safe. I just needed something…"

I was worried about mentioning Amber, but he looks softer, gentler, his eyes are wet. He reaches over and clings to me. He brushes back his hair. "Fuck, I can't have helped with how… paranoid I've been. I…"

"No, it wasn't you," I say, "It really wasn't."

"I never…ever, want you to feel like that," he says. "I never want you to feel like that again. Sookie, really, you need to talk to me. I'll try to be better too. But I don't want it to end up like this, with you bottling it up and me finding… knives in our bedroom."

"I'm sorry," I say miserably. "I'm really sorry. I'm so sorry."

Sometimes, the basics work.

"I'm so sorry."

He's holding me and shaking and stroking my hair and I hold onto him and let myself cry for the right amount of time.

"You have nothing to say sorry for," he says. "I… I wish you'd spoken to me. I really wish you'd said something."

"I didn't want you to find out like this. I'm so sorry, Rick. I'm so sorry…"

"Don't say that. Come on." He is shaking. "But… will you get rid of them, please? Will you do that for me?"

"I mean," I say, "I can try? I'm not sure of like a safe way to dispose of knives?"

He laughs then and leans up to kiss my forehead. "Fuck, it's not exactly googleable either!"

"Maybe I can pawn them?"

He laughs and covers his face. "Fuck, I'm so sorry. I just froze then. Honestly, I just locked up when I found them."

I laugh too and hug him around the middle. "I'll get rid of them. I don't like having them in the house and I know it's not a healthy way to cope."

"Have you ever used them?" I can tell from his tone that he expects the answer to be no, he thinks that he knows the answer is no, how could it be anything but no? I try not to register that the knife he's gesturing to right now, is the one I used to kill Amber.

"No way," I say. "No way, hell, I wouldn't even know what to do with them." I reach down and touch his hands. "The classes I attended were more about defending against a knife than using one. Seriously, babe, I promise I'll get rid of them."

He kisses me gently. "I love you, Sookie."

*

The knives go easily, of course. Barry gives me a suitcase that I leave with Apparently-Ivan. He leaves it in the boot of his car and I take it out whenever he takes me on a job. I leave myself with only a small switchblade that I keep and don't tell Rick about. It stays in my socks, in a big comfy pair I keep but never wear. I'm not leaving myself defenceless, I'm not leaving us without any form of protection.

I can notice the difference already. Rick is back to singing in the shower. He picks me up from work when he can, but he's not as edgy, he's just happy to see me. He's not doing it because he's terrified I'll disappear in a puff of smoke.

I take a deep breath as I glance down at my empty drawer. Nothing to see here. No secret stash. And even though what I told him was mostly lies, I feel... weird for the fact that my weapons are gone. He never found the gun, but I knew it was only a matter of time before he did. There's only so much explaining I can do after all.

Rick glances over at me, "Are you ok there?"

"Yeah," I say, "I'm just feeling a bit tired after work."

"New guy again?"

He has been enjoying the daily updates on Corey and his stupidity—particularly enjoying how Corey sliced through an exam paper diagonally during the moderation period and then tried to hide it in a cardboard box.

"New guy," I say. "Oh, sorry, Jack has insisted we don't call him the new guy, he says it's undermining."

He snorts and shakes his head. "Your boss is something else, you know?" He is in the middle of dishing out our Chinese takeout. I set out our cutlery on the coffee table and settle back against the cushions. "I really couldn't go on working for a guy like that."

"Oh, wouldn't we all like to have our boss as a friend," I say, rolling my eyes. I've met Darren, his boss, who gives the impression that his management style perhaps involves Nerf guns. "Isn't that a wonderful way to live?"

"Hey," Rick says, taking the seat beside me and passing over my kung-pow chicken, "You could make friends with Jack, you know?"

"Don't even!" I swat him and pass over his spoon. "We need one office brown-noser in this relationship only!"

*

The most stressful thing about working for Barry by far is his bizarre drop-in sessions. He seems to enjoy an existence of being equal parts friendly and threatening. Like this afternoon for example, I get a nonsense text demanding that I come out of work and get in the car outside (NOW). There's no choice after that. I had to rush out with some intense sounding excuse to try to avoid Jack's half serious, half joking, all rude line of questioning. Out of the office, there's always a car waiting for me at the end of the street. In a situation like this, I've just come to expect it. Today, I'd not so much as said 'Hi' to Apparently-Ivan when suddenly, Barry lurches out from beside Apparently-Ivan to surprise me, before awkwardly climbing out into the back opposite me while the car is still in motion. He has switched Apparently-Ivan's classical radio to a jarring techno pop channel.

"Hey, Miss. King," he says, "I just wanted to drop by for a chat."

"Is the job fake too?" I ask, refusing to react.

It's my rule of thumb with Barry, don't complain, don't react, don't get mad. Don't give him any sort of reason to make him worse. It's the little mantra I say to myself whenever I must interact with him. I mumble it in the back of my mind when he sends a text. I whisper it to myself when we talk on the phone. I need some way to cope. He likes to remind me that my life isn't my own, my habit isn't my own. My tendencies are reserved for him.

"Oh yeah," he says, "Why would I want you to go and slice up a clown? It doesn't even make sense, does it?" He laughs and shakes his head. "I mean, the circus doesn't even come to town until next summer. Did you know that?"

"No," I say. "That's crazy."

He nods and lights up a cigarette. I notice Apparently-Ivan's brow furrow in disapproval in the rear-view mirror. Barry seems to find it impossible to sit without manspreading. His legs are so far apart that it looks painful. Are legs meant to be that far away from each other?

"Yeah, so no job tonight, just a catch up," he says. "I believe we discussed travel out of state, didn't we? Last time we had a little chat?"

"Well, you did," I say.

He offers me a cigarette, and to avoid the passive-aggressive wrath of Apparently-Ivan, I shake my head. "No thanks."

"Woah," he says, "That's cold, here I am, offering you as my employee opportunities, and there you are, my employee, rejecting me. That's cold of you, Miss. King."

"I've got a lot of responsibilities," I say. "Lots on my mind, you know?"

He smirks. "Like your little job at the college? Forget it."

"See, I can't do that. It might start to look suspicious."

He shrugs, "I'm sure you could think of something. You're a resourceful woman."

"Not when I'm not cutting someone up," I say, because I know that despite his profession and despite how he likes to mess with me, I know the logistics of what I do really gross him out. It's why he flinches when I talk about leaving severed heads in parks. It's why he talked more than usual while I killed a guy in front of him. It's why he sends out someone like me instead of doing his own dirty work.

"Sure," he says, "Whatever you say, Miss. King, but we talked about that out of town work, didn't we?"

"Yes," I say.

"So, say, I give you a month, no, no, three months because I can see you wincing there, don't think I can't. Now, can you get the time off?"

"Yes," I say, because technically I have time to use. "I'd need to check with my line manager."

"Oh yeah, I get you," he says. "Check with him, but I've planned this out for you already. Three days in LA. You'd like that, right? See a bit of Hollywood? See how they do it down there?"

"If you say so," I say.

"Cool, then consider the next month time off in anticipation of that. More details to follow, as usual. But get that time off, I'd say that's the most important thing for you right now." He mimes firing a gun at me and grins that too-many-teeth grin. I hate it when he does that. It tells me that there's nowhere I can hide.

"Sure, I've never seen LA," I say. "A month is plenty notice. Thanks."

I hate how I talk when I talk to him. It's all yessir, no sir, three bags full, sir. It's not my voice. And you know, there are minutes I think I can put up with it, then in the next, that condescending smirk is making me want to puke. I don't want to be some two-bit thug on his payroll. I want to do things my way.

I think about Amber's blood on my hands. Her head resting on the ground, eyes vacant, nose ring red with blood. That's the stuff that warms my heart. Not this, not any of this right here. This is just bullshit.

Barry gets out at some strip joint downtown and Apparently-Ivan drives me back home. I sigh and cover my face with my hands.

"So now I have to worry about whether my jobs are bullshit too," I say.

Apparently-Ivan says nothing, he just sort of grunts before taking out a small spray bottle, the kind my Mother used to use when she attended her fake gardening/landscaping job, and sprays some sweet-smelling liquid into the back of the car.

"He always smoke in here?"

"Only because he knows I don't like it," he says. "He claims to be giving up, says he can only feel comfortable smoking with me…"

"He's such a…"

"Don't say it," he says, more resigned than defensive. "It'll just make you more bitter. You don't need that. You're bitter enough." He puts the bottle back down and starts the engine. "You have him figured out though, that's good. The last person he had doing this job asked a lot of questions."

The whole smoking thing must have pissed him off because he is never this chatty, particularly about Barry.

"Like what?"

"How much longer, why do I have to do this… It went on and on and on until you shot them about six months ago. His name was Kurt. He was a nice man, but stupid."

I would like to say that I remember this person. I don't. But I think Apparently-Ivan would judge me for it. So, I tell him I'm sorry and that seems to do the job. Let him think I remember every single one. He's hardier than Rick, but in some ways, men are similar.

Sorry is really doing the rounds right now.

Oh well, whatever works!

Chapter Nineteen

Another day in the office. I have a severe headache. It's raining outside, and Jack has put an irritating radio station on. Tanya is absent, Kiko is reading a book under her desk. Rajish is at the copier, humming along with the country music playing. Claudia is filing her nails and frowning—Jack has just accused her of being pregnant because she had a big lunch.

Corey is sat staring at the side of Donnie's head while he tries to show him the proper way to sort through the inbox. I can feel the irritation catching in his voice as he explains.

"So, if you look here?"

Corey keeps staring at Donnie.

He looks bored, his mouth is hanging open a little bit.

"Yeah," he says. "It's kind of simple, right?"

Donnie glances over at me and makes a face.

I can't even deal with this guy today. He's been here for three months and it's driving me crazy. He doesn't know how to do anything, and he doesn't care. I really need to know who the hell got him this job. If this isn't a case of good old-fashioned nepotism, then I really don't know what is.

I get up to grab a cup of coffee because it's genuinely painful listening to Donnie try to sincerely teach him. Despite his joking around, Donnie really does care about his job, he takes it seriously and he wants to be doing Jack's job in a few years. I guess this is like a training exercise for him? I wince and fiddle with one of the sachets of sugar.

"Sookie, can I have a word?"

I glance up and see Jack wringing his hands together, uncomfortable.

"Sure, what's up?" I ask.

"No, in G.03 outside?" He gestures with his hand.

"Ok," I say. "I'll just finish up this coffee and I'll be right in."

"Right now, please," he said.

What the heck is going on? I frown and put my half-finished cup of coffee down and follow Jack out of the office. I glance behind me and notice Donnie looking up after me. He mouths, 'What?' at me and I shrug before the door closes.

It feels weird. What's going on? What is this? Jack looks nervous, he's brought a paper and pen with him, which requires a level of forward planning that he usually just doesn't have. He opens the door to room G.03 and gestures for me to go inside. The Deputy Dean is sat in there already—Sandra McCoy, I've only ever seen her at board meetings.

"Hello, Sookie," she says.

"Hi," I say, feeling the colour rising in my face.

This side of things, I'm not used to. This is the kind of trouble I don't like. A flurry of reasons run through my head. What is this going to be about? Is it my documents? Have they found something wrong with my ID? Have they been through my records and noticed something? Is this about my work with Barry? Is this about something else? Are the police coming? I try to calm down, try not to sweat, try not to freak out and just act normal.

I haven't done anything wrong.

I haven't done anything at all.

"Why don't you take a seat?"

I sit down and put my hands on my lap to do a cursory wipe on my skirt.

Jack sidles around the table and sits down beside Sandra. He takes the lid off his pen and starts writing—I glance down and see my name and the date.

"We're sorry for calling you out on such short notice," Sandra says. "But we have a couple of questions that we hope you'll be able to answer." She leans forward and presses her palms together. "But first, is there anything you'd like to tell us?"

"Erm, no, not especially," I say. "What is this about?"

She looks disappointed, purses her lips and takes a deep breath. "This morning, it was brought to our attention that a number of students had received an email that requested their bank account details. Fortunately, a few of them reported this to IT Services, who was able to send out a memo advising them to disregard it. But there were a number of students who submitted their card details and are now suffering the consequences of this." She paused, glancing up at me. "The thing is, we've had cyber attacks like this before, but the initial corrupted email has always been from a fake account that resembles our college site but isn't. The email this morning was sent from the genuine Professional Services account."

Ok, what?

"We have looked into this further, and we have reason to believe that someone is using the college as a way of extorting money from the students in an internet scam."

"What do you think this has to do with me?"

"I asked Jack to point out the names of any member of the team who has been behaved strangely. We have a number of people to question, but your case stood out."

Jack pushes over his notebook to me. "Sookie, I've got a little list here of all the time off you've taken recently. A lot of it has been... last minute. I mean, heck, just last week, you bolted out of the office insisting you had somewhere to be out of nowhere."

"You think I did this?" I say. "Jack, I wouldn't do this."

"Can I ask you to explain these dates?" Sandra asks. "We just want to get to the bottom of this, Sookie."

I glance down at the paper. Yes, these are all Barry dates. Moments where he's had me pulled out of work at the drop of a hat and I've had to go along with it because I know he can make life worse for me.

"W-well," I can feel my voice shaking. "We're allowed to take flexible leave, it's not like this isn't time I've earned," I say. "So, this date here was to rush out to the pharmacy to pick up my prescription. The one on the 17th, I had a call from a friend who was having a crisis and needed to talk. For the 22nd, I wasn't feeling well and wanted to just go home. I didn't want to make a big deal out of it so I didn't use the usual sickness procedure."

Jack frowns. "I don't remember you feeling sick that day."

"Well, I was," I say. "I don't know what else I can say."

"What about last week?" he asks.

"Last week?"

"Yes," Sandra says. "Where did you go last week?"

"I had to go shopping," I say. "I remembered I needed to get some important stuff in for dinner. My boyfriend just got a promotion at work and I wanted to get out before things got too crowded."

Jack doesn't look convinced, neither does Sandra, and I realise that I'm going to get screwed by this. There's something they aren't telling me. My stomach winds itself painfully into a knot and I hold my breath.

"Jack tells me that you're good with IT," Sandra says.

"I'm okay, but I wouldn't know how to even do something like that.? I didn't realise knowing how to resolve an IT issue meant that I'd be accused of!"

"We aren't accusing you," she says. "But we do need to ensure this doesn't happen again. Over \$4000 was taken from the students who provided their banking information. This is very serious."

"I haven't done anything wrong." I said as calmly as I could manage.

She sighs. "Our IT team is investigating this from a technical perspective. There are a lot of members of staff with access to that email address. But honestly, your behaviour has been different, all these absences-"

"I explained those!"

"I'm not convinced by your answers," she said. "And neither is Jack here.. You understand how that must have looked?"

"I wouldn't do this," I say. "Are the police going to be involved?"

"Not yet," Sandra says. "But if we don't identify the problem here, or if this happens again, I believe that we will have no other choice. From what I understand, a less damaging version of this happened two weeks ago. An email sent again, from our central mail box, asking students to sign up for an online feature that doesn't actually exist. We think that this was the guilty person's initial attempt at checking for a response. This was sent very early in the morning. Jack tells me that you're often in the office first. Has this always been the case?"

"Yes, it's either me or Tanya," I say.

"As I understand it, your working hours don't begin until 08.30. What do you do when you arrive at 7.45?"

"I don't start working until then, when I get here early, I tend to just... wake up here," I say, "I tend to check my personal email, or like... make a list of what I need to get done in the morning. Sometimes I watch YouTube clips or something. But I don't use the printer or anything like that. This wasn't me."

Jack sighs, "Sookie, I know you have another phone. I saw messages on it talking about another job."

My blood runs cold.

"Jack, this isn't fair," I say coldly. "Sandra, what Jack is referring to is something he saw on a staff night out. I don't have another phone," I say, "I have my phone and then an old one I've needed to get rid of for ages. I don't use it. My friends send me stupid messages on it. I don't have another job."

Sandra sighs. "Can we see this other phone?"

"I sold it," I say.

She looks resigned.

"Sookie, there's not much you've given us here," Jack says. "Obviously, I don't want to think the worst of my team. But the matter still stands, someone in this office is using company property to access student information and steals. This is unacceptable and can't happen. Not here. And ultimately, you've been behaving strangely for months now. All of these sudden disappearances, strange messages on a phone you say you can't produce."

My heart is pounding in my ears. Fucking Barry. Fuck!

"I didn't do anything wrong," I say, like a miserable broken record. "So, you're firing me for this?" I say, my hands are shaking. "You're going to fire me because I've been taking my variable leave? Because I know how to fix Outlook when it crashes? This is ridiculous! I didn't do this!" Sounding upset and outraged seems to be the best solution, and a truthful one, because I really didn't do this. This job is my little piece of mundanity in this crazy life.

"We are going to launch a more thorough investigation," Sandra says gently. "We have our main specialists working on this. But, for now, as a precaution, we are taking away your access to all of our online features and placing you on professional suspension."

"Professional suspension?"

"Yes, you will be suspended on full pay. We will look into this matter further and be in touch. It may be that we discover some further information which proves your innocence and you can return to the office right away. However, it may be that you are called in for further meetings in light of what the specialists discover." She pushes a piece of paper towards me. "I need you to sign this to show that you've understood what we discussed today."

My hands are shaking as I pull the document towards me. It's a confirmation of professional suspension notice.

"This isn't fair," I say.

"We have to handle matters like this with the utmost care," Sandra says. "We don't know how many other students have been affected. I understand this must be difficult for you, but your cooperation will make things move as smoothly as possible." She offers me a thin-lipped smile.

"Sure," I say. "Sure, I understand."

Fuck, what am I going to tell Rick? How am I going to explain this? And what if I am fired? I won't be able to use this as a reference. Sure, Jack is going to sign off a reference for the apparent exam thief? Fuck. I worked so hard to get a job like this, something stable and professional. Fuck. Fuck. Fuck.

I sign the paper and feel my heart sink miserably.

"Do you know how long this will last?"

"It shouldn't be more than two weeks," she says. "But we'll be in touch."

"This really is a priority," Jack says. "We want this matter rested and put away, Sookie."

"I promise I didn't do this," I say. "This job is important to me. I wouldn't jeopardise it like that."

They nod, but don't say anything.

"What will the rest of the team think is going on?"

"Well, if they ask questions-" Jack says.

Sandra interrupts, her eyes hard. "We will tell them that you had to take unplanned annual leave due to a family emergency. We would in no way create a bad environment for you to potentially return to work into, isn't that right, Jack?"

Jack looks flustered. "Of course."

"Can I go and fetch my bag?"

"I'll do that for you," Jack says, "Do you have a coat?"

"Yeah, it's the blue stripy one," I say. "A-a raincoat."

"Righto," he says, and he sidles past me to head out of the room and back into the office.

When the door clicks shut, I say to Sandra, "What do I do if the team contact me to ask? We're a pretty close unit."

She passes me another form. "For the time being, we need to ask you to sign this."

A notice of no communication, I see, and I feel sick.

"So, if they contact me, I ignore them?"

"No," she says, "But I'd like to ask that you keep what we have discussed completely private. This could compromise the investigation and impair your case." She hands me back her pen. "As I said, the team will be informed that you've had a family emergency, so they shouldn't ask, but please keep that in mind if you do have communications with them."

"Ok," I say in a small voice. "So, I should just head home then?" My voice is shaking, and I dab at my eyes for dramatic effect.

"Yes," she says. "Do you have a way of getting home?"

"I'll catch the bus," I say. "Please let me know if there's anything I can do to help."

She smiles then and offers her hand for me to shake. "Your cooperation really is appreciated, Sookie. This is a difficult process, but we will get through it as quickly and painlessly as we can."

Jack returns with the right coat but the wrong bag.

"That's Claudia's," I tell him.

He looks irritated as he goes back in. I catch Sandra rolling her eyes. He returns with the right bag and wishes me all the best, before requesting that I hand over my staff ID badge. Wow, this is really happening then. Fucking hell. I hand it over, then I do up my coat and feel a bit of relief that they didn't have me escorted off the premises in handcuffs.

*

I lie to Rick about way too many things, so in the end I decide that when I get home, I'll just tell him the truth. I am being investigated at work. I practice the words in my head a lot, I try to make it sound like it's not such a big deal, but that proves to be almost impossible.

There's no way to make 'suspended from work' sound like it's not a potential job-loss situation.

I text Leda about it and she freaks out. Then Tammy starts texting me with loads of questions I don't know the answers to. She's halfway through telling me the number of her family lawyer before I have to call her to insist that it's not a problem.

I wish I could have just shown them my other phone. But it's a burner, suspicious, it's full of messages from Barry—also suspicious. And I don't know how seriously this will be taken. I mean, would they involve the police? How would Barry take having an employee the police are looking into? Could I end up being some anecdote Apparently-Ivan shares with my killer?

Sookie King, yeah, she was a smart girl, but found herself in trouble all the time, that's what did her in.

Ergh, no thanks.

I walk around for a while longer, pick up some groceries before heading home. I don't know what I'm going to tell Rick. I can turn on the waterworks and do it? I mean, apart from all the little unexplainable bits, I know I'm innocent. I know I didn't do this. It's just about the one thing in the world I didn't do.

I know this will pass. It has to.

I get back to the apartment and hear music playing as I get upstairs and slide my key into the door. There's the rustling of footsteps and I open the door to find myself face to face with a short, very beautiful middle-aged woman. I know her instantly, of course, from her photo on the bookshelf. This is Rick's mother, Aleida.

Her face creases into a brilliant smile when she sees me.

"Sookie, right?" she says, taking my hand. "It's so nice to finally meet you! Ricardo, Ricardo, Sookie is home."

I chuckle because nobody calls him that.

Rick pokes his head around the door. "Mom called by, so we have tamales to go with our noodles. Fusion cooking is a thing, right?" He laughs and ducks away, but I can see from his face how happy he is.

I squeeze her hand and smile, "It's nice to meet you at last. Rick is always talking about you."

She snorts, "If he is always talking about me, then why doesn't he pick up the phone more, huh?" She laughs and shakes her head. "No, I'm joking, he knows that nobody in this life has ever had a conversation with me that didn't last about two hours." She is quick to laugh, and like her son, talks as fast as she thinks. It's actually very heart-warming to see her in person. "Come through, I'm sorry for jumping out at you before you'd even taken off your shoes," she says, laughing and shaking her head. "I've become the sort of woman I used to dread whenever I went to a family party. I'm just so excited! My son dates a nice girl for over a year and I don't even get to meet her!"

"Mom! What did I tell you about scaring her off?" Veronica calls from the living room. She rushes out and hugs me tight around the shoulders. "I'm sorry, she was visiting me in dorms and wanted to drop in on you two unannounced."

"Veronica, don't you lie," Aleida says sharply, swatting her shoulder—she is shorter than all of her children and almost has to stand on tiptoe to reach her. "I called your brother this afternoon. That isn't unannounced." She smiles at me, bashful now. "What will they have you thinking of me?"

"Sookie, you'll quickly find that it's impossible to say no to this lady," Veronica says, "Come sit down."

As I sit down at my dinner table—which is looking a lot more glamourous than usual (did we have candles or did Veronica and Aleida bring those with them?)—I realise that there is no way in Hell I'm going to be able to tell Rick about the situation at work. This is going to be just another thing to lie to him about because I can't do it. I can't disappoint him like that.

Rick comes out with hot bowls of noodles and a plate full of tamales, grinning. He puts them down and kisses his mother's cheek and yup, I'm going to have to lie. I don't deserve to be a part of this beautiful family. I'm not good enough and I don't want them to see it yet.

I tuck into my noodles and prepare myself for the inevitable mom questions that will pop up. I am woefully unprepared for this, as I haven't met parents before. I never got to that level. Plus, even from a friends' point of view, my own mother was a terrible example. I could have brought anyone back to the house and she wouldn't have asked them a damn thing. Fortunately, I went to dinner at my friends' homes a lot. Mrs. Green and Mrs. Khan could question better than most FBI interrogators.

"So, Sookie, Ricardo is always talking about you, but he was not clear about what it is you do," Aleida says cheerfully. "You work in a university, right?"

This is where the pre-preparation comes in, because nobody's forever career ever included staring at a screen and taking cranky calls. But also, nobody likes the idea of their kid dating some loser in a dead-end job or someone who seems bored out of their skull by their life.

"Yes," I say, "It's administration, sort of like ensuring the students' programmes are correct and that they have everything they need to progress and graduate and stuff. It doesn't sound very interesting when I say it like that," I add, laughing at my own expense.

"No, no, that is important work," she says. "Did you go to college yourself?"

This is another one I'm prepared for. Everyone goes to college; it's becoming much rarer not to. But I mean, it isn't the be-all and end-all. I mean, college would have been nice, but I only wanted to go because my best friend from childhood did. I don't think I would have done much and would probably have ended up in the same sort of job, anyway. And come on, Lisa goes to college and she's famously stupid, Amber went to college and she's *dead*.

"No," I say, "I was always working from when I finished high school, I never really found the time and now, to be honest, I'm not sure it was for me. But it's nice to see other people go through that process."

"That's lovely," she says.

I know she won't ask about family straight away; I'm sure Rick has prepared her with my made-up but still depressing backstory. Time to regain control of the conversation.

"These tamales are amazing," I say, "Have you always made them yourself?"

"Oh, aren't you sweet?" she says, "Yes, my mother taught me, I have tried to teach my children, but alas, I'm not that good a teacher."

"It's the greatest disappointment of my life," Rick says sadly.

Veronica shrugs, "I can't fry an egg without burning it so don't look at me."

"Oh well, I can cook for all of you, I suppose!" She shakes her head and takes another bite. "Do you cook at all?"

"I can," I say, "But Rick is better."

"You must be terrible," Veronica says.

Her mother swats her again, "Manners!"

I laugh, "No, no, it's all good! It's something I fell out of practice with, but I'd like to get back into. Cooking, I mean, this relationship sometimes feels a little one-sided." I reach across to squeeze his hand as he insists that it's not, it's really not.

"It is good to share," Aleida agrees, "When I dated Ricardo's father, he loved to cook for me and kept his apartment wonderfully clean. Then as soon as we got married, wham, he stopped taking care of himself at all and expected me to wait on him hand and foot!"

At the mention of their father, I notice Rick and Veronica exchange a nervous glance.

"That's no good," I say, looking to shift the subject away, "My old roommate Leda has this girlfriend, Tammy, she's from a super-rich family and doesn't know how to do the most basic things for herself. It's where half their fights come from."

This makes her laugh. "Is Tammy very academic? Sometimes these things go hand-in-hand, the better the grades, the worse the life skills. Their big sister, Maria is like that. She has a doctorate in radiology but forgets to eat if she's stuck in a good book. When she went away to college, I was afraid she'd lose her head somewhere."

"I've heard that," I say, "Actually Tammy is very academic, she's doing her masters in psychology but also can't make her own sandwiches." This earns a laugh from around the table. "Leda once found her putting margarine on mouldy bread."

"Oh no!" Aleida gasps, "That would stress me out. How could you leave someone alone like that?"

"I've met Tammy and can confirm that I once saw her cross a road without looking because she thought she saw Blake Lively," Rick says, smirking.

"Oh, Blake Lively is beautiful," Aleida says, "I'd like to meet her."

"Not at the cost of your life, Mom!"

We all start laughing and I forget about the investigation and stupid Jack and just find myself settling into this, this situation I was always so nervous of. I could really get used to being a part of a family like this one. And that's not going to happen if I keep telling lies.

*

After Aleida and Veronica head home, Rick hands me a cup of coffee as I finish unloading the dishwasher. He kisses my cheek.

"Sorry, Mom can be kind of intense."

"No, no, she was very sweet."

He looks happy. "I'm really glad she met you. I've wanted to do it for ages, but with her living upstate, there just wasn't the right opportunity, you know?"

"I'm really glad I got to meet her, you're always talking about her, I kind of felt like we'd met already." I rest my head on his shoulder. "This evening was lovely, it really was. Thanks for this... So, listen, I have kind of some bad news, I'm sorry I didn't say before, but I was just so excited to meet your mom that it kind of slipped away."

He looks concerned. "What's up?"

"So, first you have to promise not to freak out..."

"Sookie, in the history of that phrase, I think with absolute certainty that it has never, ever, ever worked. So, I'll do my best, but no promises." He folds his arms, "What's happened?"

"I've been suspended from work," I say, "On full pay, so don't worry about the rent."

He opens his mouth, but I hold up my hands to stop him.

"Someone in the department has been conning students out of money," I say. "They are investigating it. I'd left for the day when it was used. I'm hoping this will be resolved soon."

"Sookie, they can't do this, can they?"

"They have," I say, "There's honestly nothing else I can do at this point. I'm sorry to get dragged into this drama." I hug myself around the middle. "I'm not scared. It'll be fine. I mean, I wasn't off selling them, so I have nothing to worry about. Yeah, it kind of freaked me out earlier. I was a mess-"

"Why didn't you call me?"

"I didn't know how to say it," I admit. "I was so upset that I'd let you down."

"You haven't." He smiles so gently that I feel even worse. I don't deserve this. I really don't deserve any of this right now. He hugs me tight and brushes back my hair. "I love you so much. This will blow over. You haven't done anything."

I wish he could say this about every part of my life, that I could come to him innocent and sweet and… without any of the stuff that stains me and everything I touch with that same, familiar red. But, at the end of the day, there's only so much I can do.

I deserve to be happy. Don't I?

Chapter Twenty

Darren, the world's best boss has given the OK on Rick working from home a few days a week. This has created an environment so nice that I forget that I'm in so much shit at work. It's the kind of peaceful living you just don't get with an 8-5.

Some people would feel too freaked out by the thing at work to sleep peacefully in their bed. But some people haven't lived with homicidal feelings since childhood and it shows. This feeling of tension about work doesn't bother me. I've dealt with worse. And I know I'm going to have to come up with some wild story about needing to go to LA soon, but that's out of mind for now. I have another two months off from Barry and his bullshit.

I get to sleep in—something I never do. I sleep all damn morning. It's the best. As a teenager who missed out on the later years of being a teenager, I never really got to appreciate a lie-in the same way. It's good. Waking up without alarm clocks, just the sun creeping through the blinds. A kiss on the forehead as Rick murmurs 'goodbye, babe' before he leaves for work. This has been an amazing two weeks.

On days he works from home though, it's much better. There's something so safe about waking up beside him, listening to his heartbeat. Sleeping fitfully and then wandering out of bed, eyes half open to make us coffee, trying to find something you could call breakfast. Having the time to talk, watch shitty cartoons in bed, spend the morning doing nothing.

"You ok?" he asks.

"Why wouldn't I be?"

He laughs and rests his head on my shoulder.

"Do you want to do something today?"

"Something like what?"

Rick leans down and raises an eyebrow. "Like, head out somewhere nice, like a date, hit up the town, drive out somewhere pretty."

"Aren't you supposed to be working?"

"Oh, wow, I see your priorities," he says, leaning down to tickle my side. "You don't want to have any fun with me? You wanna stay home and watch me work?"

"Don't tickle me! Hey! You know I hate that! Hey!"

*

I guess we're both ditching work!

Rick is humming as he riffles through a rack of albums, I have no idea what it is that he's humming but he's trying his best. I chuckle to myself and slink over, resting my head on his shoulder.

"Found anything good?"

"A few good things, nothing I can afford."

"I can get it for you on my student con-artist salary?"

He laughs and nudges me. "I'm glad you can joke about that so easily."

"Life is better with humour." I shrug my shoulders and step back. "I'm going to look at the magazines. You want to meet me there?"

He nods and goes back to that tuneless humming, sometimes turning it into a whistle. I smile as he taps his foot, before turning and walking downstairs towards the large array of magazines. There's a poster on the wall for the upcoming Red Creek movie. It's got both Scarlett Johansson and some actress from *Riverdale* stood knee deep in red water.

I roll my eyes and pick up a National Geographic.

I wish they wouldn't market it like a goddamn action movie. Like, actual people died. I wish I could stand here for a few minutes without giving it another thought. I wish I could forget they were making this fucking thing at all. But I can't and, ever the narcissist, I find myself fishing through the rack for a film and TV magazine.

I lean against the wall and flick through until I find an article about it, her, the film about her. I feel my stomach twisting into a knot as I read a quick update, an interview with the director, glance at the photos from the set, of the cast. I want to look at this objectively. The location isn't my hometown. I doubt there will be as much rain. I doubt the humidity will come across. I bet the woods will look more *Twilight* than they ever were.

But it looks enough like home to create a hole in my heart.

They haven't filmed at my old school because holy shit, could you imagine how in poor taste that would be? But they've recreated it. There it is. I touch a glossy page and remember that boring building with its mismatched bricks. I can almost smell it, the dusty books, the cafeteria food, the smell of Jason's AXE body spray, the floor polish.

You don't think you'd dwell on a thing like floor polish?

Well, then maybe you've never been far from home.

"Oh man, that movie again?" Rick says, tapping the paper. "I thought you hated all that *Making a Murderer* stuff?"

I close it instantly and put it back. "Oh, I do. It's just not for me. But this, I mean, yeah, I'm going to go and see it."

"Really?" He takes the magazine and rifles through. "I'll come with you. I just feel kind of conflicted about seeing it. It's such a sad story. She still won't say where she buried her daughter, like, not even to this day."

My heart sinks.

"Apparently, she's been approached by one of the other victim's parents more than once, but she hasn't said anything. She just said that she got rid of it."

I remember those texts.

Your friend's parents came here today, asking after you. Wanted to bury you with her.

"It's a really sad story, but I think I can handle it if you can?" I say and take the magazine from him, sliding it back onto the rack. "Come on, let's go get lunch."

*

"Let's go here," Rick says brightly.

I look up at the Orchid, the place where we met, I glance back at him and fold my arms. "Are you out of your mind?"

"No," he says, "Come on, let's go to the Orchid, it'll be funny."

"No way," I say, "Do they even do food?"

"Yes," he said, "They serve cakes and sandwiches in the day, see," he adds, gesturing to a sign hanging from the wall.

"Pfft," I snort, "They can't even be bothered to clean the floor so I don't even want to know what the hell their sandwiches will turn out like."

I go to leave, but he takes my hand and squeezes it. I look up at him and he's smiling. He winks at me. "Come on, let's check it out for just a minute."

"Ok, weirdo," I say, smirking and shaking my head. I let him lead me up the steps—the entrance looks weird without the threatening-looking bouncer, without a gaggle of drunk girls barely able to stand. He leads me inside and yes, surprisingly, the Orchid makes quite a classy affair in the day.

"Look, there's a potted plant," I say.

"Wow, that's something special," Rick says, laughing and kissing my hair. "But we aren't here for that." He squeezes my hand gently and leads me up the stairs.

There are a few people eating at these cute little tables set up around the dancefloor. The floor is still sticky, I notice, and feel regret at wearing my nice sneakers in here. The diners are all pretty old, like at least in their seventies. Is this who the Orchid caters for in the day? I'm so incredibly confused.

Rick leads me up onto the VIP deck, or where that would typically be if we were here late. It's kind of nice in the day, just a small table, vase, flowers, daylight. I go to sit down, but Rick stops me. He pulls me close to him and takes my hands in his.

"So, the Orchid has the dirtiest, stickiest floor in California," he says, "I'm stating that as a fact because I don't want to know about anywhere worse. I didn't like coming here, I lost my favourite shoes to this floor once. But, a year and four months ago, I came here on a boy's night with Miguel, who ditched me within about twenty minutes." He brushes a lock of hair behind my ear. "I was sitting around here, bored and booking a ride home, when I heard this girl claiming that she worked for the Men in Black to try to ditch some slack-jawed guy hitting on her." He laughs. "Somehow, I got lucky and I managed to convince you to see me again after that night."

"Hey, luck had nothing to do with it," I say.

He laughs and kisses me. "Sookie, I know the last few months have been turbulent. I know there have been times where I haven't been the man you needed me to be and I'm sorry about that. But, if all of this grief and craziness has taught me anything, it's that I need you with me." He goes to bend down, I grab his arm.

"Rick, the floor!" I'm laughing, feeling tears brimming in my eyes.

"Hey, hey, let me do this," he says, getting down on one knee. "Sookie, I love you, I want to spend my life with you." A small wooden box comes out of his pocket, he lifts it up towards me, opening it. Inside is a round golden ring with a black pearl centre, surrounded by tiny bright diamonds. "I want to give you the kind of life you deserve." He smiles then, that warm, happy smile that makes me feel so…"Will you marry me?"

And I'm crying as I leap down and kiss him, holding his face in my hands, feeling that dumb peach fuzz against my fingers. I know I'm crying, my voice coming out high and loud and breathless.

"Yes! Yes! Oh my God!"

The world seems to slow down and all the old people eating around little tables, the sticky floor, the bad lights, the pot plants, all of them disappear in an instant.

It's just me and him.

That's what I want forever to be.

Chapter Twenty-One

Darren, the world's best boss has given the OK on Rick working from home a few days a week. This has created an environment so nice that I forget that I'm in so much shit at work. It's the kind of peaceful living you just don't get with an 8-5.

Some people would feel too freaked out by the thing at work to sleep peacefully in their bed. But some people haven't lived with homicidal feelings since childhood and it shows. This feeling of tension about work doesn't bother me. I've dealt with worse. And I know I'm going to have to come up with some wild story about needing to go to LA soon, but that's out of mind for now. I have another two months off from Barry and his bullshit.

I get to sleep in—something I never do. I sleep all damn morning. It's the best. As a teenager who missed out on the later years of being a teenager, I never really got to appreciate a lie-in the same way. It's good. Waking up without alarm clocks, just the sun creeping through the blinds. A kiss on the forehead as Rick murmurs 'goodbye, babe' before he leaves for work. This has been an amazing two weeks.

On days he works from home though, it's much better. There's something so safe about waking up beside him, listening to his heartbeat. Sleeping fitfully and then wandering out of bed, eyes half open to make us coffee, trying to find something you could call breakfast. Having the time to talk, watch shitty cartoons in bed, spend the morning doing nothing.

"You ok?" he asks.

"Why wouldn't I be?"

He laughs and rests his head on my shoulder.

"Do you want to do something today?"

"Something like what?"

Rick leans down and raises an eyebrow. "Like, head out somewhere nice, like a date, hit up the town, drive out somewhere pretty."

"Aren't you supposed to be working?"

"Oh, wow, I see your priorities," he says, leaning down to tickle my side. "You don't want to have any fun with me? You wanna stay home and watch me work?"

"Don't tickle me! Hey! You know I hate that! Hey!"

*

I guess we're both ditching work!

Rick is humming as he riffles through a rack of albums, I have no idea what it is that he's humming but he's trying his best. I chuckle to myself and slink over, resting my head on his shoulder.

"Found anything good?"

"A few good things, nothing I can afford."

"I can get it for you on my student con-artist salary?"

He laughs and nudges me. "I'm glad you can joke about that so easily."

"Life is better with humour." I shrug my shoulders and step back. "I'm going to look at the magazines. You want to meet me there?"

He nods and goes back to that tuneless humming, sometimes turning it into a whistle. I smile as he taps his foot, before turning and walking downstairs towards the large array of magazines. There's a poster on the wall for the upcoming Red Creek movie. It's got both Scarlett Johansson and some actress from *Riverdale* stood knee deep in red water.

I roll my eyes and pick up a National Geographic.

I wish they wouldn't market it like a goddamn action movie. Like, actual people died. I wish I could stand here for a few minutes without giving it another thought. I wish I could forget they were making this fucking thing at all. But I can't and, ever the narcissist, I find myself fishing through the rack for a film and TV magazine.

I lean against the wall and flick through until I find an article about it, her, the film about her. I feel my stomach twisting into a knot as I read a quick update, an interview with the director, a glance at the photos from the set, of the cast. I want to look at this objectively. The location isn't my hometown. I doubt there will be as much rain. I doubt the humidity will come across. I bet the woods will look more *Twilight* than they ever were.

But it looks enough like home to create a hole in my heart.

They haven't filmed at my old school because holy shit, could you imagine how in poor taste that would be? But they've recreated it. There it is. I touch a glossy page and remember that boring building with its mismatched bricks. I can almost smell it, the dusty books, the cafeteria food, the smell of Jason's AXE body spray, the floor polish.

You don't think you'd dwell on a thing like floor polish?

Well, then maybe you've never been far from home.

"Oh man, that movie again?" Rick says, tapping the paper. "I thought you hated all that *Making a Murderer* stuff?"

I close it instantly and put it back. "Oh, I do. It's just not for me. But this, I mean, yeah, I'm going to go and see it."

"Really?" He takes the magazine and rifles through. "I'll come with you. I just feel kind of conflicted about seeing it. It's such a sad story. She still won't say where she buried her daughter, like, not even to this day."

My heart sinks.

"Apparently, she's been approached by one of the other victim's parents more than once, but she hasn't said anything. She just said that she got rid of it."

I remember those texts.

Your friend's parents came here today, asking after you. Wanted to bury you with her.

"It's a really sad story, but I think I can handle it if you can?" I say and take the magazine from him, sliding it back onto the rack. "Come on, let's go get lunch."

*

"Let's go here," Rick says brightly.

I look up at the Orchid, the place where we met, I glance back at him and fold my arms. "Are you out of your mind?"

"No," he says, "Come on, let's go to the Orchid, it'll be funny."

"No way," I say, "Do they even do food?"

"Yes," he said, "They serve cakes and sandwiches in the day, see," he adds, gesturing to a sign hanging from the wall.

"Pfft," I snort, "They can't even be bothered to clean the floor so I don't even want to know what the hell their sandwiches will turn out like."

I go to leave, but he takes my hand and squeezes it. I look up at him and he's smiling. He winks at me. "Come on, let's check it out for just a minute."

"Ok, weirdo," I say, smirking and shaking my head. I let him lead me up the steps—the entrance looks weird without the threatening-looking bouncer, without a gaggle of drunk girls barely able to stand. He leads me inside and yes, surprisingly, the Orchid makes quite a classy affair in the day.

"Look, there's a potted plant," I say.

"Wow, that's something special," Rick says, laughing and kissing my hair. "But we aren't here for that." He squeezes my hand gently and leads me up the stairs.

There are a few people eating at these cute little tables set up around the dancefloor. The floor is still sticky, I notice, and feel regret at wearing my nice sneakers in here. The diners are all pretty old, like at least in their seventies. Is this who the Orchid caters for in the day? I'm so incredibly confused.

Rick leads me up onto the VIP deck, or where that would typically be if we were here late. It's kind of nice in the day, just a small table, vase, flowers, daylight. I go to sit down, but Rick stops me. He pulls me close to him and takes my hands in his.

"So, the Orchid has the dirtiest, stickiest floor in California," he says, "I'm stating that as a fact because I don't want to know about anywhere worse. I didn't like coming here, I lost my favourite shoes to this floor once. But, a year and four months ago, I came here on a boy's night with Miguel, who ditched me within about twenty minutes." He brushes a lock of hair behind my ear. "I was sitting around here, bored and booking a ride home, when I heard this girl claiming that she worked for the Men in Black to try to ditch some slack-jawed guy hitting on her." He laughs. "Somehow, I got lucky and I managed to convince you to see me again after that night."

"Hey, luck had nothing to do with it," I say.

He laughs and kisses me. "Sookie, I know the last few months have been turbulent. I know there have been times where I haven't been the man you needed me to be and I'm sorry about that. But, if all of this grief and craziness has taught me anything, it's that I need you with me." He goes to bend down, I grab his arm.

"Rick, the floor!" I'm laughing, feeling tears brimming in my eyes.

"Hey, hey, let me do this," he says, getting down on one knee. "Sookie, I love you, I want to spend my life with you." A small wooden box comes out of his pocket, he lifts it up towards me, opening it. Inside is a round golden ring with a black pearl centre, surrounded by tiny bright diamonds. "I want to give you the kind of life you deserve." He smiles then, that warm, happy smile that makes me feel so…"Will you marry me?"

And I'm crying as I leap down and kiss him, holding his face in my hands, feeling that dumb peach fuzz against my fingers. I know I'm crying, my voice coming out high and loud and breathless.

"Yes! Yes! Oh my God!"

The world seems to slow down and all the old people eating around little tables, the sticky floor, the bad lights, the pot plants, all of them disappear in an instant.

It's just me and him.

That's what I want forever to be.

Chapter Twenty-Two

After getting some sleep, I knew I'd feel better. A bit of shut eye and I'm ok. I'm really ok.

In fact, I'm so ok I get into the hospital first thing. Getting inside turns out to be easy. It's a hospital so of course it's always slightly busy. They have a Starbucks inside, which seems crazy. I sit around there for a bit, people-watching. There are hot young doctors who hang around chatting and looking like they should be playing doctors on TV rather than actually getting their hands dirty. There's a group of PTA moms, who share a croissant between the four of them whilst looking very hungry.

At two, a gaggle of old people in hospital gowns take a very slow stroll around the corridor, all kitted out with walkers. Some chatting to each other, others steely eyed and focused on each step. It's kind of heart-warming to watch. Mostly, I'm checking to see if Mr. Silverman is among them.

He's not.

So, after the silver surfers have gone, I decide to stretch my legs. The interesting thing about walking around these sorts of wards, Frappuccino in hand, is that nobody really stops you. They assume you're grieving or walking off hearing bad news. Nobody stops me as I walk through, brazenly checking the names on doors, openly staring in at people.

Will Mr. Silverman be expecting this?

I suppose at his age and assumed fragile condition, maybe a good shock will give him a heart attack? No, that's the other thing, Barry has insisted natural-looking causes. He didn't enjoy my suggestion of 'time'. Strangely out of character, he just went really stiff and told me to do my fucking job.

Not very friendly.

I guess this Silverman guy must be a real specimen.

I find him in the end, he has a private room on the top floor. It's a pretty swish place he's got, big spacious room, a big TV, and a great view. The family appears to have saved no expense in giving Mr. Silverman the finest care money can buy.

However, the old man is deaf and blind so I doubt he appreciates these kinds of extravagances the same way he might have done before. I notice a bowl of expensive-looking fruit rotting in the corner. There's a dusty family photo by his bedside. Mr. Silverman stays in his bed, the remote to the television just out of reach.

The young and pretty nurse in particular is the nastiest piece of work I've ever seen.

I found the room because of her. In a hospital where everyone speaks softly out of grief or angrily out of emotion, there's not a lot of space for cruelty. I passed room after room, hearing crying or gentle whispering; it kind of blended in together like background noise.

"I hope you choke on that water, you disgusting pig."

It shocked me, actually shocked me.

We might think these sorts of things about someone. I know I did for Amber. But we don't say them out loud. The only time you would say something like that is if you felt…100% like you wouldn't get caught. So, I glanced in through the window and there he was, Mr. Silverman, my target, sat up in bed, drinking a glass of water, while the beautiful young nurse taking care of him stood over, smiling as she said a torrent of hateful things.

It made me feel uncomfortable, watching through the slight window above the door handle. She was so…unashamed of how vile she was being, so confident that nothing would happen. I could hear her as I passed by—anyone would hear her.

Again, I thought of telling Barry, natural causes would come with time. Whether this is his deteriorating naturally, or by the neglect expressed by his only carer.

"You're hurting me," he told her, only once as she wrenched him upright by the wrist to make him take a walk from the bed so she could change the sheets. She bundled him over to the window and cruelly told him to appreciate the view. "I have to change these sheets. They're disgusting! You're disgusting!"

"I'm sorry," he told her meekly.

I watched her take his hearing aid, claiming that it needed to be cleaned. She dropped it down the back of the television after a few minutes and left the room. She passed me in the corridor, ever the picture of professionalism.

And this is why hospitals scare the shit out of me. You can work your whole life and end up at the mercy of an actual sociopath like that. Fucking hell.

I follow her out of curiosity. She doesn't notice. She's half on her phone to her boyfriend—I guess there really is someone out there for everyone—half snapping the head off the barista in Starbucks.

The other nurses see her and try to get out of her line of vision as quickly as humanly possible.

"Any plans for tonight, ladies?" she asks.

"On shift until two," the younger of the two says awkwardly. "So, it's fridge leftovers for me and then bed."

"I'm off at seven, but I gotta take my daughter to her audition," the other says. "I can't wait to get home."

Bitch-Nurse smiles a cold, simpering smile. "Oh, you guys! I'd love to have a chilled night in like you! I have yoga after I finish, then Brian is taking me out for dinner! It'll be somewhere nice, he has very, very good taste!"

"Uh-huh," the older nurse says, her lips drawn into a tight line.

"Well, can't stop and chat," Bitch-Nurse says brightly. "You two have a nice day now!" She pats one of them patronisingly on the arm before skipping off to continue her human rights violations.

"I can't stand her," the younger nurse says furiously. "She does the barest bare minimum!"

"She has one patient, she never helps but acts like a goddamn saint."

"I hope she chokes on her oysters."

"And they take her to another hospital," the older nurse says, laughing. "Come on. We actually have work to do."

I smirk and take the stairs on my left, back up to Mr. Silverman's room.

That poor old man is paying through the nose for personalised care.

This is fucking horrible to watch.

Couldn't Barry have sent me after this bitch instead?

I return to the outside of Mr. Silverman's room to find Bitch-Nurse dragging him by the scruff of his gown back into bed. He tries to cover himself, ashamed as the robe comes undone.

"What the hell do you think I'd want to see that for? Are you proud of it or something?" she sneers, stopping to fix his clothes for him. "I could sue you for exposing yourself to me like that."

Mr. Silverman's glassy eyes are unfocused but clouded with pain.

"I was looking for my hearing aid!" he protests. "You didn't give it back!"

"I did," she says. "Honestly, you're confused again. It's here. You must have misplaced it." She hands him back the hearing aid. "I swear, if I ever get as old as you, I'd rather just die than be such a useless burden on everyone."

"Stop it," he says. "I'll report this!"

"To who?" she asks brightly. "No, really, tell me because I'm struggling to think of a single person who'd care."

It breaks my heart when he doesn't respond. He sits back on the bed, fumbling with his hearing aid.

"Can't you even manage that?" she asks, leaning down to re-attach it for him.

"Thank you, Jenny."

*

She finishes at five and goes home. Mr. Silverman is alone for most of the night. He has a buzzer, of course. But Jenny the Bitch-Nurse tends to hide it before she leaves. She skips off to her date with Brian and Mr. Silverman has to struggle to get out of bed to use the bathroom. I can only imagine the number of times he's fallen and had to wait there until someone came by.

At eight, one of the regular nurses comes by to check on him. They are usually nicer, friendlier than his usual—not that that leaves them much to work with. I suppose they must all think he's some arrogant rich old jerk for having his own personal nurse. They aren't chatty and with his limited hearing and sight, neither is he.

He doesn't muster the courage to ask the nurse who comes by at eight to help him find the television remote. I can see from his face that he really wants to. So, after she goes, I decide I can't stand it anymore. As quietly as I can, I sneak in.

The room smells slightly of rotting fruit and cleaning products.

Mr. Silverman doesn't hear me. He has his glassy eyes open, staring out of the window.

I sneak over to the wardrobe and take the remote from the top of the unit where Bitch-Nurse concealed it before leaving for the day. I place it on his bedside table and creep back outside into the corridor.

His face lights up into a smile as his hand falls upon it.

"Is anyone there?" he asks the empty room.

He switches on the TV and the news starts to play.

Geez, like his day will get any happier now.

Still, it's nice to see him looking happy. And I'm a well-adjusted person so I try to forget what I came here for. I go and get another coffee and stick around until eleven to see how many times a nurse or whatever drops by.

I'll take care of this tomorrow.

*

As I get back to my hotel room, I decide against running myself a bath. Someone slit their wrists in there, I'm about 100% sure. Much too creepy to sit in. So, I have a shower to wash away that awkward clinical hospital smell.

I order pizza to my room and sit around in bed, half watching episodes of *You* on Netflix on my tablet, half trying to plan out my next move. I have a rough schedule of when the nurses come and go. I managed to have a look at Mr. Silverman's chart—Bitch-Nurse was not careful about leaving it practically in the open. He has a weak constitution and I think an overdose of his medication would do it. He is being treated for a heart condition, so it shouldn't be too hard to get hold of some digitalis from the hospital. It wouldn't look suspicious in his system. It would look practically routine.

However, that's not what's distracting me.

I can't go and see what I've seen today and let Bitch-Nurse go without retribution.

I want to fuck her up.

Now, Barry has always been incredibly clear about what I am not allowed to do. No matter how hypocritical I find that, I've stuck to it. Well, except in the case of Amber, but that was all in his best interests to be honest. Bitch-Nurse hasn't done anything to mess with Barry. But, it'll feel wrong, just generally, if I have to go home, after killing Mr. Silverman, knowing I did nothing to that awful fucking woman.

I mean, arguably, I would need her access card to get into the medical supplies.

And, for argument's sake, I would need to be dressed as a nurse. I reckon her uniform in particular would suit me.

I smile and lean back against the very plastic-feeling pillows.

My phone flashes. There's a cute message from Rick. And my pizza's arrived in the lobby.

Sweet!

*

Day two in the hospital. Only this morning included a little detour. So, I got here nice and early and scouted out the place again. I checked on Mr. Silverman, who was being given breakfast by one of the regular nurses. I managed to get a look at the schedule and noticed that Bitch-Nurse arrives at 2pmn Wednesdays and works a shorter shift. Seriously, who organised her contract?

I hung out in the parking lot, near a phone booth, pretending to be scrolling through my phone. I kept watching out for Bitch-Nurse. From her talk, I expected her to roll in with some expensive car, or at least for Boyfriend Brian to drop her off in an expensive car. What happened was a smidge less self-flattering and so of course, she was unlikely to share it with the other nurses. Bitch-Nurse rocked up on a sticky-looking bus. She walks with her nose way up high in the air, you'd think that she'd skipped out of a limo.

She is fiddling with her headphones, scowling at the crowd of people walking alongside her. She doesn't pay much attention to her surroundings. Now, this is what I anticipated.

She walks through a narrow dark underpass where she breaks off from the crowd. As a member of staff, she could use the back entrance, but she doesn't. She wants to come around the front, to give the impression that she was dropped off at the *main* entrance. Either she's fighting with Boyfriend Brian or he never existed to begin with.

Now, the interesting thing about this narrow underpass, is that I've scouted it out already. I know that before it routes back around to the front, there's a gap where there doesn't appear to be a CCTV camera pointed this way. And they have a load of large industrial-sized bins there. Some of them are locked—possibly because they contain confidential waste or old needles or something.

I reach forward and grab Bitch-Nurse by her long ponytail and slam her head as hard as I can against the big metal bin. She cries out in alarm, legs stumbling, hands flailing uselessly. I bash her face against it again and twice more for good measure. She is disorientated when I take her bag from her. She stumbles and falls flat on her face. I poke her with my foot.

She's out cold but still breathing.

Good, sort of.

I glance around to make sure nobody is looking, nobody is coming this way, before I start heaving her up and over into the bin. Then I close the bin lid on top of her. I move two cardboard boxes that have been left to be taken away by the garbagemen from the ground and place them on top, trapping her inside.

Sweet dreams, Bitch-Nurse.

Mr. Silverman isn't getting your torture-coloured care on his last day on earth.

*

What sort of idiot doesn't lock their phone? Bitch-Nurse, that's the idiot.

I get into her phone and text the head nurse to let her know that Bitch-Nurse has a cough and won't be around. Her boss, who she has sensitively saved under the name 'Old Hag in Blue' (it took some rustling through old messages to identify her as the boss at all), texts back telling her that this isn't good enough, but I leave that fire to be put out later.

I put on her uniform and pass to get in. Then, keeping my jacket on, I go into Starbucks and sit around, just people-watching for a while. I text Rick, who is bored at work, but also looking at ties on-line.

Rick: You're going to be so impressed with the samples I got!

Me: Sure, I am.

Rick: No, seriously! One for me and a similar set for the groomsmen!

Me: How many of those again?

Rick: I'll never tell...

I smile to myself and wish I was home. I miss home so bad I could die. Well, that'd probably be what happens if I don't go along with fucking Barry and his fucking rules. I take a deep breath and lean back into the squeaky plastic chair.

Rick: Seriously though, you will like the samples! And there's not too many groomsmen, I promise! Can't have our sides looking too uneven...

Me: Hey, I have friends.

Rick: I never doubted you!

Me: Sure, sure, seems like it.

Rick: I'm sorry, I'm just teasing, promise! I know you have friends!

Me: You don't need to tell me that.

Rick: Well, did I tell you how pretty you are?

Chapter Twenty-Two

Me: It could be mentioned more.

Rick: I miss you! What are you wearing?

Me: Uh-huh. Nope!

Rick: I didn't mean it like that!

Me: Sure, you didn't!

I roll my eyes and smirk to myself, thinking about what his reaction would be if I told him I was in some nurse's get-up. Mind you, isn't that so weird that a lot of men fantasise about nurses? I get the whole, oh wow, a sexy lady taking care of me, how hot, blah-blah-blah. But surely, in the hospital, you would be feeling like shit. Why would part of your fantasy include being bed-ridden in hospital?

What is wrong with men?

I smirk and glance over as the two nurses I was spying on yesterday pass, talking in hushed whispers that clearly have bitchy undertones from here.

"Apparently she has a cough."

"A cough? She has one goddamn patient!"

"I know, I know. Hey, maybe that fancy French food disagreed with her."

"Oh, don't get my hopes up!"

It is incredible how much brighter this place seems without her. I wonder how long it'll take her to get the smell of garbage out of her hair? It's minor in regard to what I'd like to have done, but... I don't want to get caught out.

I close my eyes and glance down at the photo Rick has sent of him beaming manically from his desk, holding a package. He's captioned it 'THE SAMPLES!!!!' with more exclamation points than anything. It warms my heart.

I need this to be over so I can go.

*

The nurse's uniform stays on under the coat until late. I know roughly when somebody will come and check on him. It's every two hours. So, I wait, and I wait. I hang out by a medicine cupboard and watch how often it is checked and approached. Then I hide my coat inside it, using Bitch-Nurse's pass to get in, stock up on a few essentials and go and loiter in a toilet for another thirty minutes.

It's nearly time.

I've avoided going and looking in his room. I figured… it'd be too hard. I don't know why I'm getting like this. It's… it's sort of hypocritical, isn't it? I switch off my phones and start making my way over there. I take a deep breath and after offering a cursory glance through the little window, step inside.

I'm quiet, he's not completely deaf and I don't want him to know I'm there yet. I hold my breath and watch him as he sits absent mindedly in bed, half following the news. It's the news again. What is it with old people and the news? I slip into a corner and watch him, just really watch him for a little while. I have two hours before the next check.

All the time in the world, really.

All the time in the world.

And honestly, I'm gonna need all the time in the world. Looking at this guy—he's so old! And he's so gentle looking, I just don't see how this could be an actual job he's sending me on. In what sort of world could Barry Ames and Harold Silverman know each other?

I just don't see why I'm here…

"Is somebody there?" Mr. Silverman asks.

He must be paranoid. He's mostly deaf and blind, there's no way he can hear me, creeping around in the darkness of his hospital room.

I step closer, needle in hand.

"Barry, is that you?"

I freeze. So he was expecting something.

He turns his head and looks, almost in my direction.

"Barry Ames sent you, didn't he?"

There's no point in pretending otherwise now, so I come and sit at his bedside and touch his arm so that he knows I'm here.

"Yes," I say.

262

I expect for a split second that he might go to scream, that he might call out for someone to help him. But nobody would come. I've seen enough of that today. Mr. Silverman's white eyes seem to focus as much as they can on me and he smiles a resigned, sad little smile.

"You sound young," he says.

"I am, I suppose," I say, "At least compared to you."

This makes him laugh, it's a small, wheezy sound that seems to get lodged in his chest.

"I suppose that applies to most people these days," he says and I laugh with him. He begins to cough and covers his mouth with a handkerchief. I lean forward to pat his back gently. No, it is not lost on me how ludicrous the action is, considering what I'm here for.

"How did a young thing like you get mixed up with Barry?"

And hey, why not just tell him? He's not much longer for this world, anyway. Part of me is like, Oh God, what are you doing? But another part of me is curious. I've never…really spoken to any of the people Barry has sent me after.

He's said nothing about Mr. Silverman, just that he wants it to look like natural causes.

And I'm curious as well, what could this sweet, lonely old man have done to get on Barry's bad side?

"Oh, it's a long and disappointing story. Mostly, he caught me doing something I shouldn't have been." I notice him frown. "Nothing sleazy, hey!" I say, which gets his smile back. "I…lived in a building owned by Barry's cousin. He was a creep who took naked photos of me and a friend of mine. I couldn't get him to stop, so I killed him. I thought I'd gotten away with it, but Barry found out. He said I could work for him to pay him back."

Mr. Silverman looks thoughtful for a moment, then sad. "Little Peter is dead then?"

"Peter? Yeah, you knew him?"

"Peter Ames," he said sadly. "Yes. What a shame, he was a lovely little boy."

I frown a little. "How about you, Mr. Silverman? What did you do to piss Barry off?"

And there it is, that resigned smile again.

"Barry's my son."

I feel my heart stop.

"But...?"

"He changed his name to Ames after I left his mother when he was a little boy." He lets out a soft sigh. "It was a stupid thing. I had an affair; I left him a note and got a plane to LA. I was the cliché of a bad father. I sent money, offered to let him come up and see me. But he never forgave me for leaving. He promised he'd kill me one day. I'd almost thought he'd forgotten. I wanted to think that he had, that maybe he'd have been able to let this go. I suppose it was a foolish and selfish thing to wish for." He brushes back his little hair with his hands.

"You're really his...?"

"Yes," he said. "He tracked me down once, when he was fifteen. I think he must have stolen the car. He broke into my house and threatened my second wife at gunpoint. He was such an angry young man. Is he like that now?"

"He's more...well, geez, you're putting me in kind of an awkward position here," I say.

He looks sad. "I've always known nothing I could have said would have made things right with him."

"I could call him, say you wanted to say...?" I try.

Mr. Silverman shakes his head. "It wouldn't make any difference. Not after what I did. Not after who I let him become." He wavers a little. "Will it hurt?"

"No," I say. "He told me to make it look like natural causes. I was going to give you an injection that will put you to sleep. It's just an overdose of your medication."

Mr. Silverman smiles. "Thank you."

"That's a weird thing to say to me," I say. "Are you ready?"

"As I'll ever be."

I take his arm very gently, his skin feels like paper, dotted with bruises from restraints, injections and the rough grip of the nurse I saw earlier. He is so thin, so weak. His glassy eyes close as I insert the needle.

He lets out a soft sigh and leans back against his pillows.

"Goodnight, Mr. Silverman," I say, because I'm not sure what to say.

"Goodnight, Miss."

I sit with him for a while. I listen to the gentle rise and fall of his chest, the hum of the air conditioning. I watch the moon through the curtains. Then, when he is still, I touch his wrist and feel no pulse. Barry's father, Harold Silverman is dead.

I get up, adjust my nurse's uniform and walk out of the room and into the dimly lit corridor, closing the door behind me. There's nobody around, nobody to notice anything untoward. I can feel my phone buzzing in my jacket pocket and I ignore it. Whether it's Rick or Barry or anyone else, I don't want to talk right now.

My footsteps are calm, just one after the other.

I breathe slowly. But my heart is violent inside me. I want to panic; I want to yell and scream and cry. I don't want to do this anymore. I don't want to do this!

I've never sat and spoken to one of those people before. I'm a well-adjusted person so I don't think about the information broker he sent me after who said 'Wait!' before I shot her. I don't think about Mrs. Anderson, strewn across her staircase, covered in blood. I don't think…I can't think!

Mr. Silverman was resigned in the end. He just sat there and let me do it.

I…

The phone is buzzing in my pocket again.

I want my mother.

I get outside and manage to calm myself down enough to take my phone out of my pocket. It's Barry, of course, it's Barry. I start walking home, closing my eyes, another deep breath. The phone is still ringing. Ok.

"I've changed my mind," he says, frantic, breathless. "Don't do it. Just come back! I've changed my mind! Don't! Don't!"

My heart stops.

Oh fuck!

"B-Barry, Barry, I..."

Silence.

Then he bursts into hysterical laughter.

"Oh my God! Oh my God! Did you think I was serious? Oh man, I wish I could see your face! Oh wow! I got you! I got you, Miss. King!"

"You're fucking crazy," I say before I can really control how angry I am.

This makes him howl with laughter.

"Ivan, Ivan, take the phone," he wheezes and it breaks my heart because he sounds like his father with his caught in his chest laugh. "Ivan, seriously."

I hear the phone get shuffled around.

"I am driving," Apparently-Ivan says sharply, more to Barry than I think to me, and hangs up.

My heart is thudding in my chest and I can feel tears running down my cheeks. Fuck, I've never been made to cry by a boss before. Never. Oh my God. I lean against a wall and cover my face with my hands. I crouch down, pulling my hands over my head.

Oh God.

I feel sick.

"Oh my God, are you ok?" I hear someone ask.

I'm shaking as I get up. There's a tall, red-headed British woman bending down to check on me. She is model-thin with chunky black boots and ridiculously nice make-up. I can see a row of friends behind her, half texting, half looking over.

Man, I must look like a crazy person.

"No, I mean, yeah, I'm fine."

She looks concerned. "Are you sure?"

"Carly, come on!" one of her friends calls.

"Hold on a sec," she says, waving a hand to dismiss them.

"Yes, I'm fine."

"Long shift, huh?"

I look down and remember I'm still in a stupid nurse's uniform.

"Oh, yeah."

"Do you want me to call you a cab?"

"No, I'm fine, honestly."

"Well, ok. Take care now," she says, waving a well-manicured hand as she moves to join her friends.

I feel calmer now, letting out a deep breath as I follow the street back down to the sidewalk to get back to my creepy-ass hotel. I brush my hair out of my face and answer the buzzing phone in my pocket.

"Hello, Barry," I say stiffly.

His voice is heavy from laughter. "I'm sorry, Miss. King, that wasn't nice, was it?"

"Not particularly."

He snorts. "For the record, I wouldn't ever call you up on a job, telling you to cancel. Though we should have some sort of system for that, you know? What do you think?"

"I don't know, Barry," I say, exhausted. "Whatever you think would be best."

"Did he chat to you?" he asks, "Did he chat?"

"A bit."

"So, he told you he was my old man, right?"

"Yeah."

"How does that make you feel?" he asks, mock-shrink style.

"Gee, Barry, I don't know. How about you?"

I can picture him smirking. "Hey, I told him I'd get him one day. What am I now, a liar? My mother didn't raise a liar all on her own. I had to bump him off. I'm a man of my word."

"Wow, is that right?"

"Bet your ass it is," he says. "So, you made it look like natural causes?"

"Yeah, just an overdose of his medication. Nothing untoward."

"Good, good, knew I could rely on you, Miss. King."

"I'm going to come home tomorrow."

"Sounds good, I'll catch up with you when you're back. Enjoy LA, it's a fun city."

"I'll try."

"Thanks again, I feel like I'll be able to sleep so much better for this," he says, yawning loudly into the phone. "Goodnight, Miss. King. Have a safe flight home."

As he hung up, I found that I'd nearly gone to ask him, Hey, are you still angry with him? Your father, I mean. Are you still mad?

It's probably for the best I don't ask. I don't think I'd have found his answer particularly satisfying. I don't think he feels anything. He really is made of stone.

I need to get away from him.

Chapter Twenty-Three

I know the plane ticket was to be used to head straight home, I know I told Rick that I was heading straight home. But before I know it, I've booked a ticket to Oregon. The flight passes easily this time. I barely notice anyone around me. I don't look out the window at the wing. I don't panic. I don't feel sick as the flight begins to descend.

I take a bus and then get a taxi. I pay the driver, ignoring his questions completely. I get out, bags and all, not caring how weird it looks. Alone with my suitcase and my handbag. I don't suppose the people who usually come here, do so with excessive luggage.

Ryerson State Prison.

I could have visited. I know at first, visiting was a big no-no. But then one year, two years, three years passed, I knew she had visits from people, people who wrote her, curious people, fans... Ergh, it feels dirty to say fans, there are fans of who she was and what she did.

These are the kind of people who visit.

But then, she mentioned once that it would be possible for her to add a Sookie King onto her approved visitor list. But I didn't visit, not even after she opened the door for me. In her own, silent, cold way, that was Mother, who gave everything, asking for me to come and see her. My silence, my excuse of having 'a lot going on', that was me, her only child, who took anything and everything, saying no.

Ultimately, I think my capacity for cruelty was always more vast than hers.

I have never visited her in prison. I was always too afraid. I know how that sounds—boo-hoo, poor me, it will be so hard for me to see her in prison, where she lives, where she will live every day for the rest of her life, because of her careless and cruel child.

I'm a piece of shit.

Make no mistake.

But today, I'm a piece of shit who is going to see my mother.

"Sookie King, I should, erm, be on the list?"

The guard looks shy of forty, and has this no-nonsense expression on her face, the kind that would suggest that she has never cracked a smile in her life. She scans her files and turns a form towards me to sign.

"You know Sarah?"

Mother goes by her old name now. Sarah White. She changed it just before she had me to distance herself from her old life in Franberg. She changed it to Sylvia Taylor to honour the one person who ever escaped her knife—I know, Mother was never one for subtle.

Sarah White. She's been Sarah White since she was arrested and charged. It's like I don't belong to her anymore.

"I wrote her," I say.

No-nonsense snorts and takes my form from me. "I never get why you millennials are so obsessed with that true crime stuff."

"We're a morbid bunch," I say, flashing her a big smile which she does not return.

"Wait here. You'll be escorted through in fifteen."

I take a seat—the chairs are that kind of sticky plastic that keeps you very aware of every backside that has come before you. Glancing around at the dull grey walls, the one motivational poster of a sunrise, I can't help but feel how depressing it is. It's like a freaking stereotype for a room like this.

I glance around at the others here, there aren't many. Everyone looks sombre, like we're all heading to a funeral.

We sit in that stony silence until a tall skinny guard arrives to lead us through. The others are herded into one of those screen and telephone sets you see on the TV. I go to follow the six others in there, but Tall and Skinny stops me. I get taken into a smaller room, away from the others. There is just one screen and a very old-looking phone.

I guess Mother is kind of a high-profile serial killer. People must stare. People must get upset.

I take a deep breath as Tall and Skinny closes the door behind him, leaving me alone. I wring my hands together under the table and close my eyes for a moment to push all of this away. I try to think about the last time I saw her. Not on the news, not as an image in a documentary, I try to visualise the very last time I saw her.

I smell… the pine of the trees outside our house, the metallic sticky smell of Jason's blood. I smell anti-bacterial spray and aloe vera. And I see her, drinking tea with lemon, her flat, vacant eyes that followed me as I struggled to drag Jason's body over the threshold. I don't remember what I said to her right then. I imagine it was frantic and miserable. My best friend was dead and my world had come crashing down.

Her blankness, her distant eyes had made me feel like I'd gone mad.

She looked young for forty-six, darker than me, slim and stronger than she looked. Pretty, everyone said that about her. We were the same height back then. She kept her hair straight and short, just above her shoulders. I never saw her natural hair. She had a salon out of town she liked to go to so she could keep it like that. It made her blend in with the PTA moms better.

I think her whole look back then was based on what the other mothers did.

No jewellery and sensible shoes.

I open my eyes and see that in six years, that at least hasn't changed.

A guard escorts her in through the door on the far side of the room. She's… smaller than I remember. Still looks young for fifty-two. Still pretty. Her hair is short and wild, guess there's no salon in prison. Beige jumpsuit, not orange, that's disappointing.

She looks thin, horribly thin, I think I could hold both of her wrists in my hand. And just when I feel like my heart is going to break, Mother takes the seat opposite me, she looks up at me and smiles her crocodile smile.

She's the same.

We lift our phones and my hands are trembling. I wonder what to say, what we can say, what would be right to say right now?

"Hello." In the end, that's always the best place to start. "I'm Sookie King."

"Hello," she says pleasantly. "It's nice to meet you." She says it like we have never met, the two of us, like she isn't the woman who used to cut the crusts off my sandwiches.

"Same. So, do you get a lot of visits like this?"

"Oh yes," she says, "Particularly with the—well, I'm sure you've heard about the movie they're making about me."

"Seems in poor taste if you ask me," I say.

"Well, from what I hear, society is pretty distasteful these days," she says with a shrug. Then she turns towards the guard on her left. "Mavis, would you mind giving us some privacy?"

The dead-eyed guard I hadn't really paid any attention to, grunts something and leaves through the door she came through.

I whistle.

"So, is that your, erm, phone shop?" I ask.

"Yes," she says. "She has been very helpful during my time here." Mother sighs. "I never thought you'd actually come here."

"I was in the neighbourhood," I say, sitting back.

"Sure," Mother says. "Fiona, I'm glad you're here."

It's been so long since anyone has called me by my name. I'd almost forgotten how it sounded, how it felt. I feel… overwhelmed. It's like that seeing her, completely and utterly overwhelming. To be afraid of someone but love them dearly. To want to run away but cry at the thought of ever being apart. Just the knowledge that I'm going to have to get up and leave this room soon is devastating.

"But," she says, "I know you. You've gotten yourself into trouble, haven't you, dear?"

I laugh. "Well, thanks for the vote of confidence, Mother." I pause and lean on one elbow. "Well, since you mentioned it, not me… So, say when you were younger, say you got yourself into a tough situation, how would you get out of that? Say, if you had a dependant, someone that meant you couldn't just up sticks and run away. How would you handle that?"

She purses her lips. "Aren't you a little old to be asking me for help?"

"Hey, I'm still growing up. Aren't you at an age where you should start referring to yourself as fifty years young or something?"

"And here I hoped you'd lose that nasty sense of humour."

But she smiles as she says it.

Chapter Twenty-Three

"No such luck for you," I say.

Her eyes cast down towards my hand.

"And this dependent.... Well, should I be offering congratulations?"

I hold my ring up for her to see better. "I mean, sure, if you like."

She looks for a moment before nodding. "You look happy, Fiona."

"I am," I say, and I mean it, I want her to know that. "I have a really good life, a great life. Well, in all but one respect. This problem I mentioned."

Mother raises an eyebrow. "I think what it boils down to is a matter of priority," she says. "If it were me, I would just remove the obstacle that threatened my happiness."

I frown at her. "And what if it wasn't as simple as that?"

"What is your happy life with your dependant worth to you, Fiona?" she asks. "I'd say that you were never the sort of girl to let anything get in your way." Her hand comes up to rest against the glass between us. I touch it and try to remember how her hands felt.

"I'll keep that in mind, Mother," I say.

She smiles and her hand returns to her lap. "I saw on the news; a woman was violently decapitated and adorned with occult symbols. That wouldn't have been...?"

"Oh yeah," I say, laughing and shaking my head. "You heard about that, huh?"

"A friend of yours? I couldn't help but think..."

"My fiancé's ex-girlfriend," I say, waving my hand. "Awful woman. You wouldn't have liked her."

"The rest of your... work has been harder to keep track of."

"I mean, who keeps track of suicide and accident numbers? They happen all the time."

The crocodile smile again.

"Oh, don't they just?"

I laugh and brush my hair out of my eyes.

"Did you think I'd carry on?"

She nods. "Yes. Well, I hoped I was wrong, but I'm not often wrong so..." She never shows much, her parenting style was all shaming and sarcasm, always with a vacant stare or a sinister smile. I remember only a time or two when she was... different.

Like now, she looks sad, resigned.

It takes me back.

"Am I… taking it for granted?" I ask, "What… you gave up so I could… just waste it by carrying on. Do you regret it?"

She glances up at me, eyebrow raised. "Not even for a second."

"Oh, bullshit!" I say, pointing at her. "Bullshit, bullshit! Right there, bullshit! Mother, you live in a prison cell."

"They let me keep a garden," she says, as though that eliminates the issue of… everything else involved.

"You don't regret it? What about those long drives you used to take by yourself at night? The ones you'd take for hours and hours! What about… going somewhere that wasn't this prison specifically? You can't say that and honestly expect me to believe a word?" I'm struggling not to raise my voice. "You!"

"Fiona," she says, tapping her hand on the glass. "I don't expect you to believe a word. You never listened to a thing I told you. Why start now?" She brushes a hand across her forehead. "Yes, I am sick of this place. I'm sick of the people, the inmates, the guards, the monotony. I miss living the sort of life I had out there… I miss having my own space. I miss… I haven't thought about those drives in a long time. Yes, I miss them. I miss a lot of things. But, if it means you're out there, living a life that makes you happy… then no, I don't regret any of it. Not even for a second."

My hands are shaking. My vision blurs.

"You don't regret it? Fine! You won't regret it in another five years? Another ten?"

"Have you gone deaf recently, Fiona?"

After all this, she still knows how to make me angry.

"You won't regret it in… what is it, Mother, another twenty-five years? Is it twenty-five more years before they execute you? Will you have no regrets then?"

In all the time she's been here, we haven't spoken about that. Her death sentence. It lay unspoken between us. We didn't mention it when she was sentenced, I had no way of contacting her then. By the time she had a phone and I had an extra phone she could reach me on, I never knew how to mention it. So, I didn't. I don't know if it made it easier for me to just carry on as if it wasn't true.

She just stares at me, blank and cold as ever.

I bash my fist against the glass and cover my mouth as I start to cry miserably.

We stay like that for a moment.

I look up when I hear a soft tapping on the glass.

She is looking at me with those same cold eyes.

"Not even for a second," she says.

I wipe my eyes and laugh miserably. "You're so stubborn."

"It's been said," she says with a sigh. "Now, pull yourself together. It sounds like you have a lot to sort out when you get home."

"Oh, don't I know it?" I wipe my face furiously with my sleeve.

"And remember what I said, don't let anything infringe on your happiness if it's what you truly want for yourself." She says it like it's easy. Maybe if it was her, it'd come easier. I sigh and nod my head.

"Yeah, I know, I know."

"Visit again," she says, "If you're in town. Your... dependent, he doesn't know, about us, does he?"

"No."

"Good, I trust you to keep it that way. It'll make things easier."

"Hey, how would I even explain it?" I say, shaking my head.

"And, you remember the other bit of advice I gave you?"

I don't reply.

"I suppose you were a bit distracted. I told you to never have a child. Do you remember?"

"I remember," I say. "Trust me, I've met kids, they aren't exactly selling it to me."

She shakes her head, smaller than she was before, but just as sharp. She's made of corners, edges and all the sharpest points. I wish I could reach through the glass to touch her. Though, in truth, we never had that sort of a bond.

"I'll try to come again."

"I'll believe it when I see it."

"Goodbye, Mother."

"Goodbye, Fiona."

Chapter Twenty-Four

I am emotionally drained when I get back. I get in late. Rick is fast asleep. I slip out of my sweaty airport clothes and climb into bed beside him. I take a deep breath, take in his smell, take in the feel of his body against mine. I've missed this. I've missed this so much. My eyes are filled with tears and I cling on too tight.

This would be super romantic, however…

He flinches as he wakes up.

"Aah!" He yells and jerks and twists his body away, blinking frantically in the dark. I have to dodge an elbow and then the alarm clock which he twists in front of him like a blunt, stubby sword. "Get off me! Get out of my apartment!" I think he repeats the same thing in very swift, very furious Spanish.

"Rick, Rick, it's me!"

He blinks, calming down, twisting for the bedside lamp.

"Oh, Sookie, baby, did I hit you?" he gasps, dropping the clock and grasping hold of my face with his hands. "I'm so sorry!"

"No, no, my bad!"

"I was asleep," he says, "I didn't realise. Oh, you should've called me, I'd have come to pick you up at the airport." He yawns, a hand on his heart. "You really scared me!"

"I'm so sorry," I said. "I have travel brain, I just got into bed, I didn't think…"

"It's ok," he says. "Are you sure I didn't get you?"

"I'm fine," I say, twisting out of his grip. "Babe, seriously, you think a burglar would get into bed with you? I mean, you're hot stuff but…"

"I didn't know what was going on," he says, laughing and sliding an arm around me. "I'm so sorry. Welcome home, properly this time."

I'm laughing, curling in. "Why did you try to attack me with the alarm clock?"

He starts laughing then, tugging me in against him. "Hey, do I have to tell you that I was sleeping like, a deep, deep sleep, just five minutes ago?"

"I'm sorry," I say. "I'm glad to be home."

"Promise you won't leave without me again?" he says. "I'm totally kidding, you can."

"Nope," I say. "I don't want to go anywhere without you again."

*

"What did you think to the venues I sent you?" he asks as he tugs his t-shirt over his head. "I know it's super early, buuuut, did anything catch your eye?"

"Well, they're all beautiful," I say, lying back down on the bed. "I don't even know where to begin! Like, one looked like a not-so-haunted haunted house, one was like a really nice barn, there was a field? I guess doing the whole ceremony outside could be nice? I can't believe these prices though! Getting married is...expensive, right?"

He plops down on the bed beside me. "Well, yeah, but I only want to do this once. So, we might as well be a bit...Kardashian for the day, right?"

He is beautiful and I've missed this so much.

I sit up and kiss him on the tip of his nose.

"Yeah, I guess that could be nice."

He hugs me around the middle. "It's ok, we can take this slow! I didn't mean to spam you out while you were away."

"You didn't spam me, honestly," I say, squeezing his hand. "I just don't know where to begin with this stuff. There's so much to do and sort out and...I hadn't really considered myself as that kind of person, you know? Like...a person who is..."

"Married?"

"Yeah," I say. "I mean, I've been on my own since…I was a child. I never really thought that I'd belong to a family someday."

"Sookie," he says, "You know when you say stuff like that, it makes me want to do this…like tomorrow. Which I would, if I wasn't so concerned with the fact my mother would kill me if she missed my wedding." He kisses me, his finger under my chin. "I never want you to feel like that again. I want to give you a place, a family that you can always belong to."

"Don't even!" I say, swatting him. "You already got me to say yes, stop being so lovely!"

Rick laughs and straightens up. "I know that maybe talking all this wedding stuff is stressful because of everything happening at work. But, Sookie, baby, you're innocent. They'll have to see that, and soon too."

"I know. And hey, I'm not being reluctant because of work!" I insist.

"Well, good, because I mean, there's no rush, we're already living together and it's not like we're super religious or dying, but, I don't want to be one of those guys who slums it, you know? Is all 'yeah, babe, get whatever flowers you want', I don't want to be like that."

"Right," I say, then unable to help myself, "Soooo, what flowers do *you* want?"

He is laughing as he tackles me onto my back and kisses my face all over.

"Don't make fun of me!"

*

While Rick is at work, I buy a big notepad with a cream linen cover and scrawl 'Wedding Planning' across the top in bright red biro. Then I snapchat him a photo of it with the caption 'See! Invested AF!'. Then I lie around on the sofa, checking through the venues he sent me again. And, seriously, he has put some work in. Nobody could accuse him of pulling a 'yeah, babe, get whatever flowers you want'. These are some nice freaking venues.

Some come with their own complimentary flowers. All seem to provide seat sashes… Are those a thing? The barn looks surprisingly cosy. The lady of the manor style house, a little over the top? I think

I'd just feel silly…There are sample photos in all of the venue PDF brochures he's sent on. Nice dresses and sweet tuxes aside, it's basically like a bunch of Nicholas Sparks novels with a different glamorous setting in the background. You know what I mean, white couples embracing. Nonstop. I can't see myself in these women, in these couples. I think I'd look…silly, maybe?

I switch back to the stylish-looking hotel. Which is nice, apart from I could just see the ceremony room also being used for like, a company away day. Still, the cast of *The Notebook* look happy enough to say their 'I Dos' there so maybe I should leap down from my high horse.

There are things like this we can decide together, the venue, the menu, the…guest list. But…even that's a minefield. Rick has a big family. Like he has cousins he forgets the names of. I have these specific, bizarre fears of how wrong it's going to look with a side full of people I've acquired over the last six years. No family, no childhood friends, no old teachers—though in seriousness, who has old teachers they'd actually want to invite? I guess I could start insisting that I want a wedding that is…small and intimate and private? If only to cover for my lack of a side…

Besides, at least that's a hurdle we can cross together; there are things I definitely need to decide on independent of Rick. And unfortunately for me, it's the most memorable part, the big bit, the thing pretty much all the guests will remember about the wedding (unless something crazy happens)—the dress.

What the fuck am I going to do about the dress?

I've never been one of those girls. I've seen enough romantic comedies over the years to scare off any insecure man, but I have never thought about how I'd wear a wedding dress. Like, not even once! I mean, do I wear white? Would that be too boring? And like, what if I spill something on it? Am I going to have a super boring menu just in case I get sloppy? Red wine? White is such an unforgiving colour! Non-traditional? Would that seem too weird? Like, if I show up in…blue or red or pink or whatever, and people who haven't met me before keep asking where the bride is. That'd be embarrassing…and given the amount of money spent on the wedding, seems…counter-intuitive at best.

What the fuck am I going to do about the dress?

Why is there so much pressure on the dress?

Flicking through the pictures as the implied prices are a queasier business, one thing becomes more and more obvious—that I need back-up if I'm going to do this. I'm going to need to tell Leda that she's Maid of Honour. That's it!

*

The next day, bedraggled and exhausted, I staggered out of bed to make Rick coffee and toast before he went off to work. I had all of five minutes to myself before Barry called and wanted to meet that morning. I tried to throw him off, but it didn't work.

Travel-drained is not a good enough excuse to get on his bad side.

I left the flat, stepped down the stairwell and out of the front door. Then my stomach plummeted to my feet, as instead of Apparently-Ivan waiting for me, there was Barry, stood waiting, back against a lamppost, smoking a cigarette. Seeing him outside my apartment filled me with perpetual dread. Waving, like he's just some guy and not basically Satan.

"Hey there, Miss. King!"

"What the hell are you doing here? This is where I live," I snap at him, stuffing my hands into my jacket pockets and stomping along the pavement. He follows, still laughing, cigarette smoke getting up my nose as he catches up.

"I like to keep my people on their toes, it's not good practice to get complacent," he says. "So, I understand you took a little detour?"

"Yeah," I say. "I wanted to head off to Portland. I never go out of state much. Wanted to get some time to myself."

He raises an eyebrow, tossing his cigarette to the ground and stomping it out. "I would've thought you'd have wanted to spend longer in LA, all that shopping, chance to schmooze some celebrities," he says cheerfully.

"Not really my scene," I say.

Barry sighs. "Well, I did start to worry, maybe you were running off on me."

"Hey, I wouldn't do that," I say. "I just wanted to see that part of the country, can you blame me?" I shrug and hope he drops it. I don't want to think of anything more to say, it's none of his goddamn business where I go. "I wouldn't run off like that, Barry, come on."

"Yeah, I figured," he says. "I know you're good for it, calm your face down."

I sigh and brush my hair out of my eyes, scowling slightly. "So, what did you want?"

"I just wanted to check in, after your great vanishing act and all…"

"Hey, I didn't do anything like that!"

He smirks and shakes his head. "I'm joking, I'm joking. I wanted to check in, see how you were doing. How did you find your last assignment?"

"I didn't mind it."

"Was it a bit of a shock? Meeting my old man?" he asks. "Crushing bore, isn't he?"

"If you say so, we didn't really chat."

"He wasn't as nice as he gives out, or gave out, I guess," he says, letting out a deep breath. "I mean, what kind of man leaves his baby boy when he's just six years old? A real piece of work, that's what I reckon."

"I don't tend to sit people down for a sincere heart-to-heart before I do my work, you know? It's not a talk show."

He snorts, "You have such a nasty sense of humour, you know?"

I shrug my shoulders and glance back at him. "I didn't talk to your father. But I did see the way the nurse hired to take care of him was hurting him. I felt sorry for him, so I made it quick."

He frowns slightly, but then that shit-eating grin returns. "How did you know he was my old man?"

"He told me," I says. "He talked about you while I was sneaking around the room. His mind was mostly gone, he was very old and vulnerable."

Barry rolls his eyes. "Sure," he says. "I bet."

"Did you hire that nurse?"

"Oh, Jenny? Yeah," he says, snorting with laughter. "So, I've just got to know, but was it you who put her in that bin?"

I smirk but say nothing.

He howls with laughter, smacking me a little too hard on the back.

"Oh, man! Oh, man! She has this huge—huge bump on her head from where you pushed her! Oh my God, I couldn't get over her trapped in a bin covered in garbage. She tried to send me a dry-cleaning bill, can you believe?" He wipes a tear from his eye and snorts with laughter, hands on his sides. "Oh my God! I should've known!"

I roll my eyes. "She is vile, I dare say a trip in a bin was needed."

He smirks. "Of course she is. She's a friend of my little sister's from college. She's a nightmare! I have no idea why she trained as a nurse, but she did and I thought, hey, why not get her involved?"

"Way to give your dad a send-off, right?"

Barry shrugs. "He wasn't my dad. And he's definitely not any-more. Anyway, tell me, Miss. King, what did you reckon to Portland, to LA? Nice to get a change of scenery, right?" He's trying to bait me.

"Sure," I say. "Could be something to consider in future, no plans for that at the moment."

"Yeah, I guess," he says. "Your fiancé, Rick Fumero seems pretty settled around here, you know?" He smirks brightly at me and I struggle to keep a straight face, a calm face, the face he wants me to show.

I feel sick. I knew, always knew that he'd keep tabs on us. I knew he'd know Rick's name, what he looked like, etc. I knew this was bound to happen. But I wanted it to go unspoken between us. I want-ed it to be one of those truly terrible things that just stops...

"Oh yeah," I say. "He is."

Barry grins, delighted. "He not in today?"

"No," I say. "Come on, don't do that."

"Does he really not know that side of you?" he asks, leaning down to take my hand and hold it up to his face. My skin crawls. "I mean, that's harsh, considering the suddenly much more serious nature of your relationship..."

I raise an eyebrow and retract my hand. "Does Mrs. Ames know everything you do?"

"No way, I'm not stupid," he says. "So, showing up at your little love nest is not appreciated unless it's Ivan, huh?"

"Ivan sits in the car," I say. "He's a gentleman."

"Woooo," he says, laughing. "Okay, okay, boundaries crossed and understood. Gotcha. So, are you up to another job or are you going to drag your feet?"

*

Irritation levels now suitably high, I go and meet Leda with a new job to complete next week and a headache. Barry is waving cheerfully as he dashes off somewhere else. He yells 'Seeya round, Miss. King' as he crosses the corner and I see Mo Gills from the corner shop look up with the kind of nosey interest you only really get with old ladies.

I wonder if she thinks I'm having an affair. Pfft, as if!

It's official. I can't deal with him acting like this, showing up at the apartment. How long before he puts himself into a situation where I come home and find him in my goddamn living room, sat talking to Rick?

How long before…

He is making it very easy to follow Mother's advice.

I need to get rid of him. I've more than had enough of this. I can't have him in our life. I don't want to give Rick the kind of marital bliss that sometimes involves my maniac gangster boss dropping by, dumping himself into my life just to fuck with me and push boundaries or whatever his other shitty excuse was…

It was enough before the engagement, but now it's becoming oh so very clear, that he needs to get the fuck out of my life!

"You look distracted," Leda says. "Am I boring you?"

"Yeah," I say, "I'm bored to death."

"Oh, stop that," she says. "I went and bought you a few of those glossy magazines!" She brandishes one at me dramatically. "When else do you get to buy these, eh?"

I lift one up and frown slightly. "I don't even know where to begin."

"And I could help you," she said, "If you make me Maid of Honour…"

"And if I don't?"

"Then you're on your own, I guess," she says, flicking through the pages idly. "But I'd want me on the side."

I laugh, "You know you're Maid of Honour, right?"

Leda throws her arms around my shoulders and hugs me tight. "Thank you! Thank you! Thank you! I promise I'll do a good job!"

"I really do need your help, I have no idea where to start. Rick has been great, but I know I should be more… hands on, I guess?"

"What sort of things has he planned?" she asks.

I shrug helplessly. "Well… I don't know. Why do you know all about this stuff?"

She snorts. "Oh, come on! I grew up with chick flicks as my life's blood," she said. "And me and Tammy talk hypothetically about it all the time."

"Really?"

"Tammy has horrible taste, but the big bucks," she says. "I'm about ninety-eight percent sure she wants a cheetah print veil…"

"I can't tell if you're kidding."

"I can't tell if she's kidding," Leda says. "Ok, so, come and look at this!" She plops the magazine down on my lap. "The dress is the most exciting bit, so why don't we start there? That way we can't get on top of whatever Rick has started with. Do you know the kind of dress you'd like? Are you going conventional? A-line? Mermaid?"

"Hold your horses," I say, swatting her hands away and glancing down at the magazine.

It's weird seeing stuff like this. I've never really been… like a flashy dresser. My wardrobe choices could never be described as 'extra' and a wedding dress doesn't come more 'extra' than that. I look at these pages and there's variety, there's patterns, flair, sleeves, no sleeves, tight decorated bodices, high collars, flowing skirts, veil, no veil… How does anyone know where to begin?

"I think the best thing to do would be to just look and see if there's something you really like. Or can at least imagine wearing yourself."

"Sure, easy for you, you could rock all of these looks."

"Oh, shut up, Sookie and look at the dresses!"

"I don't think any of these are me though," I say, holding up the magazine for her. "I mean, could you see me in this get-up?"

The dress in question is ivory white, with a flowing chiffon skirt and a tight, sleeveless bodice with gaping cleavage and sequins on every surface.

"I mean, I don't think I've ever seen you in a skirt," Leda says, laughing. "But yes, to be honest. You'd look magical. Would you wear a white dress?"

"I mean, yeah," I say, "I suppose so. I don't know… Yes? Actually, that might look awful!" I laugh nervously and frown, peering down at it again. "Don't you think it would be a bit, oh look at me, look at me?"

Leda raises an eyebrow. "Sookie, you do know it's a wedding, right?"

"Ok, ok, whatever, well, it might be a bit too much. Do they do other colours? Like white-ish? Not blinding white, I'll be scared to eat or drink anything!"

"Well, you could get it in champagne?"

"What the hell is champagne colour? Like yellow-ish green? Or…"

"Hold on, page… 12?"

"Hey, Leda, why don't you just tell me which one you think would look best?"

"I mean, sure," Leda says, "I'll pick you out the best three. And while we're on the topic, I'm Maid of Honour, who else are we having?"

"Just you and Gabbie."

"What?" she says, "No, you have to have three! It'll make it way awkward if it's just me and Gabbie, like, oh, Sookie prefers Leda because she only has two good friends."

"Who would you suggest?"

"Well, Tammy looks lovely in a variety of!"

"No, Leda."

"Oh, come on, just hear me out!" she says, pleading. "Tammy has never looked bad in a picture…ever! She's tall, sophisticated, elegant!"

"The two of you will just get into a fight and it'll be awkward."

"We've actually," she says, proudly, "been getting on pretty well as of late, pretty well. Some could say-"

"Who would say?"

"-The best we've ever gotten on. We've been back together for a year properly now."

"Congratulations."

She sighs, "Ok, maybe not Tammy. But, I mean, I know you're Ms. Private, but don't you have anyone else you might want to ask? Gabbie and me will buy our own dresses so it's not like money would be an issue? Anybody else?"

For stupid reasons, I think about Beth, in her dorm room at Yale. Then that familiar wave of depression hits as I realise that an invitation to go to the wedding of Sookie King, could ruin everything I have now. Besides, like an invitation from Sookie King would mean anything to Beth. There's no reason why those two people should have met. There's no reason at all.

"No, there's nobody else. I'd ask Carmella, but I don't think she'd go for it."

Carmella was my first boss, who hired me even though I was a terrible, terrible waitress. She was patient. She never asked questions even though I was covered in scars and it took me three weeks to get used to responding to my own name.

Carmella is the first person Sookie King *knew*. There's no history of this person before that. God, my wedding is going to make me look like either Little Orphan Annie, or a Fake-Not-Real-Secret-Agent-Person.

"Well, you never know..." Leda pauses, then bites the lid of her pen. "Actually, she would probably rather just come along and enjoy herself. Maybe try to shave Rick's beard...She'll be so excited about this, have you told her?"

"Yup, she cried and yelled down the phone," I say, laughing. "She was pretty excited, started asking me about dates and venues...Then, I got a lecture for not knowing any of that stuff..."

"Well, you have to get on this," Leda said. "I mean, are you planning on getting married again?"

"No," I say, "I mean, we could always get divorced in like...ten years' time, just so we could re-marry each other."

"How Elizabeth Taylor of you," she says, rolling her eyes. "I happen to think an A-line dress would suit you. It basically suits everyone. I had my heart set on you rocking a mermaid-style dress, but alas, I saw you roll your eyes."

"I'm all hips!" I protest. "It would look obscene!"

"Obscene, or a dream," she says, pointing her biro at me.

"Obscene, I just said that," I say, nudging her in the side. "I like the floaty dresses. I think that would suit me." I point at the first one on the page that I *think* is A-line.

"Sookie, that has shoulder-pads!" Leda protests. "Do you even *want* to get married?"

*

After wedding dresses and bouquet shopping, there is something for me to do after all. Something I can do just fine, without worrying about whether or not there should be shoulder-pads or petticoats, or lace or chiffon. This is something as natural to me as using the john, as kicking back on a Sunday morning, as…breathing.

I know who acquired P.J.'s phone from the crime scene. I know who helps Barry avoid any real trouble, who is always there to tip him off about a raid or any potential trouble. I've seen him in the warehouse. It was when they sent me after Vincent Cho, the young police detective, that I put two and two together. The picture of Cho was one taken of him on patrol with his partner. A partner, I had seen knocking around the warehouse with Barry's fellas.

A little digging and it was easy enough to find Officer Andrew Connington, Conn to his friends. A corrupt cop as corrupt and stereotypical as they come. He has the icy blonde hair of the Hitler Youth and the bulging blue eyes of a TV heroin addict. He is built like a BEAST—his muscles look like separate entities on his Instagram. Way too many shirtless shots…I didn't need to see that.

I find out from his social media that he's from Sacramento and went to LA to try to make it as a movie star. Apparently after that obviously didn't work, he moved upstate to Santa Cruz and joined the police. I bet he lasted all of five minutes before he started accepting under the table deals.

I watch out for Conn from outside the station. I figure that's as good a place as any to start. He's weirdly public and private about his social media. It's all very showy, without actually giving that much away. I'm sure an expert in these things could point out how staged his photos are, but I'm not that person and it'd look way too creepy to ask someone else about it.

So, I wait. Having the time to do this sort of thing is one of the few daily benefits of being turfed out of my old job. I get a bagel, people-watch, catch some sun. I even manage to make the time to go through those darn venues again.

I close my eyes and brush back my hair and wait, just wait.

He comes out after a while. Plain clothes, but I recognize him better that way, really. He stands out and he walks around like he thinks he's all that. I watch him leave the station and wander out into the side car park. I make a note of his personalised number plate and let him drive on for now.

This will take some planning to get right.

If I'm going to free myself from this, I need to start with Conn the Corrupt Cop. I know he knows who works for Barry. I know he knows how to get at them. If I can get rid of Conn and make it look like just one of those unfortunate accidents, then I can start removing people very, very quickly.

Barry won't be able to find someone else as quickly. They've worked together for years, Apparently-Ivan has let that slip more than once. If I get rid of Conn, I have free rein to do what I want. I can scare the shit out of Barry, get rid of his people, his guys, really slowly, just to make him panic. I can get medieval, send a message, make him think his whole life is totally fucked.

But, I suppose that's just hypothetical for now.

Getting rid of Conn is also kind of like revenge.

A big "fuck you" for getting me involved with a no-good gangster like Barry Ames.

Chapter Twenty-Five

All of a sudden, my life is a mess of dutiful, excitable wedding planning and dutiful, excitable murder planning. I have a near complete schedule for failed actor turned corrupt cop, Andrew Connington. I also have an appointment at a wedding dress shop in a week's time—Leda got very insistent, despite my constant reminder that we aren't booking anything until I know what's happening with work.

"I can't believe you've picked her and not me," Gabbie teases for the not the first, but the *third* time that day.

The three of us are sitting around a café table, looking through glossy magazines and Leda's Pinterest account. Little Lucas is sat in a highchair beside her, enamoured apparently with Leda and her long, long hair.

"See, even this little guy prefers me," Leda says, laughing and leaning down to pinch his cheek to make him giggle. "You are adorable, yes! Yes, you are!"

"Leda, people talk, please, he's not a dog," Gabbie reminds her for the third time. "Sookie only picked you because you have no childcare commitments, you know."

"I wouldn't say that," Leda says. "I bought magazines! I'm organising her!"

"Sorry, Gabbie, but, I wouldn't say Leda has *no* childcare commitments," I add. "I mean, Tammy walked into traffic the other day because she thought she saw Blake Lively."

Gabbie snorts with laughter. "I don't know how she's made it this far."

"Also," Leda adds. "What did she think was going to happen? Blake Lively is going to leave Deadpool for her?"

"Maybe," Gabbie says. "I mean, she somehow persuaded you to keep taking her back."

*

We have a venue, or at least we do in theory. Rick got very excited but I won't let him book it until we know what's happening with my job. Which is annoying because come on! How many weeks do they need to realise I didn't do it? I've started low-key looking for new jobs, but it's going to be so hard with fake qualifications and apparently no references…

I think Rick has maybe reserved the venue. He has a tell. He talks a lot faster when he's lying. And he makes the very notion of the lie seem like a joke. It's kind of adorable. He lies like a little kid.

I scroll through my phone and glance at the photos again. There's a cliff and some trees, and an old swing hanging from a tree. It's basically like something out of a fairy tale. There's so much I want to do, that we want to do. But alas, the job thing again.

So aggravating.

From F: *You are so lucky you never had to plan a wedding.*

From M: *You can always just live in sin if it's too much for you.*

When did you get funny, Mother?

I smile and roll onto my back, sliding my secret phone back under my pillow. Rick is working today and then he's going out with Miguel after work, so I basically have the whole day to myself. I'm enjoying the free time, or I think I would if I didn't keep stressing about Barry asking me something stupid. Thanks to Leda's planning and Gabbie feeling more chilled out regarding parenting, we're well ahead with my part of the wedding planning.

Like, I very nearly have a dress.

Operation Kill Officer Conn is ahead of schedule and the next stage of my plan isn't due to go off until tomorrow night so… long bath?

Long bath is well deserved.

*

Conn the Corrupt Cop is partying out with a few of Barry's guys, or targets as I've come to think of them. He hangs out with them in a club Barry partially owns for two hours. I'm hanging out in the bar across the street, it's quiet enough so I can sit and have a vodka soda without having my focus ruined by loud assholes or creepers trying to sit with me.

I'm in no mood to pretend to be on business for the MIB tonight.

He comes out to smoke often enough. Sometimes he hassles young women way out of his league for a conversation over a cigarette (unsuccessfully). It's not the boldest or the worst strategy I've seen. His bug-eyes pulse in his head whenever he talks to a girl. I wonder if the bulgy eyes are telling of another type of bulge… Scratch that, I don't want to know.

This drink has turned to ash in my mouth.

Rick texts to say he's going to be out late. That suits me just fine. I make something up about going to the gym super late. I think that will be enough for him to buy. I've insisted that going to the gym is a major solitary thing for me.

Yup, I joined a gym. That's another part of wedding planning, it's going to the gym a few times a week to get into better shape for the dress. Not Leda's suggestion—God, I would never be friends with someone who makes 'suggestions' like that, could you imagine??—but more of a thing for me. I want to look fucking amazing in my dress.

But away from that now!

Back to fucking disgusting Officer Conn.

He staggers out for another cigarette, hands fumbling on the lighter. He's got that target with the dodgy nose with him. The two of them are shooting the shit, one of them spits on the ground like it's perfectly acceptable and not a 10/10 disgusting thing to do. Corrupt Conn is leaning against the wall, all smiles and bulging eyes as he checks out like… all the women who pass him on their way into the club.

Just as I'm thinking it's getting too late for me to stake him out, he waves the boys goodbye and swaggers off down the street. They stay and I leave a tip and follow him out into the night.

I keep a comfortable distance from him, sticking to the other side of the road. He is humming loudly, walking real confident, all shoulders swinging like an ape. Guys like this probably never see danger coming their way. You'd think as a cop, he'd be all up on that, Mr-On-Guard-Practically-Sherlock-Holmes-Can-See-Trouble-A-Mile-Off, but with him, it's just the opposite. He thinks of himself as a regular American Hero. Being a cop has just made him more untouchable.

He can swagger around town, pointing a gun at whoever he wants, taking bribes however he chooses, and thinks he's big and tough enough to bounce off whatever comes his way.

I really like killing guys like that.

I like to show them that they should be scared, like the rest of us.

Cop Conn stops and gets into his car—wow, corrupt *and* irresponsible—which he's parked along the roadside. He sits in the front seat for a few minutes, blinking way too slowly and clearly trying to sober up enough so he can go home. I keep back, just watching his car, pretending to be on the phone.

He gets out and staggers on over to the trunk of his car, which he starts fumbling through lazily. I tug my hood up and creep up behind him. I can see he's going through a gym bag. I steady myself and creep closer and closer. Now, this one has to look like an accident. So as much as I'd like to really fuck him up, I can't. If I fuck him up, then whatever I may or may not do next, Barry will suspect and see coming.

I want him to feel like death is following him around.

I want him to get scared.

I mean this last year has been fucking terrifying for me. Every time that phone goes off, I feel like I could sink into the floor, like my body is being pierced by a hundred tiny needles. I want him to know what that's like.

So, I creep up behind Cop Conn and say, 'Hey'.

He turns to face me, eyes bulging, face in a twisted half smile. That's when I smash the crowbar I'm carrying into the side of his head. The blow knocks him, but he doesn't quite fall. So I smash him with it again. This time he falls like a ton of bricks, backwards into the car. I just have to tuck him into the back of his own trunk and close the lid and voila, he's mine.

Car accidents can be done later, as long as they are done quickly, it shouldn't matter too much coroner report-wise.

I can drive when I need to. I don't think I could parallel park, but I know I could crash this car well enough. It's something I've become pretty good at. I take it up into the hills near his apartment to at least give the impression he was driving home drunk—no different to what he would have done anyway, minus stalling twice in a red light; hey, I don't actually have a licence.

Then I park up at the top of a hill overlooking a construction site. They're building some tacky hotel here, part of some sleazy chain. I figure that's a good enough final resting place for a creep like this. Maybe his ghost will even haunt the place.

I open up the hatch and drag his barely conscious body back into his front seat. One of his eyes is bleeding and more... bulging than its friend. It's super gross. I tell him so as I tuck him into his seat and buckle him in for dramatic effect. I put his foot on the gas pedal and press down. He doesn't really know what's happening as he starts to move towards the edge.

I think he says, 'huh' or 'what' before I slam the door shut and watch him and his car move off the edge and smash down into the ravine below. The best part of this whole thing is that this is my fucking speciality—right after doing it Mother's way. This is what I freaking do. I cause deaths that look like accidents. And Barry won't remember that because he thinks he's tamed me. He thinks I'm some fucking gun he can shoot off wherever he wants.

He'll see this and think accidents happen. He'll cover his back. He'll have to fucking rush to do it because this guy, Conn—fucking Conn—he was very obvious about what he was. I sure hope that his superiors don't find anything... uncomfortable after this.

Mind you, that would concern Conn the living, breathing, corrupt as fuck cop. In regards to Conn, the dead cop, well, I can't imagine there would be anything suspicious about his death. Just embarrassing really. I mean, cops aren't meant to be drunk drivers.

They sure aren't.

From whatever burned out pieces of him remain, there will be enough alcohol in his blood to start up a forest fire. I light a cigarette and start to walk back down the hills into civilisation so I can get an

Uber home. I even break out into a jog, just to give the impression that I've been to the gym.

And you know what? I do feel better.

I feel so fucking *good*.

*

The news about Corrupt Conn the Cop travels fast. I hear about it from Apparently-Ivan first. He comes to meet me from the supermarket to drive me to see Barry the very next day. See, that's respect for someone's life and boundaries. I buy him a Kit-Kat and brandish it at him as he fidgets with his shitty music.

"Leave me alone," he says, but accepts the Kit-Kat, anyway.

We drive for five minutes, get stuck in traffic for another five, when Apparently-Ivan's phone rings.

Apparently-Ivan, like me, has two phones. I've seen them in the glove compartment when he reaches in there for a new CD. One, I guess is his personal phone—don't think we're quite ready to start a work-based WhatsApp group yet, but maybe one day if I'm lucky. And there's another phone. His 'work' phone. And this I know is a call from Barry. I know that ring tone. Apparently, Barry likes to give his unwilling employees the same phone.

It's a ringtone I've come to dread.

"That's Barry. You should answer that," I tell him.

He scowls at me in the rear-view mirror before switching on his Bluetooth.

"Yes, boss," he says.

I do enjoy that he sounds as irritated talking to Barry—who arguably ruined his life—as he does when he's talking to me, who has, in the majority of ways, done absolutely nothing to him.

"Ivan, if you're with Miss. King, take her home," Barry says, sounding colder and more alert than I've ever heard him talk. "I don't need to see her today. I need you to come here now. I need to take care of some damage control. You need to come to Conn's place. There's shit we need to get rid of. Like now. Right now. You understand?"

I see Apparently-Ivan's brow furrow.

"Ok."

"No," Barry snaps. "You need to get here now. I can't go alone. I need… backup. Ok? Get your ass here."

He hangs up abruptly.

I realise that Conn must have stuff that Barry needs to stay hidden. Drugs, files, I don't know what. But I'll bet it's stuff that wouldn't quite make sense in the home of a respectable young police officer, no matter how bug-eyed.

I bet Barry is shitting his pants.

"I'll hop out here," I tell Apparently-Ivan. "Don't worry about dropping me back. I needed a ride into town today, anyway." I reach up and pat his shoulder. "And eat that Kit-Kat, I got it for you and from the sound of that phone call, you're gonna be needing it."

He grunts at me, but I see him tearing open the wrapper with his teeth as I get out of the car when he pulls out. As Apparently-Ivan disappears off into the traffic, I find myself with this… buzzing feeling in my stomach. This is happening. This is all systems go from here.

And Barry and Apparently-Ivan can tear Conn's place apart destroying any connection to the mob that they find. But they aren't going to find his phone. Maybe they'll hope it was destroyed when his car went over the edge of that cliff.

But it wasn't. I have it right here.

And let me tell you, Conn's phone—which I have access to thanks to Conn's fingerprint (before it was no doubt, burnt beyond plausible recognition)—is basically a little portal into Barry's world. And it is one I intend to exploit the *fuck* out of.

*

Victory lap achieved and groceries purchased—you wouldn't believe how often those two things go hand in hand—I take a nice long shower. Meeting with Barry avoided and his empire almost completely communicated to me by Conn from beyond the grave, I was sure this day couldn't get any better.

On that, I was very wrong.

Very wrong.

The phone is ringing so loud I can hear it over the running water. I get out, awkwardly fastening a towel around myself, wiping my hand frantically as I lift the phone and see 'Unknown Number' flashing across the screen.

Surely, Barry would know better than to contact me on my actual phone, right? Or has this whole thing…unhinged him faster than I realised? Heck, maybe he was especially attached to Conn. It wouldn't surprise me. Shitheads love shitheads love…well, you get the picture.

I let it go to voicemail and twist my hair up into a towel.

I'm fixing my face in the mirror when my phone kicks off again. Same 'Unknown Number' flashing across the screen. Who answers to that? Ever heard of just leaving a message? I watch it burn itself out before switching over to voicemail.

"Hello, Sookie, I do hope this is the correct number. This is Sandra McCoy, we spoke last month regarding your suspension."

Heart in mouth, despite doing nothing (at least in this one area of my life) wrong, because I have a guilty conscience 4 life, I sit down on the edge of the bathtub.

"The Faculty greatly appreciates your patience during this difficult time. Your cooperation has been an asset and I understand how hard this must have been. Needless to say, we would very much like for you to return to work. I can discuss this matter with you in person, I was hoping you would be available to come for a meeting with me today, if you are available? My office is on the fourth floor. I'm available until three. Please give me a call back on..."

I fucking knew it!

I knew this idiotic witch-hunt could only last so long!

"Hi, is this Sandra McCoy?" I ask when she picks up, clipped and professional as ever. "It's Sookie King, I'm sorry I missed your call."

*

It feels like forever since I've been to this building. Walking inside and waiting at reception, just a stone's throw from my old office. I can see them through the window, just vaguely, but I recognise Jack stomping around, hands on hips—probably telling Claudia off for absolutely nothing again.

"Sookie?"

I look up and see Sandra stood there waiting for me, all pinched and proper, professional real estate agent smile.

"Hi, Sandra," I say, standing up and accepting her very firm handshake.

"So good of you to come in, particularly given the short notice," she says. "Did you get parked alright?"

"Oh, I don't drive," I say, "But I just about remembered the way in."

She has the manners to at least look embarrassed. "Quite. Now, why don't we head up to my office? Do you take coffee? My assistant will get some."

"Ok, sure," I say, "That'd be nice." I glance over my shoulder as we walk towards the elevator and see Claudia and Kiko coming out of the office. Their eyes widen when they see me and Kiko blows me a kiss.

*

Her office is nice. I mean, really nice! There's a view of the city through this practically wall-sized window. Her desk is polished wood, none of that plastic-feeling crap. And the chairs! The chairs are so comfortable that I'm a little bit afraid I won't be able to get out of it! I mean, this is more like a plush CEO's office. I bet her PC never gives her shit either.

I smile at her nervous-looking assistant as she passes me my coffee.

"Oh, you don't take sugar, do you?" she asks.

"No, this is lovely," I reassure her.

"Thank you, Karen. Please cover my phone while Sookie and I catch up," Sandra says cordially, before settling herself back into her chair and peering over at me from the top of her rounded glasses. "So, thank you again for coming in like this."

"It's fine," I say. "These things are better in person than over the phone or by email."

"Quite," she says, "Now, I understand this has gone on longer than any of us would have liked. I sincerely apologise for that. There were several members of staff under suspicion, though admittedly, you were on suspension for the longest. Our investigation was thorough.

We wanted to be certain of what was going on before any action was taken."

"You must know that it wasn't me, right?" I say.

"Yes, the individual who was using the staff email address to trick students into providing false tuition payments was caught at the beginning of this week. He has admitted all wrongdoing and the college is taking further guidance on to how we should proceed."

"Who was it?" I ask.

"Typically, we wouldn't divulge that information, but as you'll notice who is missing from the office, I suppose it wouldn't hurt to tell you. Corey Banks, the intern. He had access to everybody's printing card at some point. And he had far more IT access than we first realised." She looks exhausted by this, and irritated. "I would like to invite you back to work, with our sincerest apologies for the way these last few months were handled."

I pause and consider this for a moment.

"I'd love to come back," I say. "But to be honest, this whole thing has been so discouraging. I mean, it was hard being accused of something like that. I feel uncomfortable coming back to work. What's everyone going to think? To be honest, I feel discriminated against."

She looks slightly panicked behind the eyes.

"I can promise that this won't affect your relationship with your colleagues. Every single one of them was under investigation as well. They all knew that."

"Yes, I appreciate that. But I was suspected that strongly that I wasn't allowed to come to work for over a month," I say. "And to be honest, I don't trust Jack not to joke around about that." I can see from the slight twitch in her expression that she knows exactly what I mean. "It's not going to be easy for me to come back to work and have him making personal comments about it every five minutes."

"I can speak to Jack," she says. "We've had a talk already about this when another member of your team returned from suspension. He will be tactful, I promise. What we want is you back in the office. Jack has reassured me that you're an asset to the team. It would be a shame for this to ruin that."

I sigh and sit back in the chair.

"He isn't really known for his tact."

"Sookie," she says, "What can we offer you to get you back to work?"

Oh, so it's like that.

I sit forward. "Well, I got engaged recently."

"I see, congratulations," she says. "Have you set a date?"

"Thank you and no, not yet. We have a date in mind. October this year actually. But as you can imagine, the wedding planning has been…a little difficult given my unstable employment situation."

I can see from the crease in her brow that she knows what I'm getting at.

"I'd be more than happy to come back to work. But there's a lot to organise, a lot to do, with planning a wedding. And then there's my honeymoon. My fiancé sort of has his heart set on taking me to Paris for three weeks. I'm not sure my annual leave would stretch to that and any other time I'd need for..."

She coughs to interrupt me. "Given your excellent conduct during our investigation and the understandable difficulties this has caused you, I am sure I could arrange for you to take…three weeks as paid leave, non-inclusive of your remaining annual leave allowance. If so, do you think you would be comfortable coming back to resume your role from next week?"

I offer her my best smile and offer her my hand to shake.

"Sandra, I would be happy to!"

Chapter Twenty-Six

You know what, fuck it—I *am* a very well-adjusted person.

*

I start small. Make up some lie to Rick about going to the gym, mentally promising that when all of this is over, I won't lie to him ever again. I'll be an open book, the kind people would want to read, not fear touching because of the stains. I head out into the night, leaving him to discuss his bachelor party with the guys. I head on over to the house of Mickey Martinez, who does the books for Barry. He lives with a boyfriend, who is fortunately out. Let's not have a repeat of Mrs. Anderson.

I watch from the front for a few minutes. It's dark and a nice enough neighbourhood that loitering may start to bother some eagle-eyed folks. I circle round back and open his garden gate very easily. Wow, he must feel pretty secure.

His back yard looks like shit, all weeds, a few dead dahlias. His patio door is open due to the hot night, so I sneak right into his house. The place is cute, or at least it would be if someone else lived here. There's takeout boxes on the kitchen countertops and two half-finished bottles of Margarita mix—like, why not just throw one away?

I pick up a knife from the rack in his kitchen and try to weigh up my options as to whether Mr. Martinez keeps a gun at his place. I don't suppose I'm going to give him the chance to use it. Keeping quiet as I creep through the kitchen and into the small dimly lit corridor, I hear the tapping of a keyboard and mismatched humming.

Peeking through the living room door, which is ajar, I spot the guy himself, Mickey Martinez, sat on his living room sofa, back facing me, working through some complex-looking Excel spreadsheets. He looks up for a second as he hears the squeak of the door hinges.. He doesn't manage to form a sentence before his very own kitchen knife comes down hard into his throat. Three short, sharp strokes with the knife and he and his laptop are on the ground, dying that cream rug red.

Seriously, cream?

Feeling particularly creative, I use the knife to draw a dollar sign in his blood onto the back of his polo shirt and leave him there on the floor.

I guess I feel a little bad for his boyfriend who's going to come home and find him like that, dead on their now very red rug. I feel bad. But not that much. Better he comes home to this than be any part of it. I mean, grief, you can work through. A knife in your skull, nope, medical science isn't there yet.

*

"So, are you thinking sleeves? No sleeves? Half sleeve?" Marsha, the saleswoman asks. She's all smiles and is motherly in a way that my own mother never was.

"Well, I'm not too sure," I say.

I wasn't sure I was going to like this: you know, the whole, buying a wedding dress in a big white shop experience. But it turns out I really do.

The store Leda picked out accepts customers by appointment only. We got given freaking sparkling wine when we walked through the door! This is like being a pseudo celebrity. I had Gabbie and Leda's support for all of five seconds until they got distracted by all the shiny fabrics and lace details and vanished to opposite sides of the room, leaving me alone with Marsha.

Marsha isn't pushy. She isn't too advice-y. And she didn't seem irritated when I gave the answer most likely dreaded by the staff in this business. You know, they say, 'What sort of dress would you ideally go for?' and I say, 'I dunno really.'

"We'll find the right dress at the right price for the right person," she said when we started combing through rack after rack of lacey white fabric. "The right person being you by the way."

I bet Marsha always makes her sale.

"You could pull off sleeveless," she says.

"Actually," I say, "I have a few…embarrassing scars on my arms, so maybe sleeves would be better."

"See, you do know what you want," she says, smiling. "Well, this is however you'd be most comfortable. But I can certainly find you a few different options with a full sleeve. And you said you wanted to wear white, right?"

"I guess, yeah, ok," I say, sitting down on a pale pink sofa. "I'd like to see some options." Marsha vanishes off into the stock room and I sip my sparkling wine too noisily.

"I think you should wear a tiara," Gabbie says, she's already drained her glass and lands beside me on the sofa with an oomph.

"No way," I say. "Short of being in a royal family, there is never an excuse for a tiara."

"Oh, come on! I think it'd look great," she says.

"Nope, no tiaras."

"Can me and Leda wear tiaras?" she asks, before shaking her head. "No, I'm kidding, I'm kidding. So, what's happening here?"

"You were meant to be sat with me, then you'd know," I say, linking my arm through hers. "Marsha is finding me some possibilities. Stick around and help me there?"

"I promise," she says, "I'm sorry! I got excited! I mean, I went all thrift store boho for my wedding. I never saw a store like this and it's super exciting," she says. "Over there, they have these heels that are like… if someone cut off our heads and piled them on top of each other. Like that high!" She tries to demonstrate with her hands.

"That is disturbing," I say. "Can you not talk about severed heads please?"

Gabbie laughs and rests her head on my shoulder. "Sorry, I'm excited! I'm so happy for you, you know?"

Marsha pops her head out from around the side of the storeroom door. "Okay, so I have narrowed it down to three. If you don't like them, I have three potential others. Here's the first one!" She comes out, holding the dress in front of her. "Obviously, you'd need to try it on before you were sure but…"

Gabbie's hand grasps mine and squeezes.

"Oh, Sookie!"

*

I decided right from the beginning that I was going to leave Apparently-Ivan alone. He's as much a victim of Barry as I am. Sure there might be others in that situation, but I don't know that for sure. I don't have time to find out. I don't particularly care.

But I went out of my way to plan the warehouse fire for a night Apparently-Ivan wasn't working, just so he wouldn't get mixed up in it. It'd be super hard to try to do it and get him out of there at the same time. So, it's easiest just to make sure he's not working Thursday and go from there.

There's a method to my madness. On Thursday night, ten of Barry's fellas are going to be sat around, waiting for a shipment of drugs. I get the impression from photos Conn took of his attendance at one of these evenings, that the boys tend to sit around playing cards like some tired cliché and knocking back a few beers.

On Wednesday, I have the joy of spending my lunch break in the warehouse with Barry, prattling on about my next target. He's in an erratic sort of mood. He waves his arms around a lot more and gets lost in the middle of most of his sentences.

"You see what I mean, Miss. King?" he asks me, tapping the table in front of me.

"No," I say.

He looks broken-hearted.

"I knew it. Conn always got where I was coming from. It's so unfair," he says, holding a hand to his head and covering his eyes. "Hey, Miss. King, would you mind popping to the break room and grabbing me my juice? I just need a moment…"

"You do know that I have my actual job to get back to, right?" I ask him.

"Whatever," he says, "Just do it ok. Ivan, can you help me with the blinds in here?"

So, I get up and wander on over to the break room at the bottom of the stairs. I check the fridge and find Barry's juice box. Also in the fridge is a few packed lunches, and on the bottom shelf, a whole load of beers.

This is where my bag comes into play. I take six of their beers out of the fridge and replace them with six of my own, six that include an extra ingredient of ground up sleeping pills. These are pills I swiped from Tammy's supply ages ago—Tammy always has the good stuff. Rich people problems, am I right?

Then I close the fridge door, pick up my backpack and head on back up the stairs, Barry's juice in hand.

This small thing on Wednesday, that quite frankly ruined my lunch break, made my Thursday night at the 'gym' a whole lot easier.

I mean, taking out ten guys is hard. Taking out four, much easier. So long as none of them start to wake up. There's this one big guy, who Conn has saved in his phone as 'Fat Pat', but I can guarantee nobody has ever called him that to his face. The guy is so scary I think professional freaking fighters wouldn't want to mess with him. From the size of him alone, I don't think the pills would do all that much.

But in terms of drugging them, it's going to be a kind of lucky (not so lucky for them) dip.

Thursday night comes and as soon as people start falling asleep—I can see them snoozing in the chairs set up around the main warehouse floor through the window, not so lucky for me, Pat is one of the snoozing ones—I walk into the carpark, hood up, surgical mask (thanks Jenny) on, I head right up to the target with the weird nose, who is outside, having a cigarette.

"Hey," I call out to him.

"Oh, hey," he says, "What're you doing here?"

As last words go, those are optimistic. I shoot him through his right eye and drag his body back into the warehouse where I stash it in the little office by the pseudo reception they've got near the front door. Then I slip into the men's room and wait around for a few minutes. Sure enough, the target with the bald head comes in to take a leak.

He plays with the light switch for a moment—I've taken out the bulb—before settling on peeing in the dark. He doesn't see me in the stall behind him and doesn't make a sound further than a grunt when I shoot him in the back of the head. I drag his body into the stall behind me and lock the door to the men's room with the key I got from the reception desk. I crouch under the reception desk and wait.

The stupid target—the one who called out to Ivan the first day I got here, he comes out looking for the bald guy. He's slurring from the beer and scratching himself. He sees me staring up at him from the ground just before he gets shot.

Then I walk leisurely into the main warehouse where all the sleeping targets are. Pat is snoring and out cold—lucky for me, I guess those pills were more potent than they seemed. I look up and see the tall skinny target coming downstairs from Barry's office. He sees me as I see him. He reaches for his gun, but first yells, 'Hey! What're you!' before I shoot him in the throat.

Not my best work, but the second shot gets his head.

After that, I shoot the sleeping bums, just to make sure they don't wake up and try to escape. I take my time getting the place ready to go up in flames. I mean, I don't want there to be any trace left. I want this to be big! I set it alight, close the front door behind me and stand out of the front gates for a few minutes. Windows crack and the flames get higher and higher. I can see it rise through the window.

As the building starts to come down, I decide it's time to jog home in the dark. As I do, I take in the smell of the smoke, the sound of the sirens in the distance, the morning sun beginning to rise. Barry is going to get a call in an hour or two and that horrible feeling, like battery acid sliding down your throat, he's going to experience that tenfold.

*

"So, have the two of you set a date?" Donnie asks as he flicks through one of my wedding magazines. "I mean, that's like… the first thing you do, right?"

"Yes," I say. "Now I'm back at work, we've finalised a date. October 15th."

"Do you want me to officiate?"

"Can you?"

"No," he says, shaking his head and laughing. "I can't believe you're getting married."

"Neither can I. There's loads to do. Check this out," I say, handing him one of the magazines. "I mean, look at this. This is a seating chart."

Donnie frowns, glancing over at it. He smirks at me. "You could always not bother with one, you know? I bet people will figure out where to sit."

I nudge him. "Sure, and when you end up sat next to Rick's elderly aunt for four hours, then you can come complaining to me."

"Hey, I might like that," he teases. "Is she cute?"

*

Barry's main security is a woman called Tara. She lives alone in an apartment near the beach. For someone who runs security for a gangster, she isn't that difficult to get to. I suppose she felt she was safe in a male-dominated field, keeping her head down and living without extravagance.

I follow her out onto the beach while she's walking her dog. She goes out in the evening because she's something of a recluse. Barry communicates with her over the phone *mostly*, though he has been known to make a house-call. There are messages on Conn's phone about how amused Barry gets with how uncomfortable Tara is when he comes over. She's in her late thirties and lives with her dog.

So, you know, I could feel bad for her: if I wanted to, I'm sure I could find in her a story not dissimilar to my own. Another person roped into Barry's employment. But unfortunately for her, she's paid to keep Barry safe. So, there's not much I can do about it. I need to get rid of her.

Just like Mother said, I must understand what I'm willing to do to protect my own personal happiness.

I'm willing to get rid of her for my life with Rick. I try to think about how all of this will be over by October as I smash her head in with a rock and leave her there on the sand for the waves to come and collect. I play catch with her dog for a little while before heading back to my nice, warm home that is just getting safer and safer by the day.

*

"I don't get why you'd even want him there!" Veronica is yelling as I shut the front door behind me. Frowning, I slip off my shoes as quietly as I can. "Rick, honestly! You can't actually want him there on your wedding day?"

"I don't think it's crazy to want our dad to be a part of it, no."

"Our dad—our dad—do you seriously think of him as our dad? He abandoned us!" she snaps at him. "He made it quite clear how much he gives a crap! And what happened the last time you made the effort?"

"It's my wedding," he says, "I can invite whoever I want."

"You're going to break Mom's heart!"

"You don't!" He trails off and pokes his head around the living room door. "Sookie, hey, sorry, my sister was just leaving."

Veronica breezes past him, her big brown eyes are filled with tears and she's flushed. "Sorry, Sookie," she says, before she rushes past me and slams the front door closed behind her.

I blink at him. "Erm, what?"

Rick groans and covers his head with his hand. "I told her I wanted to invite our dad."

"Well, you did know she'd react like this."

He nods, making a miserable sort of affirmative noise. "I... I know how much it'll hurt her and Mom... but I just... I want him there. I feel like I'll regret it in the long run, you know? It's our big day. If things patch up with him in the future, he might always feel bad for not being a part of it." He takes my hand and hugs me around the middle. "Am I being naïve?"

Yes.

"Maybe a little," I say, "But I can see where you're coming from. Have you... already invited him?"

"Not yet," he says. "But... I got in touch on Facebook recently. He's going to be in Santa Cruz for a teaching conference next month. I thought maybe we could all go for dinner together. I made the mistake of suggesting Veronica come along..."

"Give her time," I say. "But I'd be up for meeting your dad."

"Thank you," he says, "I knew she wasn't going to like it. I shouldn't let it get me bummed out. But I was hoping... maybe this could reconcile them. Veronica was so little when Dad left, she doesn't have any good memories of him the way that me and Maria do."

"You have a good heart," I say. "But seriously, if it's going to happen for your Dad and Veronica, let it happen naturally. She's probably got a lot of her own issues about this. If he comes to the wedding, just be prepared that she's not going to like it."

He kisses my forehead. "I should just let you handle this, right?"

"Pfft, no way! I'm a mess with like... no relatives coming. Don't listen to me at all!"

*

I don't like the Halloween mask. It has very little visibility and looks ridiculous. Whenever I catch sight of my reflection, I internally cringe. I know that should be the least of my problems right now, but it's not really something I can shy away from. I don't feel like Michael Myers; I feel like an idiot.

Barry's suggestions have gotten even more stupid ever since he started to get really scared. He's sent his family off to four different safe houses in different parts of the world. His youngest kid is six and he's been packed off to Cuba with an au pair. What the fuck must he think is going on?

Realistically, I shouldn't complain. I know that in his paranoid brain, there's stupider, wilder things he could be requesting I carry out. So, I wear the dumb mask, even though it makes me look like fucking amateur hour and it makes it very difficult to kill the real estate agent he's sent me after. Hopefully (and I say this very lightly), hopefully the last person I'm going to have to hurt on Barry's orders.

After wearing the dumb mask and stabbing the guy to death with a big knife he provided me with, I had to string the guy up and write in red marker 'A WARNING' on the whiteboard in the man's office. I take a photo and send it to Barry, which seems to get him to stop with the frantic onslaught of messages. This whole thing has sent him right back into micro-management territory. So ergh.

*

The invitations are out. Leda had her heart set on a set of *really* lacy, frilly looking things that barely resemble paper anymore. I told her—not for the first time, I might add—to get her own darn wedding. These are simple; rustic, I suppose, would be the right word. Carmella always told me to never over-embellish a thing if it's worth doing. It always seemed like good advice. Plus, some of the typefaces on those were so hard to read.

I wanted typewriter font. Rick hates typewriter font. I joked around with him about Comic Sans just to see the abject horror on his face. In the end we settled for something between typewriter font and flouncy font. I think it's a safe place to stay in.

'You are invited to the wedding of Rick Fumero and Sookie King,'.

My wedding invitations will go out with a name that isn't mine on them. And I know it's stupid, I know that it's selfish... but when I look at these invitations, these crisp white invitations I picked out from all those many, many options, I feel this tiny, selfish piece of sadness in my heart.

Sookie King feels like another person. Sometimes I know her well, sometimes she's a stranger. Like my avatar in a video game. It's who Rick sees when he looks at me.

I hold one of our crisp, white invitations up to the light and think about all the people who won't receive one of these. Sukhy, who I'd have taken the risk and invited anyway, even if I could only exist as 'Sookie King'. I wonder if she'd have taken the risk with me and come along. Though, perhaps that's not... a healthy thing to even think about. Beth, from her likely well-organised dormitory room at Yale, Matt, all the way from NYC. And Mother, from her prison cell.

I wish they could be here with me. I take a deep breath and settle back onto the sofa as Rick browses through the channels for something to watch.

I'm proud of who I am. I deserve to be happy. I deserve this.

"You like the invitations?"

"Sure," he says, "You sure you didn't want the flowery ones though?" He smirks and wraps an arm around my shoulders. "Are you ok? You seem quiet tonight."

"Yeah," I say, resting my head on his shoulder. "Yeah, I'm fine. Excited even. What do you want to watch?"

"You know, I'm not sure I'm in the mood anymore," he says. "Do you want to just… read and have a quiet moment? I feel so relaxed tonight."

"So zen of you," I say sarcastically.

But he just laughs and rests his head on top of mine.

And I really wish I could give him better than a psycho like me, functioning under a fake name, with a long list of people who are either dead or impossible for her to contact now. I wish I could give him the sort of life that he deserves. I find myself shutting out quiet moments because it's in quiet moments that I tend to think about all of the bad, fucking terrible things that I've done, that I do.

And sure, maybe someone else would freak out about it, cry or leave and never come back to this town again.

Not me.

I'm really fucking well-adjusted.

Chapter Twenty-Seven

I'm on my lunch break, scrolling through bridesmaid dress ideas Leda has sent, when my second phone starts to ring.

"Hello?"

"Miss. King, hey, hey, hey," Barry says, and I can feel every fidget in his words—Barry is cracking up. "I can always count on Miss. King to answer the phone. Ain't that the truth, the goddamn truth, huh?"

"Sure," I say, switching phone hands. "What's up?"

"It's fucking Ivan, isn't it?" he snaps, as though this is something I should inherently know. "Y'all talk, right? You chat?"

"Chat? I mean, Barry, you have *met* Ivan, right? Tried chatting to him? He's not exactly…"

"Well, of course I have!" He sounds high, I realise, like super-super high. Barry has always been one of those people where you can imagine his expression, his posture when you hear his voice on the phone. Usually you can hear him slouched in a seat somewhere. I can picture him now, eyes wild, pacing, buzzing. I think I heard him kick over a chair a second ago. "The man is like a brick wall! Never says much more than 'ja', 'da', 'nah'—you'd tell me though? Wouldn't you? You'd tell me, Miss. King, if Ivan suddenly got *chatty*, wouldn't you? If he suddenly had lots to say? If he suddenly had lots to say about me?"

"Erm."

And I should say now, I don't like the concept of gaslighting. I understand fully and completely how fucked up it is to mess with someone else's reality. However, is understanding how bad something is enough to stop me from doing it? And like all the big moral dilemmas in my life, I'd have to answer that it would depend on the thing and the situation!

Like, I know smoking is bad for me, but I still do it. I mean, yeah, I know I'm trying to quit. I know killing people is wrong, but I still do it. Though again, I want to quit. Right after I'm done with this Barry thing. And back to this Barry thing, I know that gaslighting is wrong. I mean, I was raised by a woman who got me to behave by implying that she'd poison my friends if we were too noisy. And like all decisions, it depends on the victim.

Would I gaslight Rick or Leda or Carla… no, fuck no! Of course not.

But would I gaslight Barry? A man who blackmailed me into a hundred—I bet it's at a hundred by now—murders? Yes, yes, I really would.

"Sure, I'd tell you," I say.

"I knew I could count on you, I just knew it. My people have been dropping left right and centre, but not you, Miss. King, you're a survivor! You're a survivor like me."

"Sure am," I say. "Boss, I gotta get back to the office."

"Right, you go. Yeah, I gotta go too. You take care of yourself, Miss. King."

He's cracking like an egg.

I know the signs.

I've seen a guy's mind unravel before. This is how it began with Jason back when I was still Fiona Taylor. Jason, who I had known since I was five, had been one of my best friends right up until the night when I stabbed him to death and dragged his body through the woods. *Unrelated.* Jason got like this. He got… paranoid, he got irrational. He started seeing conspiracies everywhere. He got into watching people, assuming they were assuming all sorts of stuff about him. Admittedly, Barry is probably progressing through this a lot faster than Jason. Jason never, thankfully, had access to Class A drugs. But they both acted the same way. They buzzed and panicked until that dangerous, rapid-fire anxiety which had pointed at everyone before it found its target.

In Jason's case, that target was our friend, Beth. He became obsessed with the idea that Beth was talking to the police about us. He was convinced she was wiretapping all of our conversations.

Barry's target, apparently, is Ivan.

This could be a problem.

*

Tonight, also just so happens to be the night we're having dinner with Rick's dad. He has the wedding invitation in his jacket pocket, if things go well. If not, as I said to him earlier, we'll leave, knowing that the olive branch was extended. I haven't told Rick that Veronica called me to talk about their father—who she refers to as 'Martin' or 'Bastard'. I sort of admire her rage. I couldn't imagine Rick or their gentle mother having that kind of fire.

"Sookie, you have to promise not to buy into the bullshit he's serving out," Veronica had said—like Barry, you can usually imagine Veronica's face and body language through hearing her talk on the phone. "He's a showman, he likes showing off and acting like everybody's best friend. It's so fucked up."

Personally, I can't stand people like that. And I can't say that I'm feeling amazing about meeting the man who abandoned Rick and his siblings. But… as everyone keeps telling me, relationships, especially marriage, are all about compromises.

Potentially inviting this shit-stain of a human is one of those compromises.

I have never seen Rick this nervous… like ever! He's checked his hair in the mirror no less than five times. He's wearing a suit. He insisted on helping me pick my outfit—something he has never done. It's strange to see him like this considering how happy and casual he was about me meeting his mother, as compared to this… strange, restrictive panic at meeting his father.

"Dad is very punctual," he says as we pull up outside the restaurant. "I know it seems a little paranoid to get here this early but trust me, I want to be here first, to meet him, you know?" He fixes his tie for the third time in the last hour and checks his face in the rear-view mirror.

"Do I look weird?" he says. "Why do I look weird?"

"Is your tie cutting off circulation to your brain?" I ask, then regret seeing his nervous expression. "Rick, it's going to be fine. Ok? Just take it easy."

317

Amber had never met Rick's father. In fact, Rick's father has never met any of his girlfriends. He's never met any of Rick's friends since he was five or six years old. Rick's father is from Texas originally and works as a high school teacher. His name is Martin Mackenzie, which makes him sound like the protagonist of a series of children's books about a cowboy.

"Sorry," he says, "I'm just nervous. It's been so long since I've seen him."

"It'll be ok," I say. "Shall we go inside?"

"Sure. Sure. Ok. Erm, are you sure my beard doesn't look…?"

"Rick!"

I know Martin Mackenzie met Aleida when they were in college. His parents didn't approve of the match, to the point that Rick has never met his grandparents on his father's side.

I know. More red flags. Who'd have thought?

The restaurant is a fancy hipster-style steakhouse which Rick spent ages researching online. It's not too crowded or too noisy. I can see him scanning the tables already, just in case his father has already arrived. I reach down, take his hand and squeeze gently. A small reminder to say, as I have been for the last few days, 'It's fine. You can calm down'.

"We have a reservation under the name Mackenzie," he says.

"Oh, hold on, let me check… Yes, yes," the teenager behind the counter says, "One of your party has already arrived. Follow me please."

"See, told you," Rick whispers.

Upon reaching the table by the window overlooking the carpark, I can feel beads of sweat on Rick's hand. He bites his lip. He rubs his head. I have never, ever seen him this nervous. At the table is a plump, middle-aged white guy, with thinning blonde hair and a thick moustache.

"Dad," Rick says.

"Rick, my boy!" He jumps to his feet and embraces Rick like an old friend, squeezing him around the shoulders. He beams at him, blue eyes bright. "Well there, I like the beard! It suits you!" He glances at me. "And you must be Sookie!"

"Yes, I!"

He interrupts to declare that he is a 'hugger' and pulls me in tight against him, giving me an uncomfortable squeeze.

"Great to meet you, great to meet you, Sookie. Call me Marty, everyone does."

"Erm, thanks, Marty," I say, feeling a little violated from the very tight hug and a little irritated by the creepy way he keeps saying my name.

"Ah, yeah, I can see we're going to get on," he says. "And Rick, very nice work. I see you've inherited my taste for gorgeous women." He nudges Rick and gives him a creepy wink, before laughing and touching my arm. "Sorry, sweetheart, I like to kid around. I'm just excited to meet you and see my boy here." He laughs and claps Rick on the back. "I'm a people person, me, love a catch-up!"

Ho-ly *shit*. This guy is a massive creep! Why is it that when someone is a 'people person', this just equates to way too much physical contact, a lot of rapey arm touching and having them say your name quite a lot? For the love of…

"Take a seat, take a seat," Marty says, taking his chair. "Feast your eyes on this menu. Nice place you've found here, boy."

"Oh, it's not a problem," Rick says. "Dad used to take me to the best steakhouses when I was a kid," he tells me. "So, I always try to return the favour when we see each other."

"That's nice," I say, trying not to think about how Veronica told me that the last time Rick saw his father he was only seventeen and had saved up tips to take him out for dinner.

"So, Dad, how have you been?" Rick asks eagerly, taking a seat beside him. "Was the conference fun?"

"Oh, yeah, it was good, very good in fact," Marty says. "I always get roped into attending those things, never any good, but it's nice to get out of town. And it's good timing that the conference landed me back in California." He glances briefly at the empty chair on my right. "So, erm, little Ronnie didn't fancy tagging along tonight?"

I can see the panic on Rick's face.

"Erm, no, she really wanted to though," he says, lying through his teeth. "Sorry, Dad, she had classes. She couldn't catch a break."

"Good work ethic, just like her old man," Marty says, tapping his robust stomach. "Would've been nice to see my little girl. She has a lot of funny ideas about me," he adds for my unfortunate benefit. "Would've been nice to talk, now that she's grown up, sort of set her straight, you know?" He looks up at me and smiles. "I mean, I'm a nice guy, I'm not a bad father."

Thankfully, the waiter arrives to take our orders, and I feel relief swim over me because I am not going to sit here and enable him into thinking that he's done nothing wrong and Veronica had wanted to be here under any circumstances.

"I'll have a No. 5," Marty says, tapping the menu. "I'd like it well-done with curly fries and a salad. He'll have the same," he says, gesturing to Rick with one hand. Rick's smile wavers slightly, before he gives a little false chuckle and shrugs. "And, Sookie, what about you? Don't tell me you're one of those figure-obsessed salad eaters?"

"Definitely," I say (I'm not), "I'll have the Caesar salad with added halloumi."

Marty snorts, shaking his head. "You girls and your diets!" He smiles at the waiter, as if he and the other men are all in on a huge joke. My skin begins to itch. Now, this guy, Rick's father aside, could really benefit from putting his head in an oven. He should do it now. Like *right* now. "I'll have a beer with mine, you pick which one," he says brightly to the waiter.

"I'll have a Coke," Rick says, before Marty can do any more deciding for him.

"And I'll have a glass of white wine," I say, "You can pick which one," I add.

Marty laughs and claps a hand on my back. His fingers feel like four bloated sausages and I vaguely consider detaching them from his palm.

No, come on. Best behaviour.

"So, Sookie, what do you do?"

"I'm an administrator," I say, "I manage student programmes from enrolment to graduation-"

He interrupts me, because of course he does, to talk about how good it is to work in education. "It's nice to finish a day's work and know that you're benefitting society, helping the next generation along the way to getting it right," he says.

"Well," I say, "I don't know much about that. But I'd say Rick's work is a lot more valuable." Yes, Rick, your son, who you haven't asked one thing about; I don't say it, but I think it's in my tone. I know it is, because Rick squeezes my hand under the table.

"Oh, yes, still with that book place?" he says, and it's disgusting. He's like a child, he can't even muster a level of politeness to sound genuinely interested. He's filling a space, ticking a box. He's not even looking at him, he's already glancing over to the bar.

"Yeah," Rick says. "It's going well actually, so!"

"You know, Sookie," Marty interrupts, clearly Rick had used his 30 second slot and I find my nails biting into my palm. "This boy couldn't get his head out of a book when he was a kid. I'd be hassling him to come and kick a ball around outside, but all he'd want to do is read." He pats Rick's back again, laughing. "When he left college, I knew it'd be something with books. I imagined I'd see him behind the counter at Barnes and Noble, maybe catch something of his in print one day. You're writing a novel, aren't you, son?"

"No," Rick says. "I'm…"

"Ah, our drinks! Good man, good man," he says to the waiter, beaming and weirdly getting up to take his beer from the tray instead of, you know, just waiting and letting the poor guy set it out, like a normal person would. The waiter, now struggling to balance the tray, and fighting to hide a very visible frown, passes Rick his Coke and me my wine.

I've rarely been as grateful for booze.

"So, what do you teach?" I ask, because I don't want to have to listen to him hassle Rick about a novel he's definitely not writing. And clearly, this old fuck likes to talk about himself.

"I teach mathematics at Northampton Academy," he says, smiling this shit-eating grin like he's expecting me to say 'Oh wow' or something. When I just nod—clearly not the reaction he wanted—he adds, "It's a very prestigious private school."

"Math teacher," I say, taking a sip of wine. "That must be rewarding work."

"Oh, it is," he says, "I'm taking our Mathletes to Nationals this year."

"No way," Rick says brightly. "Dad, that's amazing!"

He shrugs, still smirking.

"I'm proud. My wife, Lizzie is the principal at Northampton, she's really pushing for funding for more academic competitions, rather than your typical football season. Though, our boy, Tommy, did make varsity this year."

I can see the disappointment in Rick's face, and it breaks my heart.

"We're very proud. His big sister, Molly hates him playing football, she's going through a rebellious phase. You know how teenage girls can be." He smiles, twinkly eyed, one of those happy fathers who brags about his kids. "She's involved in all these petitions and human rights type things. She's so mature for her age and she has such a big heart. I keep telling her, 'Molly, you can't handle every crisis. You should enjoy being sixteen'—but there's no telling her that, of course."

This is cruel, this is the worst. And I hate seeing Rick smiling through, I can see him juggling with asking a follow-up question, just to be polite or changing the subject. I can see him desperately wanting to change the subject.

"They are great kids," Marty continues. "I really am blessed. You guys will get it when you have a family of your own. Whenever I go to a game, see my boy catch that ball, I get this tight feeling in my heart. I'm so goddamn proud. I want to tell everybody, you know, everybody in the stands, that's my boy! That's my son." He chuckles and takes a sip of his beer. "Hey, you know, you two should come up and stay with us sometime," he says. "It'd be great for you to meet your little brother and sister. And you've got to have Sookie here meet the rest of the family. I mean, I doubt Aleida gave you the best impression of-"

"Are you serious?" Rick says.

Marty blinks in surprise. "What was that?"

"Are you seriously asking me to come and stay? It's just, you didn't seem too keen for me to meet your new wife and your new kids last time."

Marty's smile vanishes and his lip curls into a frown. "Do you have something to say?"

Rick folds his arms. His eyes are cold and hard. "Dad, the last time we met up, do you remember? We finished our meal, we were talking by your car. You said you wanted to see me more. Then Molly came over, she was out with her friends and she spotted you. Do you remember what you said?"

"Rick, I apologised for this," Marty says, but the colour is rising in his cheeks, he's glancing around nervously, embarrassed. "You're exactly like your mother, she could never let things go-"

"You said, 'this is Diego, he's a former student of mine'." His voice crackles slightly as he says it and he's squeezing my hand tight, way too tight.

"I apologised."

"You didn't let me meet your new kid. You didn't hug me. You dismissed me, like I was some stranger, you said—and I remember this exactly, you said, 'It was nice running into you, Diego. Take care now' and left me there in the parking lot while you drove off with your new kid and your new life that clearly doesn't embarrass you the way me and my sisters do."

His hands are shaking.

"I apologised," Marty says. "Molly was only ten. I didn't want to confuse her."

"You apologised after Mom called you," he snaps. "You drove off thinking you'd done absolutely nothing wrong!"

"Rick, there's no need to shout," Marty says, his voice in a hushed whisper. "I don't even know why you had to drag Aleida into it in the first place. You know she loves nothing more than!"

"I was only seventeen, Dad, I was a kid and I came home in tears. How would... Lizzie-" He says the name like it's a type of poison, "-react if Tommy or Molly came home crying because of something *you* did?"

"Rick, I spoke to your mother and then I apologised to you. What do you want me to say?" he says, his neck is nearly purple now. "Tommy and Molly know about you and your sisters now, my little *familia*." Rick flinches. "They're old enough to understand it better. Molly even learned Spanish last year, she's a bright girl, I'm sure you would all get along."

"Then why," Rick snaps, "Why is it that you never call? You never write? You don't make the effort? Are you ashamed of us?"

Marty doesn't answer right away and, in that pause, is absolutely everything Rick likely feared. Rick gets to his feet, he shakes his head.

"Rick!" Marty calls.

Rick fumbles with his wallet and dumps crumpled dollar bills on the table. Then he reaches for my hand and we get up and go.

"Rick!" Marty calls after him.

My heart is pounding in my chest as we walk right out of the restaurant, other diners glancing up as we walk, curious, unable to look away from the car crash. One of the waiters goes to say something but Rick pulls us past him. As we reach the front door, sausage-like fingers reach out and grab hold of my arm.

"Wait!" Marty says, he's redder now, embarrassed. "Rick, come back. Let's talk. Think about how this looks!"

I see Rick turn and I see in his expression, he's in so much pain. I think he'd stop and listen and go back, despite the pause, despite it all. So, I let go of Rick's hand and turn and push Marty off me hard.

"Keep your fucking hands *off* me," I say, and, in that moment, it frightens me how much I sound like Mother. "You leave him alone. You've done enough."

And I know from his expression that I must look fucking crazy, because he steps back and that redness in his face is replaced by a very ghastly white.

I reach down, take Rick's hand and walk away.

*

"Am I stupid?" he asks.

He's lying with his head on my lap on our bed. It's the first he's spoken since we left the restaurant. I tried to go a few times to get him some coffee, some water, but he held my hand so gently and just shook his head.

"No," I say. "He's your dad, it's natural for you to want him around."

"You saw him," he says. "He treats me like a dog he doesn't want anymore." His eyes are bright, so bright and so full of pain. I reach down and brush his hair off his forehead.

"Can I say something? Something you might not want to hear?"

He smiles and wipes a hand across his face. "Go on then."

"He's human waste," I say. "He's nothing. He's an arrogant old bastard who can't and won't ever give you the kind of relationship you want from him and you deserve." His eyes fill with tears. "But I promise, if we leave him there, in that moment, just leave him there forever, you won't ever feel like that again. Not ever. I won't allow it."

He sits up and hugs me tightly around the shoulders.

"I love you," he says in a small, broken voice. "Don't ever leave me."

"I won't. I'm right here. I'm right here."

*

I'm going to stop. I'm going to stop doing all of this once Barry is gone and the two of us are married. I want to give him a future he can be proud of, one where the only gangsters he has to deal with are the ones in films or on TV. I want to give him a home where he never feels unwanted or unloved.

I'll stop soon, I tell myself as I finish hammering Jean Luc's head to Barry's front door.

It hangs there miserably, like a twisted Christmas wreath. He has long hair, which means he's perfect for dangling. It's going to scare the shit out of whoever finds it. And this should be indication enough for Barry to get his family out of California. I don't really fancy breaking into his house while his wife and kids are home.

So, take the hint, you coke-brained idiot and get them out of here.

*

"So, are you going to change your last name?" Carla asks as the two of us sit back in the hot tub at the back of the lodge. It's my bachelorette party and I turned it into a weekend in the hills.

"Yeah," I say. "I mean, King was from my parents. I never see them. I don't talk to them, so I don't see the point in keeping hold of it, you know?"

She smiles and pulls back her hair. "I guess that makes sense. The wedding is getting close now. Are you nervous? Excited?"

"No way," I say, "Maybe a little nervous, but it's all planning-related stuff."

"Erm, no!" Leda says, striding towards us. She very recently went ahead and dyed her hair silver after talking about doing so for the last three years. It's wound up on top of her hair in a bun so tall there's a resemblance to a somewhat elderly Marge Simpson. "There should be no planning-related worries, between me and Rick, this wedding is on track." She climbs into the tub and prods me in the arm.

Carla laughs, "Damn, Leda, you should be my wedding planner when the time comes."

"I'd do an amazing job too," she says. "Tammy always tells me that I have amazing taste."

"Except in girlfriends," I say.

She rolls her eyes and leans forward to get herself closer to the bubble jets. "Seriously though, what planning is making you nervous, Sookie?"

And sure, it's not like I can say, well, I have a month and a half to finish off a rather sizable hit-list, so I shrug and say something about fitting into my dress, which starts Leda off on a rant about how I look incredible, but also, shall we go jogging together every Wednesday morning if I'm starting to worry about fittings and stuff.

I reach over and hug her.

"Yeah, that sounds nice."

*

Andre Jiro is a piece of shit politician who takes payments for letting dodgy deals go through or pulling the wool over people's eyes. He's worked with Barry for years. It actually shocks me how high an asshole like Barry's connections go.

Still, this guy is a massive waste of space. His politics are backwards and his creepy ads on the back of buses make me want to vomit. He has a big house with his wife and kids, but also has an apartment downtown where he must go to relax. That's the easier one for me to hit up, and to be honest, I'd rather not bust in on his family home and traumatise a little kid.

Like I'm always saying, I'm not a monster.

So, I break into his place and hide out in a wardrobe for a little while. It's a nice way to spend my afternoon off. I have a bit of a relax, look at some potential wedding shoes Leda sent me, and am getting ready to call it a day and get back out through the bathroom window, when the slimy suit comes home.

He is on the phone, snapping at someone over his schedule for tomorrow. It's kind of funny, he is spending his last minutes alive on this earth, moaning about shit he won't be off doing tomorrow, anyway. I creep out and as he finishes on the phone, I shoot him in the back of the head. His blood splatters across the kitchen cabinet and the pot of coffee he was brewing, definitely ruined. I drag his body through the kitchen to the living room, where I mess it up a little more. I hack off his nose and put it in his mouth. His breath stinks of onions.

I am about to leave, when I hear someone else in the apartment.

Now this freaks me out because I was here for like… forty minutes alone and I didn't hear anything. Though, as I remind myself, I was making sure I was completely quiet before. This was someone, now making themselves known to me.

Frowning and keeping my gun close, I creep through the apartment and I find a locked door. That comes open quickly enough and inside, well, what I find inside makes me even more relieved I put a bullet through that bastard's head.

There is a girl in there. She can't be older than high school age. She can't speak English, I think she may be Ukrainian. The room stinks of sweat and vomit. She is wearing crude lingerie that doesn't suit her teenage ballerina frame, she's been gagged and her wrists and ankles are bound with rope.

Upon seeing me in the mask, the girl screams into her gag. I suppose even in her predicament, someone breaking down the door wearing a mask is not good practice. I can't take it off though, I want a clean slate. Nobody is going to see me like this, except Barry right at the end, because I'm a sucker for dramatics. Though seeing how frightened she is, how miserable she is, I wish I'd picked something less intimidating than just a black balaclava.

I have to let her out. This disgusts and frightens me and reiterates so loudly and so clearly why I can't continue to work for a man like that. This girl, this young girl definitely came into the Senator's life because of Barry.

The only English word she seems to know is 'No' which she screams at me over and over again when I take off her gag. She tries to bite my hand as well, which explains the nasty bruise above her eye. This is a girl who is always going to fight like hell. I hold my hands in defence to her, shaking my head.

"Won't hurt you," I keep saying. I wish I'd learned some Russian from Apparently-Ivan, she might have understood a little of that, maybe? "I won't hurt you. Rescue. I'm going to let you go."

She breaks down into hysterical sobbing. I hush her, calm her down, which is hard considering I am not about to take the mask off anytime soon, nor is she able to understand anything I am saying. I untie her hands and let her out of the room. She is shaking, holding her arms around herself. I take one of the Senator's jackets and drape it around her shoulders. When she sees his body on the ground, she lets out a snarl like a fury and kicks him as hard as she can, once and then twice, aiming squarely for his throat. Then she begins to cry again.

*

I saw her on the news a few days later. I had wondered if I'd ever see her again, ever since I left her with his cell phone and pointed to the late-night diner across the road, telling her the best I could that she'd get help there. Then, just three days later, I was sat in the break room with Kiko and Claudia, bitching about new regulations, when the wide, frightened eyes of that young girl met mine on the TV screen.

She was wearing a smart, comfortable-looking sweater. She'd washed her hair and wore it up in a tight blonde ponytail. She was speaking very rapidly while a translator spoke over her.

"Senator Andre Jiro kept me against my will," the translator explained as she spoke. "I was taken from my country, from my home and my friends and forced to reside at his home in California for six weeks. He beat me. He assaulted me. I thought I was going to die."

"Oh my God," Claudia said, "I heard about this the other day. I voted for that guy last year. This makes me feel sick!"

"What happened again?" Kiko asked.

"Senator Jiro, he got killed in his house last week," Claudia explained, "They think it was gang related. You hear a lot about that these days-"

Sure do.

"Anyway, whoever killed him, discovered he'd been keeping a girl there, against her will. It turns out he was involved in human trafficking." She leant closer in her seat. "That's her. God, she looks so young."

"How did you escape from your situation?" the reporter asked.

"My guardian angel rescued me," she said. "It was a woman all in black. She wore… a mask on her face. She helped me. She came and let me out."

"You say a woman helped you?"

"Yes," she said. "I am thankful. I would have died there if I had been forced to stay. That man wanted to kill me. He told me that he had done it many times before."

*

I get a call from Barry as I walk home. He's calling a meeting of all his people together, Ivan won't be picking me up because he's not invited. And it's hard not to burst out laughing while we're still on the phone.

Barry has unravelled. He's unravelled fast. He hasn't just sent his family out of California, but he's sent them to three separate locations. He tells me frantically that he's frightened Ivan or whoever this is, is planning on killing off all of his offspring.

He's *convinced* it's either Ivan after him—particularly with the rescue of the young girl in Jiro's apartment—or it's another gang. He wants to get everyone together to talk about it.

"What should I tell Ivan if he asks?"

"Why would he ask? God, use your brain!" he snarls at me before hanging up.

A text comes in five minutes later with a time and a location. Or rather, he's telling me where my targets will be gathered.

I text Rick telling him that I'm going out with Leda and not to expect me back until late-late.

I've got a really fucked-up plan for this one. I'm actually pretty excited about pulling it all together. Hey, if this is my last round with my hobby, then yes, I'm going to have a bit of fun with it. Plus, the press is under the impression that this is gang related.

Which basically gives me the right to be as savage as I want.

329

Chapter Twenty-Eight

On a list of places you would rather not be tonight, Warehouse 28 should definitely be right up tip-top of the list. It's becoming increasingly funny how much a rabbit mask can scare people who are, you know, supposed to be credible gangsters.

A hoodie and a creepily realistic rabbit mask I bought from the market a while ago and I have my Michael Myers outfit. Since Barry had sent the location and time, it made it oh so easy to get there an hour in advance, scout out the place, check for cameras, check for bugs.

Then I nailed all the windows shut and went back outside to get a good vantage point. There was a tree. Honestly, it was comical; I was up in a freaking tree, watching them start to arrive. I kept the creepy mask aside because visibility wise; it isn't the best, and put the balaclava back on. I'm not the best shot, but from certain ranges, how am I supposed to miss?

The first two guys came on their own, it was a nice clean shot, direct, to the point. Then I climbed down from the tree and dragged the bodies aside. That was how it worked for the first two. They were early birds and that gave me enough time. See, it doesn't *necessarily* help everyone to be early for everything.

After that, a group of them arrive together. There are four of them, four targets. They stand around the front door, talking loudly together, when I shoot the one with the denim jacket in the back of the head. His brains are all over the door and the others. They start screaming and yelling. One of them has a gun which he fires indiscriminately in the air. I shoot him in the leg, the others sort of gather around him. One of them is now frantically knocking on the door. I get out of the tree, crouching now as I move closer.

The guy knocking at the door is shot in the back of the head as he pounds and yells as loud as he can. God, what a voice.

The one who is still able to walk is trying to snatch the gun from his injured friend, who is grasping it tight to his chest, refusing to let go. They are scuffling, arguing louder and louder. I shoot the guy on the ground in the head and then put on the rabbit mask.

The last man standing is trying to prise the gun out of his friend's dead hands. I approach slowly and the colour drains from his face as he sees me. It really is a creepy mask, but he starts howling in terror. He staggers back, forgetting the gun and just runs. He isn't fast, I can see the side of his jeans darkening as he sprints away. I shoot him in the base of the spine and as I reach him, he's groaning in terror, trying to find the voice to scream for help.

"No! No!" he moans as I turn him over with my boot.

He screams when I stab him. I sometimes forget that they do that. He screams and the sound pierces my ears before it's dragged from him forever. I take out Conn's phone and see how many others are coming before it's just me, Ivan and Barry left.

Four.

I smirk. He really was getting low on people.

*

Barry arrives last. He's got this other guy, Marco, driving him around. I've stashed my rabbit mask inside my backpack and meet him from half-way down the street. I wave and see him frown. Marco is young, he walks with his hands tight in his pockets like a bratty teenager.

"Hey, Miss. King," Barry says. "You're late."

"I had things to do," I say.

His eyes narrow. "Yeah, like what?"

He's at that level of unravelling that I can see he's going to be suspicious of just about everyone, except Marco apparently, who I think must be a new addition.

"My job, my real job," I say.

He snorts and rolls his eyes. "Well, you best have your head in the game. I need everyone to be on their best..." He frowns as he notices footprints on the ground. He flinches and steps back. "Hey, is it quiet to you?"

"No," Marco says. I can see that he's from the Corey strand of lackey.

"Shit," I say, "Shouldn't everyone be here already?"

Barry looks pale now. He steps back and then grabs hold of my shoulder, holding me in front of him. "Shit! Shit, Miss. King, you keep in front, Marco, stay from behind. Look around. Shit… Shit… Is that blood?" He's noticed a stain in the dark and starts trying to shine his phone light onto it.

I don't need to wait and check, I know it's blood. It's part of the reason I have a lot of tension in my arms right now.

Barry fumbles with the lock and lets himself into the warehouse, pushing me in front of him. I keep my gun close and contemplate whether I should just shoot him here. Barry lets out a horrible gasp when he sees them. I've piled up the bodies of his guys right in the centre of the warehouse. All on top of each other, bleeding out and bullet-riddled.

"Oh fuck!" I say—I think I've turned out to be a really good actress. Maybe I won't need to seriously think about who should play me in a movie, huh…

"Oh my God! Leroy and Kyle! Oh my God, oh my God!" he gasps, pushing past me and bending down near them. "Oh fuck, oh fuck, who did this to you, boys?"

Me and Marco sort of stand next to each other, both looking equally uncomfortable as Barry groans and covers his head, half talking to the corpses, half muttering to himself. I hear him say Ivan's name a lot and he curses him. He curses again and again, bashing a fist on the ground.

In the next moment, he's on his feet. He storms towards us and grabs me by the wrist.

"That crazy Russian fuck is going to kill me," he says. "Moral high horse! I should've known he'd find out in the end… Oh fuck, oh God!" He pulls me along after him, out of the front doors. "Marco, hey, Marco," he snarls.

Marco is struggling to keep up with us.

"Burn this place up. We need it gone. If this is another gang, heck, if it's not, I can't have this being spread around as the sort of thing that happens to me. I just can't! I can't!" He's shaking. "You need to burn this place up! Burn it to the ground."

"Erm, yeah," Marco says, already looking like he has a list of questions but is unsure of how to actually vocalise them. I don't blame him. Barry isn't the sort of boss you relish having to ask for anything from.

"Then you go and get that Russian FUCK and bring him to my place, ok? Me and Miss. King will be there waiting for him."

"Russian…?"

"IVAN! Go and get FUCKING Ivan!" He lets go of me and lurches forward to shove Marco as hard as he can. The kid staggers and goes dashing back towards the warehouse to start, what I suspect, will be a very poor fire.

I follow Barry to his car and shake my head when he throws me the keys.

"I can't drive."

"Bullshit," he says.

"No, seriously, I take the bus everywhere. You drive," I say and throw the keys back at him. "Also, do I have to come with you? I don't think Marco will be the best at!"

"I need you with me. What if that fucker is already waiting for me? He was at my house the other day, he discovered poor Jean Luc's head." His hands are shaking so violently now that I kind of wish that I hadn't told him to drive.

Is he going to kill us both?

I get into the passenger seat anyway and slide in my backpack by my feet.

Barry's teeth are chattering and he struggles to light his cigarette.

"Fucking bullshit, you are such a liar," he says to me. "I bet you can drive."

"Well, I can't," I say, "And why would I let you drive if I could? You're a mess."

He lets out a heavy exhale, filling the car with smoke. "You try living my life and not being a mess, Miss. King," he says. "Life is a fucking mess. You think you trust a guy and he ends up stabbing you in the goddamn back."

He tries to start the car unsuccessfully.

"Fucking bullshit."

"Why're you so sure it's Ivan?" I say, "He doesn't strike me as the type."

"He thinks I killed his daughter," Barry says. "I know he's found out. He's a sneaky motherfucker. I know he's found out somehow."

"Did you?" I ask.

He starts the car again. "She was a junkie. It was always going to happen."

"That's fucked up," I say, taking his cigarette from him.

"Oh fuck you," he snaps at me. "Seriously, fuck you. You killed my cousin and my dad. You get zero say in anything, Miss. King!"

He sounds so childish. It really does baffle me that this man has kids. Those poor little fuckers are going to be infinitely better off with Barry out of the way.

I take a drag of his cigarette. He doesn't seem to mind. He's scowling as he adjusts his lights and pulls off into the night. He jams the radio with his finger a few times before he just lets me do it. I lean back and take in the smell of the leather seats. The air-con blowing in my face. The satisfying ache of my arms as though I've just completed a good work-out at the gym.

I close my eyes—or I do for a second before Barry's foot slams down on the brake and I'm lurched forwards.

"Fucking red lights," he mutters under his breath. "This is a goddamn joke."

His phone starts to buzz and he ignores it, letting it go to voicemail. I glance down at it as it rattles along in the cup-holder. His wife, I realise.

"She ok?"

"She's being a pain in the ass," he says. "You'll get it when you're married."

"Sure," I say.

"If that fucker Ivan doesn't kill us both first," Barry adds, encouragingly.

*

I've been to his house but never inside. It's gaudy as fuck. Everything is marble, he has a leopard skin rug on the sofa. It looks like a

1960s pimp lives here. He's so wonderfully tacky. I head over to the kitchen to get a glass of water and he starts hassling me for scotch.

"I need to keep my wits about me," he says.

"Then have water, like me."

"No way," he says. "Scotch."

I do it anyway.

"And keep out your gun," he barks at me from his seat at the dining room table. "You need to be ready for when he gets here."

I roll my eyes. "So, what, you want me to shoot him as soon as he comes through the door?"

"Yes, no, I don't know!" he snaps at me, knocking back the scotch.

"So, you invited me here to maybe shoot Ivan?" I ask. "Sorry, I'm just trying to work out what you want here."

He groans and rubs his eyes. "I want you here to protect me. I don't know what's going to happen, I can't see the fucking future," he says coldly, pushing the glass towards me. "Can you get me another scotch?"

"Sure," I say.

I can see him watching me as I do it. He really does suspect everyone at this point. Every time a car goes past, I can see him flinching and going for his gun.

"That gun is shit," he tells me after his third scotch.

"Hey, you gave me the gun," I say.

"Nah, nah, get a better one. Here." He hands me one which he genuinely took out of a cabinet that contained knives and forks. "Get your head out your ass," he tells me when he sees my expression. "I don't usually keep them in there. I'm a good goddamn father."

"Hey, did I say anything?" I say. "You're in an awful mood, you know?"

He does a bad impression of me and hunches over the table to drink.

There's a knock at the door. Barry bolts upright in his seat.

"What was that?"

"It's probably Marco," I say, "I'll go check."

"Don't leave me," he says, getting up and trailing after me. He is way too close and he keeps scratching at his neck and arms. The noise is going right through me. It's unsettling.

I reach the front door and stare through the peephole. Marco is there, hands in his pockets, frowning and slightly sooty. But he's alone. I whisper this to Barry, whose face twists up in rage. He pushes me aside and yanks the door open.

"Marco, you goddamn idiot! You piece of shit! Where's Ivan?"

He yanks him in by his collar and slams him into the nearest wall, causing a 'Home Sweet Home' sign to clatter to the floor.

"Hey! Hey!" Marco protests.

"Put the gun in his face!" Barry tells me, he's practically frothing at the mouth.

"He's on his way!" Marco says, frantic. "Get the gun away from me! Boss, come on!"

Barry slaps him. "I told you to bring that Russian fuck here."

"He said I was a bad driver," he says. "He said he was eating and he'd come in ten minutes. He's huge, I didn't want to tell him different! You think he's a psychopath, what was I supposed to say? I didn't want to be in the car with him!"

"I don't think he's a psychopath!" Barry protests. "Everyone thinks that! Every goddamn person! Me and you and Miss. King, all think the same thing, Marco!"

"I know!" he wails. "I'm sorry!"

Barry lets him go and storms back into the kitchen. "Great! Well now we can look forward to a visit from fucking Ivan!" He turns on the radio loudly, the sound of the Black-Eyed Peas parading through the house. "Give him time to get ready, get a plan! Goddamn it, you're a waste of your daddy's jizz, you know that, Marco?" he yells over the sound of the radio.

Marco mutters something that sounds very, very rude under his breath. He doesn't have to worry about the ramifications of Barry retaliating anymore though. Because I creep up behind him, cover his mouth with one hand and stab him four times in the stomach and chest with the other. He contorts, grunting briefly and then goes slack in my arms.

I stuff him and the knife in a small closet on the left before heading back into the kitchen.

Barry is pouring himself another scotch when I come in, so he doesn't notice the blood on my hands. He doesn't look up when I raise the gun. In fact, the first indicator to him that anything is wrong, is the second my bullet cuts through the air and shatters the glass in his hand.

Blood and scotch.

He snarls like an animal, clasping at his injured hand.

His eyes turn to me and he realises, I think in that moment, that Ivan had absolutely fucking nothing to do with any of this.

I smirk at him and go to take another shot.

Unfortunately for me, Barry is quick. He grabs the bottle of scotch and hurls it at me. I have to duck out of the way. He grabs a bottle of olive oil and throws that as well. I dodge past the various bottles and condiments he hurls. I take a shot and hit him in the side.

Barry snarls in pain and falls to his knees.

"Fucker!" he curses.

I stand there, watching him.

"Fucking hell! I should've known."

"Don't take it personally," I say. "I was just bored of working for you."

His arm comes up fast and my bullet goes through a light bulb above us. My hands are stinging, and I realise that he's hit me with a mallet. The gun is gone. It's shot off across the kitchen floor back into the hallway. Barry takes a dive for it and I kick him hard in the back of the head. He grunts in pain and clatters to the ground. He's strong, if he gets a hold of me, this could be tricky. I try to stay out of his grip, going for the gun.

He swerves out an arm, taking a swipe for me with the mallet again. He misses me the first time and catches my leg with the other. I cry out in pain and his eyes swivel back to me. The gun forgotten about now, he uses the cabinet to drag himself to his feet. Bleeding onto the kitchen floor, he turns towards me, mallet in hand, eyes manic.

"I'll kill you, you crazy bitch!"

I honestly didn't expect him to have a lot of fight in him. Guys like Barry work out for show. And he may be an asshole and the worst, but he's not stupid. I figured he'd gotten as far as he had on his—and I hate saying this—brains. But aren't I lucky, Barry Ames is more than that.

The mallet smashes into my shoulder—thank God I picked sleeves on my dress—and sends me into the kitchen cabinet. He is panting from exertion and goes to hit me again. I roll out of the way and land awkwardly on my knees. He swings again, blow narrowly missing my head.

"Stay fucking still!" he says.

I kick him as hard as I can in his left leg and get up, punching him in the face. Glad I opted for brass knuckles as I feel his nose break under my fist. I pull back and hit him again and again and again.

The mallet comes crashing into the side of my head then and it's like my body smashes to the floor like a ton of bricks without me being involved at all. Wincing from pain and blood in my eyes, I scramble up onto my back.

Barry is panting hard now, mallet still in hand.

Oh fuck, is this going to leave a scar?

He keeps his eyes on me, mallet in hand, the other hand frantically running over the countertop, looking for the girly gun he had me put down earlier.

I spit blood out and inch back, wincing as my hand encounters what is definitely broken glass. He flinches and lurches, but keeps his hand looking for his gun.

"You're fucking crazy!" he snarls at me. "The fuck are you doing this for?"

"You're a scumbag," I hiss at him.

"Well, you're stupid and dead," he says. Gun in hand, he goes to point it down at me. Broken glass breaking skin, I reach up and stab him in the crotch with the shard. He howls like an animal and fires the gun at his dishwasher. I cover myself with my hands, dropping the glass to the floor.

Barry is screaming, swearing, all his words blur together, and he clasps bloodied hands over his crotch, sobbing out in real pain. I snatch the mallet off the ground from where he dropped it and smash it down on his shoulders to give him a taste of his own medicine. Unfortunately for me, this appears to be where he gets his second wind and he lets out a terrible roar and grabs hold of my wrist and knocks me hard onto the floor.

He's on top of me, one hand squeezing my wrist, the other one on my throat, keeping me pinned to the ground. He's going white from blood loss and his eyes are bulging out of his head. He's snarling, hissing, not quite able to form sentences, but you sort of get the impression of what he's trying to say. I'm trying to think of which in-jury to dig my nails into when there's a loud bang.

And there's a hole in Barry's head.

He falls on top of me, limp and pissing himself.

That's…super gross.

I wince, scrambling to get out from under him and standing over us is Ivan. Apparently-Ivan, smoking gun in hand.

"It's you," I say, partially because of blood loss, partially because that is factual.

"No time for your stupidity," he says. "Get up. Can you stand?"

I can, just about. My head is still ringing from the gun shots, from the blow to the head. I wince as I stand up. I glance down at Barry as he lies dead on the floor. He's so still. And so quiet. I don't think I've ever known him to be so quiet.

"I thought you don't kill people," I say, probably a little unfairly given the circumstances.

Apparently-Ivan frowns at me. "Oh, I see, you would rather you were dead."

"I had things under control."

"Your head is bleeding," he says. "Besides, I don't kill people. This is an animal." He nudges Barry's lifeless body with his foot.

"Well, yeah, but he did have kids," I say.

"They are better off," Ivan says, putting the gun down on the coun-tertop. "So, all this was really you, wasn't it?"

I nod.

He rolls his eyes at me, but I can see it there on his face. Relief. Relief is kind of like gratitude coming from him. I guess I wasn't the only one trying to get free from this life. I suppose I just wanted it more. I wonder what Apparently-Ivan will go and do now. I think about asking him, but know he'd probably just say something like 'none of your business, why all the questions?'

"Hey-" I say.

"Are you going to help me burn this place or not?" he asks, irrita-bly. "Unless you would like the police to find your blood all over the kitchen, no?"

*

It feels strange to drive home after that. Glancing out of the window, I can see the flames from Barry's home in the distance. I lean out of the window and let out a deep breath, taking in the early morning air. The hum of Apparently-Ivan's music thudding in my head. I let out another deep breath.

It's over, isn't it? It's really, truly over.

Apparently-Ivan glares at me and gestures with his hand.

"Sit properly in your seat. Are you a dog or a human?"

I sit back down and laugh, brushing my hair out of my face. "I guess I can manage to sit still. Sorry, I'm still kind of in shock."

"I do not believe you," he says, eyes on the road, same as always.

A moment passes quietly between us. Enough for me to realise that he's never let me sit up front with him before. I'm glad we finally got there in our association with each other. I find myself fighting the urge to reach out and alter the radio station. I wonder if he'd bat my hand away like Mother used to.

"So," he says, "If I hadn't assisted you back there, would you have let me go? Or did you have plans to kill me too?"

"Come on, you really think I'd do that?"

"Yes," he says. "I could never tell what a woman like you thinks."

I sigh and lean back, closing my eyes. "No, I always planned to let you run free. I figured we were both in the same boat and it wouldn't hurt to help you out. Heck, I even sped up my plans to take him out as soon as he started to suspect you."

"Well, that was very nice of you," he says in that same deadpan tone.

"It was, actually."

"You know," he says, "I wasn't the only other person he had like that. Did you think about that before you went on your little killing spree?"

"A little," I say. "But I know you. I don't know any of them. I doubted I could make them trust me enough to help or at least understand."

Ivan's brow furrows, but he doesn't respond. Not for a few minutes.

"Do you think you'll stop now?" he asks.

"Stop…"

"Stop killing," he clarifies. "I think you should stop. I think you've had enough for at least ten lifetimes."

I smile to myself. "Yeah, you think so?"

"Yes," he says. "You are not as smooth as you think you are. So, stop now, alright?" He glances over at me, still frowning, but sincere. It's the most direct he's ever been with me.

"Okay," I say. "I was planning on making Barry my last anyway. I've quit."

"Good," he says. He pulls up three blocks away from my apartment as smooth as ever. I'm always sort of struck by how much I want Apparently-Ivan to teach me to drive. I suppose I should have asked before. "I will not see you again," he says. "Have a good life, Miss. King."

"Aw, hey, you don't want to hang out after this?" I ask, but I know he's right.

He frowns at me. "It amazes me that you and Barry did not get along better. You are both very irritating."

"The wonders of cohering people, I guess, kind of put me off a sleepover," I say, as I climb out of the car.

"Oh, Miss. King," he says, raising a hand to me. "You… should think carefully before you get married. It's not right to enter a union like that with someone if you don't intend to be honest about it. It is where I went wrong. You should think about what you're putting that young man through."

We hold each other's gaze for a moment.

"Ivan, come on, I just told you, I've quit." I say. "You could try congratulating me, you know? That would be nicer."

He doesn't look convinced, but he sighs and turns back to the road. I close the door and stand on the sidewalk, watching as he pulls out of the space and joins the early morning traffic and out of my life forever. I let out a deep breath and take out a cigarette from the packet in my jacket. I think I'm owed a cigarette tonight of all nights. Another habit I'm quitting from now on.

I let out a deep breath and start to walk the short distance back to the apartment, back to Rick and our future without any gangsters darkening our door.

I've quit, I tell myself. I'm not putting Rick through this because *this* isn't what I do anymore.

I'm free.

Chapter Twenty-Nine

There's so much I can't tell you. So many things I'll never have the chance to say. So, while you're sleeping, I think I can ask, can you ever forgive me for keeping so much of myself hidden?

You smile in your sleep and mumble 'yes'. And my heart melts because that's you. That's so you. So I lean back and whisper that I'm going to tell you about her, I'm going to tell you about me, and I'll tell you about me and her.

Once there was a little girl named Sarah, who lived in a smoky little town called Franberg. Sarah had good parents, kind people who had a lot of time for church and charity. She had a pretty older sister and a lot of people who loved her.

But Sarah was born wrong.

She loved all the things she should hate. And she hated all the things she should love.

The sleepy little town she grew up in bored her. She hated the people, going about their day to day lives, stressing over their jobs and bills and tired, lazy relationships. It was boring to her. She wanted to lash out all the time. Sure, she tried to dedicate herself to other things, like running track and her school subjects. But none of it made her feel any better. Ultimately, what made Sarah feel good, was tearing the skin from another person.

She tried her best not to, but sometimes these things can't be helped.

Sarah killed her teacher one night after school. She said it was for no reason other than that she just wanted to. The woman had been rude to her, she was always treating her like a servant and acting all condescending. So she got rid of her and her school life improved.

Sarah started looking around town and saw lots of people who irritated her, who caused trouble one way or another. She got rid of them too. One by one she got rid of them until people in town started to notice. Unlike her, they didn't see how much better life had become, they only worried and panicked. There were several searches over the years for some of the people she killed, but nobody was smart enough to discover her. Eventually, one day she killed another girl. A teenager the whole town adored. The search was bigger and wider this time. Nobody wanted to give up on this girl.

That was how they found Sarah's hiding place, where she hid all the flesh, blood and bones of her victims.

After that, the police, the FBI, the CIA, the whole country turned and looked at what Sarah was doing. The media gave her another name, the Red Creek Killer. But nobody knew that behind the blood and the guts and the bravado, was just little Sarah White, age fifteen, who just wanted to destroy everything she'd ever seen.

Sometimes people got close, but nobody ever found her out.

When she got bored of it all, she decided to set someone up.

There was a man in town she knew was bad. When he was young, he'd babysat his older sister's children and their friends. He took photographs of them, naked and vulnerable. He kept the photos locked up in a box in the woods, but he didn't dig deep enough.

Sarah knew that this man was a monster and had to be stopped. So she framed him. She made sure he saw her attacking someone one night, she made sure he snatched her knife away from her. And in time, no time at all, actually, the man was caught and locked away. So ashamed of his secret being exposed, it didn't take much for him to admit to all the things the police pushed his way.

Sarah left the town of her childhood and the Red Creek Killer behind her. She moved all the way to Atlantic City. She did odd jobs, lived without the church and her family, and all those people telling her what to do. Amongst the general crime and gambling, her killings didn't stand out here. She could be savage and secretive and for the longest time she was happy.

She didn't love easily. In fact, romantically, she didn't love at all. She told me once that she saw men as an outlet, something to alleviate her boredom. I don't think it happened often. I don't think people interested her that way. I know she lived with a man for a little while.

She had his picture. I think he might have been my father. I know she would have been unkind if I asked her about it, so I never ever did.

The photograph is small, I think it was taken in a photo booth, like you get at the fair. He is dark with perfect white teeth. He smiles wide and easily. He has a strong arm around her shoulders. Sarah is staring at the camera, unimpressed, vacant. Her arms are folded.

I asked her about it once and she took it from me and put it away somewhere. I never found it again.

Sarah left Atlantic City when she got pregnant. She drove all the way to Oregon, to the sort of town she grew up in and loathed. She figured that would be as good a place as any to raise her child. She told me that she stopped when she got pregnant with me. She stopped for the longest time and wanted to stay stopped. She was content to just raise me. Fiona.

That's my name, my real name. I'm named after her grandmother, I remember her telling me once. You know the first day we met, when you introduced yourself to me, I nearly told you my real name. Fiona Taylor.

I sometimes wish things had turned out like that. I torture myself imagining how her life might have been, how mine might have been, if all her plans worked out. But there's not much to be done about it now. She passed her sickness onto me, you see. I killed an old woman when I was only three. I killed a little girl at my pre-school. I hurt a lot of people. She ended up taking up her knife again just to put me off, just to wean me off the scent of blood. For a time, she believed she'd fixed me. She thought she'd made me better. It was too late for her. She was back at it, finding homeless people off the street and cutting them to bits in our basement. But she thought I was safe.

She did so much for me and in the end, I only ever brought her pain. I wish I could tell her that I'm sorry. I really am selfish.

I know if I ask now, you'll say that you'd forgive me. Because you're kind and you're asleep. And all of this is a side of me you'll never know. Because it would hurt too much for you to leave me.

Chapter Thirty

Today's the day. The official release date of the Red Creek movie.

Rick buys popcorn and a slushie for himself, I tell him that I don't want one. It seems in poor taste to drink sugary frozen ice while watching a cinematic version of the most traumatic event of my life.

Popcorn, I think is ok.

The cinema isn't too crowded, not too loud.

"Are you ok?" he asks me.

I smile and tell him, "Of course." I kiss him softly on the mouth and squeeze his hand. "Thanks for coming with me."

"Hey, of course, this looks like it'll at least be well made and in poor taste," he says, leaning back into his seat.

I try to pretend I'm not freaking out during the stupid commercials, then during the trailers, I don't know what any of them are, I can't concentrate. I don't know if this is weirdly flattering—I mean I am about to see a movie about my actual life, who gets to see the movie version of their own life?

Mostly, I think I'm nervous.

I don't know how they'll show me in the film.

I won't be able to defend myself. This is how people will remember me.

And I suppose that's fair, because she probably didn't want her story to have a third act that was completely and entirely spent in prison and now I'm trying not to cry again. Great, the movie hasn't even started...

I disguise it with a cough and tuck my legs in close against me.

The credits start to roll and I take in a deep, long breath.

And the film starts, I suppose, right where everyone forgets it really started, with two little kids playing out at Read Creek. A little boy and his three-year-old sister, tossing rocks across the surface of the water. The little boy takes a tumble and his sister watches him drown before going back to play with her dolls.

A couple of times Rick takes my hand while the film rolls on, I don't think I notice. I'm watching as they flutter through Mother's childhood, a childhood I know so little about, she wasn't much of a talker. There are the frustratingly nice religious parents, the pretty older sister, the small town that bored her, the community that she silently loathed. There's also this really grisly scene of her killing a neighbour's cat.

Since her arrest, she has spoken to Winne Gails openly about the first murder she committed as Red Creek. She finally put a chronological order onto her confirmed kill count.

Starting, of course, with her first.

And here it is: twenty minutes into the movie, played by Sophia Lilis, Mother attacked her supply teacher, Ms. Miriam Keogh with a butcher knife one night after school. Ms. Keogh was always pestering her with extra work and just being genuinely irritating. Considering that the character is based on an actual lady, it's pretty tactless how they have her being so annoying you find yourself, as the audience just wishing she would die. So after a handful of scenes of teenage Mother suffering through Mrs. Keogh in class—it cuts to that special evening where the Red Creek killings truly began. Mrs. Keogh leaving her office at night only to be capacitated by Mother and subsequently dragged into the girl's showers and dismembered her completely.

The bulk of the Red Creek murders are sensitively played through as a gory montage. I'd say each is more ridiculous than the last, but to be honest, the director is a good match for Mother, she really was as gruesome as this. I really think, amount of blood in a body aside, nothing is that elevated, nothing is shied away from.

I think seeing this film would make her happy. Particularly the big reveal of the body parts, the event that had the name Read Creek so gruesomely changed, shown in high definition, in the most stomach-churning detail ever. Way more blood than I imagine there would have been.

Rick gags and covers his mouth with his fist. I laugh and reach over to squeeze his other hand.

The film has Randall Kayne portrayed as a disturbingly sympathetic paedophile. Lots of shots of him lurking near parks or the high school, some of him crying in a truck. Lots of setting him up, much like Mother did, I suppose.

The film focuses half on Mother, who is silent and blank, and half on Detective Morgan, the young cop in charge of the case at the time. I found out later, that he had been something of an inspiration to my own Detective Brankowski. Morgan was a looker in real life; his film counterpart, Archie from Riverdale, is a decent stand-in. The film shows Morgan is young and misunderstood by an otherwise incompetent police department. I mean, come on, he's the only one who seems to suspect the strange, scowling teenage girl who appears conveniently at all the murder scenes.

Sylvia Hardey is presented as a sort of best friend character to Mother. She is sweet and cheerful and clueless as to why her silent, blank-eyed best friend keeps disappearing on long evening walks. Seriously, this film…They slow down for her attempted murder.

We see Mother donning a red bandana—the closest she ever got to wearing a Halloween mask—and chasing her down a darkened underpass with a knife. They show her scuffle with Randall Kayne, all stuff you know if you read one of those awful books about it or anything more refutable. It's weird seeing it like this, I wonder if this is how it was for her. She was just a kid in way over her head. She rubbed so much right in the police's face and only ever had one guy suspicious of her. Did that excite her? Did it bother her? Did she worry about her parents finding out? Did she panic when she was alone at night?

When I was a kid, I was too angry with her to ask any of those things. Now I really wish I could. I don't like that the answers I get from her are the kind I have to read about in some torrid little interview with Winnie Gails or films like this. How much of this is for cinematic effect? How much of this is her?

After this, the film moves to cover the arrest of Randall Kayne, which they do very sensitively, like he was the real victim. Well, that's certainly an odd choice. I mean, the man wasn't…completely innocent.

After that, time skips ahead to Mother, now played by Scarlett Johansson, making a campfire in the woods. She sighs into the night air and tosses what looks like a human foot into the flames. She reaches down and the camera pans down to her very pregnant belly.

She winces in pain, realising that her body is going into labour. She staggers frantically back towards her car, leaving her victim to burn. Leaving me to wonder, was that actually what she was doing when she went into labour? Because if it is, that is so goddamn… typical of her. Couldn't she have other hobbies?

Then, of course (because come on), there's a classic cinematic childbirth scene, lots of bright lights, lots of Mother groaning in pain, lots of nurses telling her what to do. Then a big bright light and a baby (me) crying.

The next scene has Mother/Scarlett Johansson, holding the baby in her arms. The baby yawns and reaches up blindly. Mother/Scarlett Johansson goes to offer a finger—they jarringly cut to the bodies running red down the creek. She recoils from the baby as if burned before holding it tight against her chest.

"Who is the father?" a nurse asks.

"I don't think I caught his name," Mother/Scarlett Johansson says absent mindedly, ignoring the scandalised look on the nurse's face. "No, it's…just the two of us. Isn't it, Fiona?"

The baby yawns and closes its eyes peacefully, content.

And I know this is just a movie, I'm not deranged. But my stomach winds itself into a knot and for a moment I just want to get up and leave. I want to curl up into a ball. I want to…I mean, come on, this is my life up on screen—something anyone else would be able to object to, but I can't because, you know, *officially* I'm dead. How are they going to play this? Because you can't have me being sympathetic and also knowing full well what she was getting up to in the basement?

Will I be…just as crazy as she is? Or will I be an idiot?

How will I be seen?

I mean, I know they won't be completely honest. I know they won't show what I did to my babysitter, or the little girl I pushed down the stairs. I know that with me, this film will be fiction, not fact. But there was so much more to me than any of that stuff. There is more to me than this.

I get distracted as I hear Rick gasp.

On screen, I see Mother/Scarlett Johansson standing in the kitchen, holding rat poison over my baby food as the baby…me, I guess, screams from a highchair. Her hand falters and then she turns and frantically starts pouring both down the sink, her eyes wild and frightened. She rushes to the baby, me, and scoops me up, clinging tight as I wail against her shoulder.

I know that she felt like that more often than she'd admit when I was very small. She discussed this sort of thing with Winnie Gails after she was formally arrested. As a kid, I suspected that sometimes she wanted to…I was scared a lot…but I know that she wouldn't have hurt me because she loved me, she loves me, you can tell because I'm still here.

Mother/Scarlett Johansson struggles to hide her killer instinct as the child who plays me is replaced by a toddler and then a larger toddler. We get scenes of her polishing a knife and putting it away, of her watching me play and forcing herself to act and behave like the other mothers around town.

There's even some footage of the Red Creek Memorial services she attended. Having attended plenty of those myself, I know that this was right on the money, right down to the repetitive version of "Amazing Grace". Mother/Scarlett Johansson stands there with a quiet smile on her face. She drives home with classical music playing even though she hated music. She'd bat my hands away if I tried to switch on the radio in the car. It was why the cello case cover always seemed obvious and stupid to me.

The film follows Scarlett Johansson/Mother as she returns home, fumbling with her keys, smiling at the neighbours and blank the moment they look away. She steps inside and hears a woman snarl 'Shut up! Stop that crying!' and the sound of a slap.

She rushes into the kitchen to find a matronly looking older woman standing over a wide-eyed, red-faced toddler version of me. The woman has her hand raised again. She flusters when she sees Scarlett Jo-Mother and steps back.

"Nothing wrong with a bit of discipline," she says, brushing her hands on her skirt. "Never did me any-"

Mother steps forward and stabs her in the stomach with a bread knife. She moves forward, swiping it off the countertop and inside her victim in one fluid motion. The old woman keeps her eyes but bleeds out on the carpet. The toddler version of me sits there weeping loudly while Mother drags the woman's body down into the basement, closing the red door behind her.

Scarlett Jo-Mother sits with an expression on her face that is disturbingly close to Mother's own crocodile smile—she must have met with her at some point. She smiles as she cuts up the woman, turning her into tiny pieces in gratuitous gore and then, burns the pieces up in a convenient little incinerator.

She wipes bloodied hands on her memorial dress and ascends the stairs to wash her hands in the kitchen sink. Her weeping child stares after her and you know, I imagine how much easier it would have been if things turned out this way. With her as the ruthless killer and me as the helpless weeping child along for the ride.

She strokes the toddler's hair out of her eyes and smiles softly at her.

And this is wrong because she never touched me, not like that, never a hug, never a squeeze of the hand. Only ever a shake, a grab out of harm's way, a tug in the wrong direction. She kept her hands to herself. It was like she was afraid to touch me at all.

I can't remember how her hands felt.

I wipe my own eyes and try to detach myself from this completely.

The film introduces Sukhy, whose name they have changed to Kiran Patil as my childhood best friend. They include a few scenes of us playing together, typical kid stuff, screaming and throwing leaves, going down slides, running around.

I know this scene is coming, the one I hoped they wouldn't include. That was naïve. It was in Detective Brankowski's case notes, so of course it will feature in a big way. I've listened to the recording, they put it in a documentary about Mother two years ago. It was hard… to hear her voice again. I left my phone and every piece of her behind. The first time I heard the footage of her talking with *him* about me, about Mother… about that awful night, I had to turn it off. My hands reacted before I did, hands on the remote, screen off. I had to go and smoke outside with tears rolling down my cheeks. I hadn't been prepared to hear her voice after all those years.

And it may sound clichéd, but there's not a day that passes where I don't miss her. I miss talking to her. When something bad happens, when something good happens, I miss her. I hate that I can't talk about her, not to Rick or anyone else. I hate that I have to read about how she died in articles and in films like this, like she doesn't belong to me anymore.

We are aged up for this scene, ten years old, not barely four. I see the ten-year-old version of me falling asleep while a movie plays. Sukhy—or Kiran, I guess—rolls onto her back, bored and unable to sleep. She stretches and wanders downstairs to get a glass of water. As she reaches the bottom step, in true horror movie logic, she hears a woman singing 'Humpty Dumpty' slowly and eerily. Sukhy/Kiran wanders over to the basement, frowning in confusion and opens the door, peering down.

The lighting is good, it's dark but there's this thin, flickering light —there was never a flickering light, Mother kept everything working properly—at the bottom of the stairs, illuminating Scarlett Jo-Mother as she sits there, drenched in red, hair sticking down her back like Carrie.

She pauses, then turns, blank eyed to stare up at Sukhy.

Not hesitating, Sukhy turns and runs. The camera pans back to Mother, who grabs the knife from beside her and runs up the stairs. Sukhy dashes up onto the first floor, frightened and screaming for me.

"Fiona! Fiona! Help! Mrs. Taylor! Mrs. Taylor, there's someone!"

The child version of me rushes out of the bedroom with wide frightened eyes. She sees Mother coming up the stairs with the knife before Sukhy does. She is quick, barrelling in front of her to cause a barrier between them.

I wish I had been so brave.

I'd tried to pull her into my room. But Sukhy had been too frightened and too confused. Her legs gave out under her and she huddled into the wall, screaming and crying.

On screen, I hit Scarlett Jo-Mother and scream and lash out. I swipe at her with my nails and kick and bite. She tries to pull me aside.

In reality, I didn't. I covered her body with mine the best that I could. I screamed and cried and kept saying no over and over again. I felt her hands grasping at my shoulders to pull me aside. I bit her a few times, I think. But I was crying. I thought she was going to kill me. I'd never been so sure as I was right then.

On screen, Mother stands up and leaves us, walking into her bedroom and closing the door, leaving the two frightened children crying and clinging to each other. She returns, clean and freshly showered and tells us that we'd just had a bad dream. She escorts us back to bed and kisses the on-screen version of me on the forehead.

The on-screen version of me is placated and falls asleep.

In reality, I didn't sleep properly from that night for the next ten years.

The rest of my childhood flashes before me. Mother starts murdering homeless people and transporting the bodies around in a cello case. The child who is me watches from afar, disgusted and frightened. She keeps her friends close, but carefully keeps them away from the basement and her mother. Time follows in a montage. All too soon, I become a teenager, to be exact, I become Madeline Petsch.

Madelaine Petsch is a good actress. I guess she makes sense as Scarlett Johansson's on-screen daughter. But as if I ever dressed as glamorously as that when I was in high school! Like they haven't even stuck her in jeans and a t-shirt or something. She's dressed like a model. Nobody wore heels to my high school. But, such is fantasy.

There's a scene of Fiona and Kiran strutting down the corridors in these stripper-short dresses and big clumpy heels, laughing and talking. Matt joins them, with a perfectly styled quiff which he couldn't have had, not even on his best day. Matt (or Gary) is portrayed as he was, shy, uncomfortable in his own skin. Though they have confusingly cast someone buff as Matt and then dressed him in baggy clothes, hoping (and failing) to hide it.

Riley Sanders, who they introduce as a young Captain America looking type, is shorter than Matt. He's not played up as the nasty jock type, because you know, he died really horribly. Instead, they go with him being sensitive, pushed by his coach to be a big man on campus and out on the football field. Instead of, you know, keeping him as the nasty little homophobe he was. In fact, as it goes on, what I realise they've done is fuse Riley with...oh God, what was his name? Fred? Freddie Hankerson! We get some shots of him looking longingly at Matt, then hiding it by barging into him in the corridors.

The film has Beth (Carrie in the movie) and Lisa (Billie in the movie) as identical twin sisters, with Lisa/Billie being popular and outgoing and Beth/Carrie as bookish and a bit gothic. We get a scene of them squabbling in the girl's bathroom, fighting over make-up and the car for the ride home. In this film, we all have cars. Jason, or Jack as he is in the film, is shown last, portrayed from the off as Kiran's boyfriend. There are a few scenes of the six of us—six because Lisa is one of the gang in this story—hanging out in the woods or listening to music in Jason's ridiculously oversized car.

Our peace is broken, much like in real life, by Matt Damon or rather Pete Brankowski, a brilliant young (not so young in this) detective, with an obsession with the Red Creek murders. He is shown writing notes in his oversized car, watching Fiona and her friends as they leave the high school. They have him jogging around our street, taking breathers so he can stare up at the house. This is accurate.

Scarlett Jo-Mother is never far though. She is shown landscaping, talking to other mothers at PTA meetings. She has noticed Matt Damon hanging around but doesn't seem impressed. She only intervenes when she sees him talking to her daughter, who is flirting so unashamedly.

I wasn't like that!

Was I?

Either way, there was nothing in his notes to suggest that I was. Ew, why have they added this? Is that how Mother saw those interactions? Did she do this?

Scarlett Jo-Mother is stiff, blank eyed but not without some Black Widow sassiness as she says, "So, do you have a habit of talking to underage girls?"

You know, I think she did say something like that. Matt Damon looks suitably embarrassed and awkwardly leaves. Then Scarlett Jo-Mother and Madeline Petsch have the type of argument we never would have done in real life. It's like something out of a bad teen romantic comedy.

They even have Mother saying, 'I just want what's best for you'.

In reality, she could have *wanted* until the cows came home and longer, Mother knew she could only expect so much from me.

The party is long and drawn out. Lots of dancing, lots of bottles and red cups, no talk about Jason/Jack hitting a girl at school the day before—which is what happened by the way. They disturbingly include a sex scene between Kiran and Jack, which didn't happen. Fiona spends the party socialising and chatting and flirting.

In reality, I think me and Sukhy sat drinking beers in the garden, laughing at nothing in particular.

Goth-Beth falls out with her twin sister and leaves to go wandering through the woods, with Fiona following her. Meanwhile, Matt, who they have cast as someone buff, so he can have one shirtless scene, for reasons that betray logic, has left the party to go swimming in his boxers in a lake in the woods. He's all wet and swimming when he's discovered by Riley.

The two of them shove each other and yell. Eventually they roll around in the dirt (without getting dirty, of course) kissing. This is where Goth-Beth and Fiona discover them. The boys break apart. Riley violently yelling and storming off after slapping Matt in the face.

Matt, tearful and still shirtless, walks back to Fiona's house through the woods with her, after begging secrecy from the others. They get to her garden when, in true jump-scare fashion, Riley pops out from the dark, having followed them.

"Anything you have to say to Matt, you can say in front of me," Fiona says coldly. "Go home, Riley."

"You've told her," Riley snarls, stepping close. "You've told your friend lies about me."

"I haven't told her anything!" Buff Matt protests.

Riley is on him in a second, slamming him into the ground. He keeps hitting him and cursing, spitting. Fiona is trying to pull him away, yelling for help. Matt is bloodied up. Riley keeps hitting him, all fists, hammering down on his chest and face.

This was… this was almost as it was.

But I had a knife back then. It was Beth who tried to save him.

Riley turns and hits Fiona in the stomach, winding her and sending her to the floor. He turns to go for Matt again as Fiona wheezes and tries to get up.

Scarlett Jo-Mother steps between them and stabs him in the back with a large hunting knife. She kicks him in the back, sending him away from Matt and gagging as he begins to bleed out, onto his back. He rasps, terrified and vulnerable as she sits down on top of him and brings her knife down again and again and again and again and again.

Matt is unconscious, weak from the beating.

Fiona is watching, wide eyed and terrified. She begins to cry.

"Mother, Mother, stop!"

Eventually, when Riley resembles nothing that is human anymore, Scarlett Jo-Mother looks back at her child and asks, dead-pan, eyes blank. "Are you alright? Are you hurt?"

Fiona sobs into her hands, drawing her knees to her chest.

Mother gets up and walks towards her, offering her a blood-red hand. "Can you stand?"

She does, stumbling at first, not taking the hand reaching out for her.

"Why did you do that? Mother, Mother, oh my God!"

She covers her mouth and weeps hysterically, head in her hands.

"Mother… you promised you wouldn't!"

Mother stares at her blankly, then she picks up Riley's leg and drags him into the house and towards the basement. Movie Fiona rushes after her, her eyes wild and crazy.

"Mother! Mother, stop! Stop it! What are you doing?"

The red door of the basement opens, and Mother tosses the chunks of Riley down the stairs. Movie Fiona tries to grab her arm and shake her, but Mother freezes her out with a glance and leaves her crying in the living room.

*

The film covers the search for Riley with careful detail. His mother, played by Margo Martindale, is wonderfully tragic and stoic in her grief. There are lots of shots of Fiona looking out of her window, miserable and frantic. She tells Margo Martindale in a tiny, miserable voice that she doesn't know anything about Riley's disappearance.

"Come out to the woods," Kiran says. The two of them are hanging out, smoking on the roof, just like we used to. That's a nice touch. You know, I bet it was Mother who told them that we used to do that. Of course, I can't imagine making the climb from my bedroom window to the roof in heels as big as my face, but the heels seem something the director is very sold on.

"I can't," Fiona says quietly. "I just feel wrong leaving the house."

"You've got to come out at some point," Kiran says. "I'll be waiting when you do."

*

They include the old man, the one who I cut to bits in the woods. He's a dirty old pervert in this as well. He accosts Fiona and the gang from their huge SUV where they are all sat. He takes out his genitals and starts jerking himself off, staggering around, barely able to stand.

Kiran spooks him by driving directly at him, before turning and leaving the woods. That's another thing about this film, a lot of the footpaths we used to use, or short-cut through, have been turned into very narrow twisty roads.

I suppose they have to fit in the car sponsorship somehow.

It's what I tend to think of when I reminisce about my dead friends. Their designer shoes and their enormous Volvos.

"Do they have to zoom in on the shoes every time someone runs away?" Rick whispers to me. "Or like uses the accelerator or anything?"

"Yes," I say, "How else would we know about Nike?"

He snorts with laughter and kisses my cheek.

After the gang returns home, Goth-Beth and Fiona seem to remember that they left their school backpacks in the woods. And stupidly return to go and fetch them. The old man finds them quickly and there's a nasty gratuitous shot of him taking his dick out again.

I mean, it's nice this film has a higher male to female nudity ratio, but also ew. I didn't want to see that.

Goth-Beth screams and throws a twig at him. Then the two of them start running through the woods, school bags forgotten. The camera zooms in on their Nike trainers a lot. I'm just glad this scene didn't involve them doing it in heels. They charge through the woods and come back to Fiona's garden again. Panting and exhausted, Goth-Beth lets out a terrified scream as the old man follows them through the gate.

"Come on, girlies, Daddy has enough for both of you," he crones.

I think I do remember him talking like that.

Ew.

Scarlet Jo-Mother appears from behind a tree. I wonder if, in the context of the film, that was all she did. I mean, from this, you'd half believe Fiona was providing her victims by just going into the woods and coming out again. But she appears and stabs the man right through the stomach. She has a machete like Jason from *Friday the 13th* and holds it up dramatically after she's basically cut him in half.

This proves to be too much for Goth-Beth, who screams and turns to run back through the house. Scarlett Jo-Mother barrels after her. Goth-Beth is struggling with the front door handle, sobbing and just yanking it like that will suddenly negate the need for a key. Fiona leaps between the two of them.

"No! No! No! Please!" she screams.

And she really is good.

Mother is screaming in her face.

Goth-Beth is crying.

Mother grabs Fiona by the hair and throws her aside. She crashes into the staircase. Mother then turns and stabs Beth in the side. Beth lets out a howl of pain and crumbles to the ground. Mother raises the knife again and Fiona leaps between them at the last second.

"I'll call the police!" she staggers out. "I'll tell! I'll tell everyone!"

Mother just stares at her.

Then she puts the knife down.

"Fine, Fiona," she says. "Fine."

Fiona lets out a sigh of relief. She turns to Beth, bending down and trying to look at her bleeding side. She winces and Beth sobs.

"It's going to be ok," she tells her.

This is when the metal doorstop comes down on Beth's head.

Mother stands over them, one hand outstretched.

Fiona starts to scream.

*

"Your friend will make a full recovery," Matt Damon tells Fiona as she sits, tearful on her porch. She's wearing thigh-high boots and a jumper that is serving as a dress. She's also cuddled up against him.

Which again, I didn't ever do!

"Did you see what happened?" he asks her.

"No," she says in a tiny voice. "I didn't see anything."

*

I hate that they have Brankowski's notebooks, I hate that they have his interviews with her. It means they can take her voice, her words and warp them into whatever this is. I don't like it. I can feel Rick's hand in mine, but it makes me feel frozen. They have a few scenes of Kiran and Brankowski working together, word-for-word interviews between them. There were a lot of them.

I know from reading up on it that Sukhy's parents argued against it, but Brankowski, ever organised in all the ways it didn't help him to be, had acquired her written consent. It didn't help any that Sukhy was fifteen, a minor. Her signature was all it took for these interviews to make it into the films.

"I feel scared for Fiona, Detective," Kiran says on screen. She fidgets with her arm in a way that Sukhy never would have. "Do you really think this will help her?"

"Yes, Kiran," Matt Damon lies, "I promise it will."

*

It all happens sooner than I expect. I know none of the things that happened in between Riley's death and Mother being exposed will ever come to light. It's her gift to me. But as soon as it starts to happen, I want to get up and leave the movie theatre. I imagine walking right out the door. I imagine a reality where Fiona and her friends carried on with their boring high school life. That life may not have been exciting, but it was safe, and it was enough. I imagine that Fiona went off to college and broke off contact with her mother. Mother eventually got bored of doing all of those things and she settled down into her boring job. I imagine sometimes they... sometimes we talk on the phone, every now and then.

And it's boring, but it's alright.

But I stay in my seat and I watch the film end.

Fiona, Kiran, Jack, Gary and Billie are sat around a campfire in the woods, just like we were that night. They are swapping beer and if

362

they're Kiran and Jack, swapping spit too. As the night gets later, Gary leaves to go home. After he leaves, it begins to rain, they suggest going to Fiona's house.

She is reluctant. But with the others teasing her, they cave.

Scarlett Jo-Mother is out, so they settle down in the living room. Billie is fussing over her hair and Jack is going through the liquor cabinet while Fiona supervises. Kiran takes the opportunity to creep downstairs into the basement. She glances behind her suspiciously and, taking out her phone, begins to take photographs of the basement.

At first it's just the stairs, the walls, the tools. But as she gets to the bottom of the steps and looks out into the darkness, her phone light lands on a human torso on a table. She cries out in alarm and muffles it with her hand.

Everyone in the cinema jumps as a piercing scream comes from behind Kiran. She turns to see that Billie has followed her. She runs back upstairs with Kiran in hot pursuit. Billie is crying and yelling and trying to leave through the back door. She's crying and fumbling with her cell phone, which is of course, out of battery.

Battery or reception, it's always one or the other.

"Did you know what was down there?" Billie is yelling at Fiona, who has gone completely pale. "There's a fucking dead body!" She manages to get the door open and goes running out into the night, with Jack following after her.

Fiona covers a hand over her mouth.

"I know," Kiran says to her. "Fiona, I've always known."

Fiona starts to cry. "She-She's not well, she's..."

"I know," Kiran promises, taking her hand. "It's alright. Look, there's a detective who can help. I've been working with him."

"No, I'll get!"

"He understands, please. He wants to help us. We just need to send him this evidence. It's going to be ok. I'd never let anything happen to you."

Then the front door clicks closed and slowly coming into focus from the dark, there she is, Mother. In the dim light of the moon, we can see a knife in her hand.

"Oh dear," she says blankly. "I'm afraid you'll have to go now."

She comes forward for Sukhy/Kiran and like before, Fiona leaps in front of her like a shield.

"Mother, no!" She glances back frantically at her friend. "Kiran, run!"

Kiran looks frightened, but grasps hold of Fiona's hand. "Not without you!"

Fiona looks terrified, her eyes are wild and scared. "Mother, you can't! You can't!"

"Get out of the way, Fiona," Mother says. She raises the knife. Fiona grabs hold of a glass from the kitchen counter and smashes it against her head. Mother stumbles and Fiona and Kiran run from the house into the woods, screaming.

Mother gets up and wipes the blood from the side of her head.

Her eyes are blank and crazed.

The camera flickers back to Kiran and Fiona running through the woods—impressive in the heels they're wearing. Kiran is yelling for Jack, while Fiona tries to get her to be quiet. She's frantic, looking around for her mother in the dark. The camera jerks around wildly to show how frightened and paranoid she is in this moment.

Jack and Billie come running, frantic. The group of them are gathered in a small and convenient-looking clearing. Billie is crying miserably. Fiona is trying to shush them all.

"Kiran, what the fuck is happening?" Jack yells.

"Guys! Guys, shut up! Shut up a second!" Fiona says frantically. "Listen, we have to get out of here! She's coming!"

Kiran lets out a horrified scream as the light of her phone falls on a fifth person stood with them in the clearing. Mother stands beside them. Quick as a flash, she stabs Jack in the head. He groans in agony and falls to the ground, a suspiciously large amount of blood etching out over the grass. The music is loud, pounding. Rick covers his hands with his mouth.

Kiran is screaming, Fiona is yelling and crying, reaching down to Jason/Jack's body, weeping and trying to put pressure on his wound. Billie takes off into a run.

Mother chases after her. She catches her easily. Billie falls to the ground with Mother on top of her. In the scuffle, Mother has dropped her knife. Billie howls, "HELP! HELP!" at the top of her lungs. Mother grabs a rock and bashes it down on her skull, knocking her silent. She goes to raise her hand again when Kiran grabs hold of her from behind.

"No!"

The two of them are fighting now, grappling over Billie's unconscious body. Mother rakes her nails down the side of Kiran's face. She cries out in pain, covering her eyes. Mother grabs hold of her knife and manages to pin Kiran to the floor.

"Wait! Wait!" Kiran is yelling.

Then she screams in terror as she gets stabbed, the blow cutting through her shoulder.

Fiona is beside them, frantically pulling at her mother's arms, grabbing at her hair, trying to pull her off Kiran. Kiran is sobbing, her bloodied arms over her head to try to protect her face.

"Please! Please!" Fiona keeps begging, sobbing miserably. "Please! No! No! No! Leave her alone! Please!"

Mother swings out at her, knife in hand. Then she turns and stabs Kiran in the head, smashing through her skull just above her eyebrows. She is panting from exhaustion, bleeding from the cuts and scratches all over her.

Brushing a hand over her head, she glances back at her daughter and says, "Things can be replaced." Then her eyes widen in horror as her gaze falls on Fiona, who is bleeding profusely from the neck.

I watch my cinematic self, lying there, legs curled into her chest. Her hand clasping at the wound in her neck, voiceless and reaching miserably for Kiran. She's red-eyed from crying. Helpless. In that way she always feared she would be.

I'm wiping the tears from my face as I watch.

Mother keeps saying, 'No'. She bends down and clasps her child to her, holding her head. "Fiona, no, no. God. Oh God." She's trying to see the wound, but Fiona won't let go. She isn't fighting, she looks resigned. She gasps uselessly, unable to speak. Her breathing is erratic. She is looking at her mother when she dies.

The camera cuts to flashbacks, all sporadic and from Mother's point of view. There's Fiona as a baby. Fiona as a toddler. An excited child. A sulky teenager. Soft, sentimental music begins to play and Mother begins to sing "You Are My Sunshine" very, very softly as the sirens sound in the background.

The camera cuts to black and some words on the screen tell me what I already know.

Sarah White was responsible for the deaths of 59 individuals, including her daughter, Fiona. She currently resides on death row.

The credits roll and as they start showing photographs of all of Mother's victims, my heart clenches like a fist as I see my own face for a second and have to cover my eyes with my hands. I lean forwards in my seat as the cinema lights come on and I rest my head in my hands.

"Hey," Rick says softly.

I look up and see him smiling down at me. He squeezes my shoulder gently.

"Are you ok?"

For what isn't the first and won't be the last time in our future together, I smile and lie as I say, "Yeah, Rick, I'm fine."

Epilogue

As the guys get the drinks from the crowded bar—a favourite haunt of Rick's while he was in college, he tells me—I sneak another glance down at my wedding ring. There it is, gold and bright and *mine*.

I got married today and everything is just…perfect.

A send-off back in Santa Cruz and now we're in New Orleans for the start of our honeymoon and I wouldn't change a damn thing. I mean, yes, the music is too loud and the floor is too sticky, but that's just like the day we met. Why not start the honeymoon off like that? Luis comes and takes a seat beside me, grinning and putting down my beer.

"Rick's bringing the rest," he says. "Man, I can't believe you guys are all married and stuff!" He laughs and nudges me playfully. "You gotta take care of my boy, ok?"

"Hey-hey, I said the vows, didn't I?" I nudge him back.

Rick glances over at me from the bar and smiles and I'm…helpless.

You know, maybe I'm being sentimental, but getting married is, unsurprisingly, super romantic. He wants this life with me and I want…to make it a good one. I don't want seedy gangsters hanging on, I don't want to disappear into the night and try to squeeze the blood out of my clothes.

I want something…safe and warm.

I want to give him the home he deserves.

I take a deep breath and slowly take a sip of my beer.

I'm sure I can renounce my old ways, I can put the past behind me, get rid of my knives, use my knowledge of how to get rid of blood stains for domestic cleaning reasons only.

We can have a life together, a really good, really happy life. We can have problems like any other couple, we can fight over…crockery or watching the game on the weekends or the usual stupid things couples fight about.

I can become the person he needs me to be, the person he thinks I am. I can do it for love.

I mean, how does it go again?

Love is all you need.

But then… this guy in a red baseball cap bumps into Rick on purpose as he's on the way back from the bar with our drinks. "Hey, watch it, buddy," Rick says.

The guy reels around to look at him, his red face twists into an ugly smirk and he says, "No Espanyol, pal."

Rick rolls his eyes and goes to walk away.

"Hey, don't you give me that look," the guy snarls at him, grabbing Rick's shoulder and jerking him back. "Show some respect for an American citizen, you fucking Mexican."

The drinks slide off the tray and shatter on the floor.

Rick twists out of his grip, frowning now. "Get off me."

"Learn some manners," the guy says, smirking that awful smirk again.

I feel my nails bite the hardened skin of my palms and I'm on my feet, one hand on Rick's shoulder.

"Hey! Hold it there!" The red-headed waitress rushes over and gets between the two of them. She tells the guy, 'Larry', I hear her call him, to go home, or he'd be banned. The guy looks embarrassed and saunters off with his friends to get his coat. "He's drunk, I'm sorry," she says to Rick. "You ok, mister?"

"I'm fine, nothing that hasn't happened before," Rick says, shaking his head.

"I'm so sorry, sir, we've had problems with Larry before, he's the owner's brother…Here, let me get you some fresh ones, I'll bring them over to your table. Y'all sat over there?"

"Yeah," Rick says. He squeezes an arm around me. "You ok, Sookie?"

"I'm sorry you had to put up with that," I say. "It's bullshit."

"Clearly the staff here have to be trained to handle him," he says, glancing over at the guy who is glowering at him as he struggles with his too-small leather jacket. "Ergh, would you look at the fucker?"

"Ignore him. The wannabe Hell's Angel tub of lard," I say.

Rick laughs and takes a seat, squeezing my hand.

"Sorry," Luis says, "He's given me trouble before as well. I fucking hate that guy, man."

"Oh well," Rick says, "He's got to spend the rest of his life looking like that, so let's forget about it."

The new drinks come and Rick leans over to kiss my hair.

"And I get to spend the rest of my life with my lady wife."

"And poor Sookie gets to spend the rest of her life with you," Luis teases.

We say cheers and crash our bottles together. As Luis is talking—something about his sister's terrible fiancé—I glance back and notice Larry leaving without his friends, he's squeezed into his jacket and out the back door, alone.

All alone.

"Sorry, Luis, sorry," I say. "Babe, I've just missed a call from Leda," I say. "I'm just going outside to call her back. Be five minutes?"

"Sure," he says, kissing the side of my head. "I'll keep your seat warm for you." He slides across into it and offers me a dorky thumbs up and I love him, I love him so much that it actually makes me ache.

There it is again.

Helpless.

I am so helplessly in love with you, Rick.

So, obviously there is no way in hell that I'm letting some drunk bastard speak to you like that.

I slip out through the back door and spot Larry turning down the next street.

I follow him, tugging my coat around the lower half of my face as I walk out into the night.

Am I a hypocrite? I consider as I turn the corner and, as luck would have it, spot Larry taking a shortcut down a dimly lit alley.

No, not a hypocrite.

I'm doing this for love.

And how does it go again?
Love is all you need.

Acknowledgments

In 2018 I completed *Down Red Creek* as part of the global National Novel Writing Month (NaNoWriMo) challenge. On that November 30th as I sat sneakily reading over my first draft on my lunch break, I never imagined that in nine months' time it would be out there in the world as a published novel.

And like anyone who can be just a little too obsessive about their writing, even after I finished the book, I couldn't get Fiona out of my head. I found myself wondering what she did after *Down Red Creek* ended. What sort of antics was she finding herself in at age twenty? How well did the whole 'not killing' thing go after the story ended?

I mean, anyone who's worked in retail or an office finds themselves suppressing the urge to kill occasionally, right? You get your entitled customer demanding a discount for no reason, the aggressive drunk who could barely slur their order together at a crowded drive-thru, the office manager who likes the sound of their own terrible jokes. I found myself wondering – what would an actual killer do in these kinds of situations?

Then one day I was chatting with my soon-to-be-father-in-law about the book, and he said, 'So, what did she do next?' – and I realised that I really wanted and needed to write that story.

There are so many people who helped make this novel a reality with their incredible support so here we go:

Firstly, my fiancé, George, who read the draft of this novel chapter-by-chapter and listened to me reading this in my terrible American accent. You are the most patient, brilliant man I know, and I really couldn't have finished this book without you.

I'd like to thank my excellent proof-reader, Elise, whose incredible attention to detail and vital comments made this novel a reality. Thank you for spotting all the silly mistakes I became utterly nose-blind too! I seriously cannot recommend Holloway With Words enough as a proof-reading service. Also, I'd like to thank my best friends, Amanda and Kate, for always being so supportive of me and my work! Kate, I'm sorry for all the travel sickness I've contributed to over the years for sending you things to read on your very long commute. Amanda, your excitement over my work always motivates me so much more than you'll ever know.

I want to thank my family for supporting my writing, especially my mum for chatting through ideas and plot-holes on my lunch breaks and my dad who is so easily proud of me that it makes me want to work harder to make that happen. My siblings, Charlotte—who loves serial killers so much, it's a little disturbing—and Ieuan, who makes me a better writer by refusing to hear spoilers, while also helping discuss ideas for my work. I'd like to thank my grandparents—especially Grandma—for reading my very gory book.

A huge thank you to my ridiculously cool soon-to-be-in-laws, Joy, Ian, and Mili, who asked what Fiona did next, and prompted me to write a whole series about the life and times of a serial killer. An enormous thank you to the FBL squad! I can't tell you enough how much I miss working with you all every day. Remember that 6 months we were all in the same office? Dream office, am I right?

I would also like to express my thanks to my editor, Mark, and all his hard-working colleagues at Sulis International for making this series a reality.

Thank you to the Francis W Reckitt Trust that allowed me to finish this novel in beautiful surroundings at Tŷ Newydd Writing Centre's Nant Cottage – it was a privilege to write a novel somewhere so many other great books have been written.

And finally, a massive, immeasurable thank you to all of you who purchased and read *Down Red Creek*. Your kind comments and reviews are my lifeblood. I hope you enjoy this sequel just as much, because I have so much more of this story to tell. Keep your eyes peeled for news about the third book in the Red Creek Series, coming soon!

About the Author

Rachael Llewellyn is an English writer living in Wales where she is completing her PhD at Swansea University, exploring memory and folklore in the novel. Her short fiction has appeared in many publications including FreckledInk, Terror House Magazine and anthologies for both the University of Warwick and Aberystwyth University.

Impulse Control is her second novel and is the sequel to her debut novel, *Down Red Creek* (Sulis International, 2019).

Read an excerpt at the end of this book of Book Three of the Red Creek Series.

Join the Sulis Newsletter for preorder and publication dates.

https://sulisinternational.com/subscribe/

If you enjoyed this book, please consider leaving an online review. The author would appreciate reading your thoughts.

You can follow the author on Twitter at @FumigatedSpace

A Preview of Book Three of the Red Creek Series

Chapter One

I came across Meredith Andrews through my husband. There was a fundraiser Rick was invited to through a publishing friend of his. One of the joys of being married is both always having and always being a plus one. Rick is better at these things, he knows how to network, how to charm. Of charm, I have a limited amount, so I tucked myself into one of the corners with a glass of complimentary wine, when this pinched, irritated voice catches my attention.

"No, no, no, Marie-Lucia, if you can't be bothered to do it correctly, why bother wasting my time at all?"

I turned to one of the nearby tables where a tiny old woman was sat, cigarette in hand, scolding a very uncomfortable looking middle-aged woman.

"I'm very sorry, Mrs. Andrews, I'll get you some more…"

"No, you've done quite enough. You."

I pointed up at myself as I realised, of course, she was beckoning me with one heavily bejewelled finger. "Me?"

"Yes, you, who else," she snapped. "Do you work here or not?"

And you know… in the end, you just have to sit back and take that old-school racism in your stride. I mean, what's the alternative?

"No," I say, "I don't work here. I'm here with my husband."

"Ah," she says, not quite capable of looking apologetic. "I see. Meredith. Meredith Andrews." She says it expectantly, like I should know exactly who Meredith Andrews is. Then she confusingly offered me up the beckoning hand like the queen offering her glove to kiss.

"Oh, hello," I say.

Within just a few minutes of conversation, I found out that Meredith Andrews was a big deal at that *particular* event, or if you listen to her for long enough, the whole of California. In just five minutes, she mentioned not once, not twice, but five times in total, that she was founder and primary donor of this charity. She referred to my husband as 'that handsome Italian man' and then told me twice that I had 'a look' of her childhood maid.

I listened, bemused and unsure of how to get away from her exactly. Like I said, I have a limited amount of charm and grow more prone to sarcasm by the minute with old bigots who like the sound of their own voice.

"Mrs. Andrews, I've got your hot plate here."

"Ah, that looks less likely to poison me," she said. "It was nice meeting you, Dana, was it?"

"Yes," I said, despite that sincerely not being the case.

I watched as her servant helped her into one of the chairs. Within a few seconds of observing them, I saw Meredith purposefully spill her cup of coffee over the poor woman's hands as she set up her napkin on her lap.

"Mrs. Andrews-!" the woman cried out in alarm, wincing in pain.

The old woman leant forwards and whispered, just loud enough for her maid and me, I suppose, eavesdropping, to hear. "You can always go back to whatever third world country you crawled out of."

Then Rick came and found me with a fresh glass of champagne and insistence that I come and meet Bob or Bart or… well, it began with a B. I was a little distracted. I'd already starting planning how I was going to kill Meredith Andrews.

*

As I sit, somewhat cramped in Meredith Andrews's closet, preparing an adrenaline shot in the dark, I find myself considering my life choices. I mean, it's that or I could think about how weird it is that Meredith Andrews owns the shiny snake-skin boots of a cowboy. But I've always been slightly self-centred. How many times have I promised myself that I wouldn't do things like this anymore?

Maybe once every week since I was fifteen.

I said I'd stop when I ran away from home. I said I'd stop when I got married. I wonder if I say it enough perhaps one day it will come true. Like—oh yeah, good example—last year I had to share a very small office with a woman named Angelica. Angelica was not the best desk-neighbour for a lot of reasons. For one, she liked to brush her hair at her desk, pelting me with long red strands which had Rick jokingly ask more than once, if I was having an affair with The Little Mermaid. Also, she would make personal calls at least every hour. And finally, and most relevantly, she had a *very* serious dairy allergy, but refused to stop eating chocolate. It was all I ever heard about, all day from 8.30 until 5.

It was annoying! She would arrive for work, make a personal call, then grumble about how she wanted chocolate, but it was *soooo* bad for her, oh no! Then she'd vanish for ten minutes to make a personal call on her phone, return with two bars of chocolate, eat them and then moan about how bad it was for her, whilst itching her skin until the end of the day.

Angelica knew the chocolate was bad for her, terrible for her even, from a health perspective. But she couldn't stop herself from indulging. For her it was the kind of joy that seemed worth the risk.

It's the same for me.

I know it's bad for me, morally. I know that killing is wrong. Sin seems a strong word for it, but I know that ethically, it's a big 'NO'. I know that if I was ever discovered, my very nice, very comfortable life would be ruined beyond repair. I know that it would end my marriage. I know that it would ruin Rick's life as there would be no way anyone would believe he didn't know or at least suspect. If all of that is what I'm risking, then surely it should be easy for me to just stay at home and… I don't know, read a book?

It should be.

But I honestly can't help myself. For me, it really is the kind of joy that makes the risk seem worth it. For me, this is chocolate.

I can hear faint snoring coming from a few paces away.

Show-time.

So, getting up, careful to avoid the boots and various dusty smelling coats, I creep out of the closet and into the old lady's bedroom. The closet door screeches very slightly on the hinges. I freeze up, but the snoring stays the same. It's a good tell, but honestly, I never would have taken the old woman for a snorer.

Squinting in the dark, I move closer to the bed. I can see her from here. Meredith Andrews is lying in the centre of a plush looking double bed. She's wearing one of those Colonial looking white nightgowns that looks like it should be incredibly itchy. Maybe that's why she's always in such a bad mood. I doubt I'd get a good night's sleep wearing one of those things to bed. Upon closer examination, I see that she has her hands folded neatly in front of her like a very old, pointy doll.

I suppose as murders go, this isn't that bad.

She's got to be… what, a hundred?

No, she's not a hundred. I know she's eighty-three.

She's eighty-three, she likes to abuse her staff and threaten to have them deported whenever they try to stand up to her. Two years ago, charges were brought against her but dropped just as swiftly. Apparently, she had hit the daughter of her gardener in the face with her walking stick and partially blinded the child. She's unpleasant to speak to and with her money and excellent choice of health care, she'd probably have lived another ten to fifteen years, doing pretty much the same stuff.

It makes more sense to just draw a fine line under her life from where she is now.

I don't fancy being mistaken for a maid from her youth at another of Rick's fund-raisers.

I have to fiddle with the high collar of her nightgown to inject her with the adrenaline shot. I was right, the fabric really was itchy. Ew, how does she sleep wearing something like this? Well, I suppose that's not something she needs to worry about anymore.

I know I gave her enough to finish her off, so I pocket the syringe and slip over to the door. The corridor is empty. There's music playing somewhere in the house, downstairs, I think, in the kitchen. I am good at being quiet, I always have been. Though in an old house like this, the floorboards creak and the pipes shudder. It's a little unsettling, but I keep in mind that anyone else in the house wouldn't be sneaking around on tip-toe like me. They'd be bold about it, and sure of themselves, taking purposeful strides. I take a deep breath and make my way through the dark.

It's a little tough not to be distracted by this place. Meredith Andrews decorated her home the way that rich old ladies always seem to in films and on TV. There are doilies—I saw them when I was in her living room—there are odd looking ornaments and a very poor taste model on her bedside table—there are also a lot of weird looking family portraits hung up around her home. There's this one—ah yes, I noticed it on the way in—which looks like it was taken in the 1930s, of a mother and her two children. And one of the kids, the younger girl, looks so unashamedly bored. She has her bottom lip stuck out in protest and is clearly rolling her eyes at the camera, very unimpressed. Her expression is especially funny due to the rather adorable looking older sister stood with her arm around her, beaming, delightedly at the camera.

I wonder if one of them was Meredith, come to think of it.

I sort of want to take the picture with me as a souvenir, to remember it better and also because I really do think it would look amazing in my hallway. But, alas, souvenirs are how idiots get caught. So the photograph of the unimpressed child remains, and I make my way downstairs.

In the dim light of the downstairs hallway, I slip over to the living room. I peek through the door and see that nobody is inside. There's a sudden ripple of laughter coming from the kitchen. It startles me, but not badly. Then I reach over and slide the window open a little higher—this was my entrance into Meredith's tastefully decorated home.

Climbing out through the window feels so high school, I think to myself as I struggle to let my leg over the ledge. It's a bit of a squish. Come to think of it, I was such a brazen teenager that there wasn't an occasion where I didn't just walk straight through the door. I chuckle and lift myself out and onto the ledge. It's not a long way down, I just need to be careful about how I land. Why didn't I sneak around more as a kid? Awkwardly shifting my weight, I wince as the baby starts to kick.

I groan and decide to save my leap down until my little invader decides to keep still. One kick. Two kicks. Three kicks. Right up against my bladder as well. Thanks for that.

I hear someone talking in the hallway back in the house and decide to take my chances and just climb down. I land awkwardly on my ankle and walk it off, one hand on my stomach, wincing as I go. It's best to get out of here. I'm hoping the old woman won't be discovered until morning. As for me, I have a bathroom to get to and a husband to beat home from work.

*

I am aware that I shouldn't be keeping up with my hobby in my current condition. There are lots of rules with pregnancy, I've come to find, and most contradict each other. Some people say you can keep up an active lifestyle, running, swimming, yoga, the works—on the other end of the spectrum, you have Karen from the Planning team, who said she wanted to report her co-worker to social services for taking the stairs whilst pregnant.

Some people say to avoid spicy foods completely. Others say not to. Some people treat you like you're some fragile wounded soldier who must be spoken to very slowly and simply. Others treat you like you're a spoilt brat for complaining about your swollen feet and near constant need to pee.

It's not like I can google 'how to keep up any homicidal habits while you're pregnant'. So, I've been trying to make my own rules. I've been targeting victims who are old and annoying and unlikely to give me much of a fight. I've been pacing myself. I've been keeping my knives to myself if I'm not in the mood.

I mean, sure, it's getting harder to lose myself in my hobby as of late. It's hard to relax and enjoy your work when you keep bumping your stomach on things. Or you look down from a lifeless body and get that constant reminder of the life growing inside you. You're trying to make a speedy escape through a window and your little interloper starts pressing down on your bladder. You end up thinking all sorts of things, you know, the usual, 'Oh my God, why am I doing this?' and then more specific fears like 'What if I get caught?' 'Should I be doing this?' 'Should someone like me be having a baby?' etc.

And sure, I'm a hormonal mess right now. So, I could let these moments really get to me. There are times they do get to me and there's no avoiding that. All I can do then, is take a deep breath and reassure myself that it's not like I'll be bringing the baby along with me on nights like this in the future.

I mean, I'm not a *monster*.

About the Publisher

Sulis International Press publishes select fiction and nonfiction in a variety of genres under four imprints: Riversong Books, Sulis Academic Press, Sulis Press, and Keledei Publications.

For more, visit the website at
https://sulisinternational.com

Subscribe to the newsletter at
https://sulisinternational.com/subscribe/

Follow on social media
https://www.facebook.com/SulisInternational
https://twitter.com/Sulis_Intl
https://www.pinterest.com/Sulis_Intl/
https://www.instagram.com/sulis_international/